# POKÉMON ADVENTURES
## BLACK & WHITE

**8**
VOLUME EIGHT

Story by
**Hidenori Kusaka**

Art by
**Satoshi Yamamoto**

# & WHITE

A STORY ABOUT YOUNG PEOPLE ENTRUSTED WITH POKÉDEXES BY THE WORLD'S LEADING POKÉMON RESEARCHERS. TOGETHER WITH THEIR POKÉMON, THEY TRAVEL, BATTLE, AND EVOLVE!

SOME PLACE IN SOME TIME... A YOUNG TRAINER NAMED BLACK, WHO DREAMS OF WINNING THE POKÉMON LEAGUE, RECEIVES A POKÉDEX FROM PROFESSOR JUNIPER AND SETS OFF TO COLLECT THE EIGHT GYM BADGES HE NEEDS TO ENTER NEXT YEAR'S POKÉMON LEAGUE.
ON THE WAY, BLACK MEETS WHITE, THE OWNER OF A POKÉMON TALENT AGENCY, AND THE TWO TRAVEL TOGETHER.
MEANWHILE, A MYSTERIOUS ORGANIZATION NAMED TEAM PLASMA, WHOSE KING IS A YOUNG MAN NAMED N, URGES PEOPLE TO GIVE UP THEIR POKÉMON AND RETURN THEM TO THE WILD. WHAT IS THEIR ULTERIOR MOTIVE? THEN TEAM PLASMA STEALS A MYSTERIOUS DARK STONE FROM THE NACRENE MUSEUM AND KIDNAPS MOST OF THE GYM LEADERS! BLACK VOWS TO RESCUE THEM AND BEGINS TRAINING HARD WITH BRYCEN...
IN THE MEANTIME, BLACK HAS EARNED HIS SEVENTH GYM BADGE AND IS READY TO PURSUE HIS EIGHTH...BUT THE POKÉMON LEAGUE OPENING HAS BEEN PUSHED UP AND NOW IT'S TOO LATE FOR HIM TO ENTER! THEN, WHEN HE WITNESSES A FIERCE BATTLE BETWEEN N AND GYM LEADER ALDER, BLACK DECIDES TO TAKE ON N HIMSELF...BUT THEN BLACK'S POKÉMON MUSHA ABANDONS HIM!
IN THE MIDST OF ALL THIS UNCERTAINTY AND CHAOS, THE CURTAIN RISES ON THE BEGINNING OF THE POKÉMON LEAGUE...

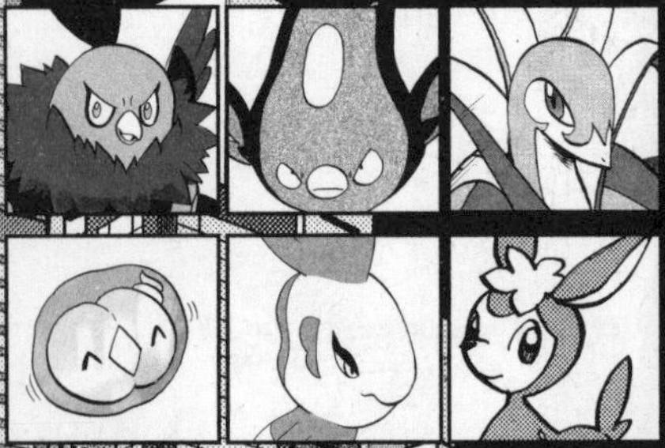

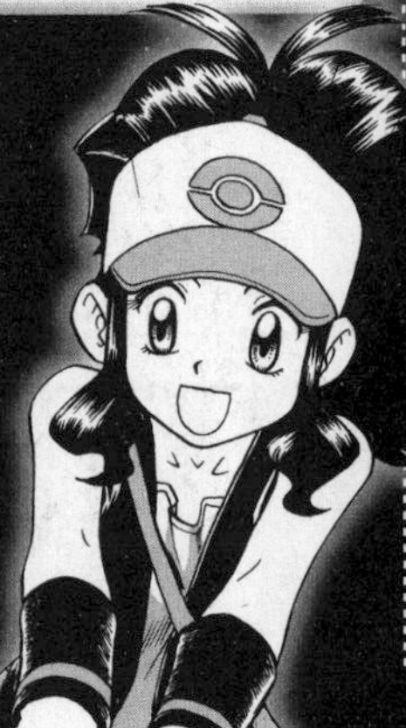

**WHITE**

THE PRESIDENT OF BW AGENCY. HER DREAM IS TO DEVELOP THE CAREERS OF POKÉMON STARS. SHE TAKES HER WORK VERY SERIOUSLY AND WILL DO WHATEVER IT TAKES TO SUPPORT HER POKÉMON ACTORS.

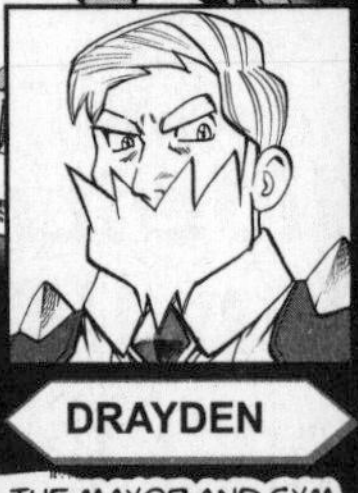

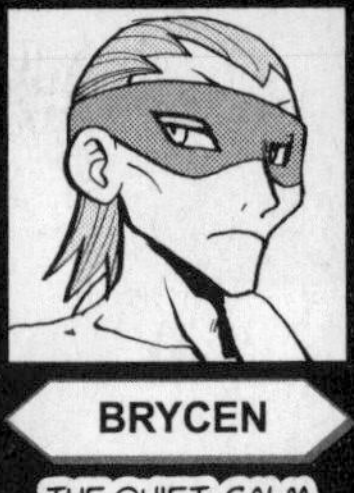

**DRAYDEN**

THE MAYOR AND GYM LEADER OF OPELUCID CITY. SPECIALIZES IN DRAGON-TYPE POKÉMON.

**BRYCEN**

THE QUIET, CALM GYM LEADER OF ICIRRUS CITY.

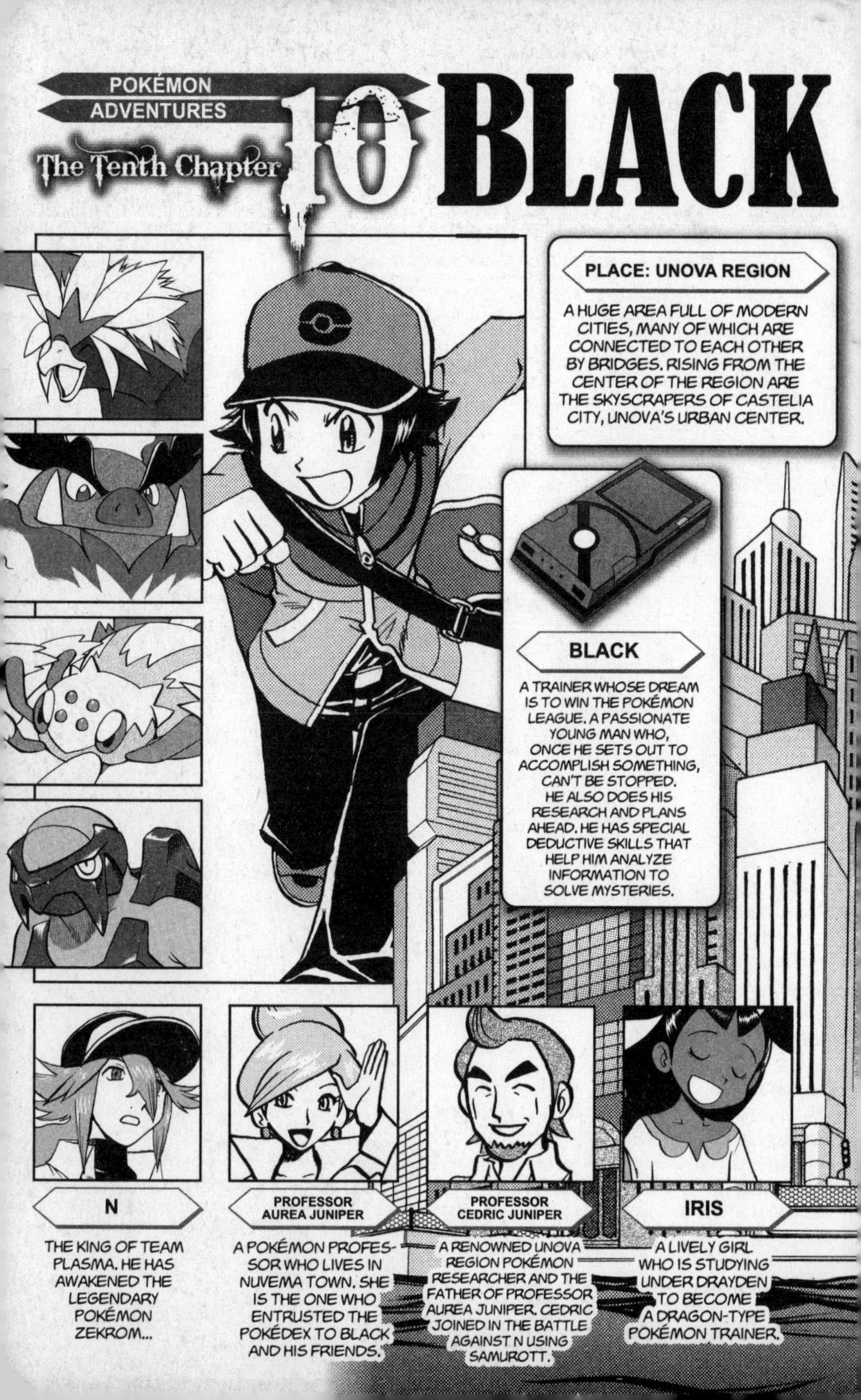
POKÉMON ADVENTURES
The Tenth Chapter
10
BLACK
PLACE: UNOVA REGION
A HUGE AREA FULL OF MODERN CITIES, MANY OF WHICH ARE CONNECTED TO EACH OTHER BY BRIDGES. RISING FROM THE CENTER OF THE REGION ARE THE SKYSCRAPERS OF CASTELIA CITY, UNOVA'S URBAN CENTER.
BLACK
A TRAINER WHOSE DREAM IS TO WIN THE POKÉMON LEAGUE. A PASSIONATE YOUNG MAN WHO, ONCE HE SETS OUT TO ACCOMPLISH SOMETHING, CAN'T BE STOPPED. HE ALSO DOES HIS RESEARCH AND PLANS AHEAD. HE HAS SPECIAL DEDUCTIVE SKILLS THAT HELP HIM ANALYZE INFORMATION TO SOLVE MYSTERIES.
N
THE KING OF TEAM PLASMA. HE HAS AWAKENED THE LEGENDARY POKÉMON ZEKROM...
PROFESSOR AUREA JUNIPER
A POKÉMON PROFESSOR WHO LIVES IN NUVEMA TOWN. SHE IS THE ONE WHO ENTRUSTED THE POKÉDEX TO BLACK AND HIS FRIENDS.
PROFESSOR CEDRIC JUNIPER
A RENOWNED UNOVA REGION POKÉMON RESEARCHER AND THE FATHER OF PROFESSOR AUREA JUNIPER. CEDRIC JOINED IN THE BATTLE AGAINST N USING SAMUROTT.
IRIS
A LIVELY GIRL WHO IS STUDYING UNDER DRAYDEN TO BECOME A DRAGON-TYPE POKÉMON TRAINER.

# Pokémon™ Adventures Black & White

8 VOLUME EIGHT

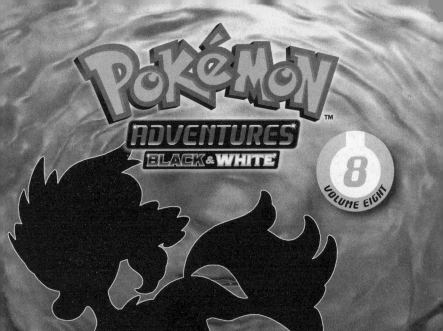

# CONTENTS

Pokémon Adventures Black & White

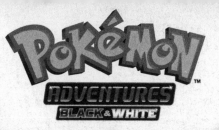

GOTHITELLE

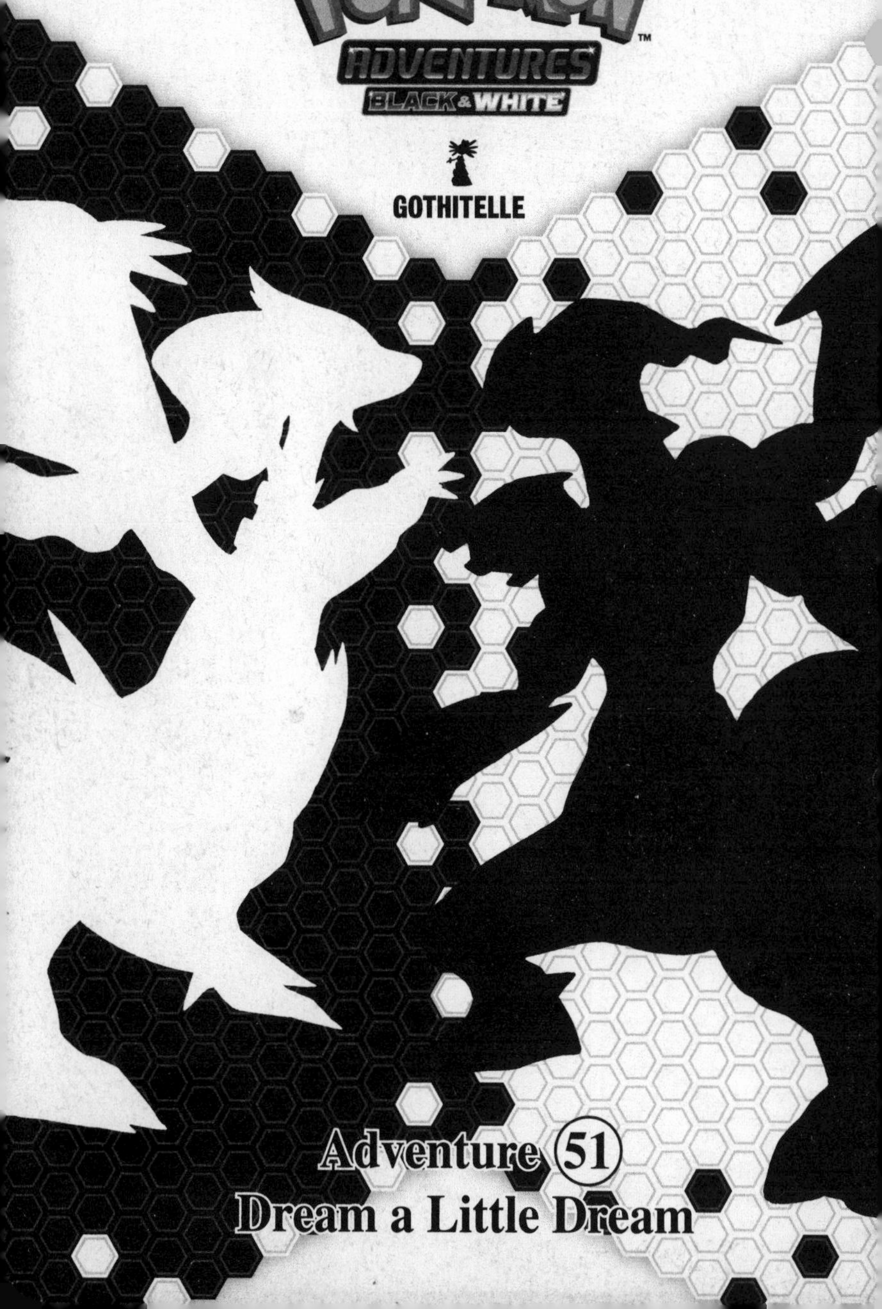

# Adventure 51
# Dream a Little Dream

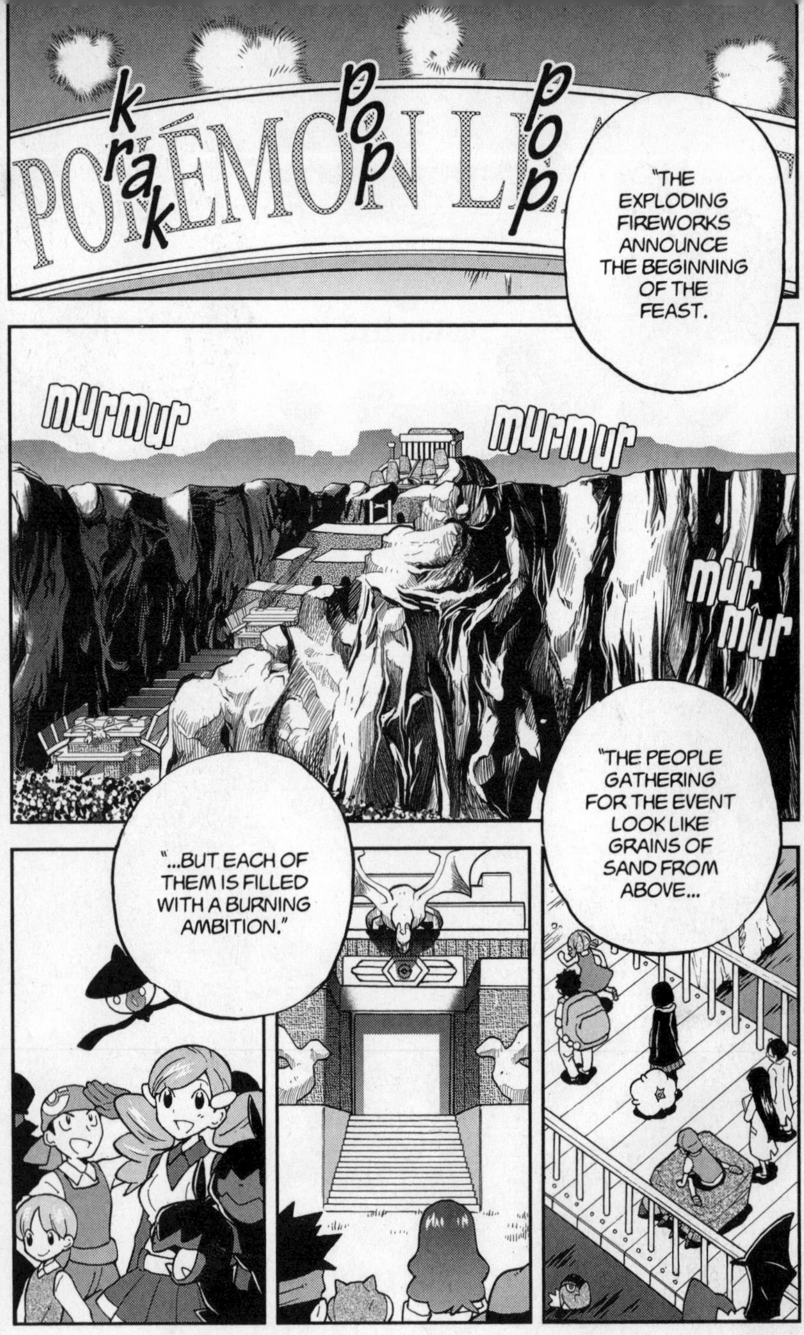
POKÉMON
krak
pop
pop
"THE EXPLODING FIREWORKS ANNOUNCE THE BEGINNING OF THE FEAST.
murmur
murmur
mur mur
"THE PEOPLE GATHERING FOR THE EVENT LOOK LIKE GRAINS OF SAND FROM ABOVE...
"...BUT EACH OF THEM IS FILLED WITH A BURNING AMBITION."

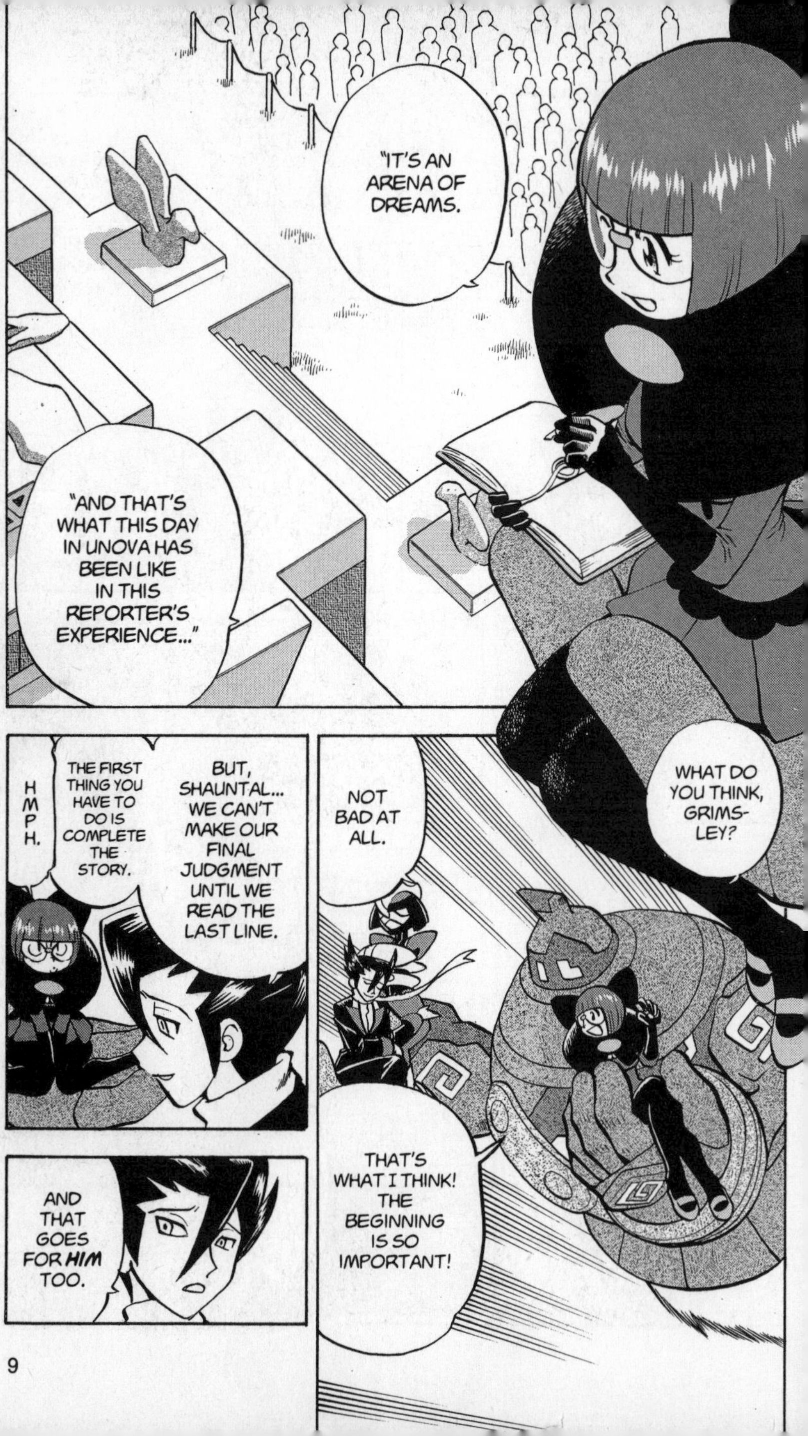

"IT'S AN ARENA OF DREAMS.
"AND THAT'S WHAT THIS DAY IN UNOVA HAS BEEN LIKE IN THIS REPORTER'S EXPERIENCE..."
WHAT DO YOU THINK, GRIMSLEY?
NOT BAD AT ALL.
THAT'S WHAT I THINK! THE BEGINNING IS SO IMPORTANT!
BUT, SHAUNTAL... WE CAN'T MAKE OUR FINAL JUDGMENT UNTIL WE READ THE LAST LINE.
THE FIRST THING YOU HAVE TO DO IS COMPLETE THE STORY.
HMPH.
AND THAT GOES FOR **HIM** TOO.

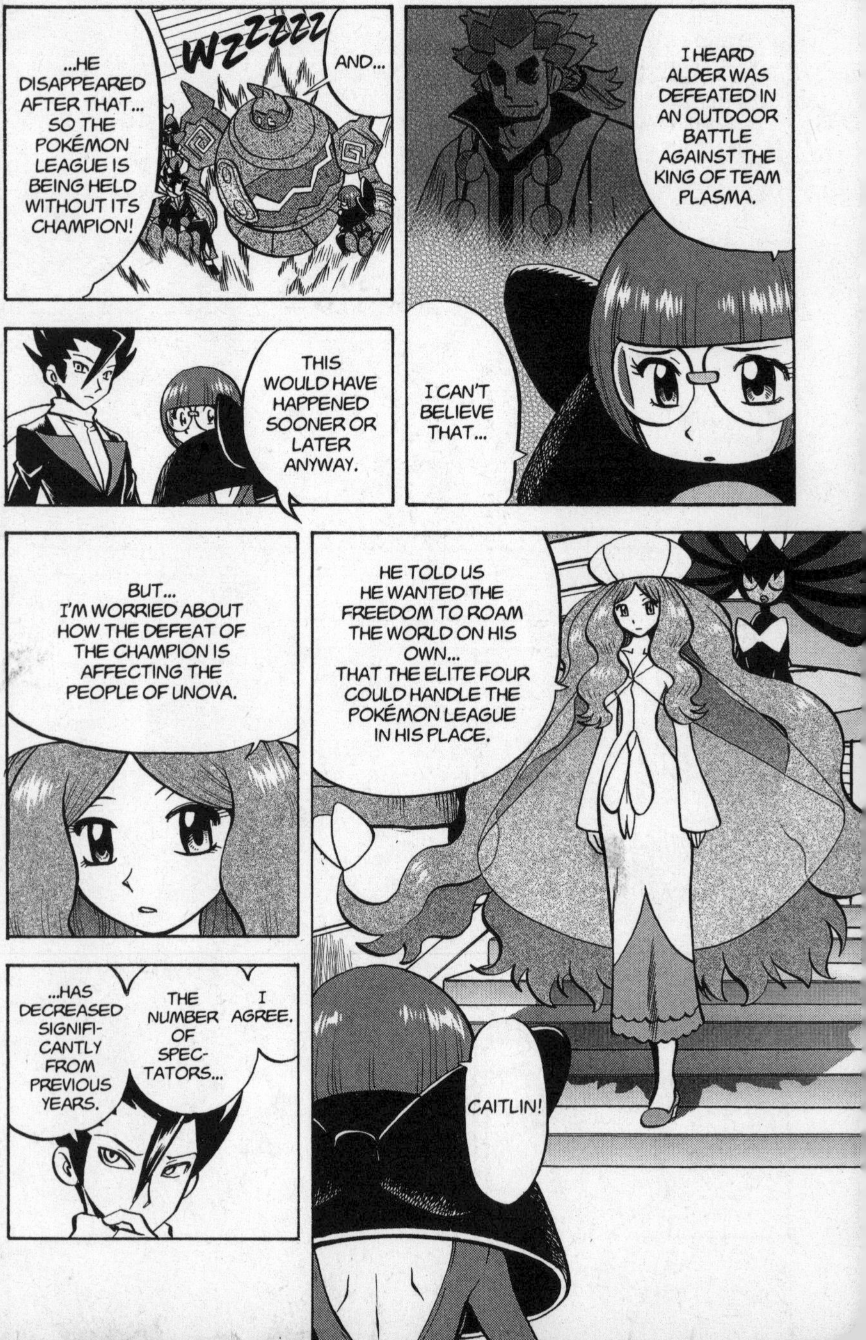
I HEARD ALDER WAS DEFEATED IN AN OUTDOOR BATTLE AGAINST THE KING OF TEAM PLASMA.
I CAN'T BELIEVE THAT...
AND...
WZZZZZ
...HE DISAPPEARED AFTER THAT... SO THE POKÉMON LEAGUE IS BEING HELD WITHOUT ITS CHAMPION!
THIS WOULD HAVE HAPPENED SOONER OR LATER ANYWAY.
HE TOLD US HE WANTED THE FREEDOM TO ROAM THE WORLD ON HIS OWN... THAT THE ELITE FOUR COULD HANDLE THE POKÉMON LEAGUE IN HIS PLACE.
CAITLIN!
BUT... I'M WORRIED ABOUT HOW THE DEFEAT OF THE CHAMPION IS AFFECTING THE PEOPLE OF UNOVA.
I AGREE.
THE NUMBER OF SPECTATORS...
...HAS DECREASED SIGNIFICANTLY FROM PREVIOUS YEARS.

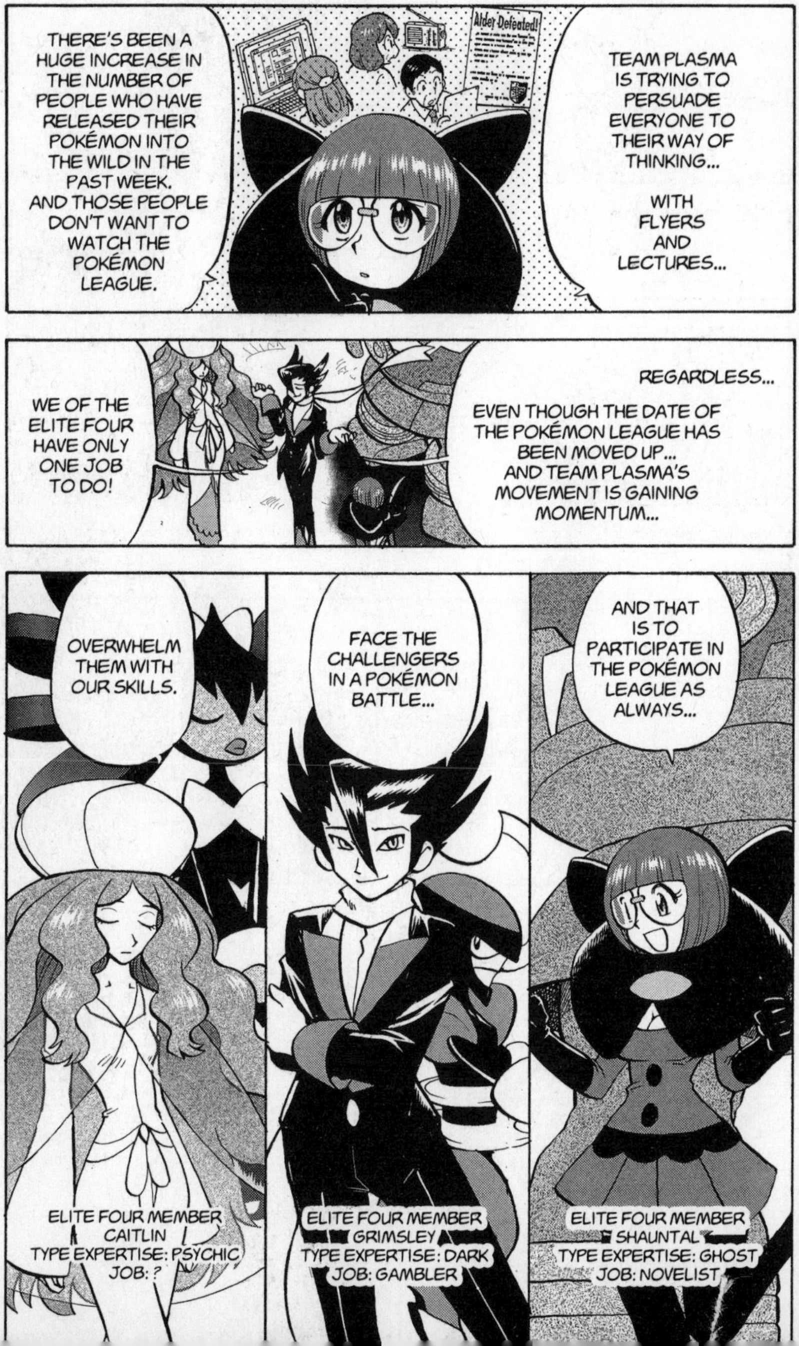
Alder Defeated!
TEAM PLASMA IS TRYING TO PERSUADE EVERYONE TO THEIR WAY OF THINKING...
WITH FLYERS AND LECTURES...
THERE'S BEEN A HUGE INCREASE IN THE NUMBER OF PEOPLE WHO HAVE RELEASED THEIR POKÉMON INTO THE WILD IN THE PAST WEEK.
AND THOSE PEOPLE DON'T WANT TO WATCH THE POKÉMON LEAGUE.
REGARDLESS...
EVEN THOUGH THE DATE OF THE POKÉMON LEAGUE HAS BEEN MOVED UP... AND TEAM PLASMA'S MOVEMENT IS GAINING MOMENTUM...
WE OF THE ELITE FOUR HAVE ONLY ONE JOB TO DO!
AND THAT IS TO PARTICIPATE IN THE POKÉMON LEAGUE AS ALWAYS...
ELITE FOUR MEMBER SHAUNTAL TYPE EXPERTISE: GHOST JOB: NOVELIST
FACE THE CHALLENGERS IN A POKÉMON BATTLE...
ELITE FOUR MEMBER GRIMSLEY TYPE EXPERTISE: DARK JOB: GAMBLER
OVERWHELM THEM WITH OUR SKILLS.
ELITE FOUR MEMBER CAITLIN TYPE EXPERTISE: PSYCHIC JOB: ?

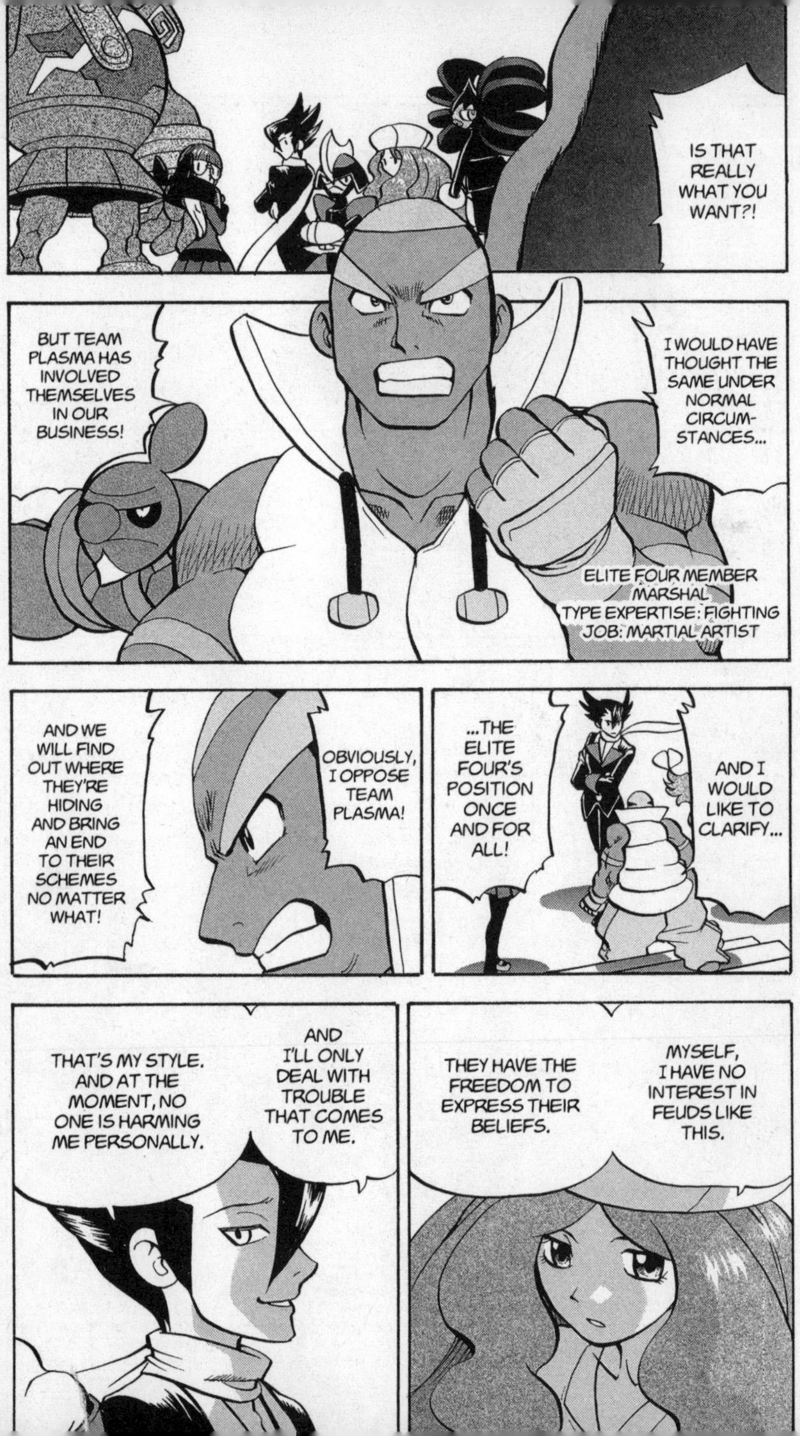
IS THAT REALLY WHAT YOU WANT?!
I WOULD HAVE THOUGHT THE SAME UNDER NORMAL CIRCUM-STANCES...
BUT TEAM PLASMA HAS INVOLVED THEMSELVES IN OUR BUSINESS!
ELITE FOUR MEMBER MARSHAL TYPE EXPERTISE: FIGHTING JOB: MARTIAL ARTIST
AND I WOULD LIKE TO CLARIFY...
...THE ELITE FOUR'S POSITION ONCE AND FOR ALL!
OBVIOUSLY, I OPPOSE TEAM PLASMA!
AND WE WILL FIND OUT WHERE THEY'RE HIDING AND BRING AN END TO THEIR SCHEMES NO MATTER WHAT!
MYSELF, I HAVE NO INTEREST IN FEUDS LIKE THIS.
THEY HAVE THE FREEDOM TO EXPRESS THEIR BELIEFS.
AND I'LL ONLY DEAL WITH TROUBLE THAT COMES TO ME.
THAT'S MY STYLE. AND AT THE MOMENT, NO ONE IS HARMING ME PERSONALLY.

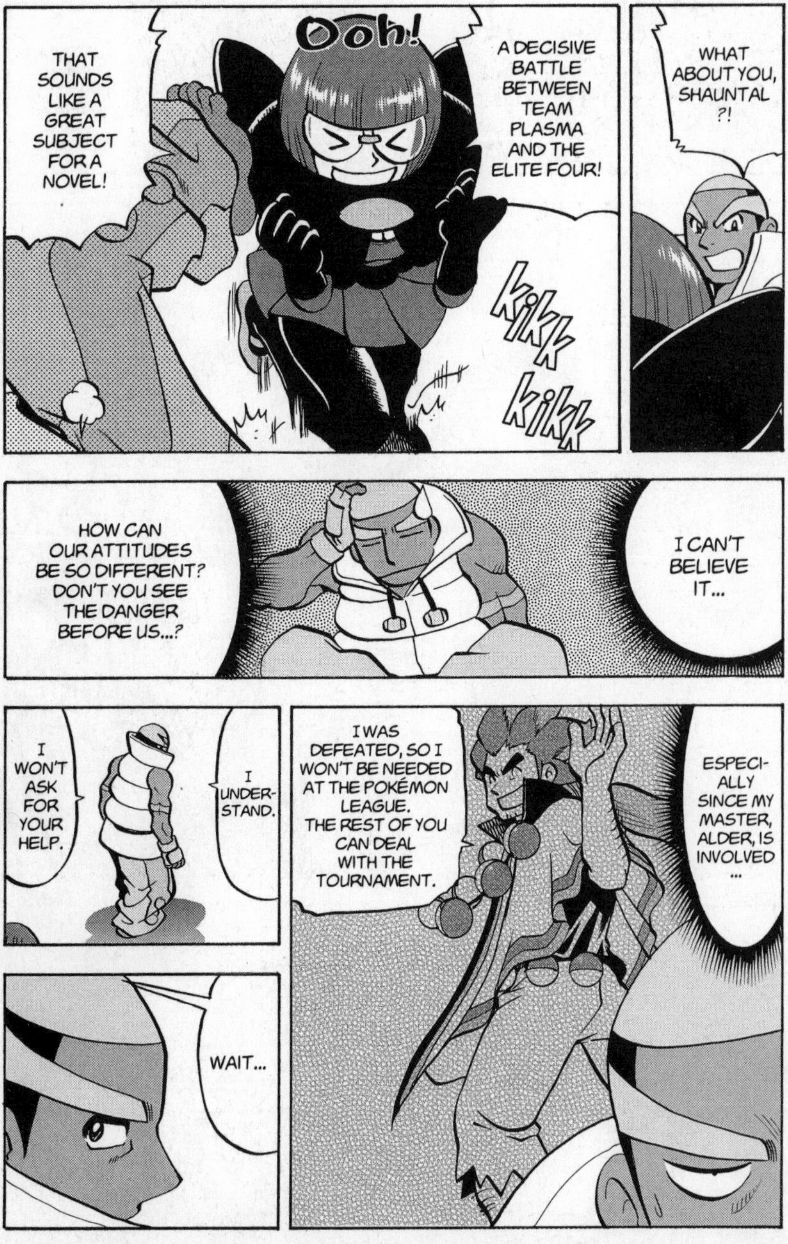
WHAT ABOUT YOU, SHAUNTAL ?!
A DECISIVE BATTLE BETWEEN TEAM PLASMA AND THE ELITE FOUR!
Ooh!
THAT SOUNDS LIKE A GREAT SUBJECT FOR A NOVEL!
kikk kikk
I CAN'T BELIEVE IT...
HOW CAN OUR ATTITUDES BE SO DIFFERENT? DON'T YOU SEE THE DANGER BEFORE US...?
ESPECI-ALLY SINCE MY MASTER, ALDER, IS INVOLVED ...
I WAS DEFEATED, SO I WON'T BE NEEDED AT THE POKÉMON LEAGUE. THE REST OF YOU CAN DEAL WITH THE TOURNAMENT.
I UNDER-STAND.
I WON'T ASK FOR YOUR HELP.
WAIT...

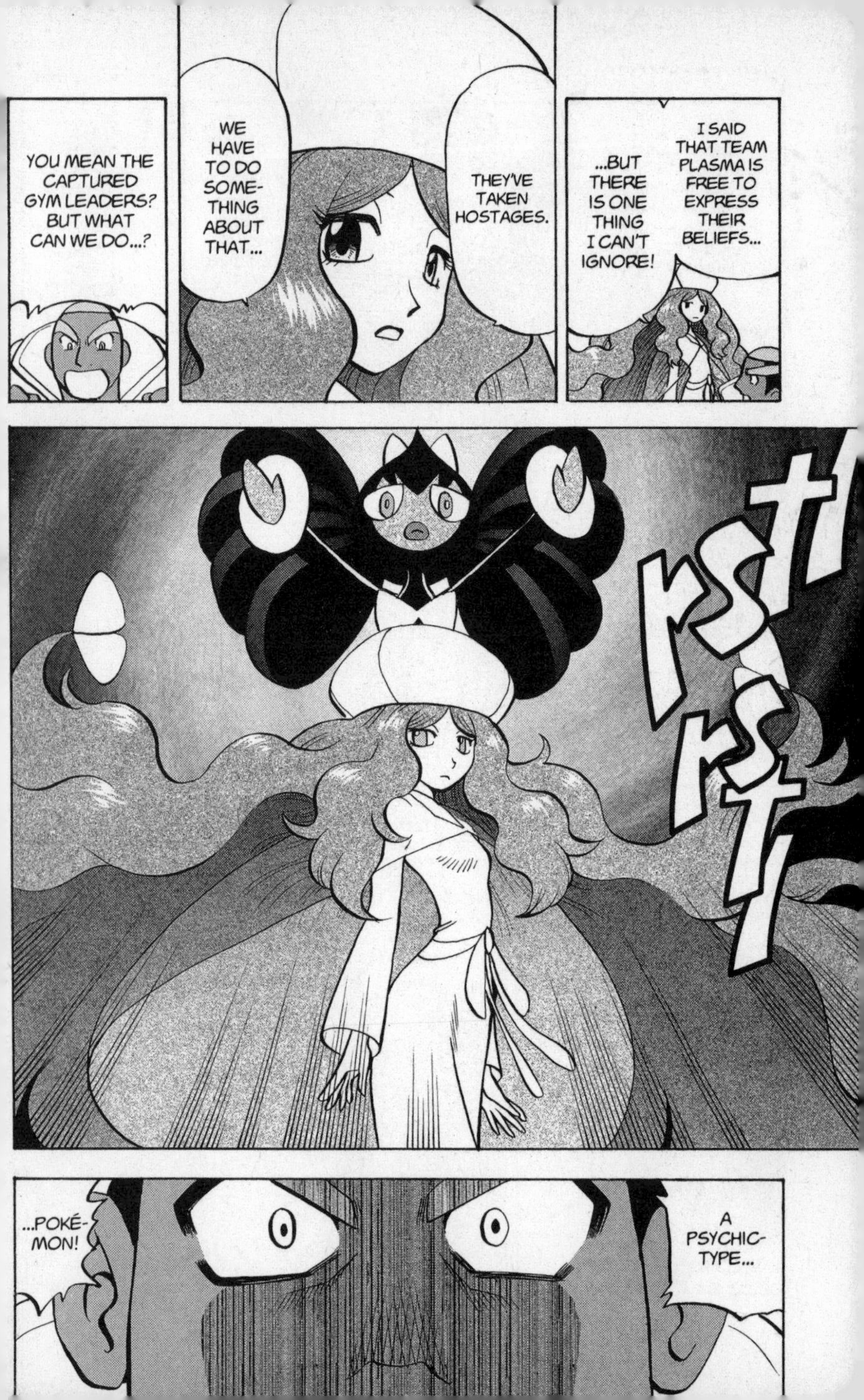
I SAID THAT TEAM PLASMA IS FREE TO EXPRESS THEIR BELIEFS...
...BUT THERE IS ONE THING I CAN'T IGNORE!
THEY'VE TAKEN HOSTAGES.
WE HAVE TO DO SOME-THING ABOUT THAT...
YOU MEAN THE CAPTURED GYM LEADERS? BUT WHAT CAN WE DO...?
A PSYCHIC-TYPE...
...POKÉ-MON!

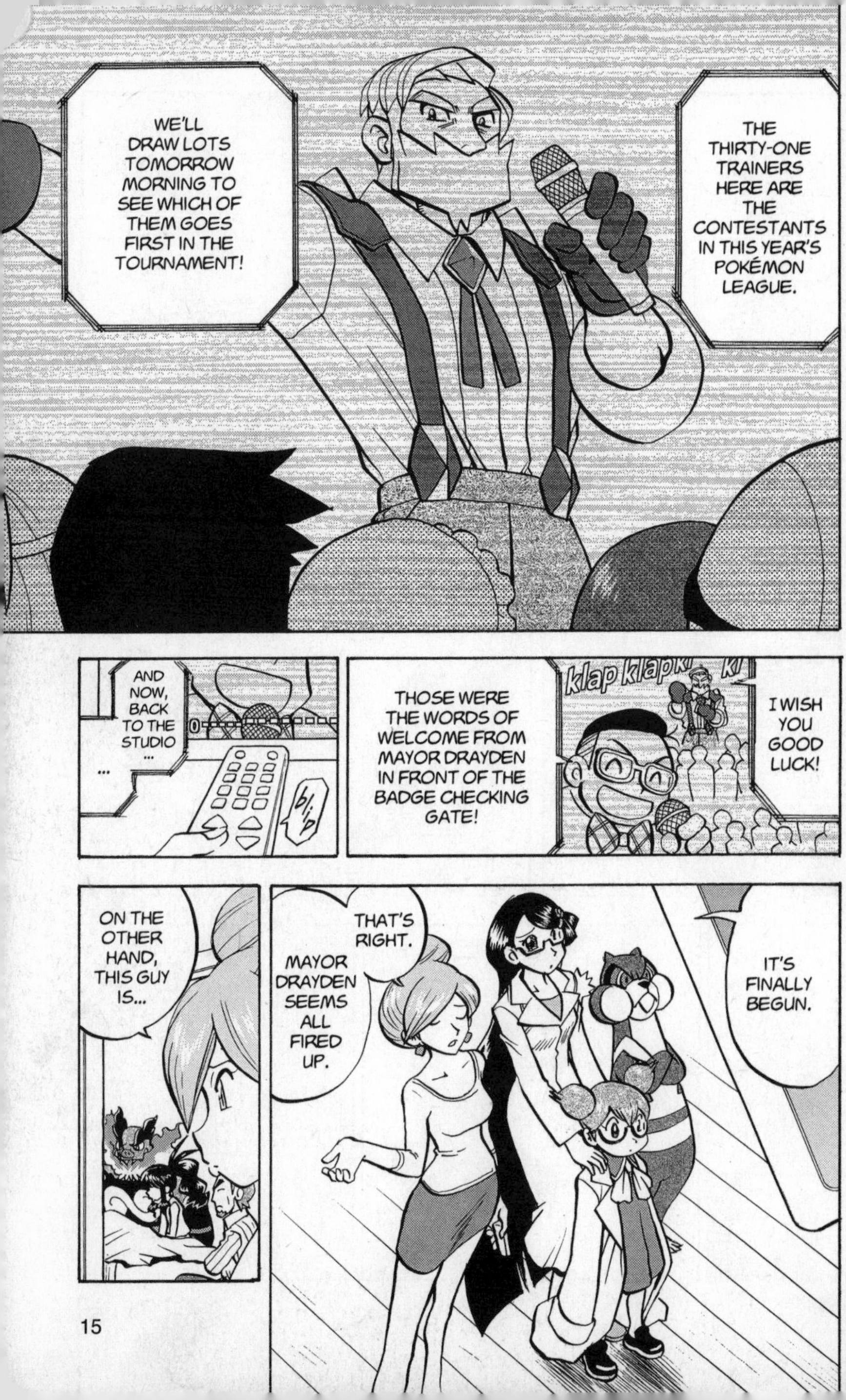
THE THIRTY-ONE TRAINERS HERE ARE THE CONTESTANTS IN THIS YEAR'S POKÉMON LEAGUE.
WE'LL DRAW LOTS TOMORROW MORNING TO SEE WHICH OF THEM GOES FIRST IN THE TOURNAMENT!
klap klapki ki
I WISH YOU GOOD LUCK!
THOSE WERE THE WORDS OF WELCOME FROM MAYOR DRAYDEN IN FRONT OF THE BADGE CHECKING GATE!
AND NOW, BACK TO THE STUDIO ...
...
blip
IT'S FINALLY BEGUN.
THAT'S RIGHT.
MAYOR DRAYDEN SEEMS ALL FIRED UP.
ON THE OTHER HAND, THIS GUY IS...

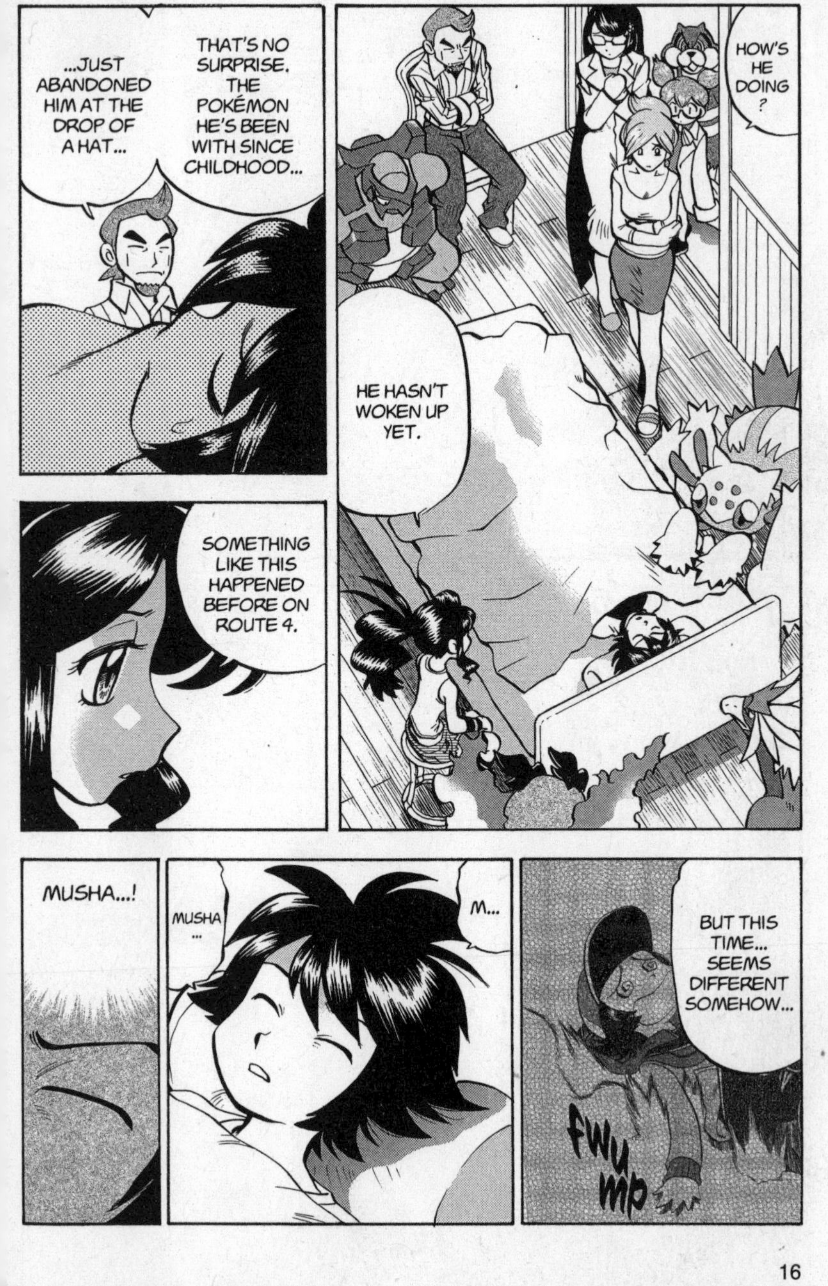
HOW'S HE DOING?
HE HASN'T WOKEN UP YET.
THAT'S NO SURPRISE. THE POKÉMON HE'S BEEN WITH SINCE CHILDHOOD...
...JUST ABANDONED HIM AT THE DROP OF A HAT...
SOMETHING LIKE THIS HAPPENED BEFORE ON ROUTE 4.
BUT THIS TIME... SEEMS DIFFERENT SOMEHOW...
fwump
M...
MUSHA ...
MUSHA...!

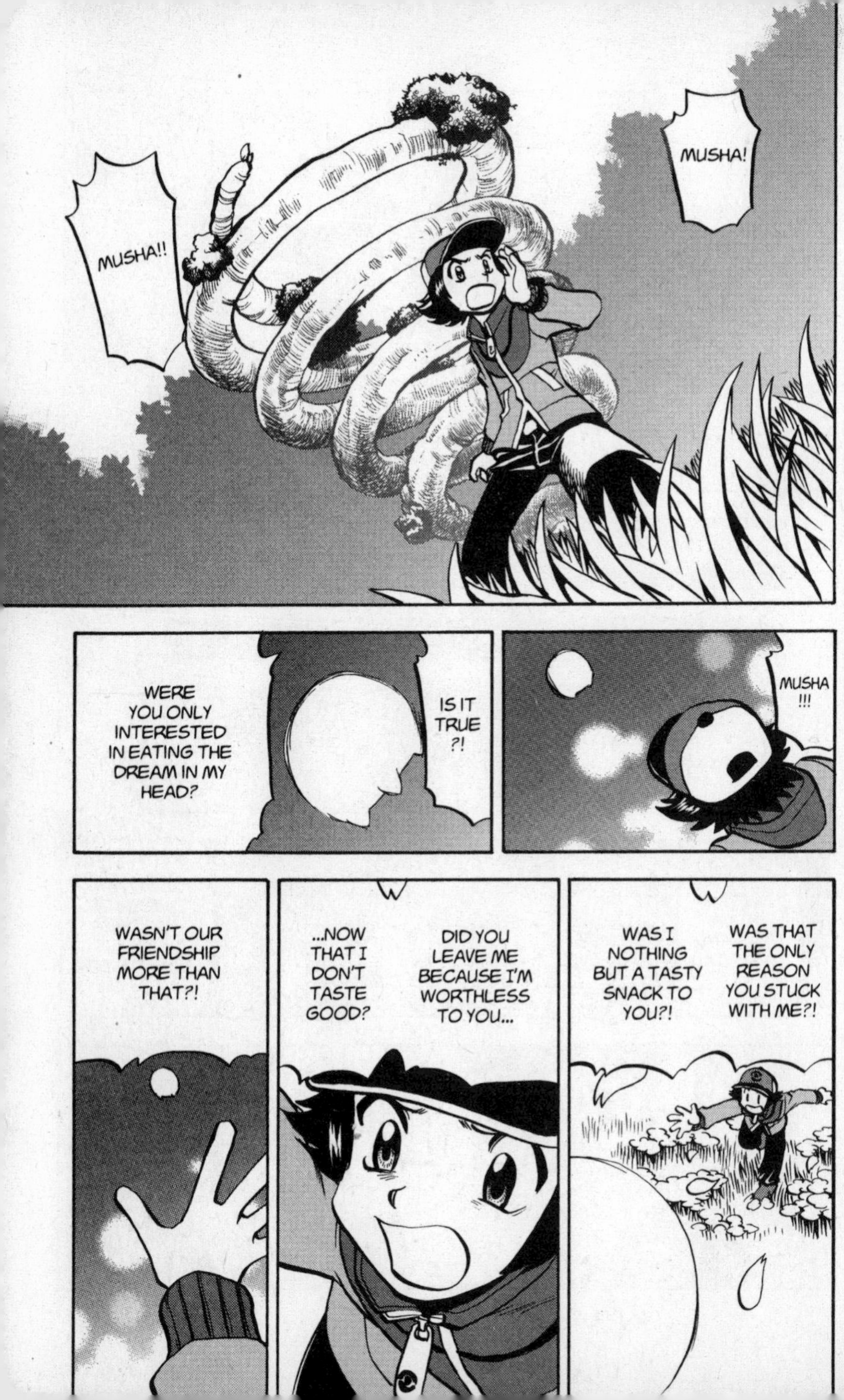
MUSHA!
MUSHA!!
MUSHA !!!
IS IT TRUE ?!
WERE YOU ONLY INTERESTED IN EATING THE DREAM IN MY HEAD?
WAS THAT THE ONLY REASON YOU STUCK WITH ME?!
WAS I NOTHING BUT A TASTY SNACK TO YOU?!
DID YOU LEAVE ME BECAUSE I'M WORTHLESS TO YOU...
...NOW THAT I DON'T TASTE GOOD?
WASN'T OUR FRIENDSHIP MORE THAN THAT?!

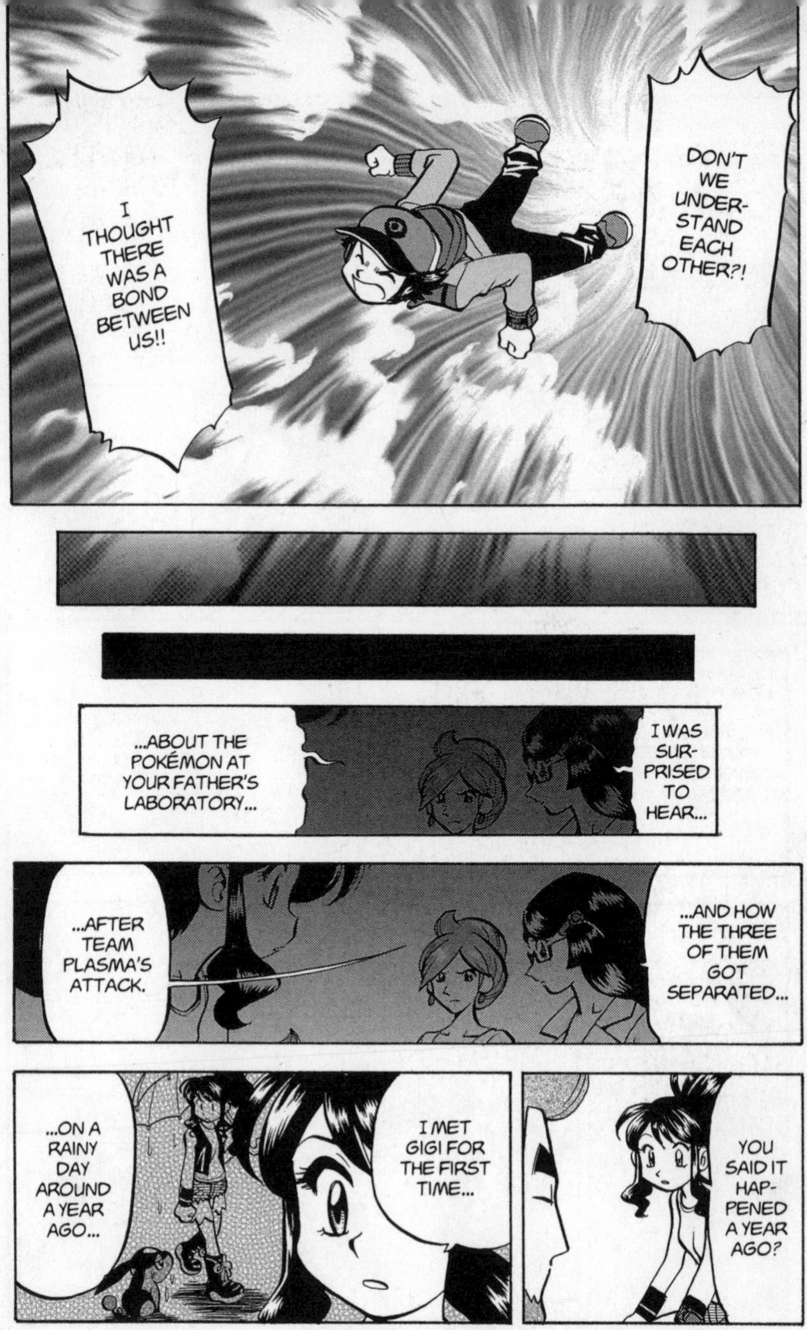
DON'T WE UNDERSTAND EACH OTHER?!
I THOUGHT THERE WAS A BOND BETWEEN US!!
I WAS SURPRISED TO HEAR...
...ABOUT THE POKÉMON AT YOUR FATHER'S LABORATORY...
...AND HOW THE THREE OF THEM GOT SEPARATED...
...AFTER TEAM PLASMA'S ATTACK.
YOU SAID IT HAPPENED A YEAR AGO?
I MET GIGI FOR THE FIRST TIME...
...ON A RAINY DAY AROUND A YEAR AGO...

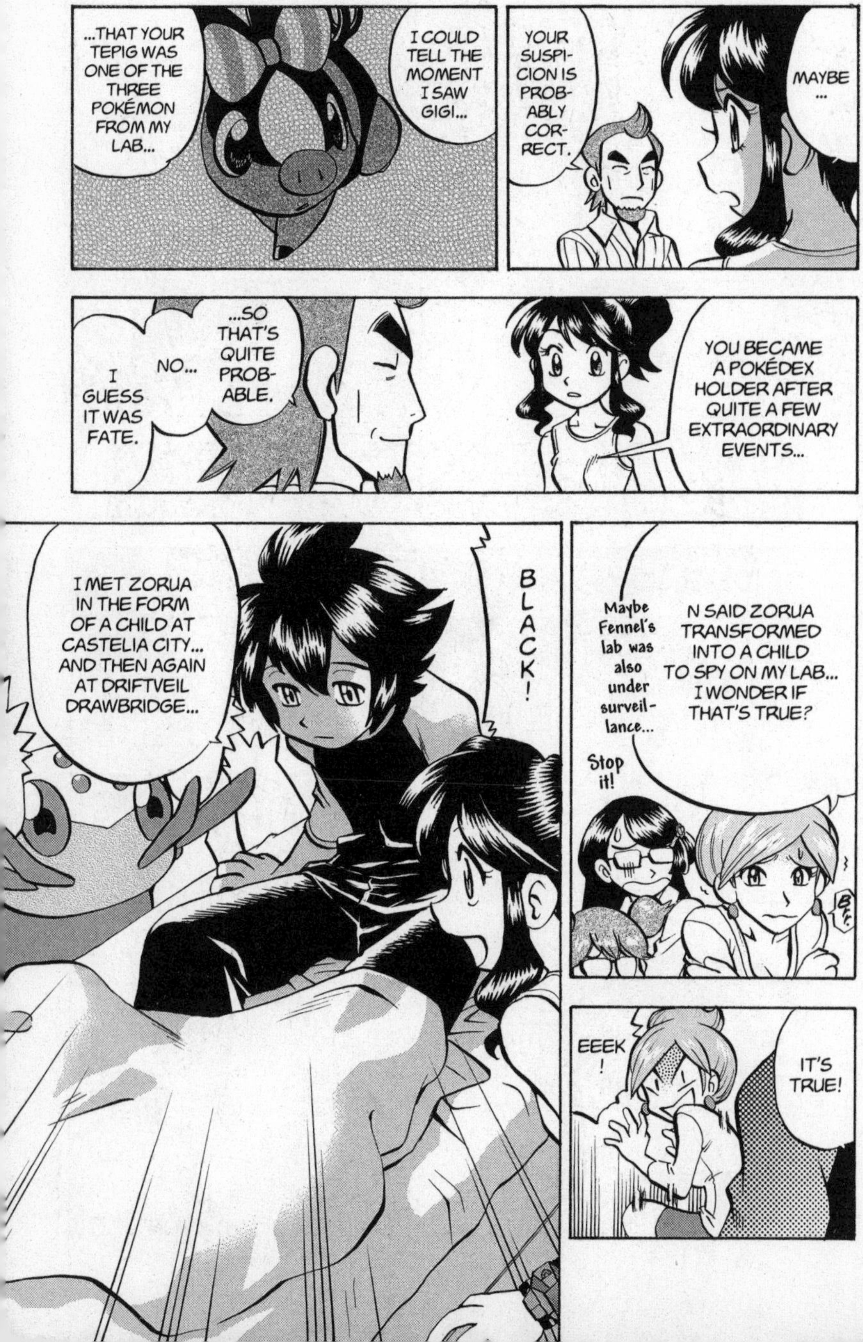
MAYBE...
YOUR SUSPICION IS PROBABLY CORRECT.
I COULD TELL THE MOMENT I SAW GIGI...
...THAT YOUR TEPIG WAS ONE OF THE THREE POKÉMON FROM MY LAB...
YOU BECAME A POKÉDEX HOLDER AFTER QUITE A FEW EXTRAORDINARY EVENTS...
...SO THAT'S QUITE PROBABLE.
NO... I GUESS IT WAS FATE.
N SAID ZORUA TRANSFORMED INTO A CHILD TO SPY ON MY LAB... I WONDER IF THAT'S TRUE?
Maybe Fennel's lab was also under surveillance...
Stop it!
IT'S TRUE!
EEEK!
BLACK!
I MET ZORUA IN THE FORM OF A CHILD AT CASTELIA CITY... AND THEN AGAIN AT DRIFTVEIL DRAWBRIDGE...

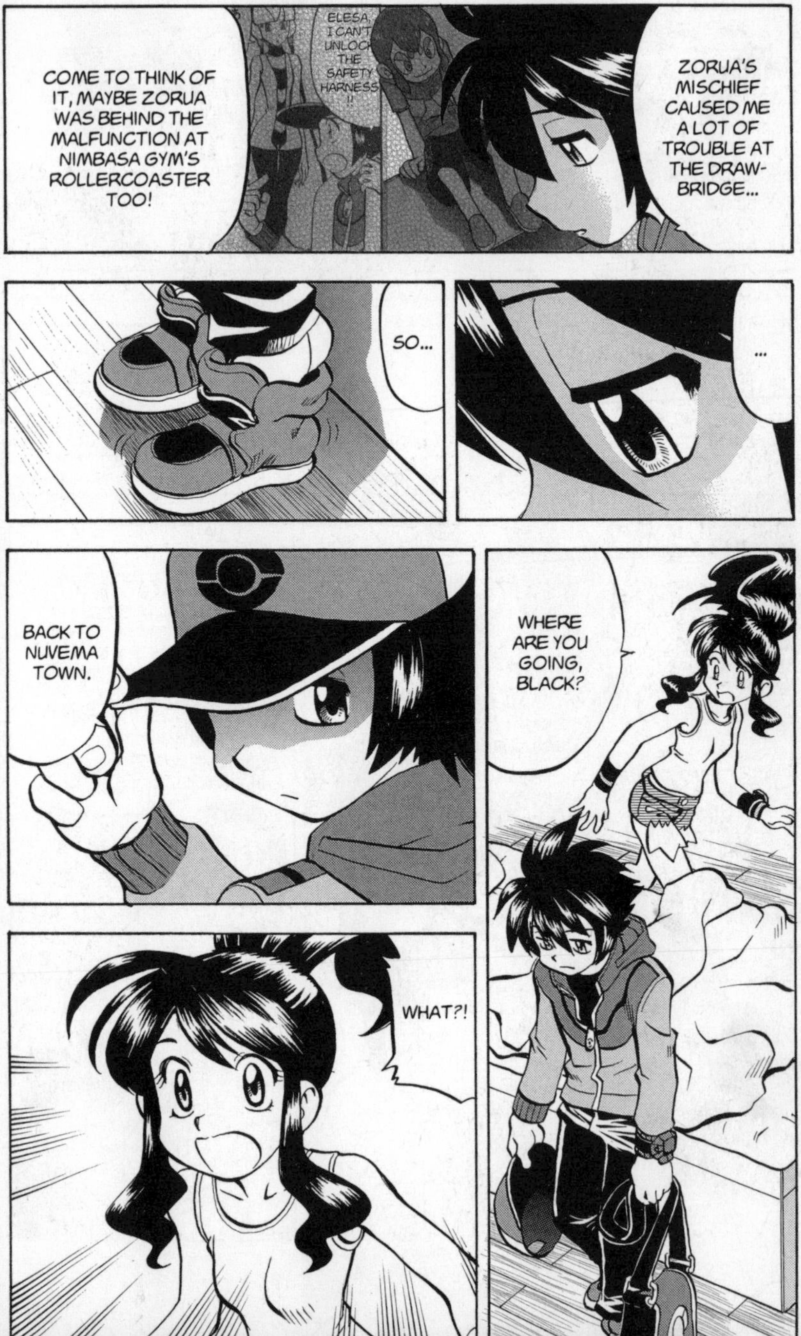
ZORUA'S MISCHIEF CAUSED ME A LOT OF TROUBLE AT THE DRAW-BRIDGE...
ELESA, I CAN'T UNLOCK THE SAFETY HARNESS!!
COME TO THINK OF IT, MAYBE ZORUA WAS BEHIND THE MALFUNCTION AT NIMBASA GYM'S ROLLERCOASTER TOO!
...
SO...
WHERE ARE YOU GOING, BLACK?
BACK TO NUVEMA TOWN.
WHAT?!

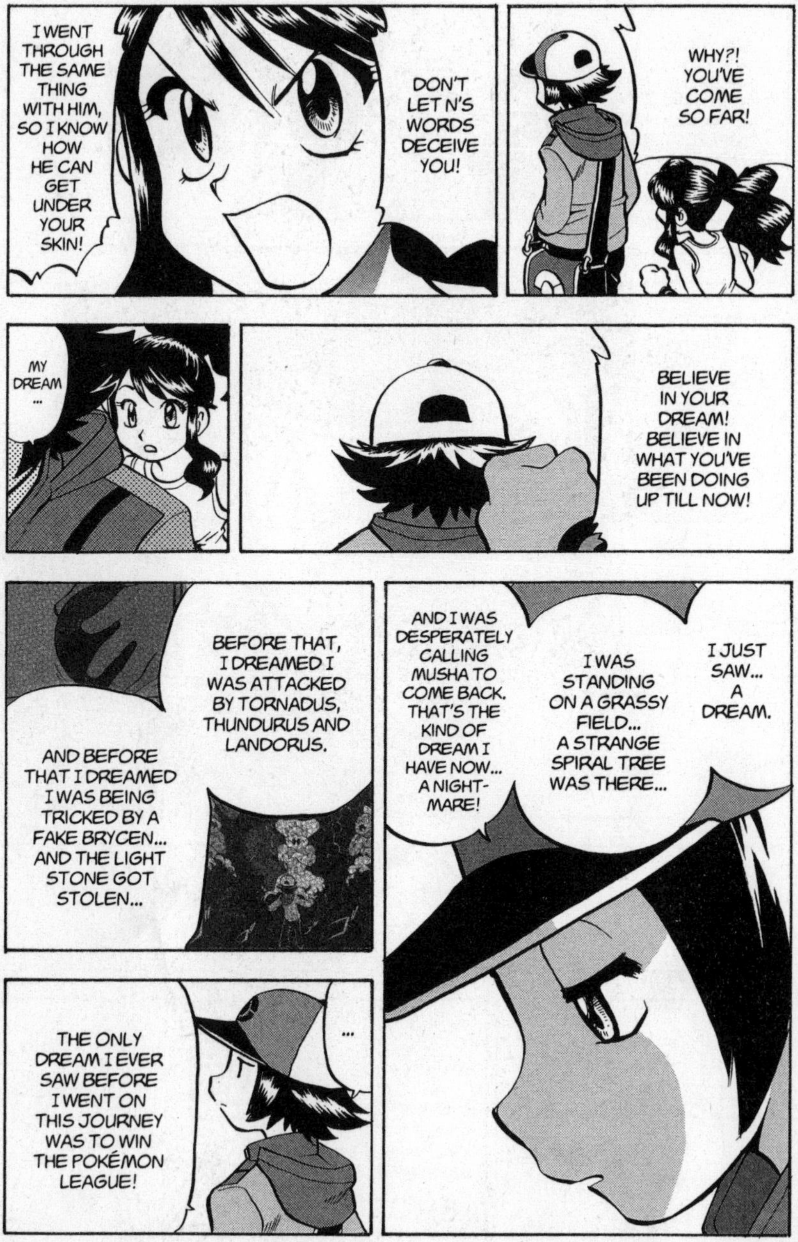
WHY?! YOU'VE COME SO FAR!
DON'T LET N'S WORDS DECEIVE YOU!
I WENT THROUGH THE SAME THING WITH HIM, SO I KNOW HOW HE CAN GET UNDER YOUR SKIN!
BELIEVE IN YOUR DREAM! BELIEVE IN WHAT YOU'VE BEEN DOING UP TILL NOW!
MY DREAM...
I JUST SAW... A DREAM.
I WAS STANDING ON A GRASSY FIELD... A STRANGE SPIRAL TREE WAS THERE...
AND I WAS DESPERATELY CALLING MUSHA TO COME BACK. THAT'S THE KIND OF DREAM I HAVE NOW... A NIGHT-MARE!
BEFORE THAT, I DREAMED I WAS ATTACKED BY TORNADUS, THUNDURUS AND LANDORUS.
AND BEFORE THAT I DREAMED I WAS BEING TRICKED BY A FAKE BRYCEN... AND THE LIGHT STONE GOT STOLEN...
...
THE ONLY DREAM I EVER SAW BEFORE I WENT ON THIS JOURNEY WAS TO WIN THE POKÉMON LEAGUE!

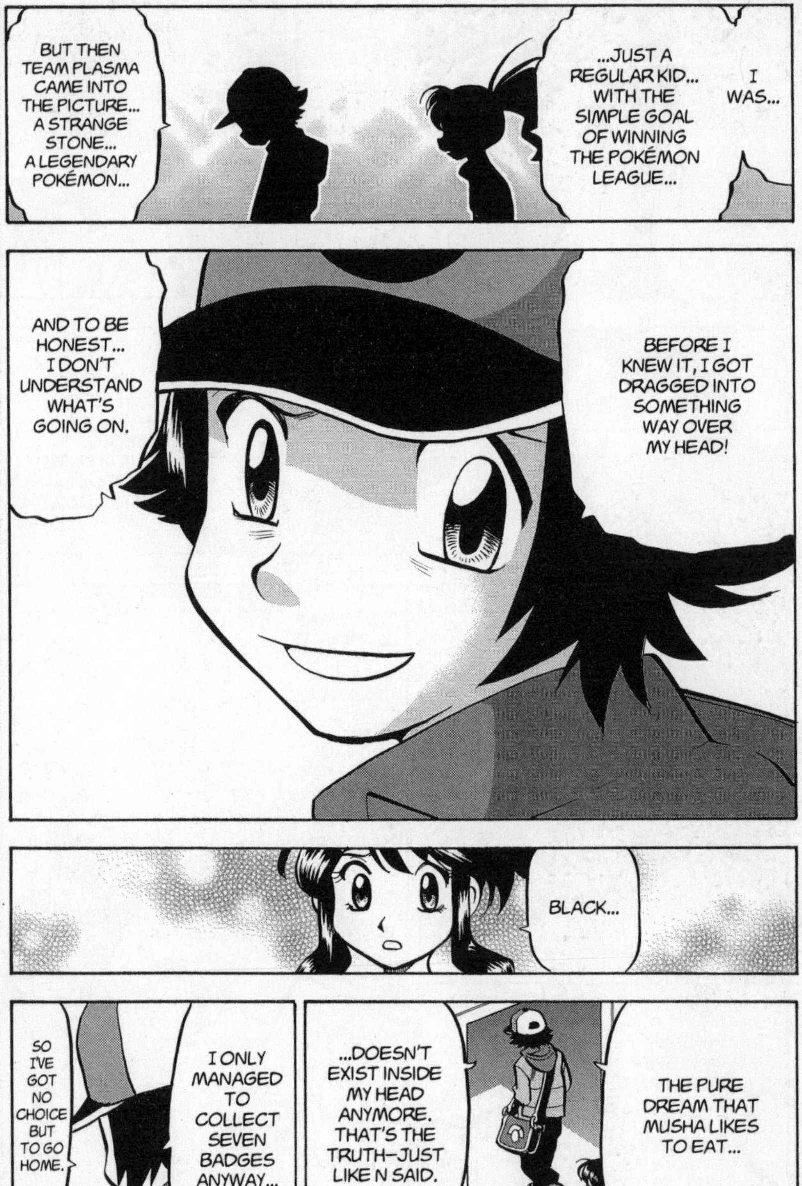
I WAS...
...JUST A REGULAR KID... WITH THE SIMPLE GOAL OF WINNING THE POKÉMON LEAGUE...
BUT THEN TEAM PLASMA CAME INTO THE PICTURE... A STRANGE STONE... A LEGENDARY POKÉMON...
BEFORE I KNEW IT, I GOT DRAGGED INTO SOMETHING WAY OVER MY HEAD!
AND TO BE HONEST... I DON'T UNDERSTAND WHAT'S GOING ON.
BLACK...
THE PURE DREAM THAT MUSHA LIKES TO EAT...
...DOESN'T EXIST INSIDE MY HEAD ANYMORE. THAT'S THE TRUTH—JUST LIKE N SAID.
I ONLY MANAGED TO COLLECT SEVEN BADGES ANYWAY...
SO I'VE GOT NO CHOICE BUT TO GO HOME.

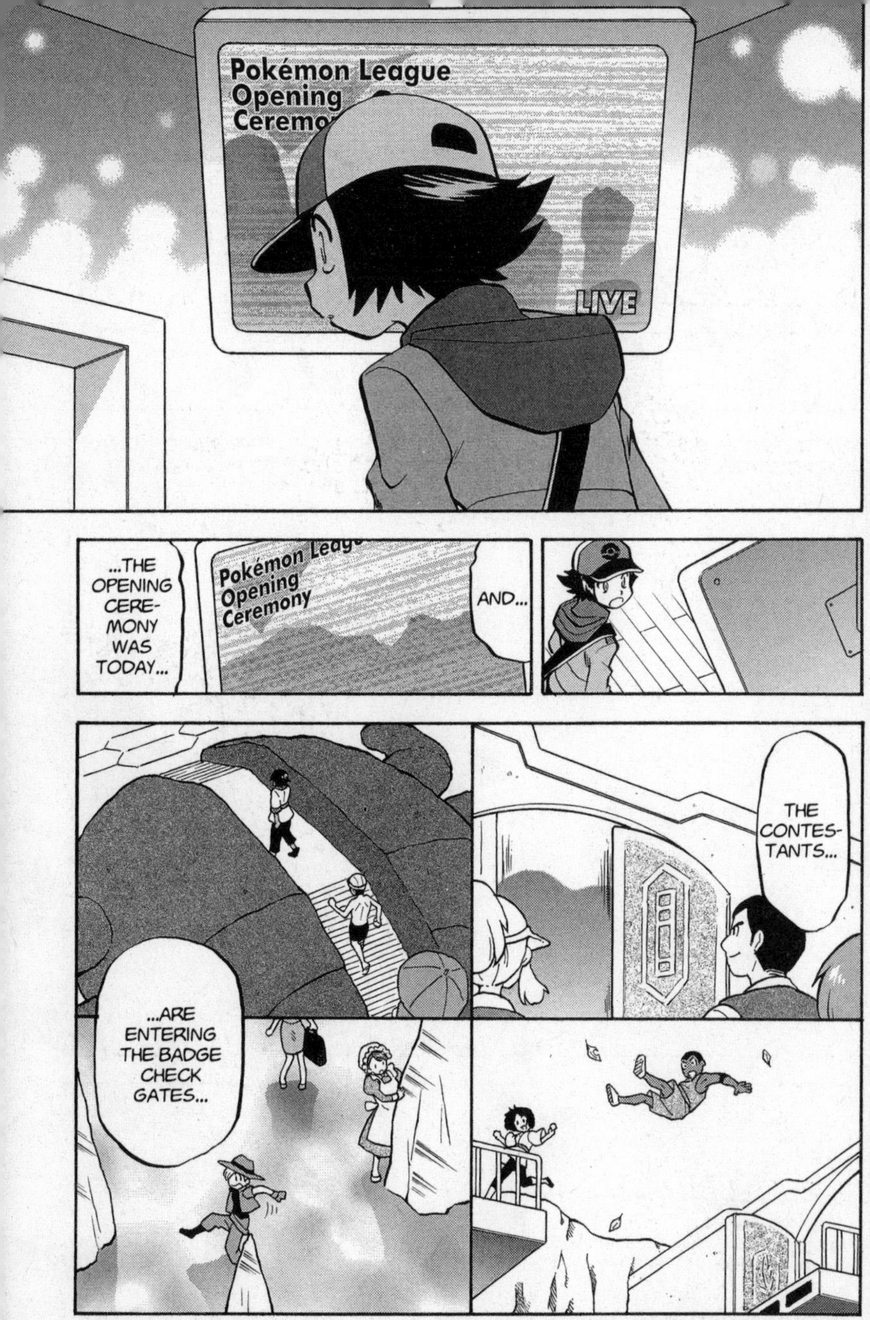

Pokémon League Opening Ceremony
LIVE
Pokémon League Opening Ceremony
AND...
...THE OPENING CERE-MONY WAS TODAY...
THE CONTES-TANTS...
...ARE ENTERING THE BADGE CHECK GATES...

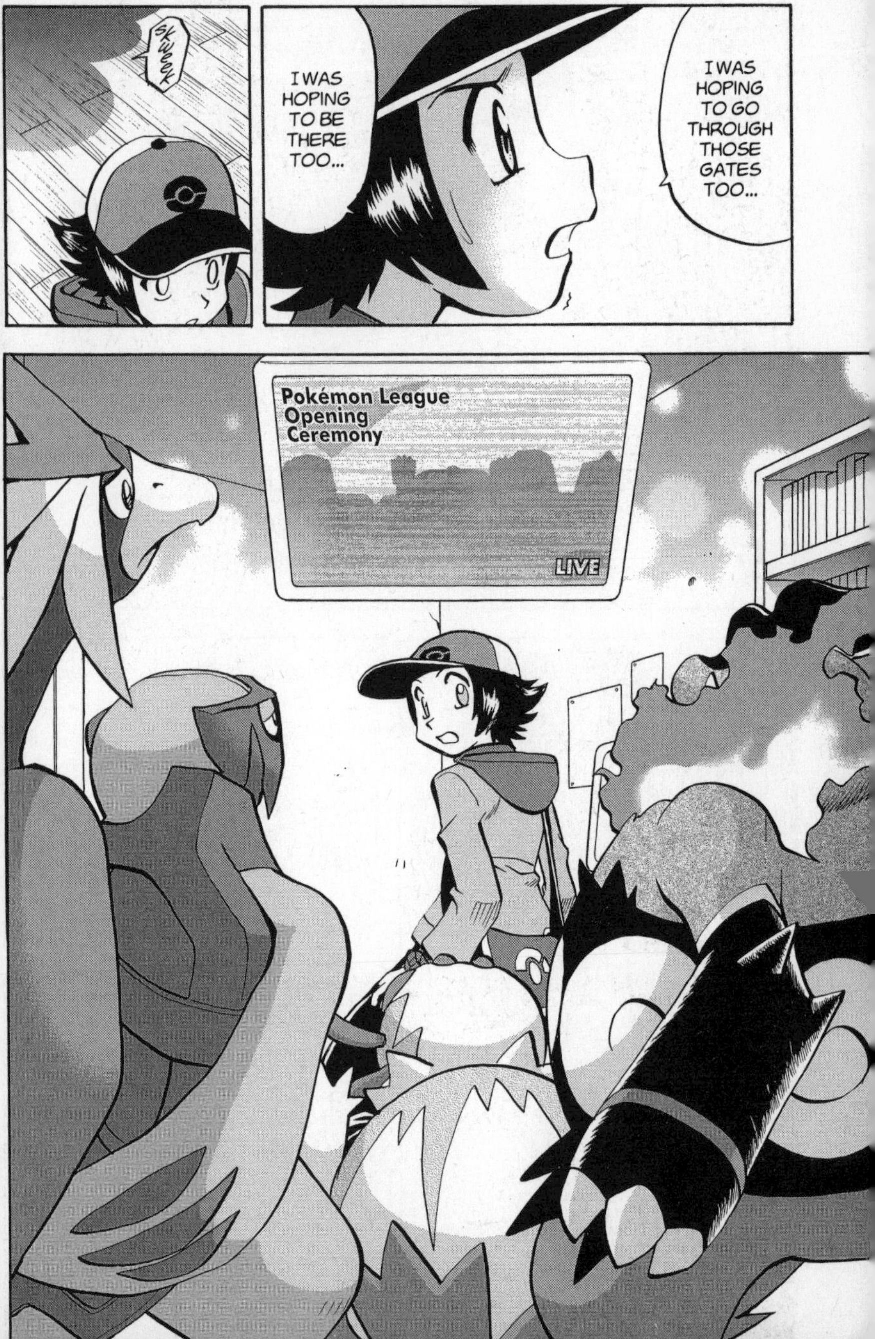
I WAS HOPING TO GO THROUGH THOSE GATES TOO...
I WAS HOPING TO BE THERE TOO...
SKWEEK
Pokémon League Opening Ceremony
LIVE

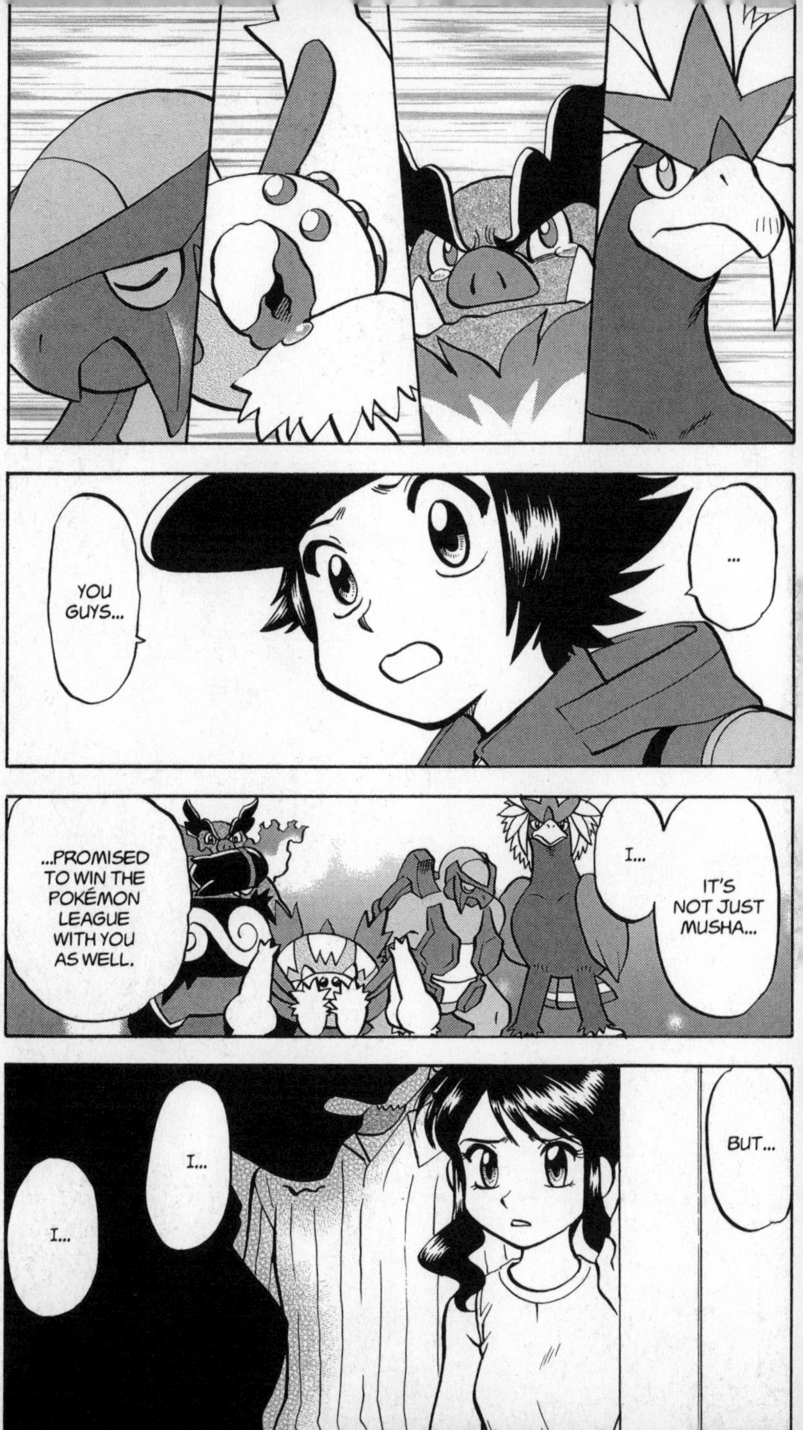
...
YOU GUYS...
I...
IT'S NOT JUST MUSHA...
...PROMISED TO WIN THE POKÉMON LEAGUE WITH YOU AS WELL.
BUT...
I...
I...

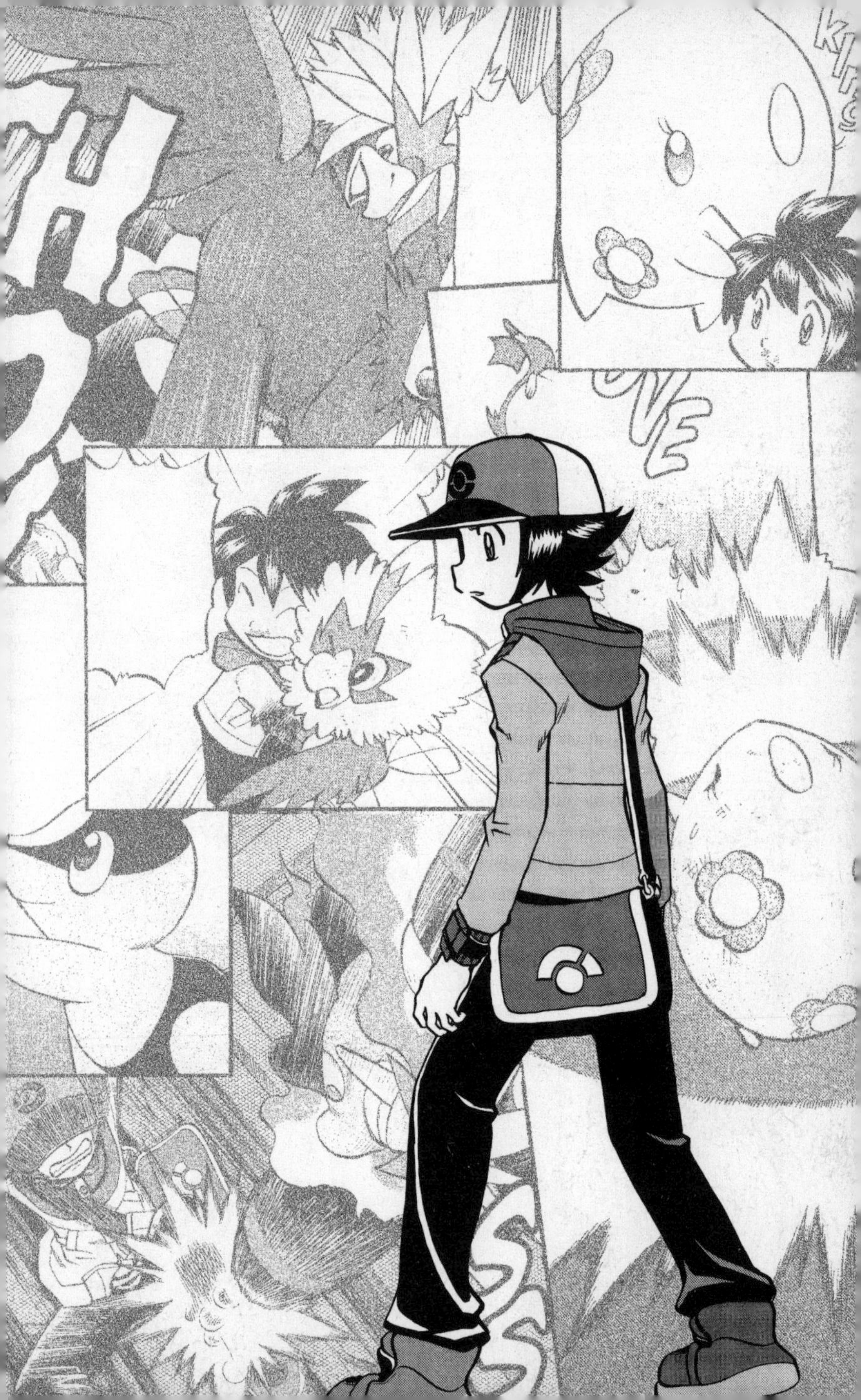

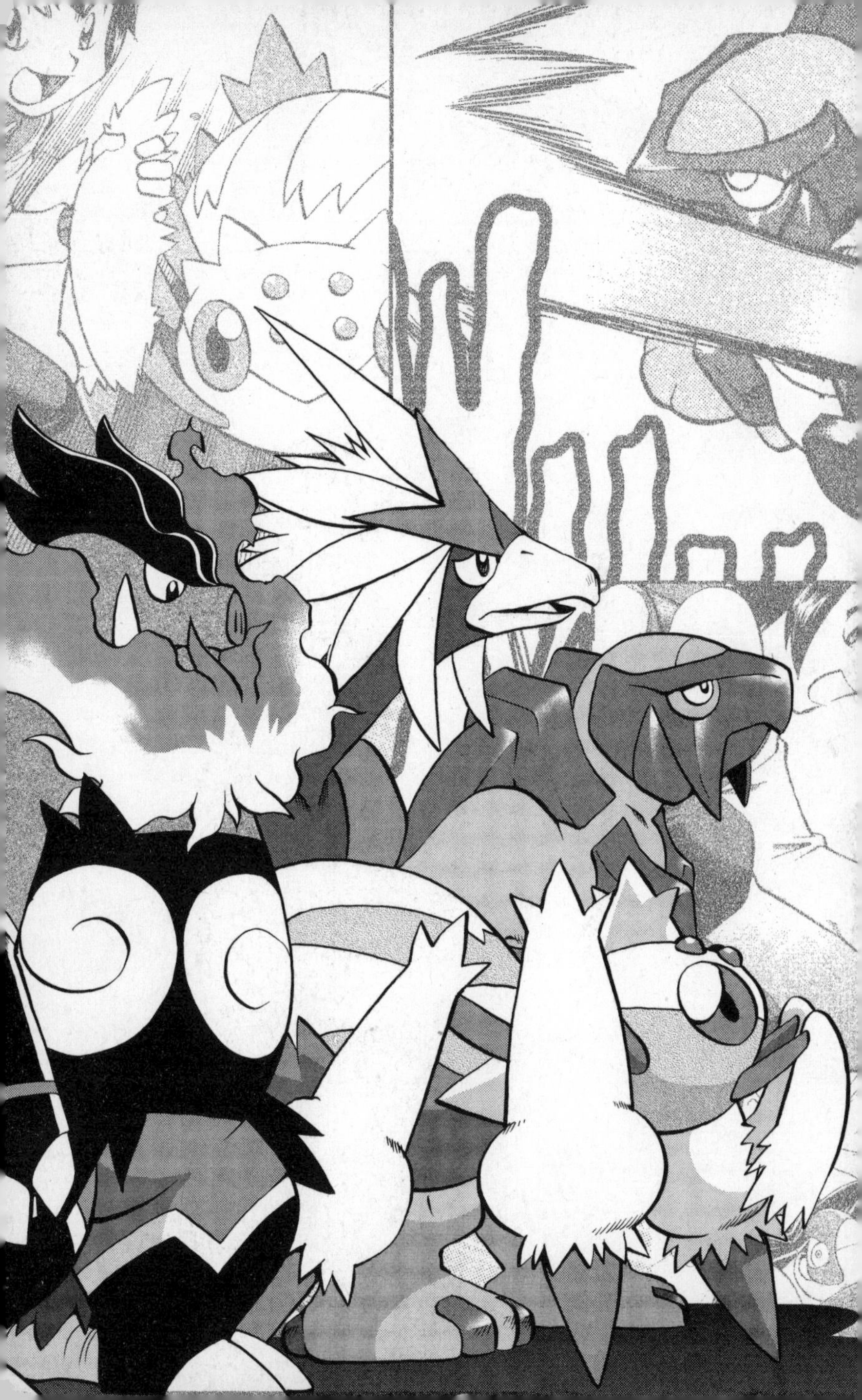

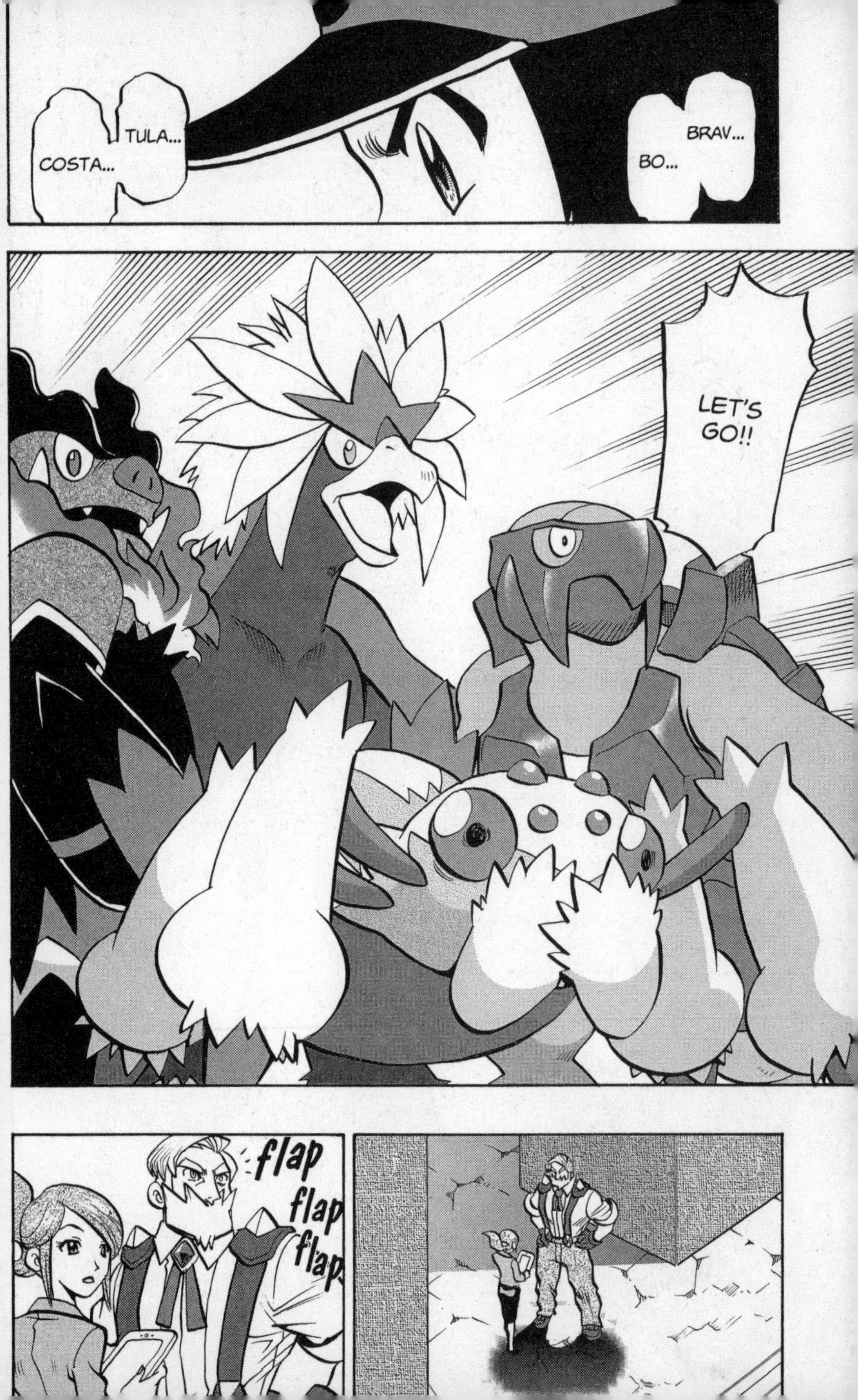
BRAV... BO...
TULA... COSTA...
LET'S GO!!
flap flap flap

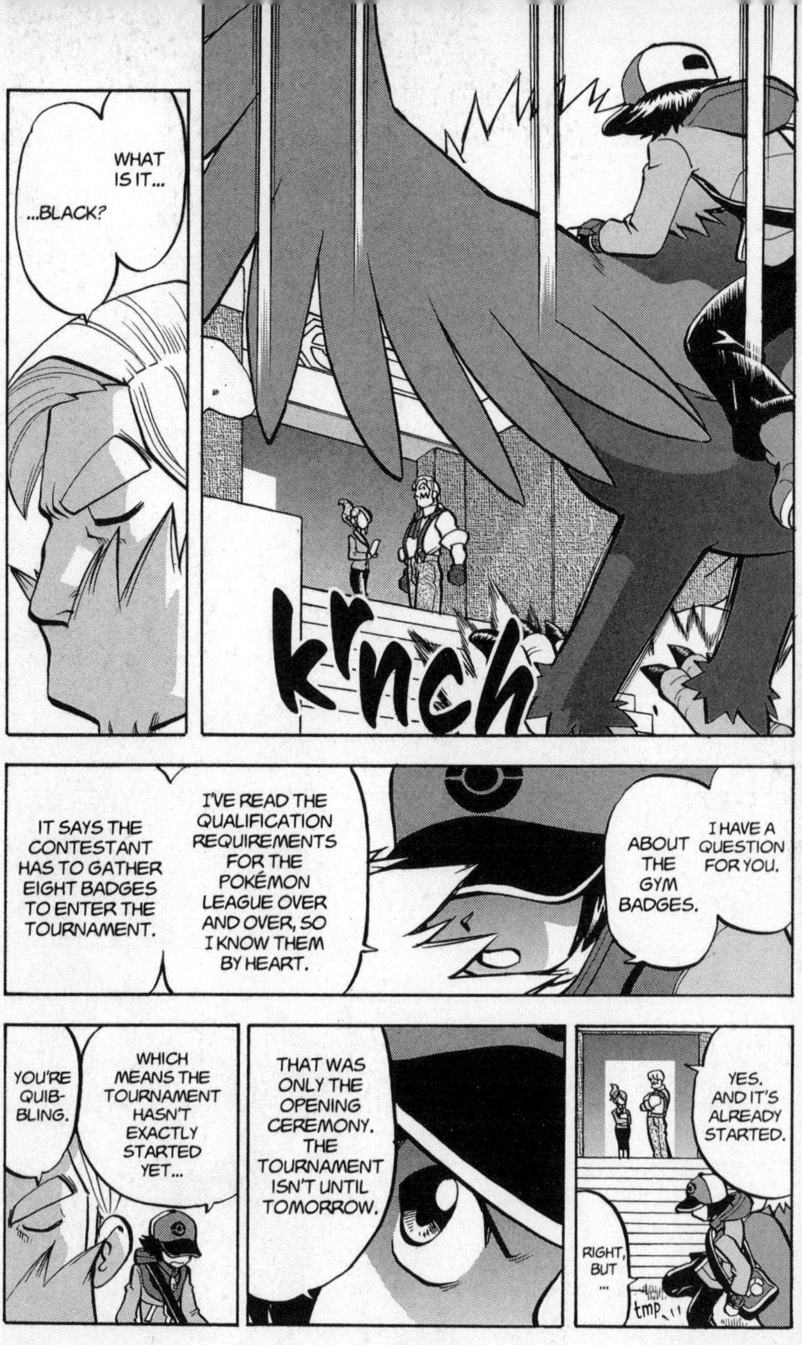
k'nch
WHAT IS IT...
...BLACK?
I HAVE A QUESTION FOR YOU.
ABOUT THE GYM BADGES.
I'VE READ THE QUALIFICATION REQUIREMENTS FOR THE POKÉMON LEAGUE OVER AND OVER, SO I KNOW THEM BY HEART.
IT SAYS THE CONTESTANT HAS TO GATHER EIGHT BADGES TO ENTER THE TOURNAMENT.
YES. AND IT'S ALREADY STARTED.
RIGHT, BUT ...
tmp
THAT WAS ONLY THE OPENING CEREMONY. THE TOURNAMENT ISN'T UNTIL TOMORROW.
WHICH MEANS THE TOURNAMENT HASN'T EXACTLY STARTED YET...
YOU'RE QUIB-BLING.

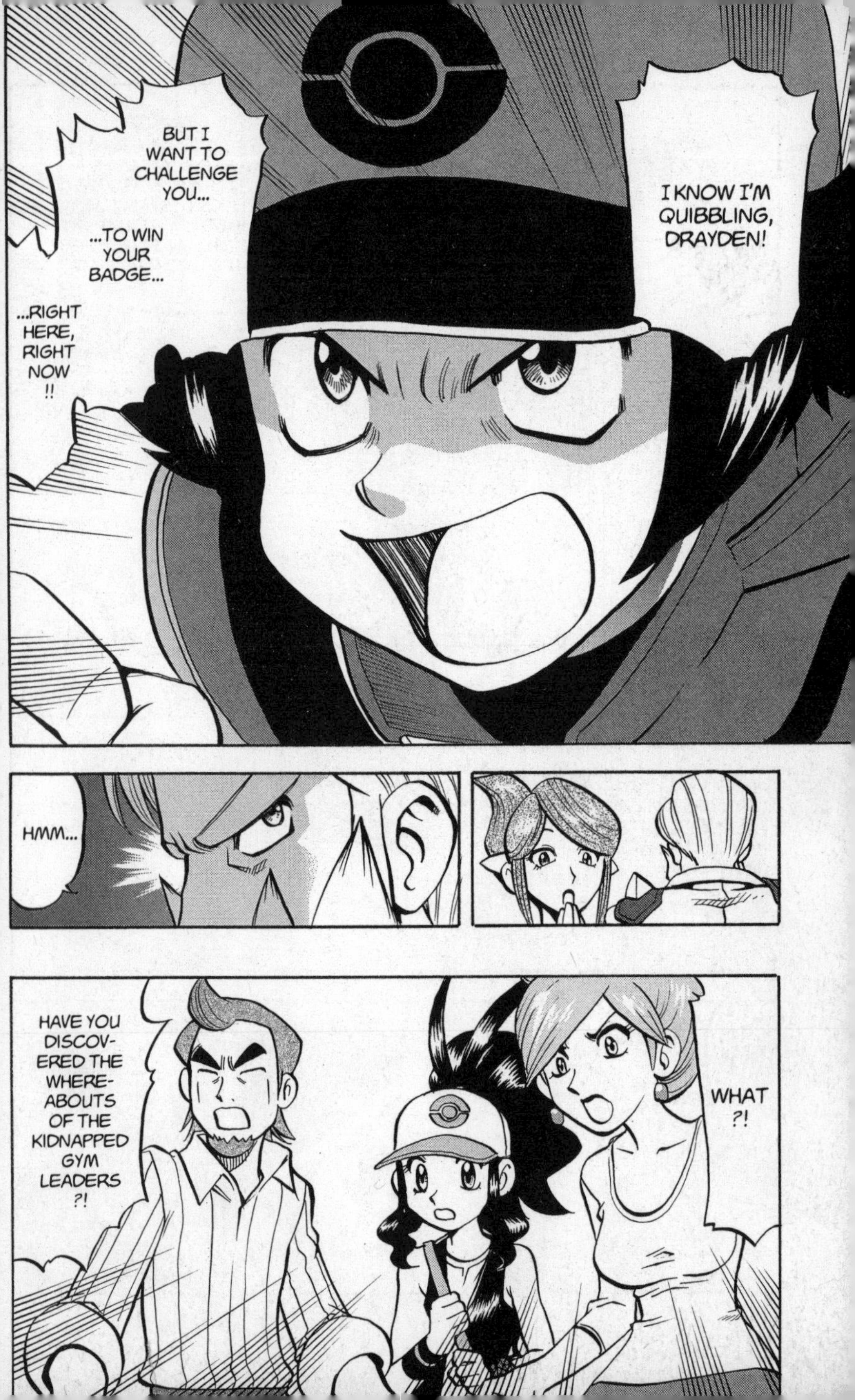
I KNOW I'M QUIBBLING, DRAYDEN!
BUT I WANT TO CHALLENGE YOU...
...TO WIN YOUR BADGE...
...RIGHT HERE, RIGHT NOW !!
HMM...
WHAT ?!
HAVE YOU DISCOV-ERED THE WHERE-ABOUTS OF THE KIDNAPPED GYM LEADERS ?!

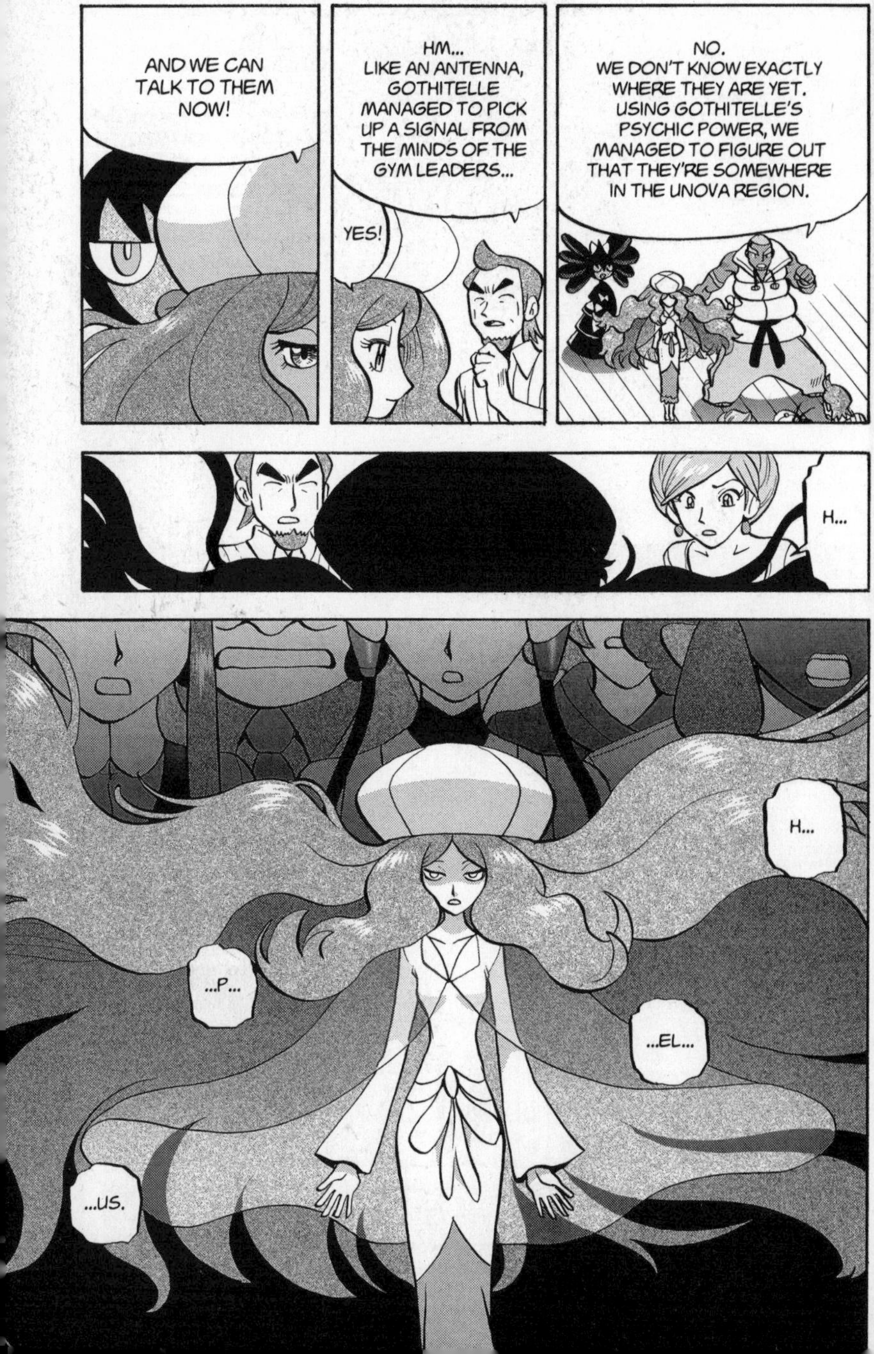
NO. WE DON'T KNOW EXACTLY WHERE THEY ARE YET. USING GOTHITELLE'S PSYCHIC POWER, WE MANAGED TO FIGURE OUT THAT THEY'RE SOMEWHERE IN THE UNOVA REGION.
HM... LIKE AN ANTENNA, GOTHITELLE MANAGED TO PICK UP A SIGNAL FROM THE MINDS OF THE GYM LEADERS...
YES!
AND WE CAN TALK TO THEM NOW!
H...
H...
...P...
...EL...
...US.

# ADVENTURE MAP

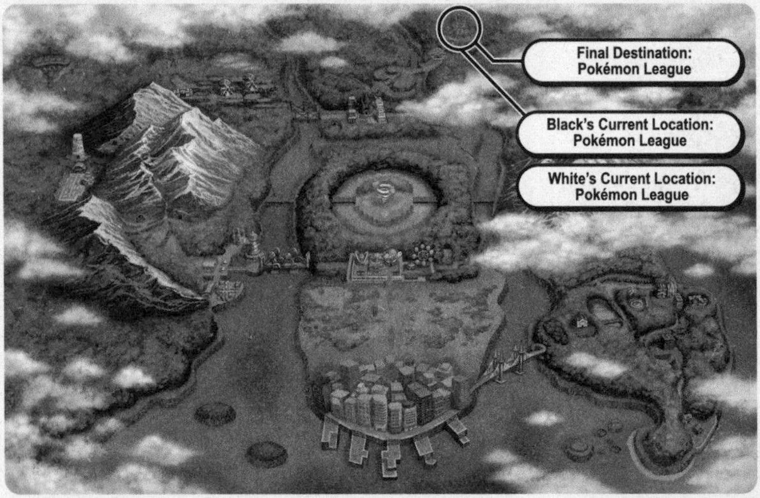

Final Destination:
Pokémon League
Black's Current Location:
Pokémon League
White's Current Location:
Pokémon League


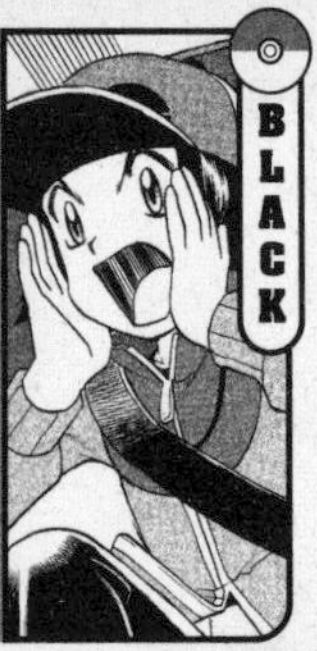

BLACK


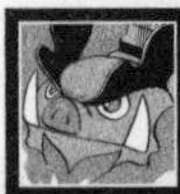

**Bo**
Mega Fire Pig Pokémon
Emboar ♂ | Fire | Fighting
Lv.46 Ability: Blaze

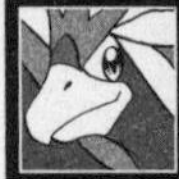

**Brav**
Valiant Pokémon
Braviary ♂ | Normal | Flying
Lv.56 Ability: Sheer Force

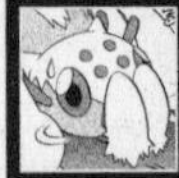

**Tula**
EleSpider Pokémon
Galvantula ♂ | Bug | Electric
Lv.56 Ability: Unnerve

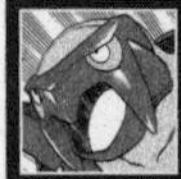

**Costa**
Prototurtle Pokémon
Tirtouga ♂ | Water | Rock
Lv.40 Ability: Solid Rock

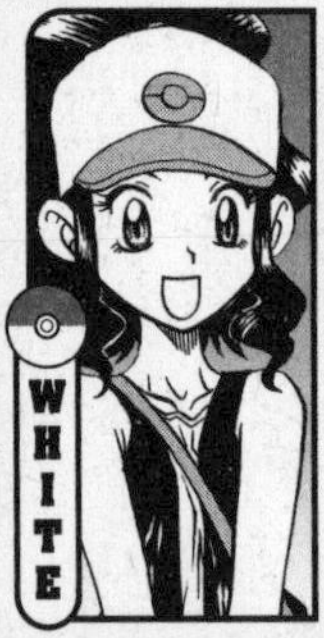

WHITE


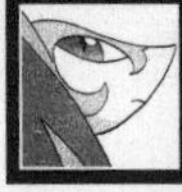

**Amanda**
Grass Snake Pokémon
Servine ♀ | Grass
Lv.37 Ability: Overgrow

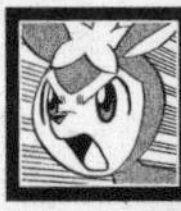

**Darlene**
Season Pokémon
Deerling ♀ | Normal | Grass
Lv.31 Ability: Chlorophyll

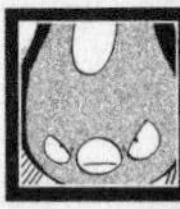

**Dorothy**
Trap Pokémon
Stunfisk ♀ | Ground | Electric
Lv.34 Ability: Limber

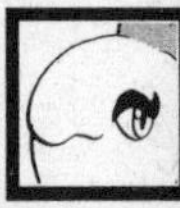

**Nancy**
Caring Pokémon
Alomomola ♀ | Water
Lv.35 Ability: Healer

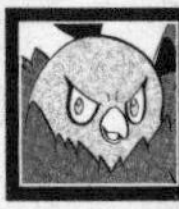

**Barbara**
Diapered Pokémon
Vullaby ♀ | Dark | Flying
Lv.39 Ability: Big Pecks

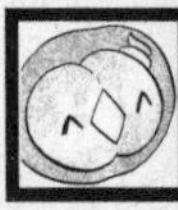

**Solly**
Cell Pokémon
Solosis ♂ | Psychic
Lv.29 Ability: Magic Guard

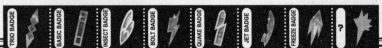

TRIO BADGE · BASIC BADGE · INSECT BADGE · BOLT BADGE · QUAKE BADGE · JET BADGE · FREEZE BADGE · ?

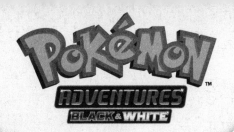

Pokémon™ Adventures Black & White

DRUDDIGON

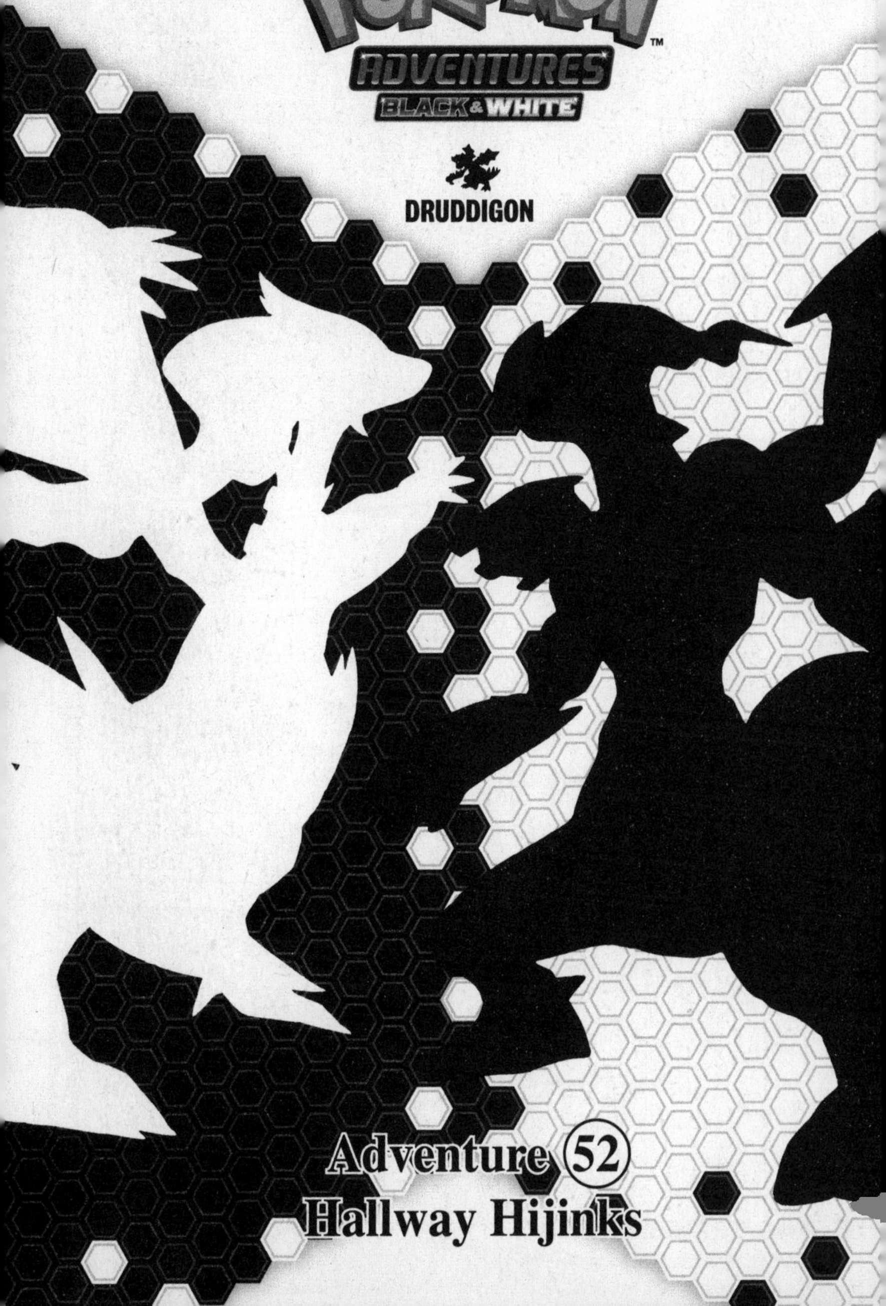

# Adventure 52
# Hallway Hijinks

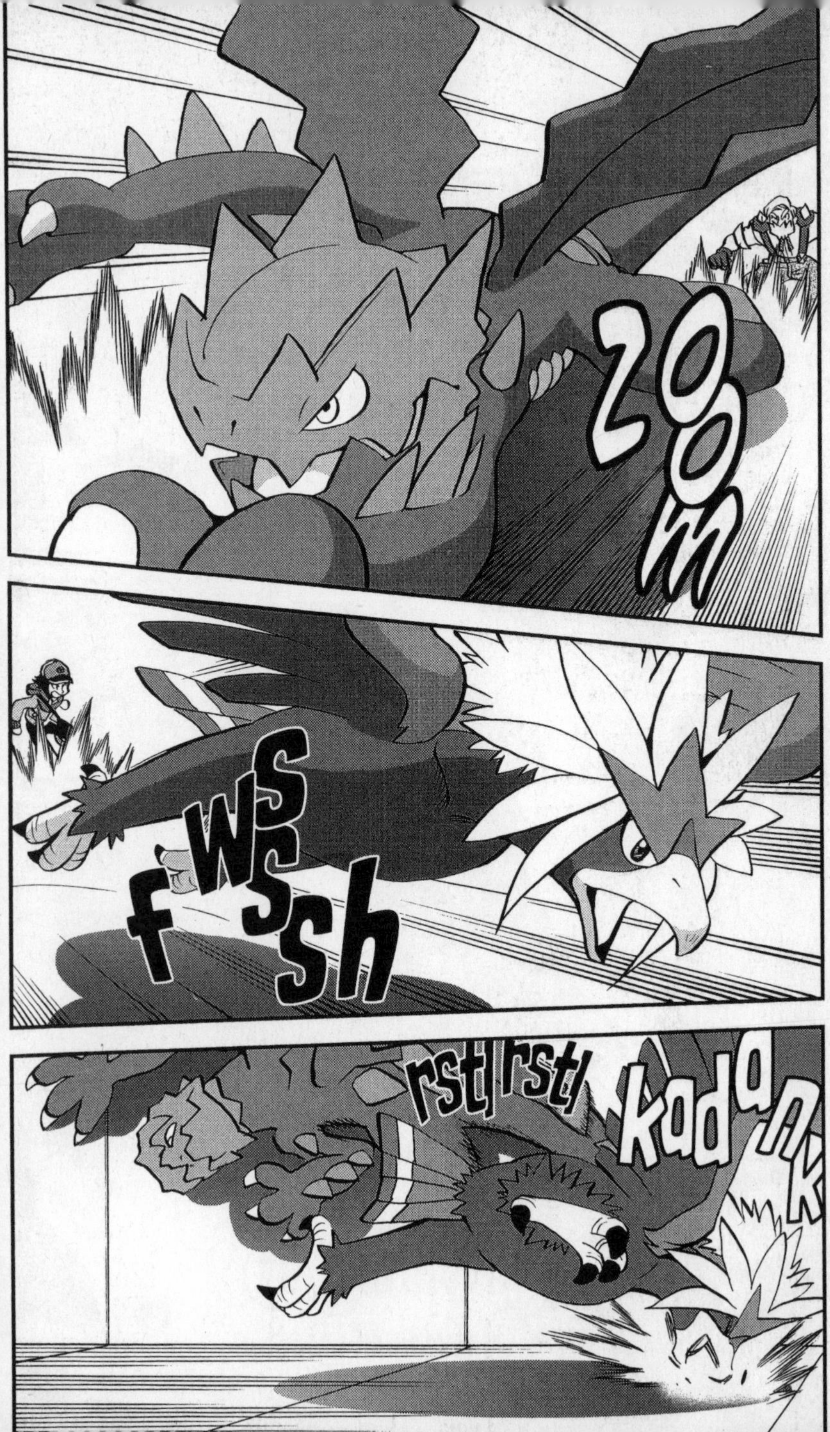
zoom
fwssh
kadank
rstl rstl

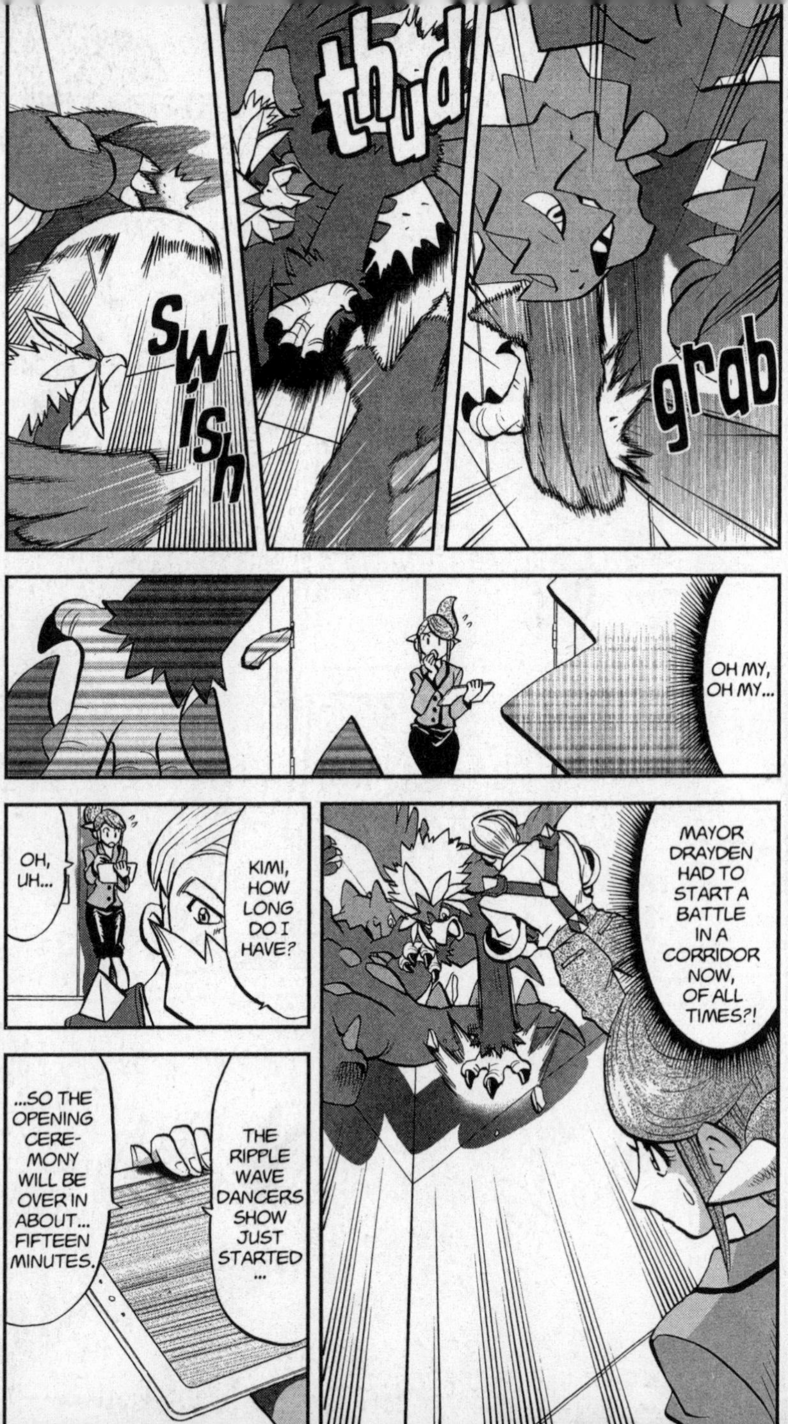
grab
thud
swish
OH MY, OH MY...
MAYOR DRAYDEN HAD TO START A BATTLE IN A CORRIDOR NOW, OF ALL TIMES?!
KIMI, HOW LONG DO I HAVE?
OH, UH...
THE RIPPLE WAVE DANCERS SHOW JUST STARTED...
...SO THE OPENING CEREMONY WILL BE OVER IN ABOUT... FIFTEEN MINUTES.

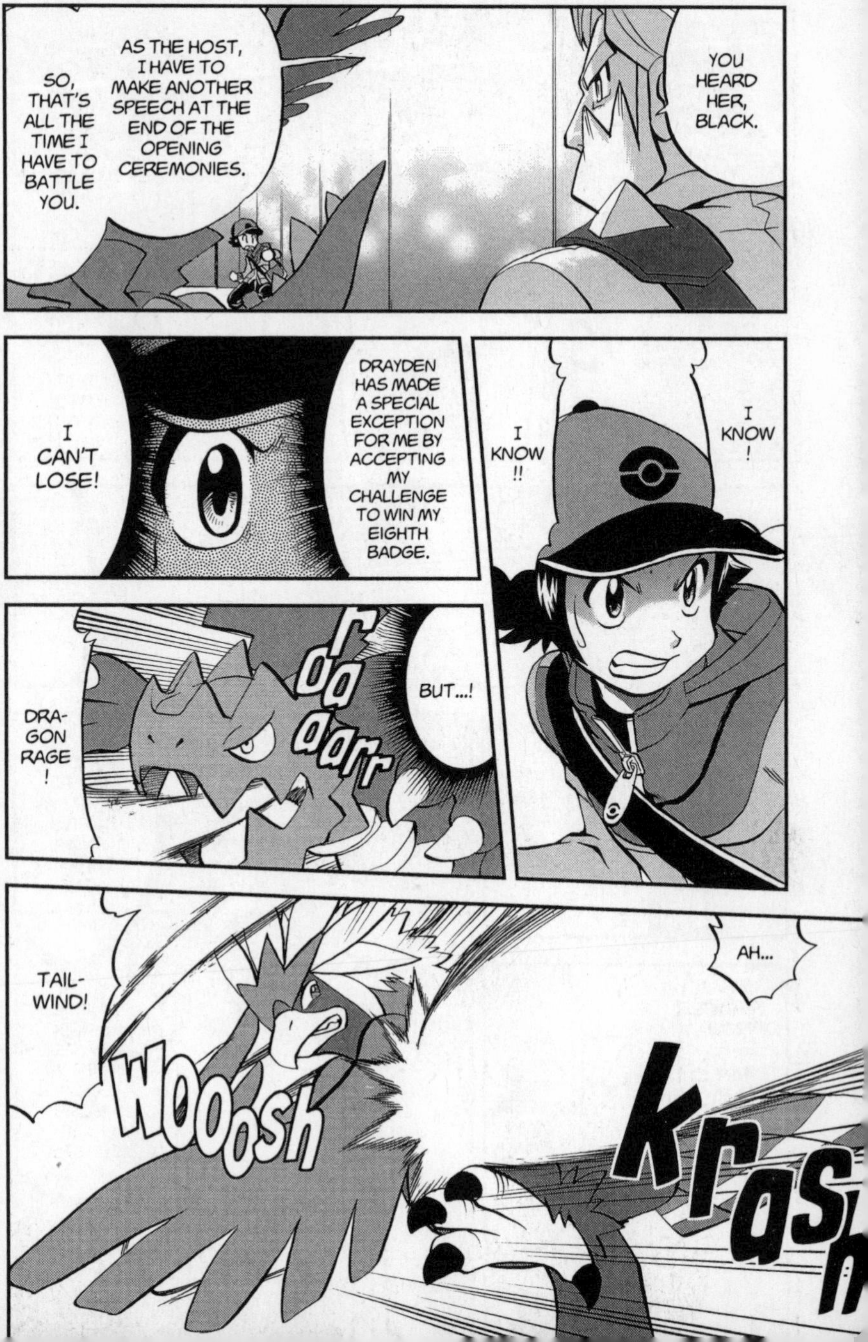
YOU HEARD HER, BLACK.
AS THE HOST, I HAVE TO MAKE ANOTHER SPEECH AT THE END OF THE OPENING CEREMONIES.
SO, THAT'S ALL THE TIME I HAVE TO BATTLE YOU.
I KNOW!
I KNOW!!
DRAYDEN HAS MADE A SPECIAL EXCEPTION FOR ME BY ACCEPTING MY CHALLENGE TO WIN MY EIGHTH BADGE.
I CAN'T LOSE!
BUT...!
roaarr
DRA-GON RAGE!
AH...
krash
TAIL-WIND!
WOOOsh

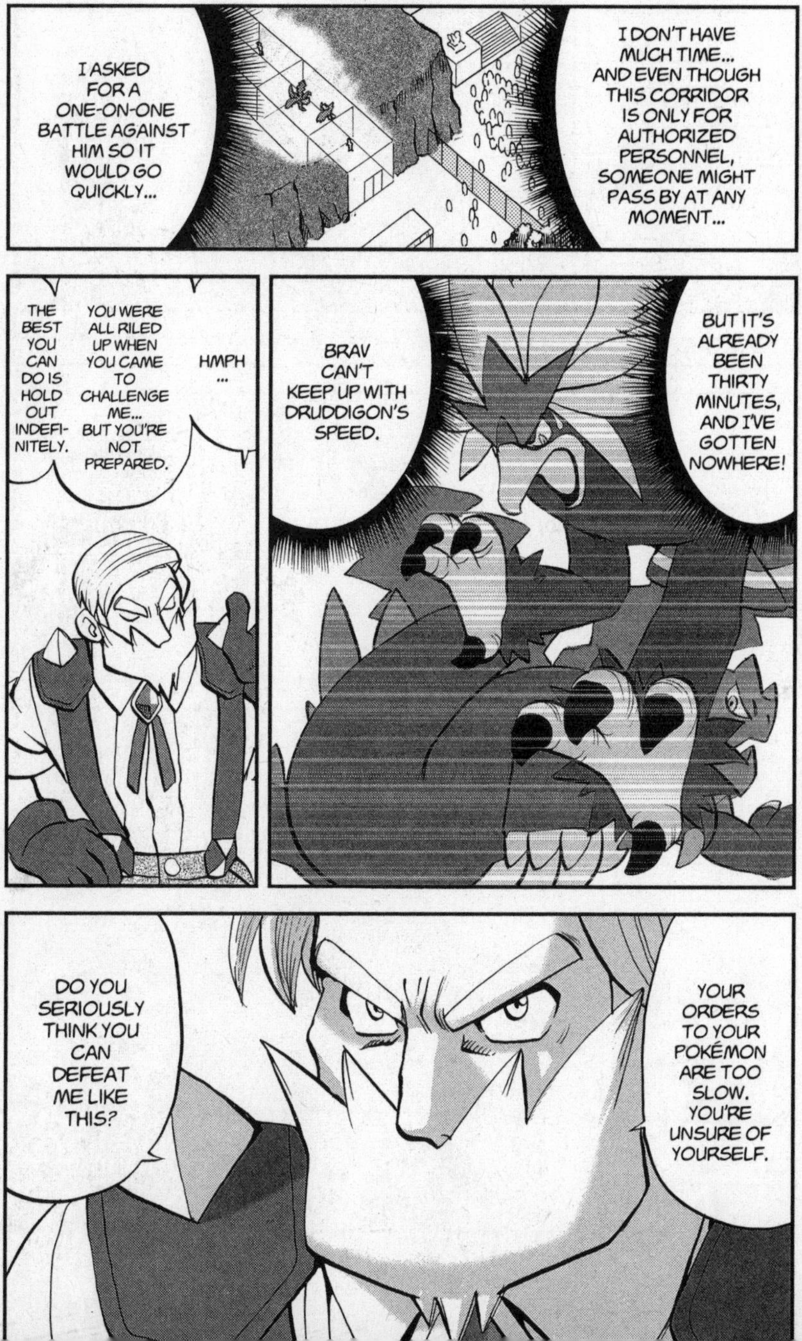
I DON'T HAVE MUCH TIME... AND EVEN THOUGH THIS CORRIDOR IS ONLY FOR AUTHORIZED PERSONNEL, SOMEONE MIGHT PASS BY AT ANY MOMENT...
I ASKED FOR A ONE-ON-ONE BATTLE AGAINST HIM SO IT WOULD GO QUICKLY...
BUT IT'S ALREADY BEEN THIRTY MINUTES, AND I'VE GOTTEN NOWHERE!
BRAV CAN'T KEEP UP WITH DRUDDIGON'S SPEED.
HMPH ...
YOU WERE ALL RILED UP WHEN YOU CAME TO CHALLENGE ME... BUT YOU'RE NOT PREPARED.
THE BEST YOU CAN DO IS HOLD OUT INDEFI-NITELY.
YOUR ORDERS TO YOUR POKÉMON ARE TOO SLOW. YOU'RE UNSURE OF YOURSELF.
DO YOU SERIOUSLY THINK YOU CAN DEFEAT ME LIKE THIS?

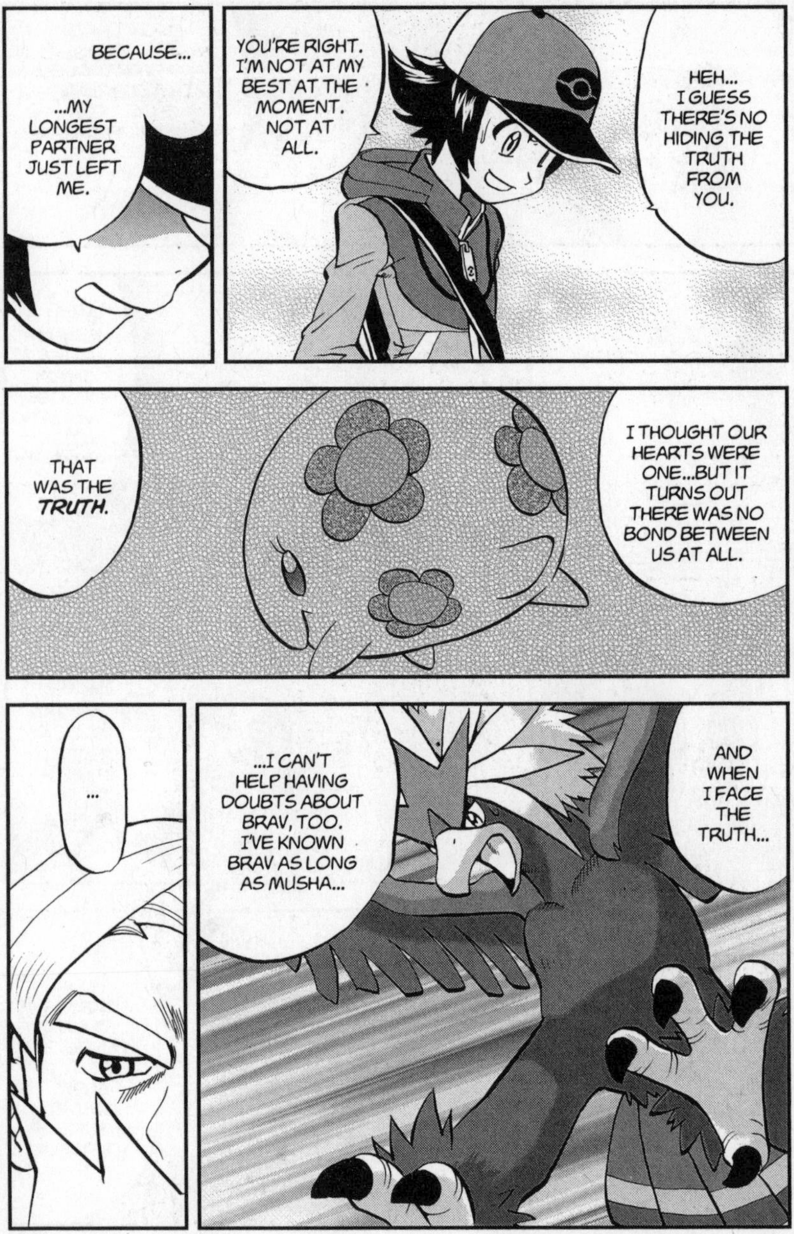
HEH... I GUESS THERE'S NO HIDING THE TRUTH FROM YOU.
YOU'RE RIGHT. I'M NOT AT MY BEST AT THE MOMENT. NOT AT ALL.
BECAUSE...
...MY LONGEST PARTNER JUST LEFT ME.
I THOUGHT OUR HEARTS WERE ONE...BUT IT TURNS OUT THERE WAS NO BOND BETWEEN US AT ALL.
THAT WAS THE ***TRUTH***.
AND WHEN I FACE THE TRUTH...
...I CAN'T HELP HAVING DOUBTS ABOUT BRAV, TOO. I'VE KNOWN BRAV AS LONG AS MUSHA...
...

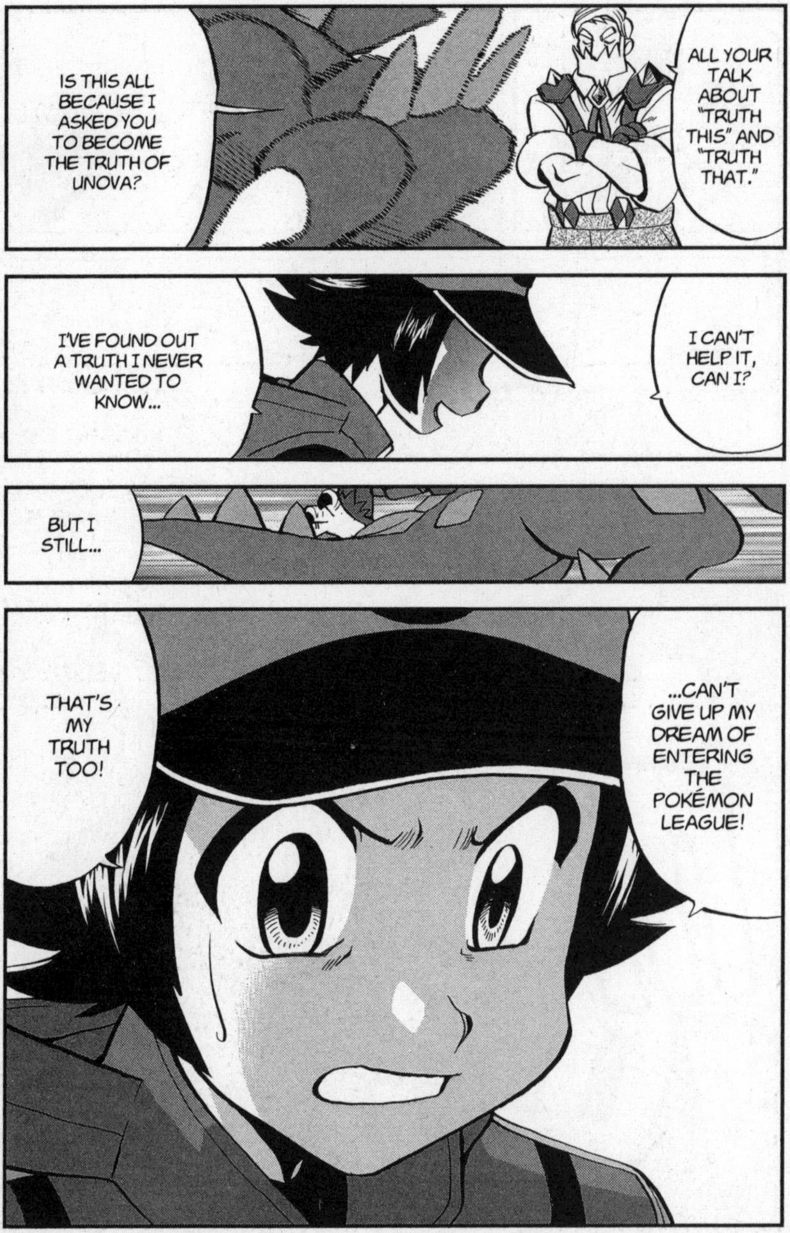
ALL YOUR TALK ABOUT "TRUTH THIS" AND "TRUTH THAT."
IS THIS ALL BECAUSE I ASKED YOU TO BECOME THE TRUTH OF UNOVA?
I CAN'T HELP IT, CAN I?
I'VE FOUND OUT A TRUTH I NEVER WANTED TO KNOW...
BUT I STILL...
...CAN'T GIVE UP MY DREAM OF ENTERING THE POKÉMON LEAGUE!
THAT'S MY TRUTH TOO!

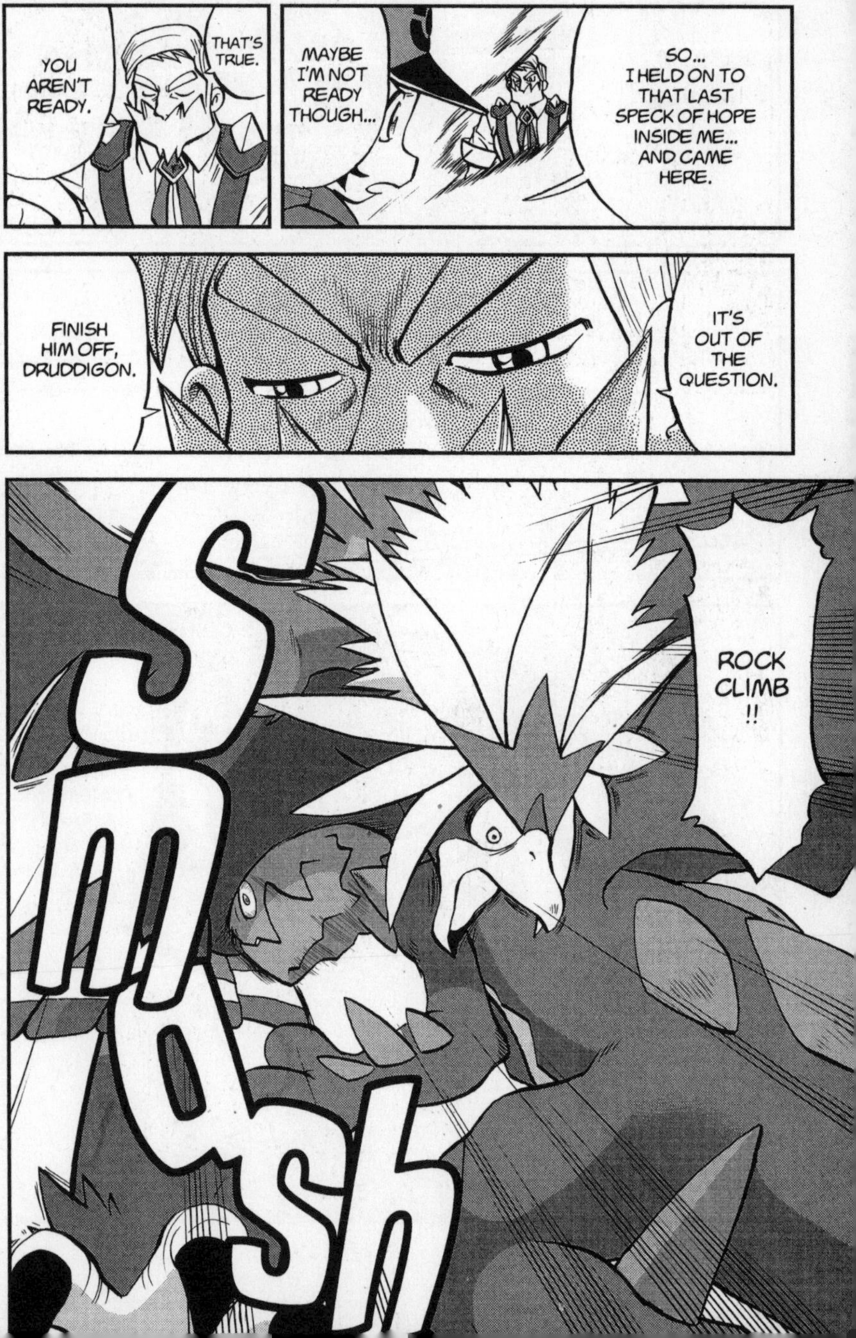
SO... I HELD ON TO THAT LAST SPECK OF HOPE INSIDE ME... AND CAME HERE.
MAYBE I'M NOT READY THOUGH...
THAT'S TRUE.
YOU AREN'T READY.
IT'S OUT OF THE QUESTION.
FINISH HIM OFF, DRUDDIGON.
ROCK CLIMB !!
Smash

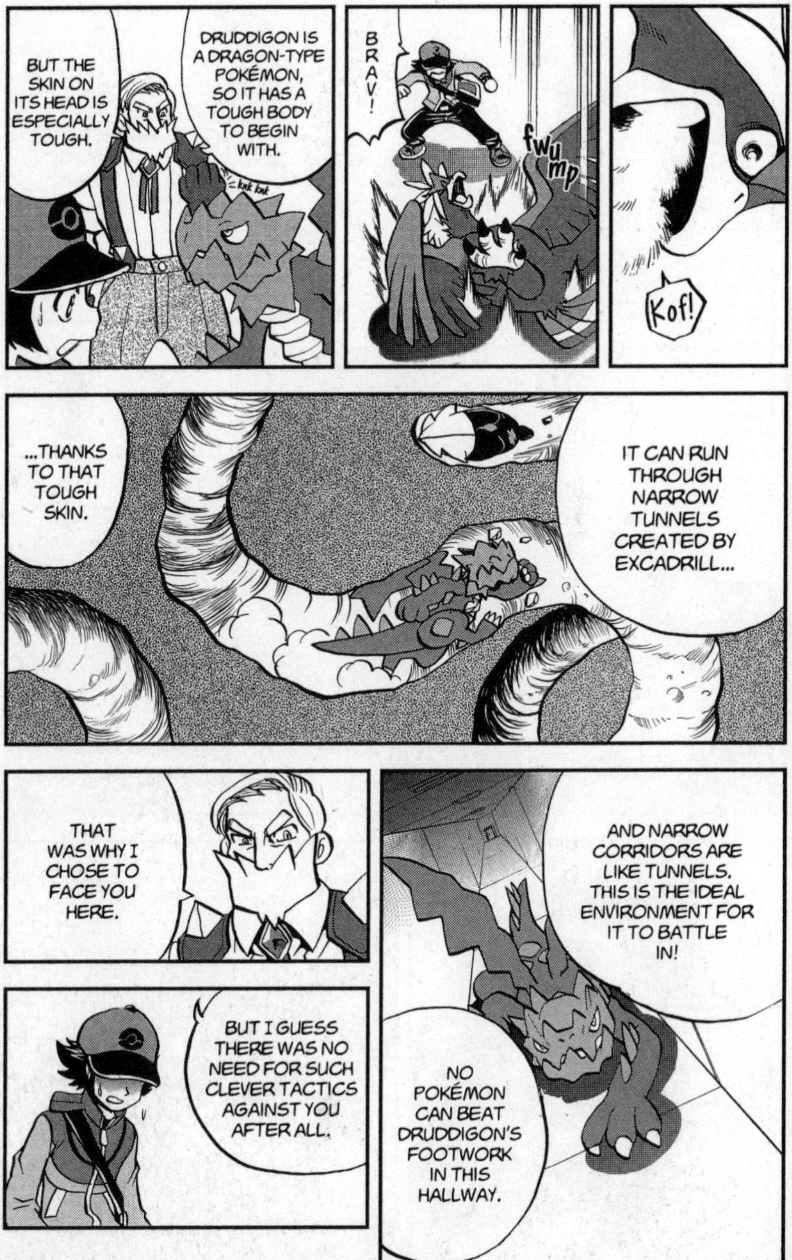
Kof!
BRAV!
fwump
DRUDDIGON IS A DRAGON-TYPE POKÉMON, SO IT HAS A TOUGH BODY TO BEGIN WITH.
BUT THE SKIN ON ITS HEAD IS ESPECIALLY TOUGH.
knk knk
IT CAN RUN THROUGH NARROW TUNNELS CREATED BY EXCADRILL...
...THANKS TO THAT TOUGH SKIN.
AND NARROW CORRIDORS ARE LIKE TUNNELS. THIS IS THE IDEAL ENVIRONMENT FOR IT TO BATTLE IN!
NO POKÉMON CAN BEAT DRUDDIGON'S FOOTWORK IN THIS HALLWAY.
THAT WAS WHY I CHOSE TO FACE YOU HERE.
BUT I GUESS THERE WAS NO NEED FOR SUCH CLEVER TACTICS AGAINST YOU AFTER ALL.

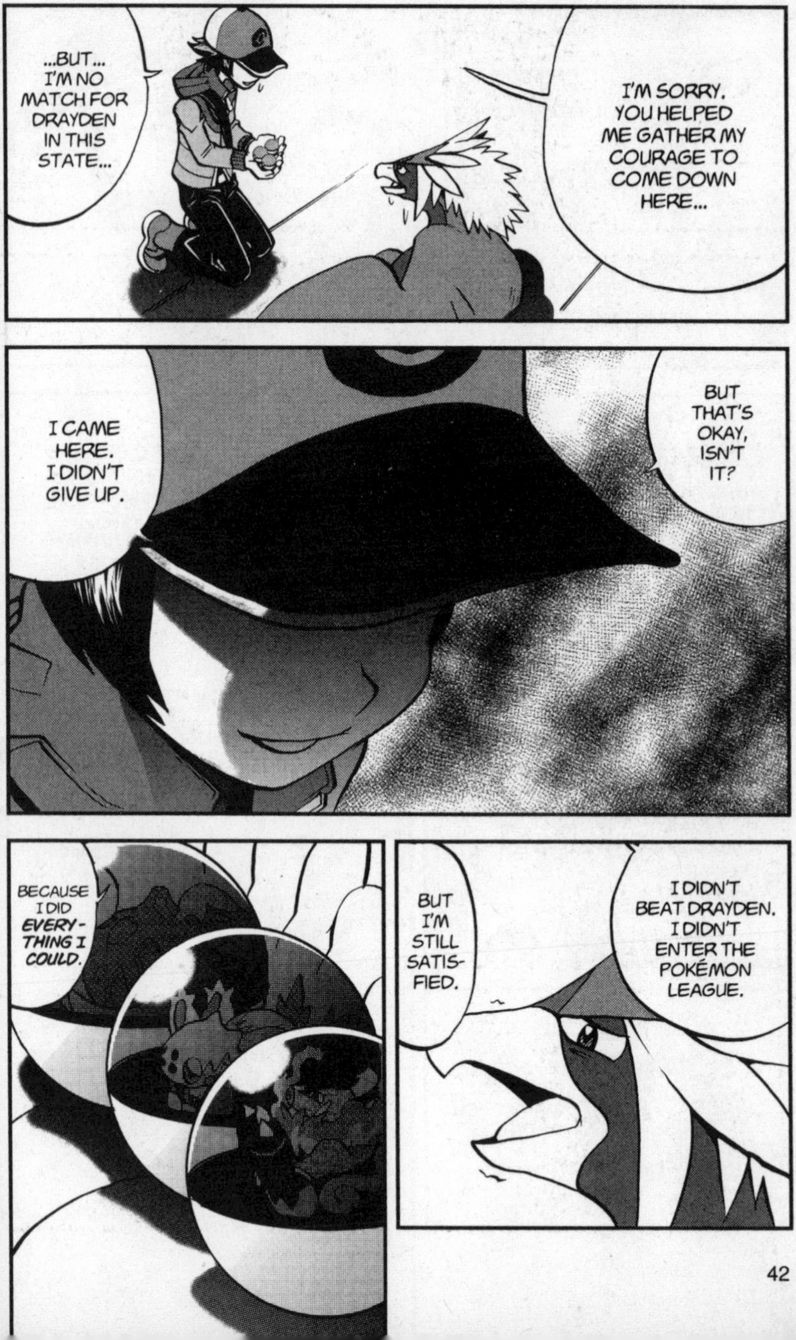
I'M SORRY. YOU HELPED ME GATHER MY COURAGE TO COME DOWN HERE...
...BUT... I'M NO MATCH FOR DRAYDEN IN THIS STATE...
BUT THAT'S OKAY, ISN'T IT?
I CAME HERE. I DIDN'T GIVE UP.
I DIDN'T BEAT DRAYDEN. I DIDN'T ENTER THE POKÉMON LEAGUE.
BUT I'M STILL SATIS-FIED.
BECAUSE I DID *EVERY-THING I COULD.*

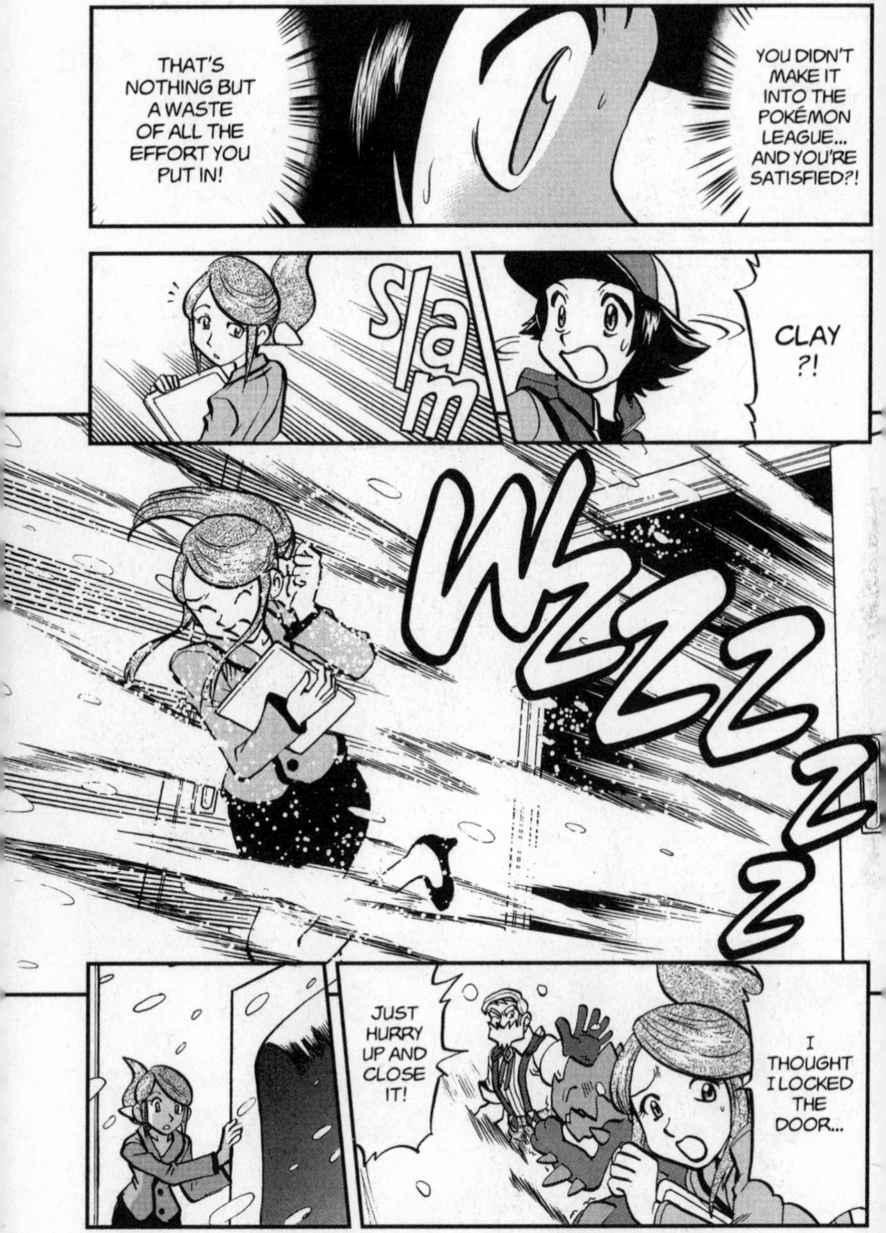
YOU DIDN'T MAKE IT INTO THE POKÉMON LEAGUE... AND YOU'RE SATISFIED?!
THAT'S NOTHING BUT A WASTE OF ALL THE EFFORT YOU PUT IN!
CLAY ?!
slam
WHZZZZZ
I THOUGHT I LOCKED THE DOOR...
JUST HURRY UP AND CLOSE IT!

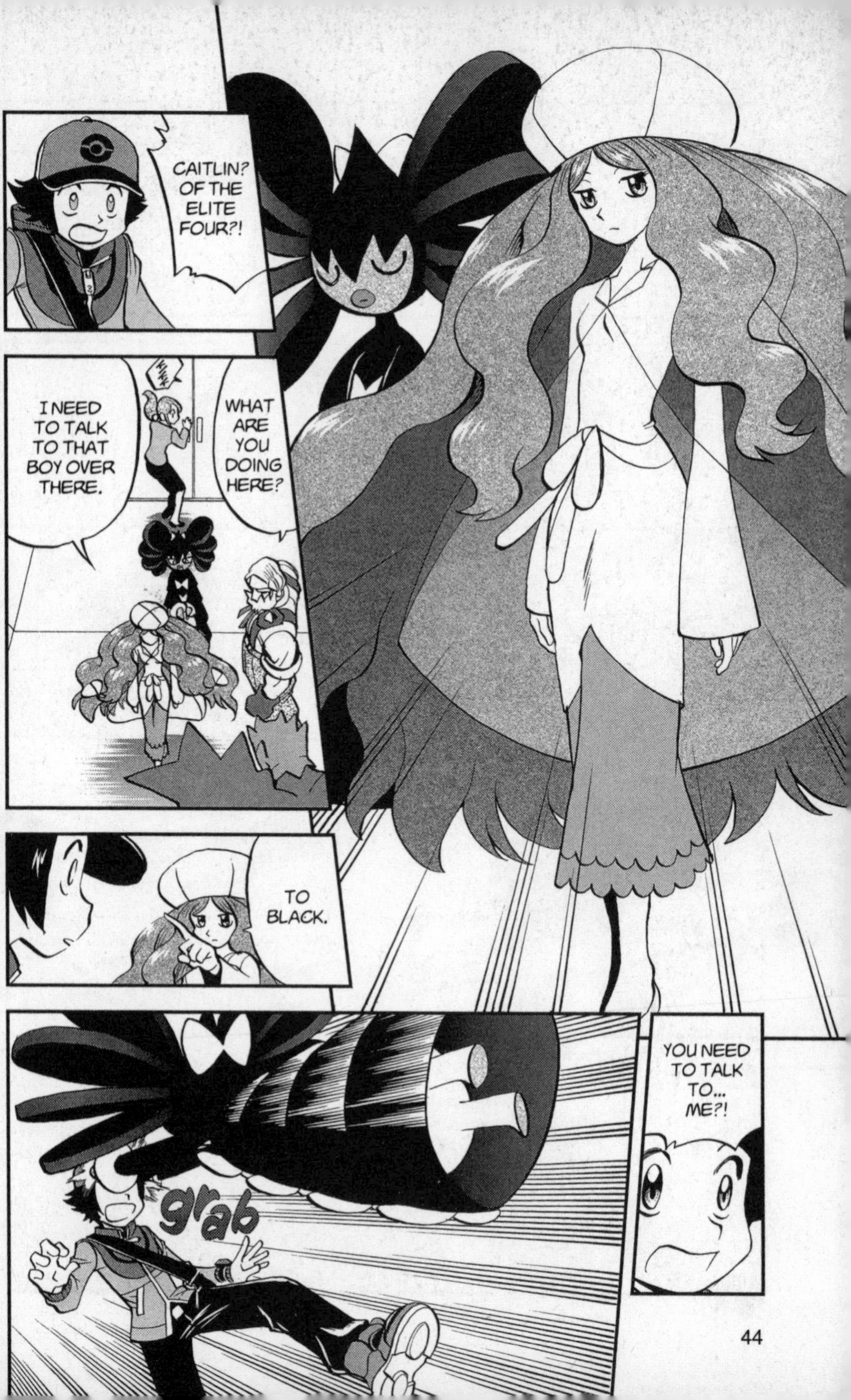
CAITLIN? OF THE ELITE FOUR?!
WHAT ARE YOU DOING HERE?
I NEED TO TALK TO THAT BOY OVER THERE.
TO BLACK.
YOU NEED TO TALK TO... ME?!
grab

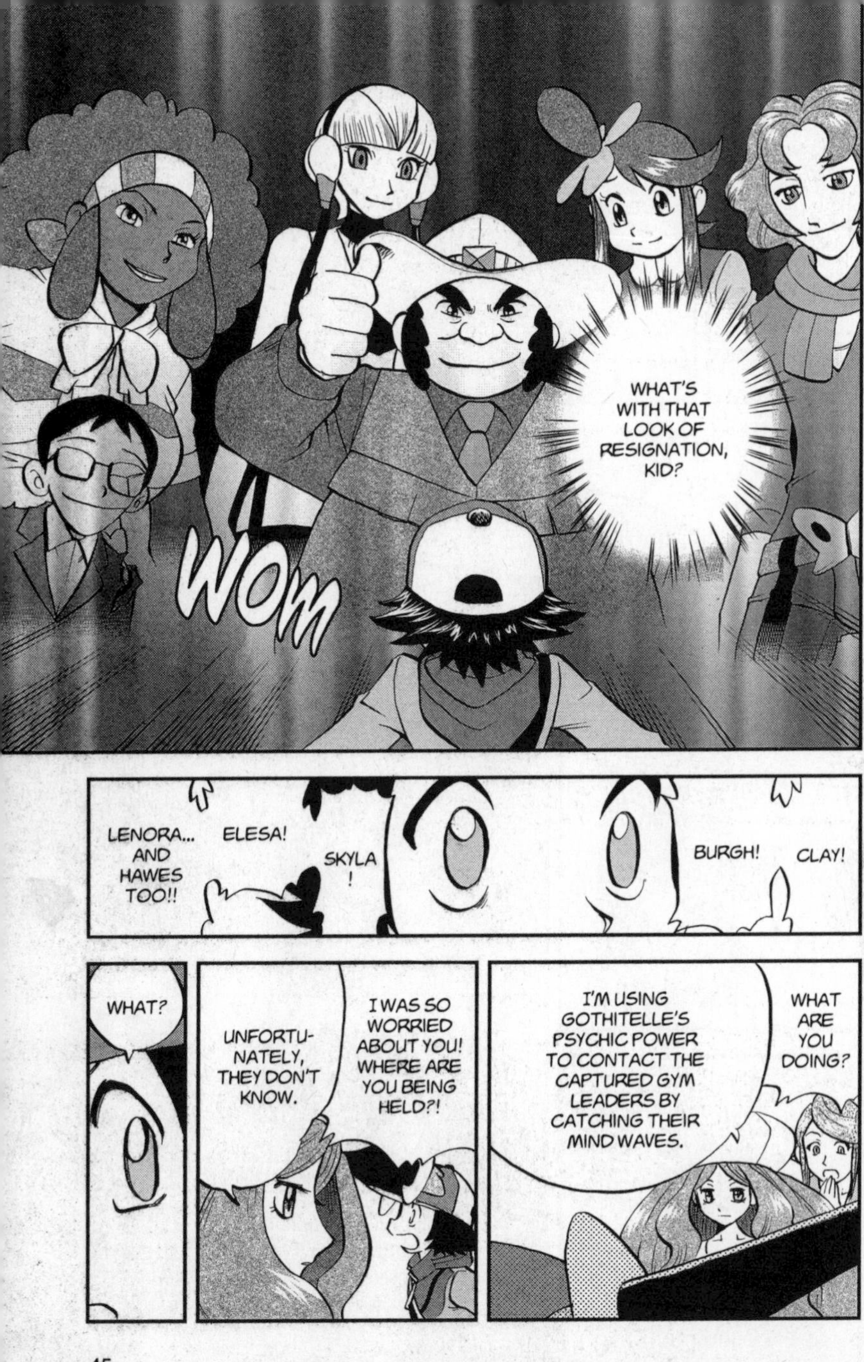
WHAT'S WITH THAT LOOK OF RESIGNATION, KID?
WOM
CLAY!
BURGH!
SKYLA!
ELESA!
LENORA... AND HAWES TOO!!
WHAT ARE YOU DOING?
I'M USING GOTHITELLE'S PSYCHIC POWER TO CONTACT THE CAPTURED GYM LEADERS BY CATCHING THEIR MIND WAVES.
I WAS SO WORRIED ABOUT YOU! WHERE ARE YOU BEING HELD?!
UNFORTU-NATELY, THEY DON'T KNOW.
WHAT?

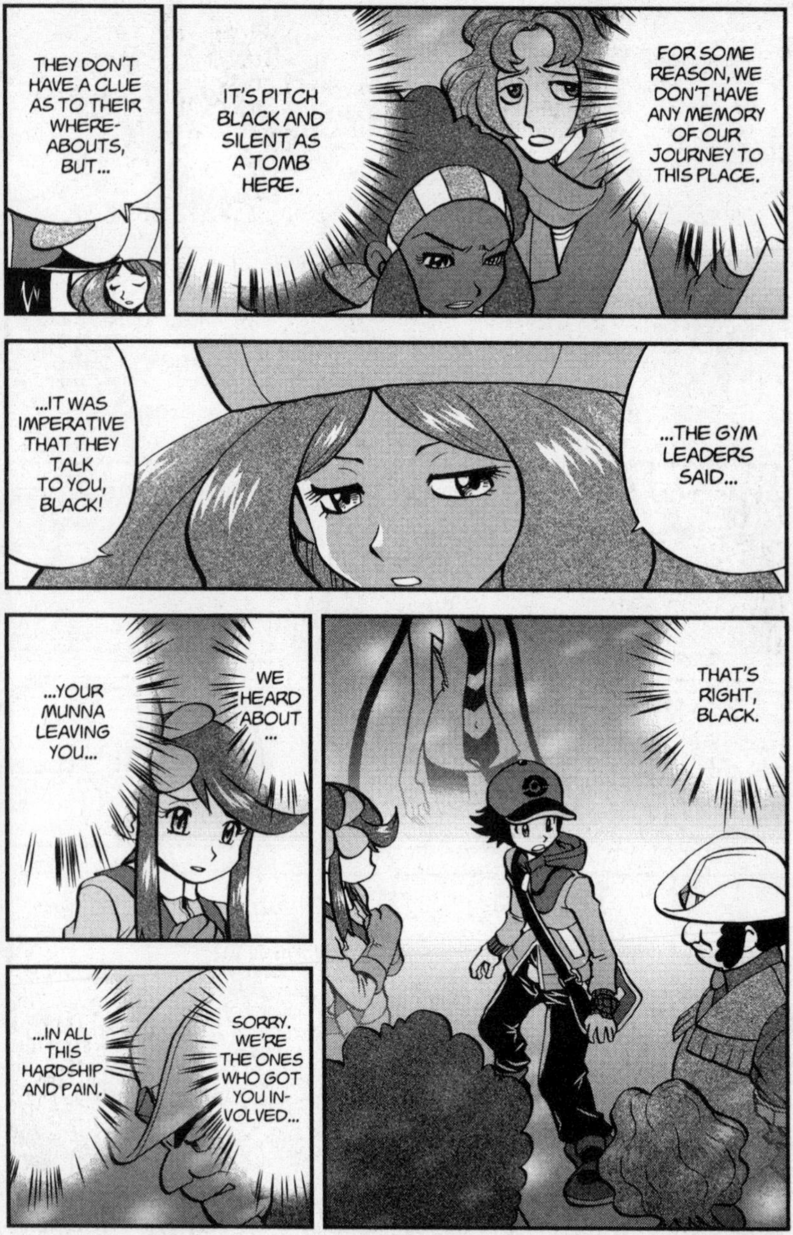
FOR SOME REASON, WE DON'T HAVE ANY MEMORY OF OUR JOURNEY TO THIS PLACE.
IT'S PITCH BLACK AND SILENT AS A TOMB HERE.
THEY DON'T HAVE A CLUE AS TO THEIR WHERE-ABOUTS, BUT...
...THE GYM LEADERS SAID...
...IT WAS IMPERATIVE THAT THEY TALK TO YOU, BLACK!
THAT'S RIGHT, BLACK.
WE HEARD ABOUT...
...YOUR MUNNA LEAVING YOU...
SORRY. WE'RE THE ONES WHO GOT YOU IN-VOLVED...
...IN ALL THIS HARDSHIP AND PAIN.

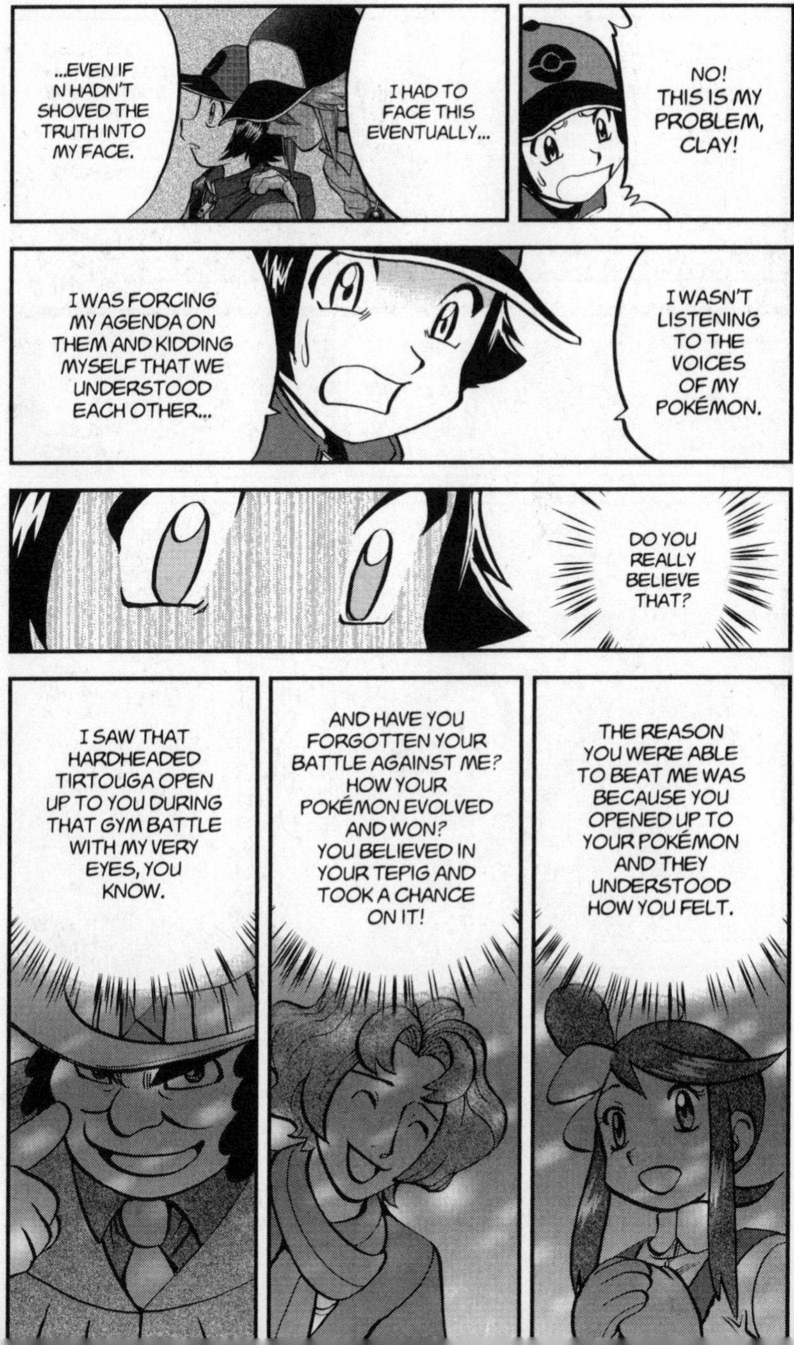
NO! THIS IS MY PROBLEM, CLAY!
I HAD TO FACE THIS EVENTUALLY...
...EVEN IF N HADN'T SHOVED THE TRUTH INTO MY FACE.
I WASN'T LISTENING TO THE VOICES OF MY POKÉMON.
I WAS FORCING MY AGENDA ON THEM AND KIDDING MYSELF THAT WE UNDERSTOOD EACH OTHER...
DO YOU REALLY BELIEVE THAT?
THE REASON YOU WERE ABLE TO BEAT ME WAS BECAUSE YOU OPENED UP TO YOUR POKÉMON AND THEY UNDERSTOOD HOW YOU FELT.
AND HAVE YOU FORGOTTEN YOUR BATTLE AGAINST ME? HOW YOUR POKÉMON EVOLVED AND WON? YOU BELIEVED IN YOUR TEPIG AND TOOK A CHANCE ON IT!
I SAW THAT HARDHEADED TIRTOUGA OPEN UP TO YOU DURING THAT GYM BATTLE WITH MY VERY EYES, YOU KNOW.

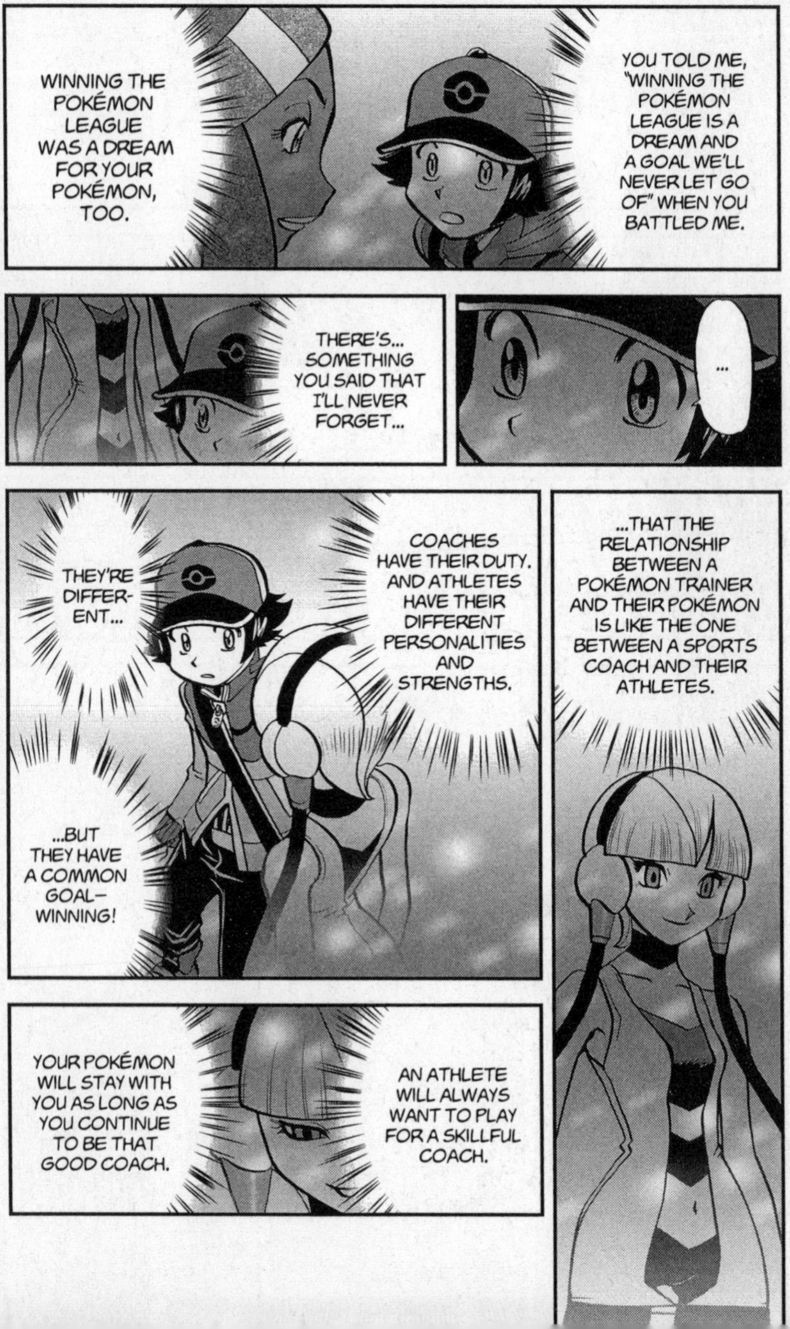
YOU TOLD ME, "WINNING THE POKÉMON LEAGUE IS A DREAM AND A GOAL WE'LL NEVER LET GO OF" WHEN YOU BATTLED ME.
WINNING THE POKÉMON LEAGUE WAS A DREAM FOR YOUR POKÉMON, TOO.
...
THERE'S... SOMETHING YOU SAID THAT I'LL NEVER FORGET...
...THAT THE RELATIONSHIP BETWEEN A POKÉMON TRAINER AND THEIR POKÉMON IS LIKE THE ONE BETWEEN A SPORTS COACH AND THEIR ATHLETES.
COACHES HAVE THEIR DUTY. AND ATHLETES HAVE THEIR DIFFERENT PERSONALITIES AND STRENGTHS.
THEY'RE DIFFERENT...
...BUT THEY HAVE A COMMON GOAL—WINNING!
AN ATHLETE WILL ALWAYS WANT TO PLAY FOR A SKILLFUL COACH.
YOUR POKÉMON WILL STAY WITH YOU AS LONG AS YOU CONTINUE TO BE THAT GOOD COACH.

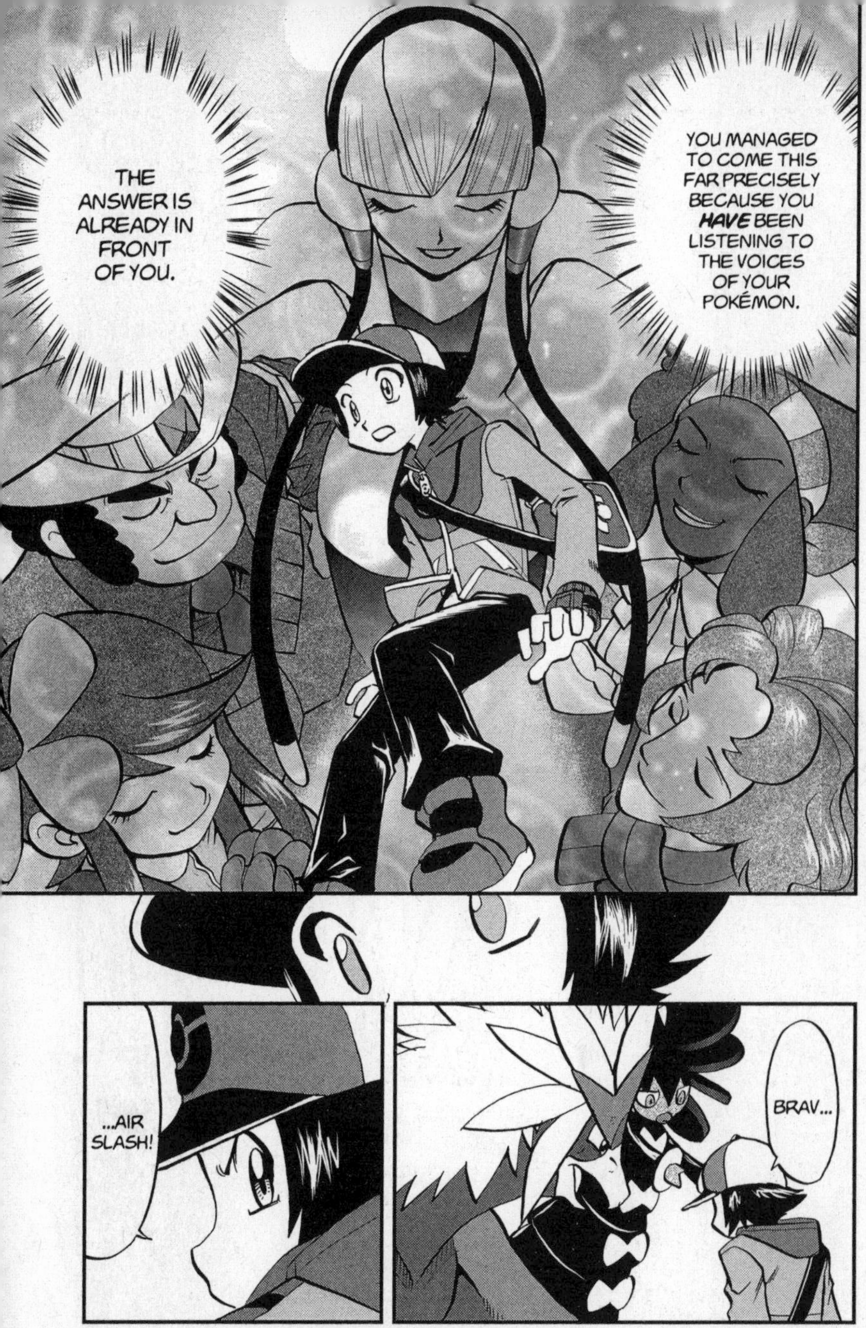
YOU MANAGED TO COME THIS FAR PRECISELY BECAUSE YOU HAVE BEEN LISTENING TO THE VOICES OF YOUR POKÉMON.
THE ANSWER IS ALREADY IN FRONT OF YOU.
BRAV...
...AIR SLASH!

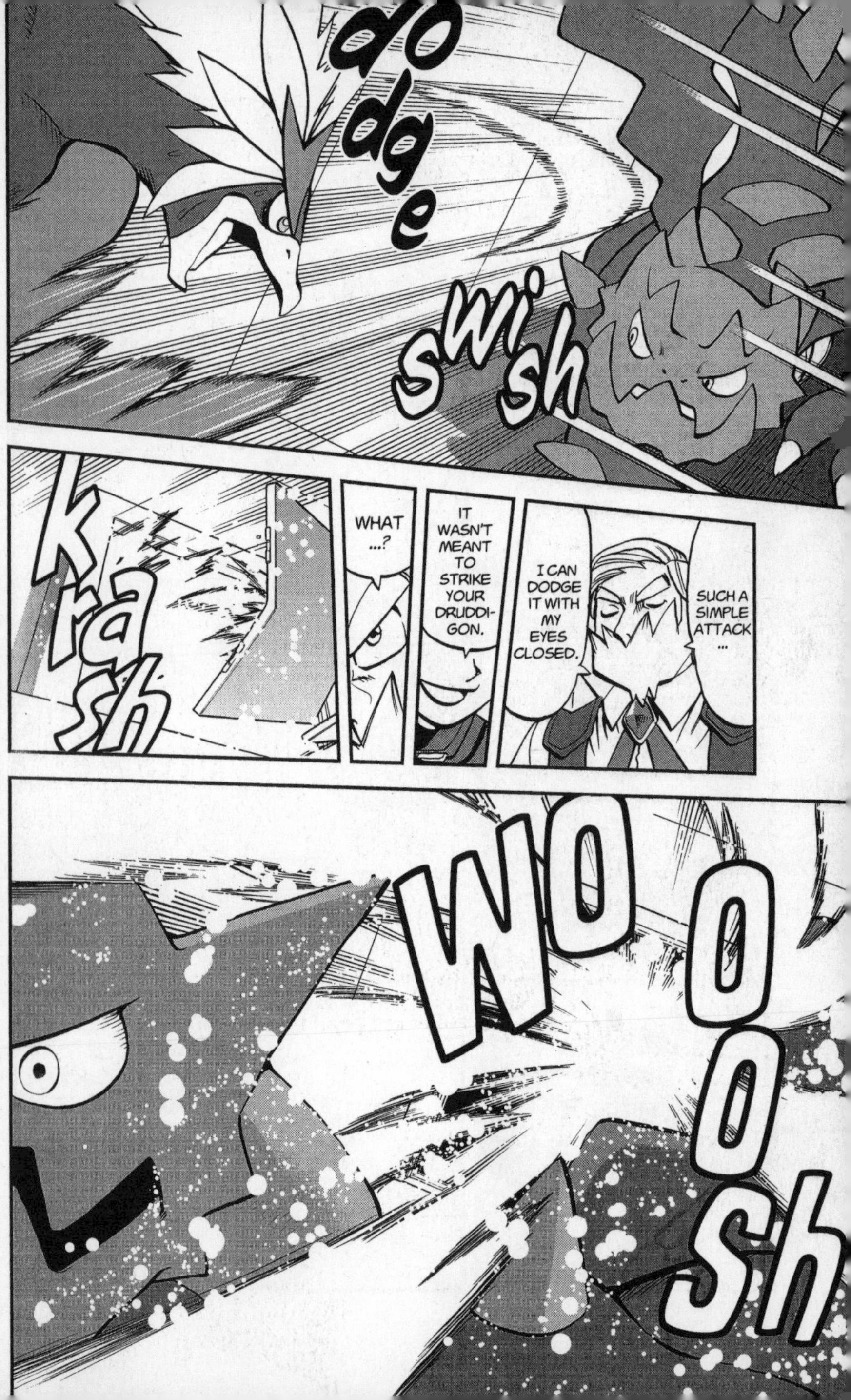
dodge
swish
SUCH A SIMPLE ATTACK ...
I CAN DODGE IT WITH MY EYES CLOSED.
IT WASN'T MEANT TO STRIKE YOUR DRUDDIGON.
WHAT ...?
krash
WOOOSh

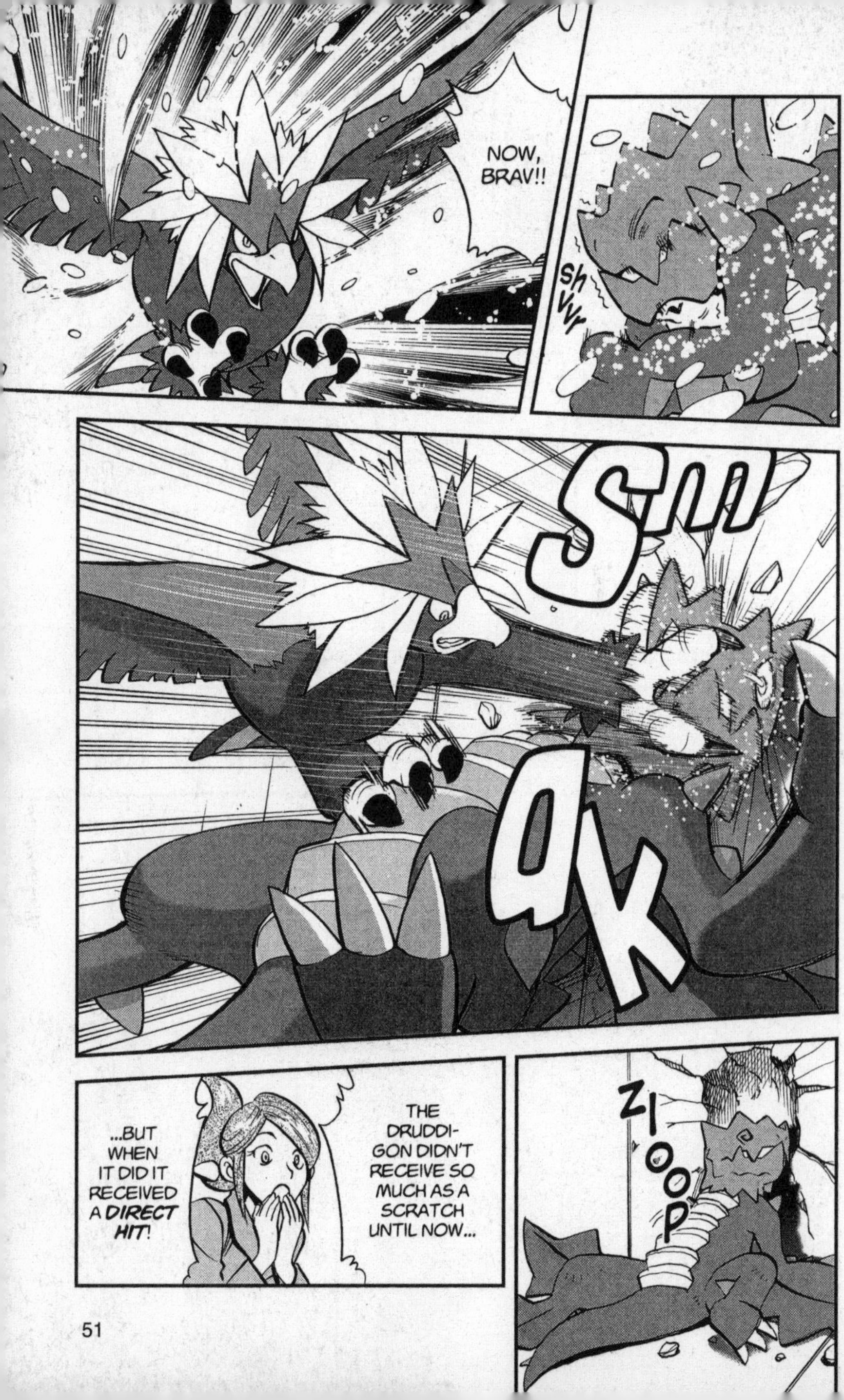
shvvr
NOW, BRAV!!
SMAAK
ZIOOOP
THE DRUDDIGON DIDN'T RECEIVE SO MUCH AS A SCRATCH UNTIL NOW...
...BUT WHEN IT DID IT RECEIVED A **DIRECT HIT**!

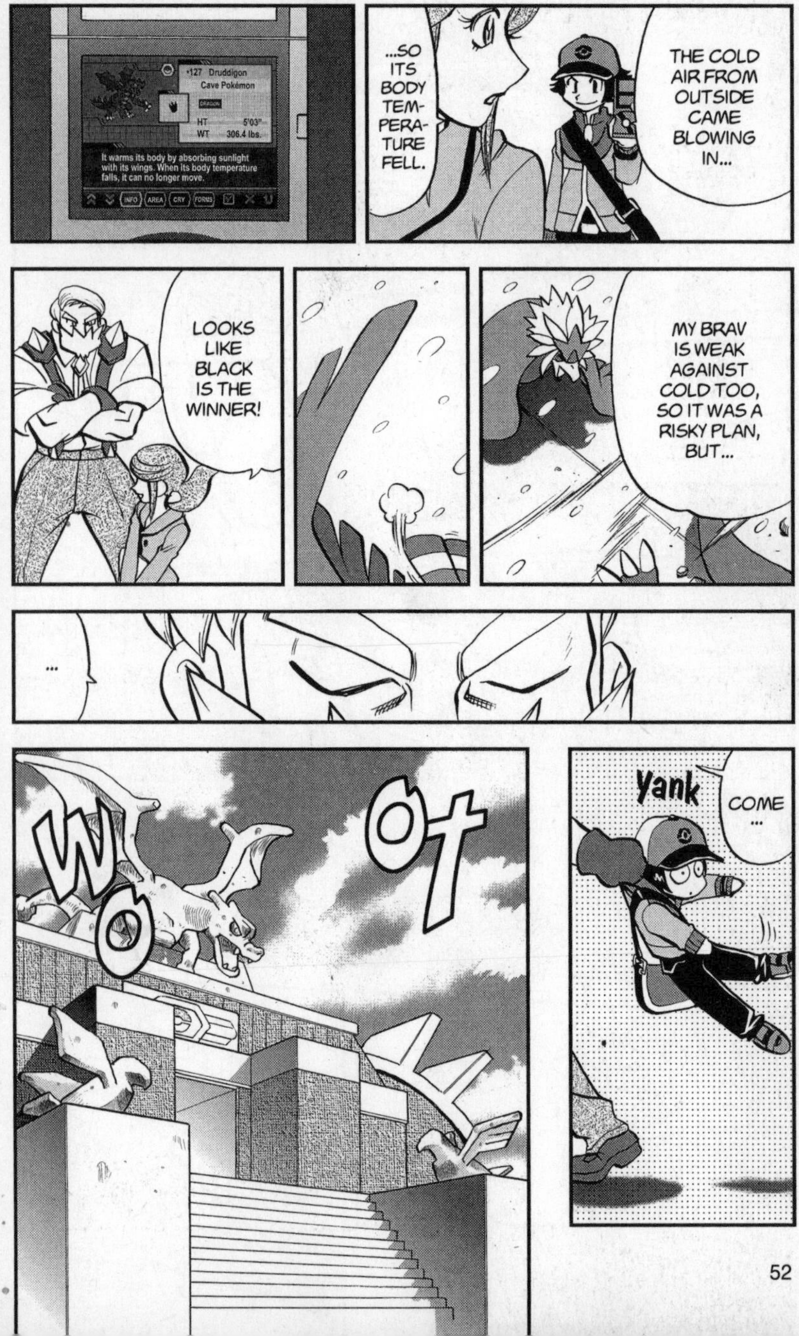
THE COLD AIR FROM OUTSIDE CAME BLOWING IN...
...SO ITS BODY TEMPERATURE FELL.
127 Druddigon
Cave Pokémon
DRAGON
HT 5'03"
WT 306.4 lbs.
It warms its body by absorbing sunlight with its wings. When its body temperature falls, it can no longer move.
INFO AREA CRY FORMS
MY BRAV IS WEAK AGAINST COLD TOO, SO IT WAS A RISKY PLAN, BUT...
LOOKS LIKE BLACK IS THE WINNER!
...
Yank
COME ...
WOOT

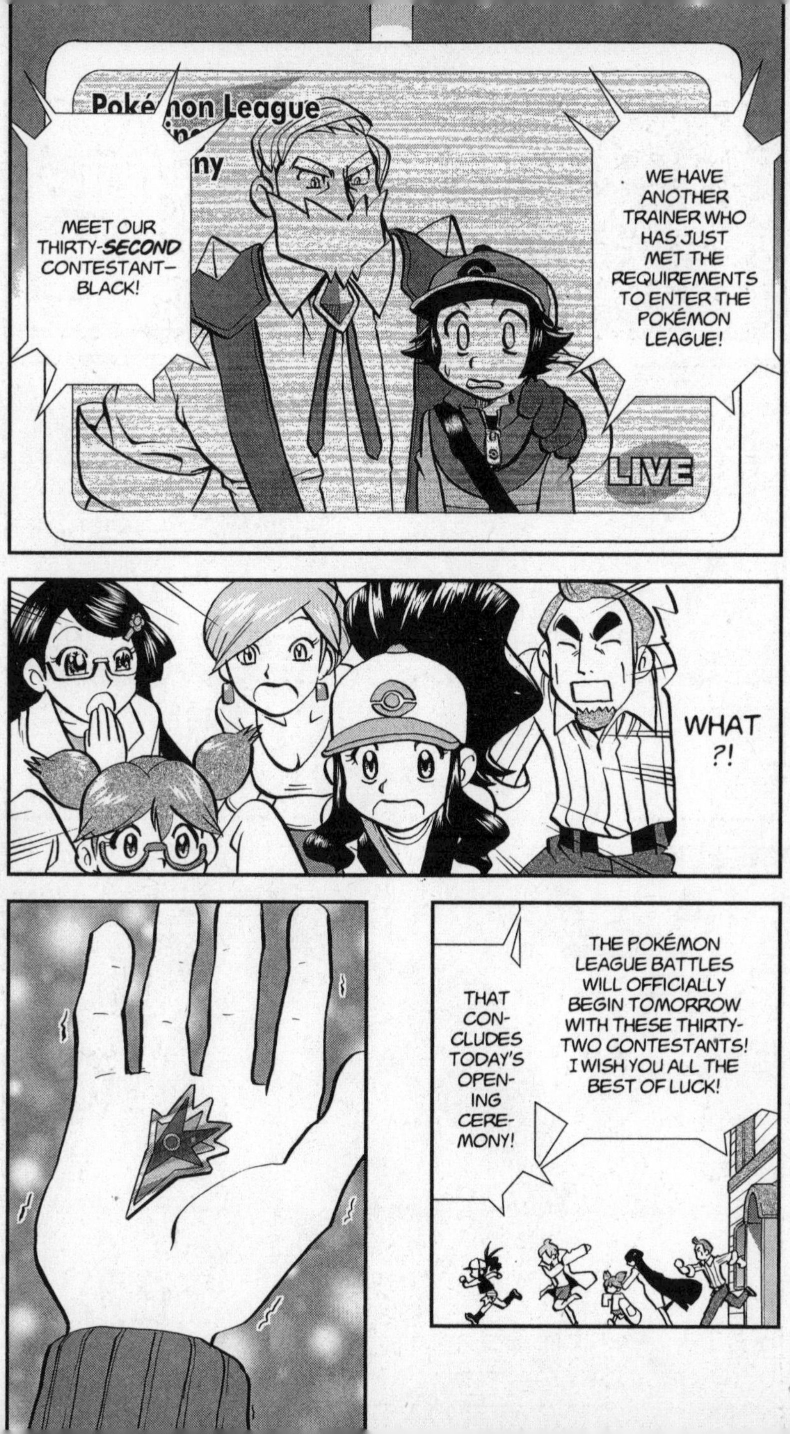
Pokémon League
LIVE
WE HAVE ANOTHER TRAINER WHO HAS JUST MET THE REQUIREMENTS TO ENTER THE POKÉMON LEAGUE!
MEET OUR THIRTY-*SECOND* CONTESTANT—BLACK!
WHAT?!
THE POKÉMON LEAGUE BATTLES WILL OFFICIALLY BEGIN TOMORROW WITH THESE THIRTY-TWO CONTESTANTS! I WISH YOU ALL THE BEST OF LUCK!
THAT CONCLUDES TODAY'S OPENING CEREMONY!

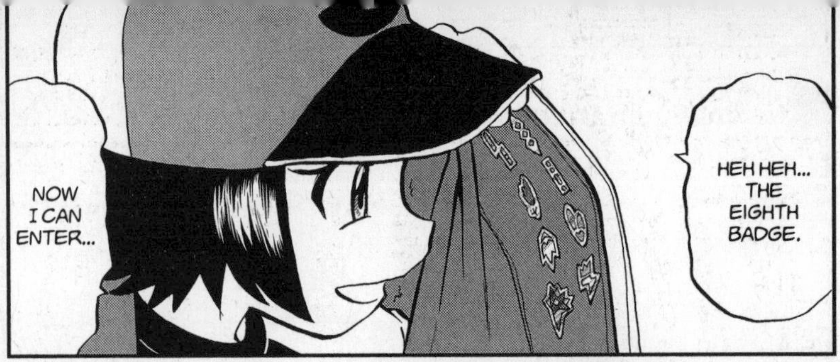
HEH HEH... THE EIGHTH BADGE.
NOW I CAN ENTER...

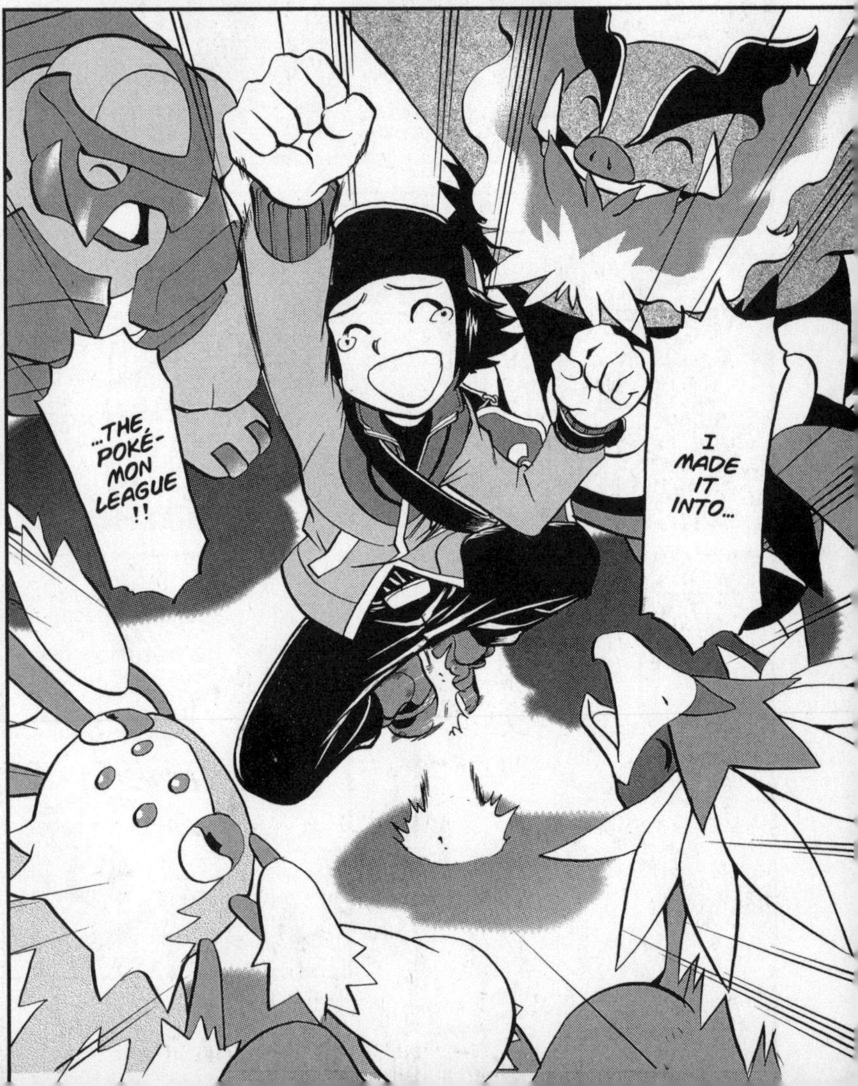
I MADE IT INTO...
...THE POKÉ-MON LEAGUE!!

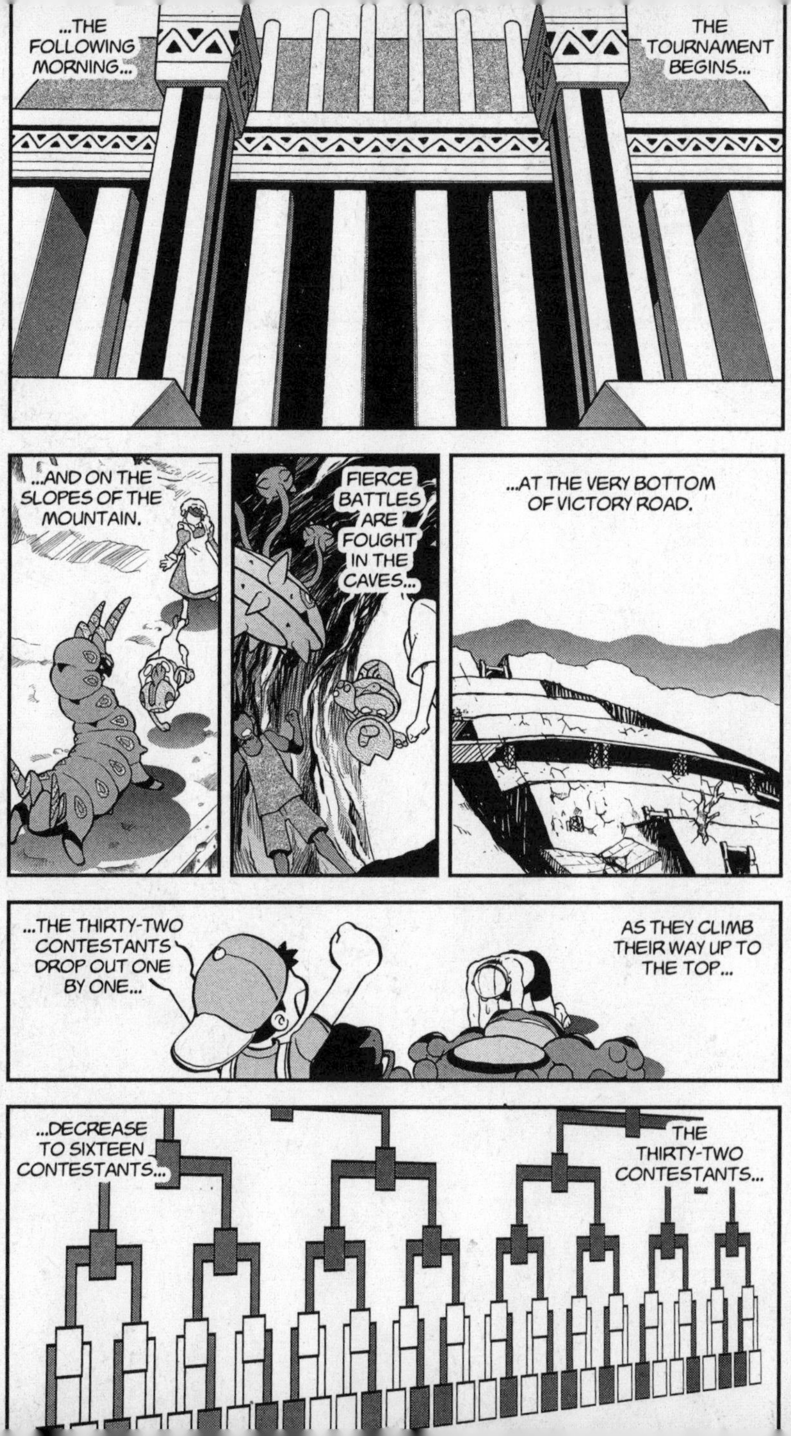
THE TOURNAMENT BEGINS...
...THE FOLLOWING MORNING...
...AT THE VERY BOTTOM OF VICTORY ROAD.
FIERCE BATTLES ARE FOUGHT IN THE CAVES...
...AND ON THE SLOPES OF THE MOUNTAIN.
AS THEY CLIMB THEIR WAY UP TO THE TOP...
...THE THIRTY-TWO CONTESTANTS DROP OUT ONE BY ONE...
THE THIRTY-TWO CONTESTANTS...
...DECREASE TO SIXTEEN CONTESTANTS...

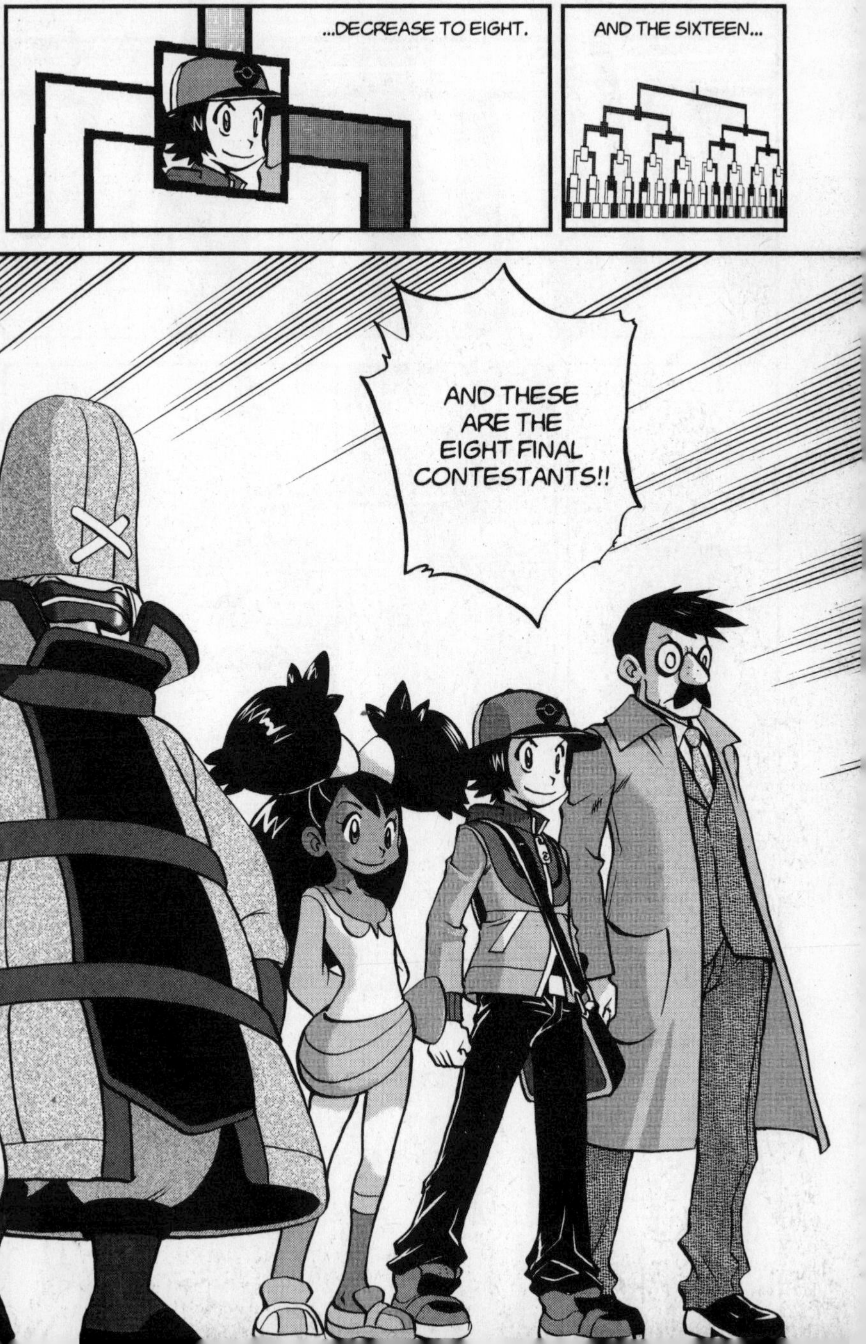
AND THE SIXTEEN...
...DECREASE TO EIGHT.
AND THESE ARE THE EIGHT FINAL CONTESTANTS!!

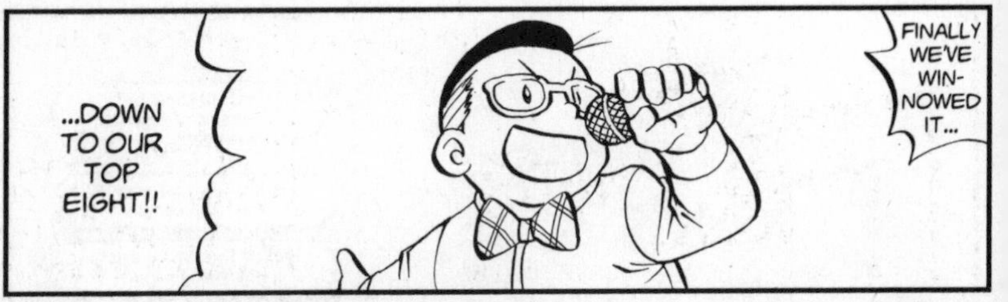
FINALLY WE'VE WIN-NOWED IT...
...DOWN TO OUR TOP EIGHT!!

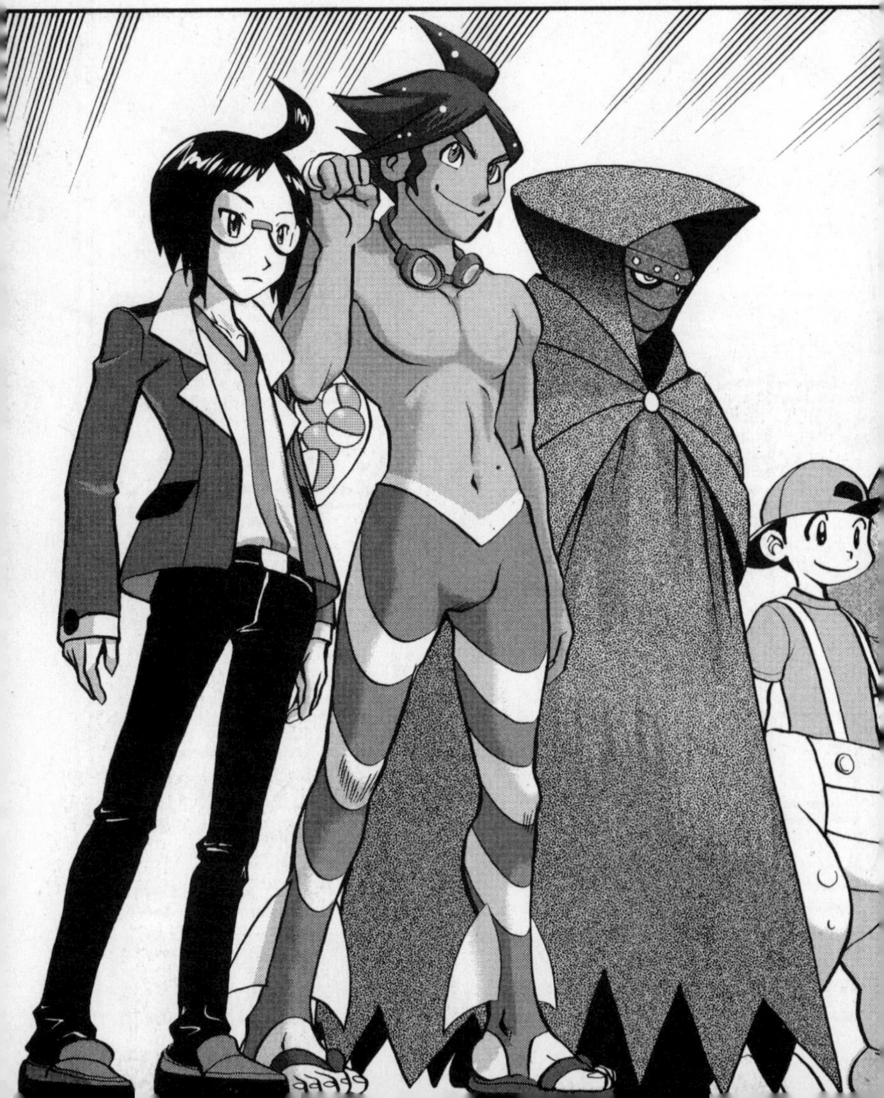

# ADVENTURE MAP

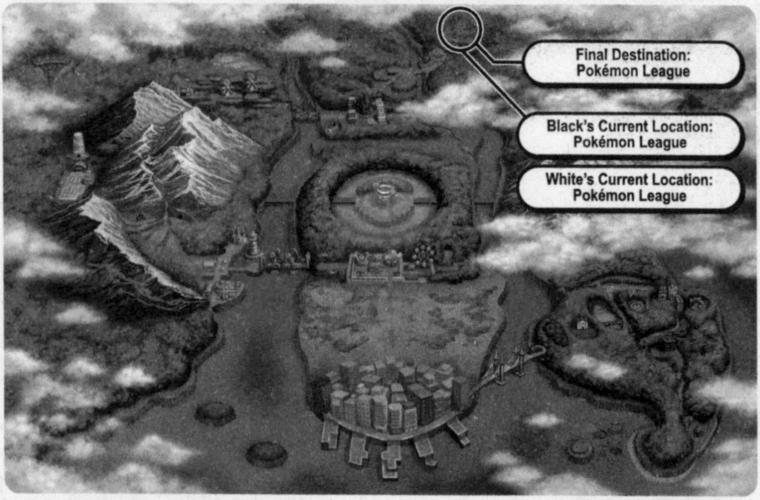

Final Destination: Pokémon League
Black's Current Location: Pokémon League
White's Current Location: Pokémon League


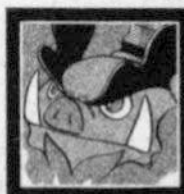

Mega Fire Pig Pokémon **Bo**
Emboar ♂ Fire Fighting
Lv.47 Ability: Blaze

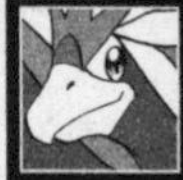

Valiant Pokémon **Brav**
Braviary ♂ Normal Flying
Lv.57 Ability: Sheer Force

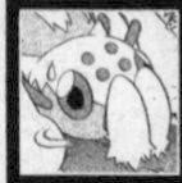

EleSpider Pokémon **Tula**
Galvantula ♂ Bug Electric
Lv.57 Ability: Unnerve

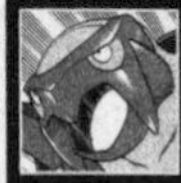

Prototurtle Pokémon **Costa**
Tirtouga ♂ Water Rock
Lv.41 Ability: Solid Rock

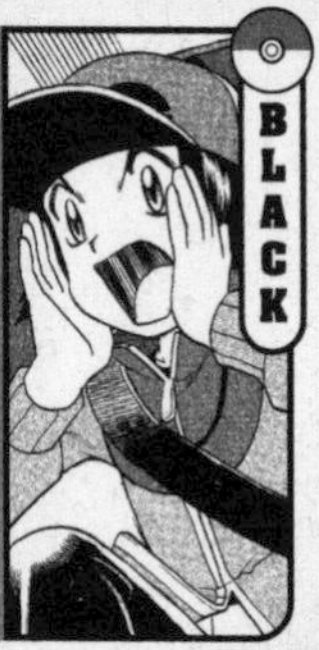

BLACK


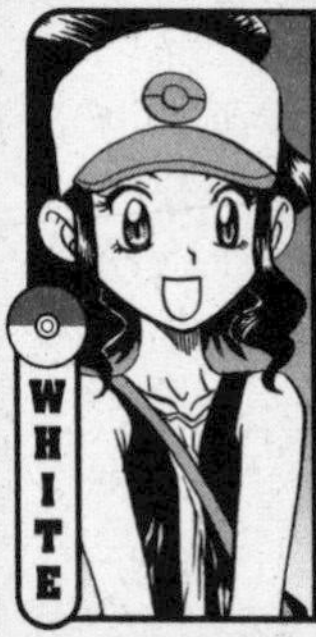

WHITE


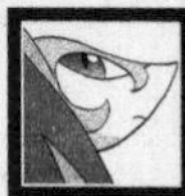

Grass Snake Pokémon **Amanda**
Servine ♀ Grass
Lv.38 Ability: Overgrow

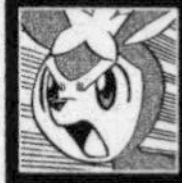

Season Pokémon **Darlene**
Deerling ♀ Normal Grass
Lv.31 Ability: Chlorophyll

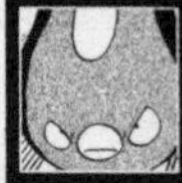

Trap Pokémon **Dorothy**
Stunfisk ♀ Ground Electric
Lv.34 Ability: Limber

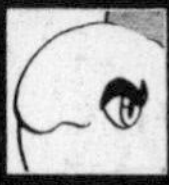

Caring Pokémon **Nancy**
Alomomola ♀ Water
Lv.35 Ability: Healer

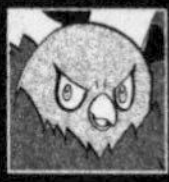

Diapered Pokémon **Barbara**
Vullaby ♀ Dark Flying
Lv.39 Ability: Big Pecks

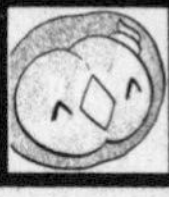

Cell Pokémon **Solly**
Solosis ♂ Psychic
Lv.29 Ability: Magic Guard

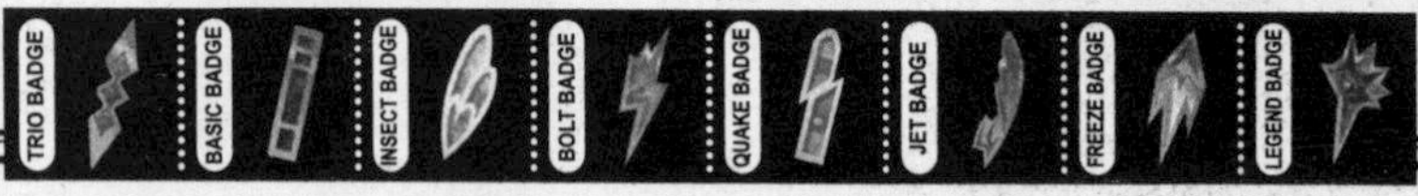

TRIO BADGE
BASIC BADGE
INSECT BADGE
BOLT BADGE
QUAKE BADGE
JET BADGE
FREEZE BADGE
LEGEND BADGE

POKÉMON™ ADVENTURES BLACK & WHITE

CROAGUNK

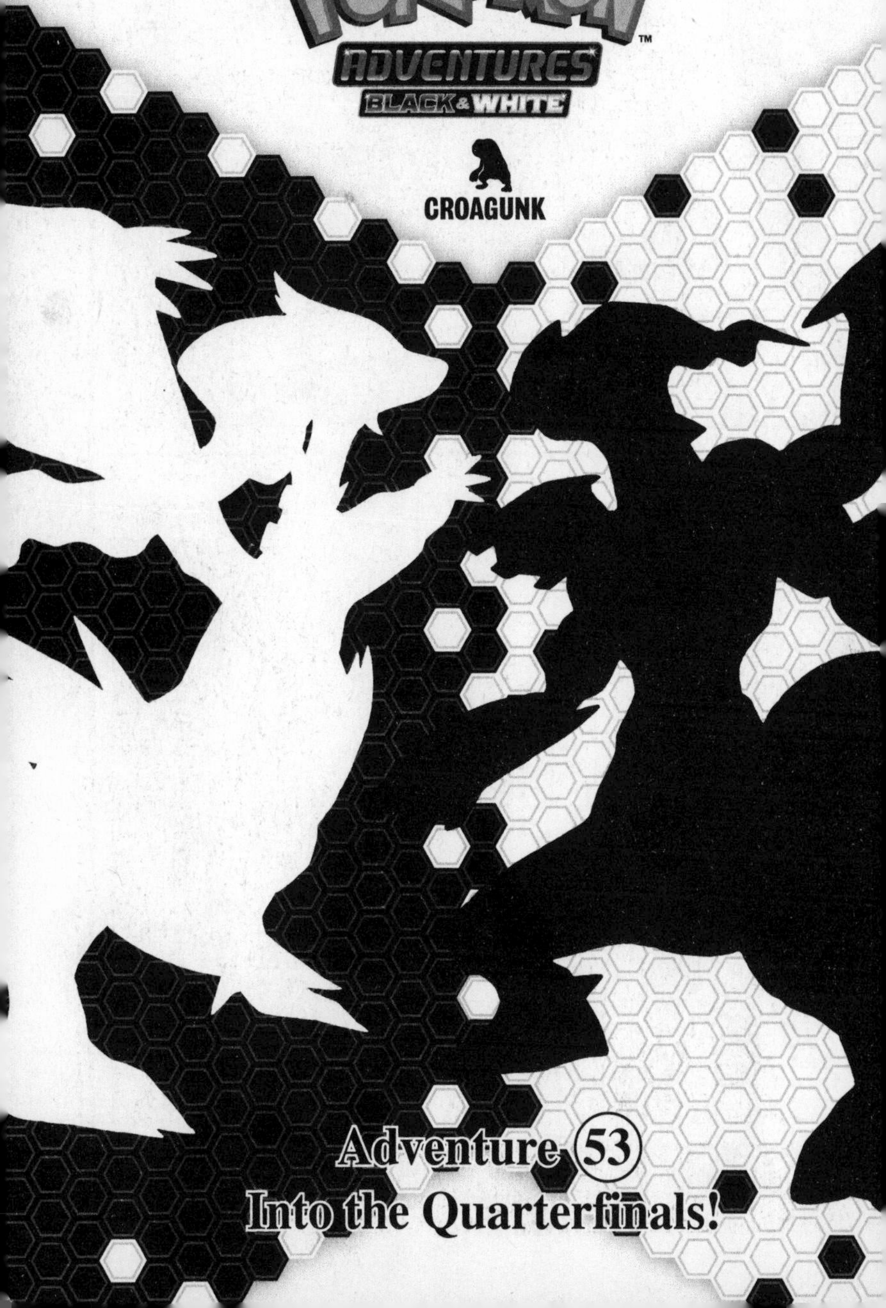

# Adventure 53
## Into the Quarterfinals!

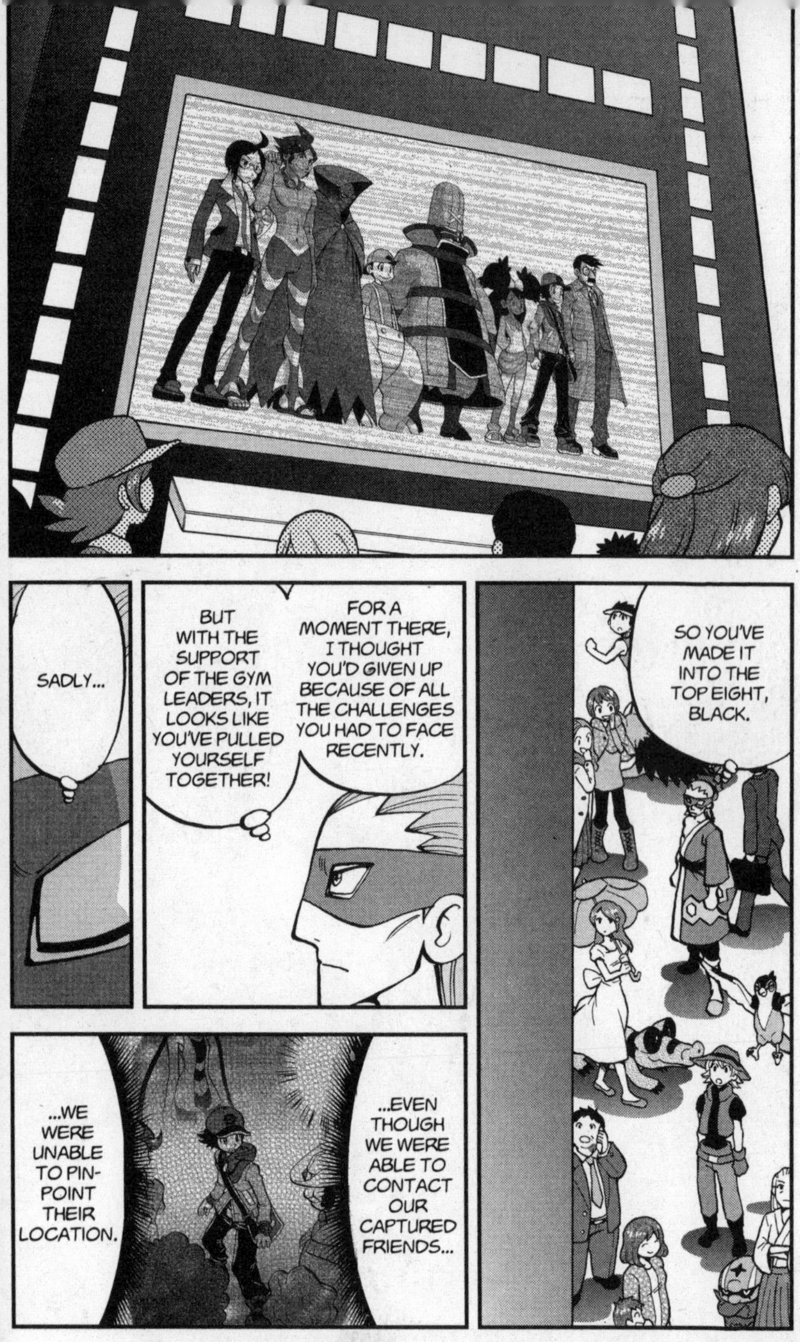
SO YOU'VE MADE IT INTO THE TOP EIGHT, BLACK.
FOR A MOMENT THERE, I THOUGHT YOU'D GIVEN UP BECAUSE OF ALL THE CHALLENGES YOU HAD TO FACE RECENTLY.
BUT WITH THE SUPPORT OF THE GYM LEADERS, IT LOOKS LIKE YOU'VE PULLED YOURSELF TOGETHER!
SADLY...
...EVEN THOUGH WE WERE ABLE TO CONTACT OUR CAPTURED FRIENDS...
...WE WERE UNABLE TO PIN-POINT THEIR LOCATION.

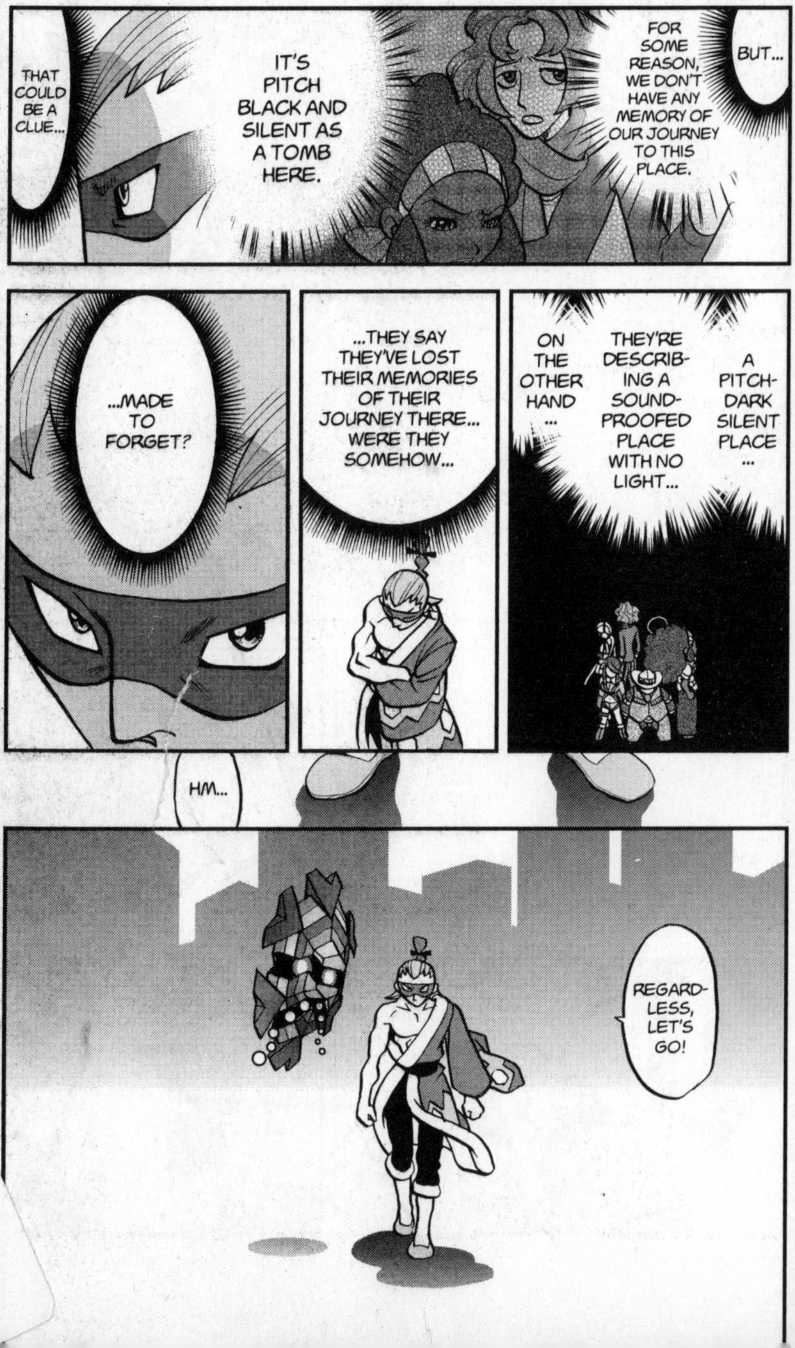
BUT...
FOR SOME REASON, WE DON'T HAVE ANY MEMORY OF OUR JOURNEY TO THIS PLACE.
IT'S PITCH BLACK AND SILENT AS A TOMB HERE.
THAT COULD BE A CLUE...
A PITCH-DARK SILENT PLACE...
THEY'RE DESCRIBING A SOUND-PROOFED PLACE WITH NO LIGHT...
ON THE OTHER HAND...
...THEY SAY THEY'VE LOST THEIR MEMORIES OF THEIR JOURNEY THERE... WERE THEY SOMEHOW...
...MADE TO FORGET?
HM...
REGARDLESS, LET'S GO!

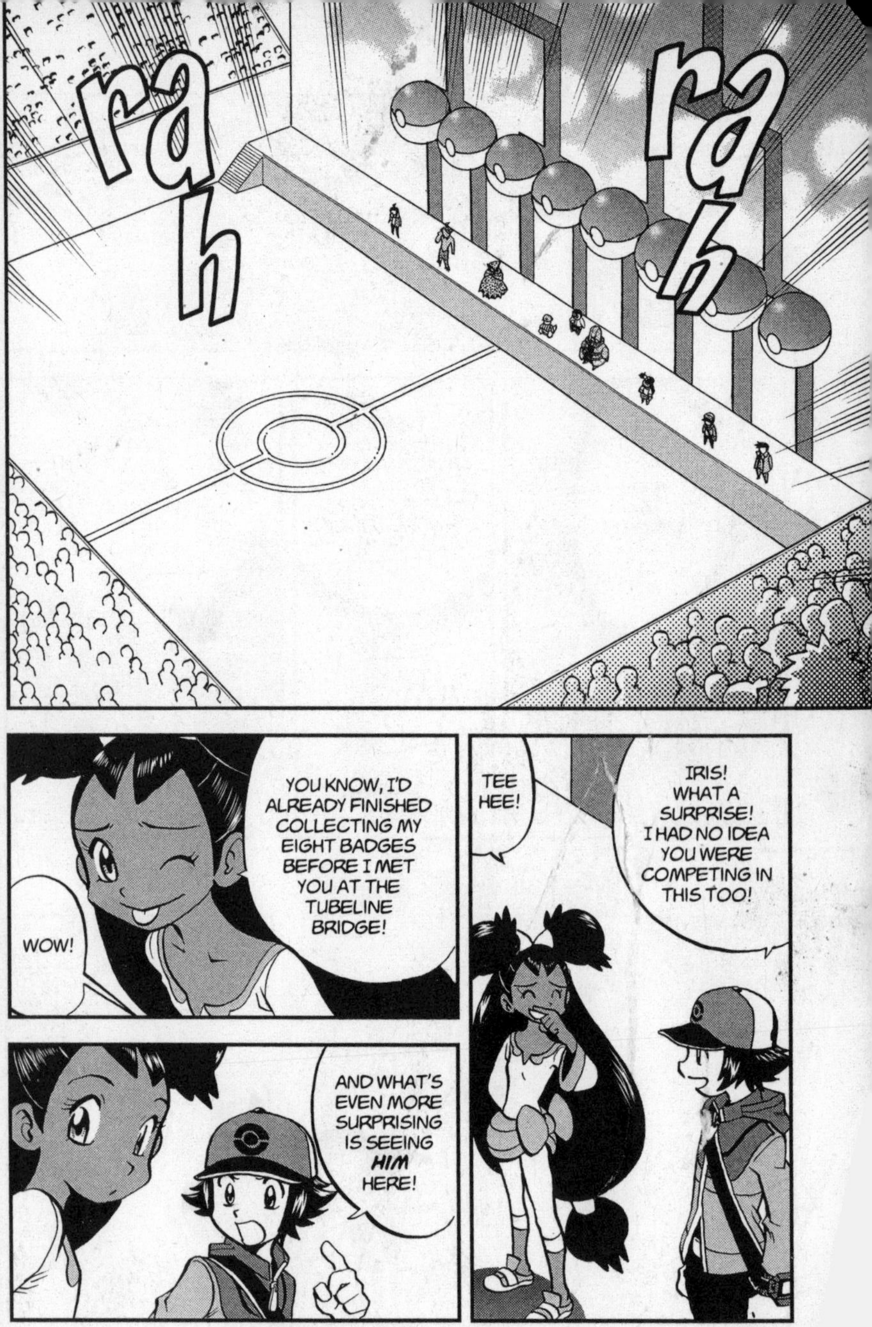
rah
rah
IRIS! WHAT A SURPRISE! I HAD NO IDEA YOU WERE COMPETING IN THIS TOO!
TEE HEE!
YOU KNOW, I'D ALREADY FINISHED COLLECTING MY EIGHT BADGES BEFORE I MET YOU AT THE TUBELINE BRIDGE!
WOW!
AND WHAT'S EVEN MORE SURPRISING IS SEEING ***HIM*** HERE!

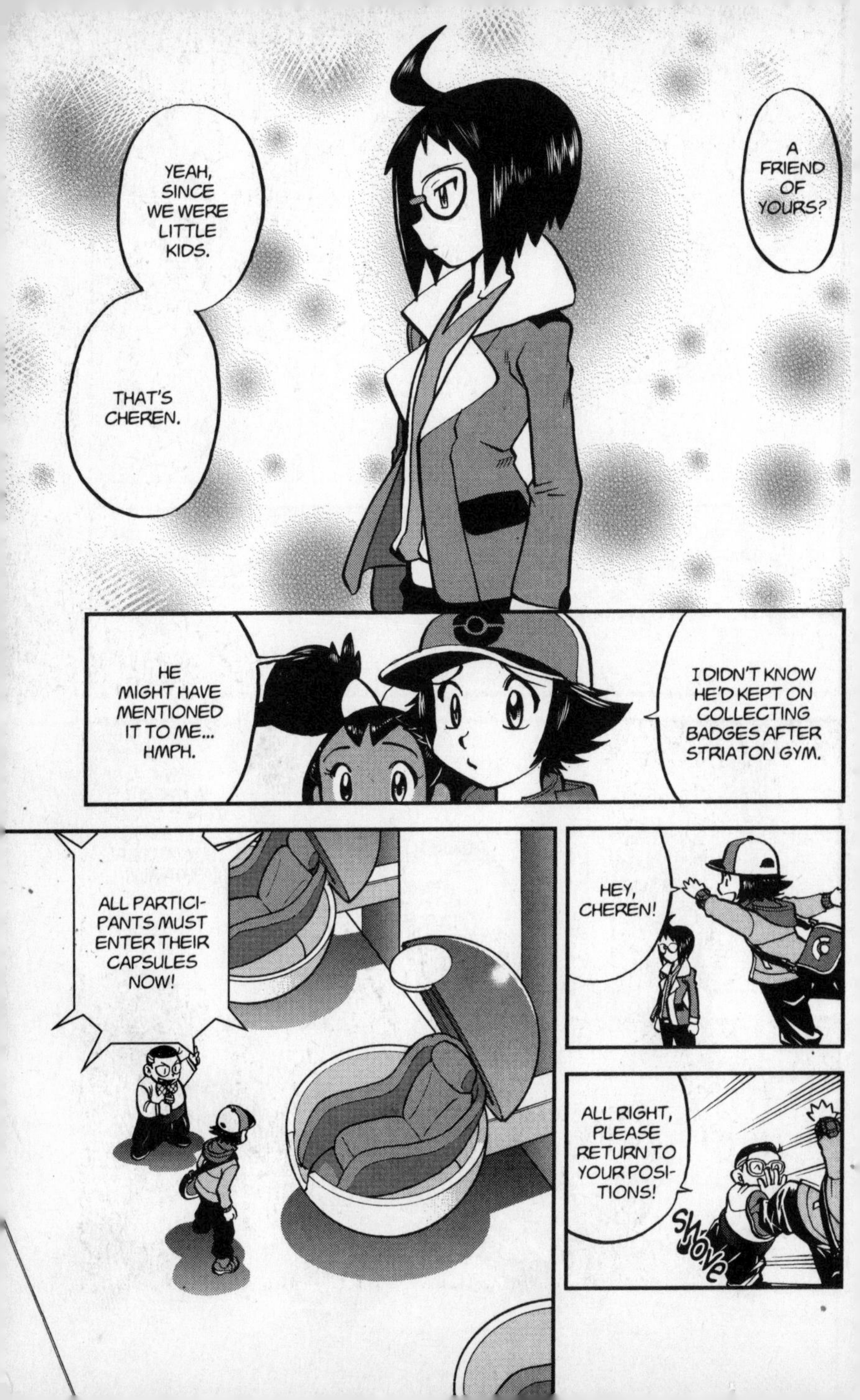
A FRIEND OF YOURS?
YEAH, SINCE WE WERE LITTLE KIDS.
THAT'S CHEREN.
I DIDN'T KNOW HE'D KEPT ON COLLECTING BADGES AFTER STRIATON GYM.
HE MIGHT HAVE MENTIONED IT TO ME... HMPH.
HEY, CHEREN!
ALL RIGHT, PLEASE RETURN TO YOUR POSI-TIONS!
SHOVE
ALL PARTICI-PANTS MUST ENTER THEIR CAPSULES NOW!

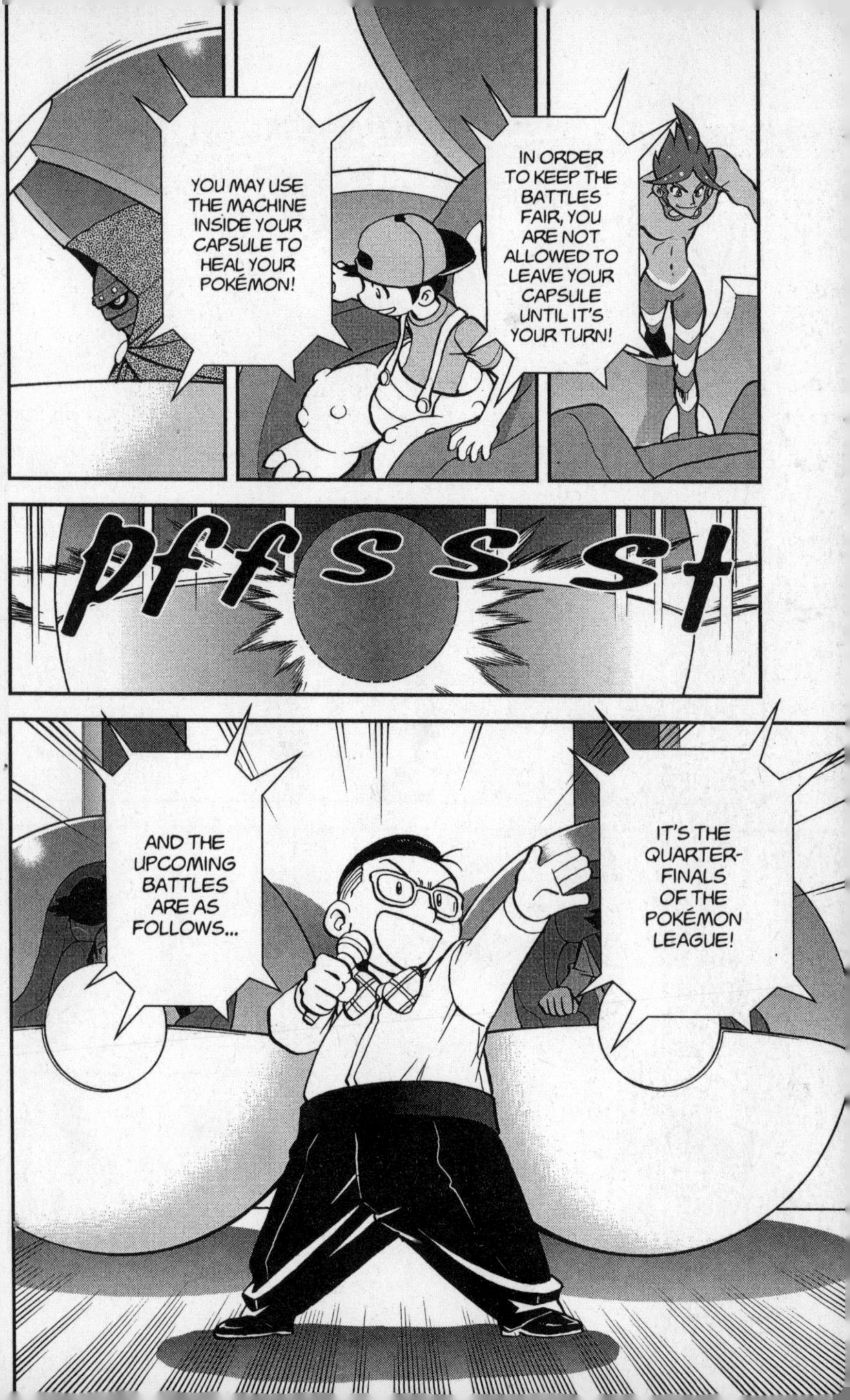
IN ORDER TO KEEP THE BATTLES FAIR, YOU ARE NOT ALLOWED TO LEAVE YOUR CAPSULE UNTIL IT'S YOUR TURN!
YOU MAY USE THE MACHINE INSIDE YOUR CAPSULE TO HEAL YOUR POKÉMON!
pfssst
IT'S THE QUARTER-FINALS OF THE POKÉMON LEAGUE!
AND THE UPCOMING BATTLES ARE AS FOLLOWS...

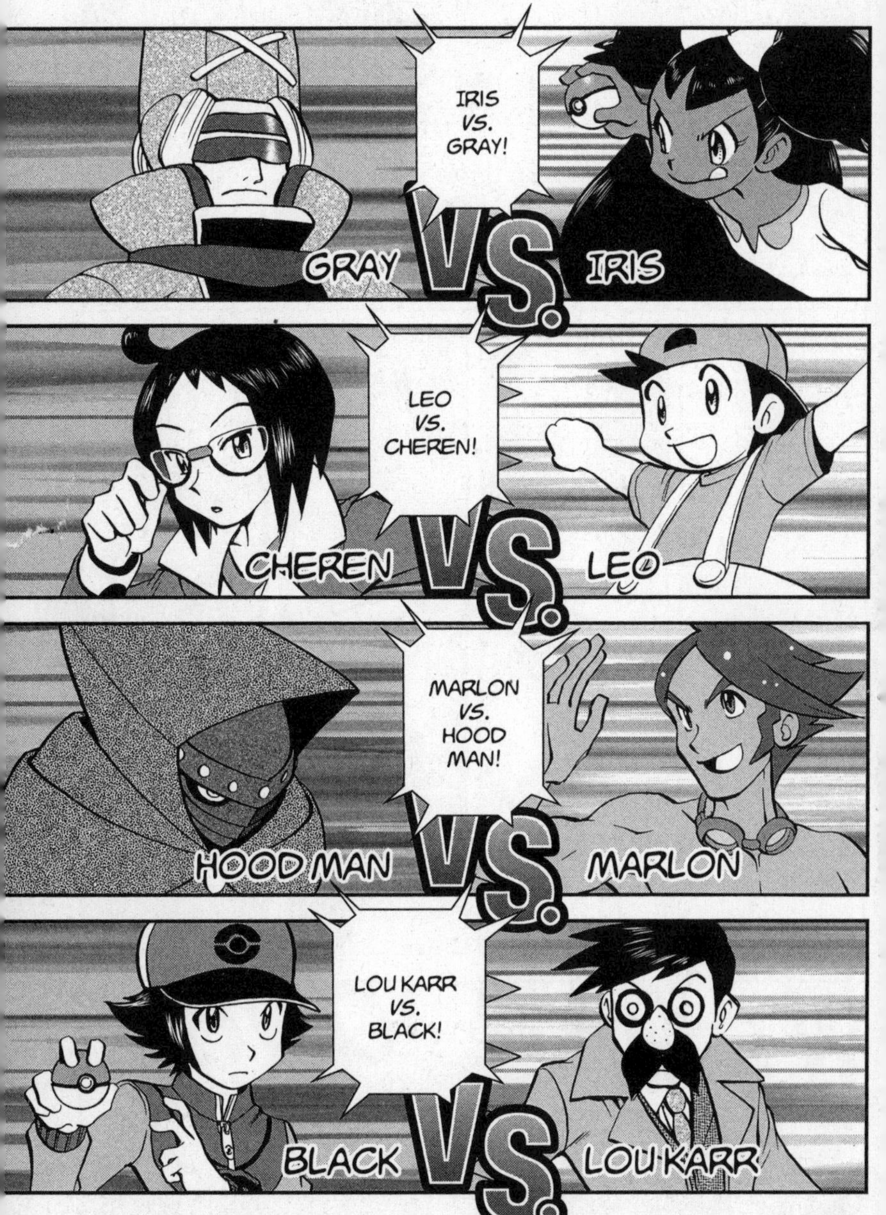
IRIS VS. GRAY!
IRIS
VS.
GRAY
LEO VS. CHEREN!
LEO
VS.
CHEREN
MARLON VS. HOOD MAN!
MARLON
VS.
HOOD MAN
LOU KARR VS. BLACK!
LOU KARR
VS.
BLACK

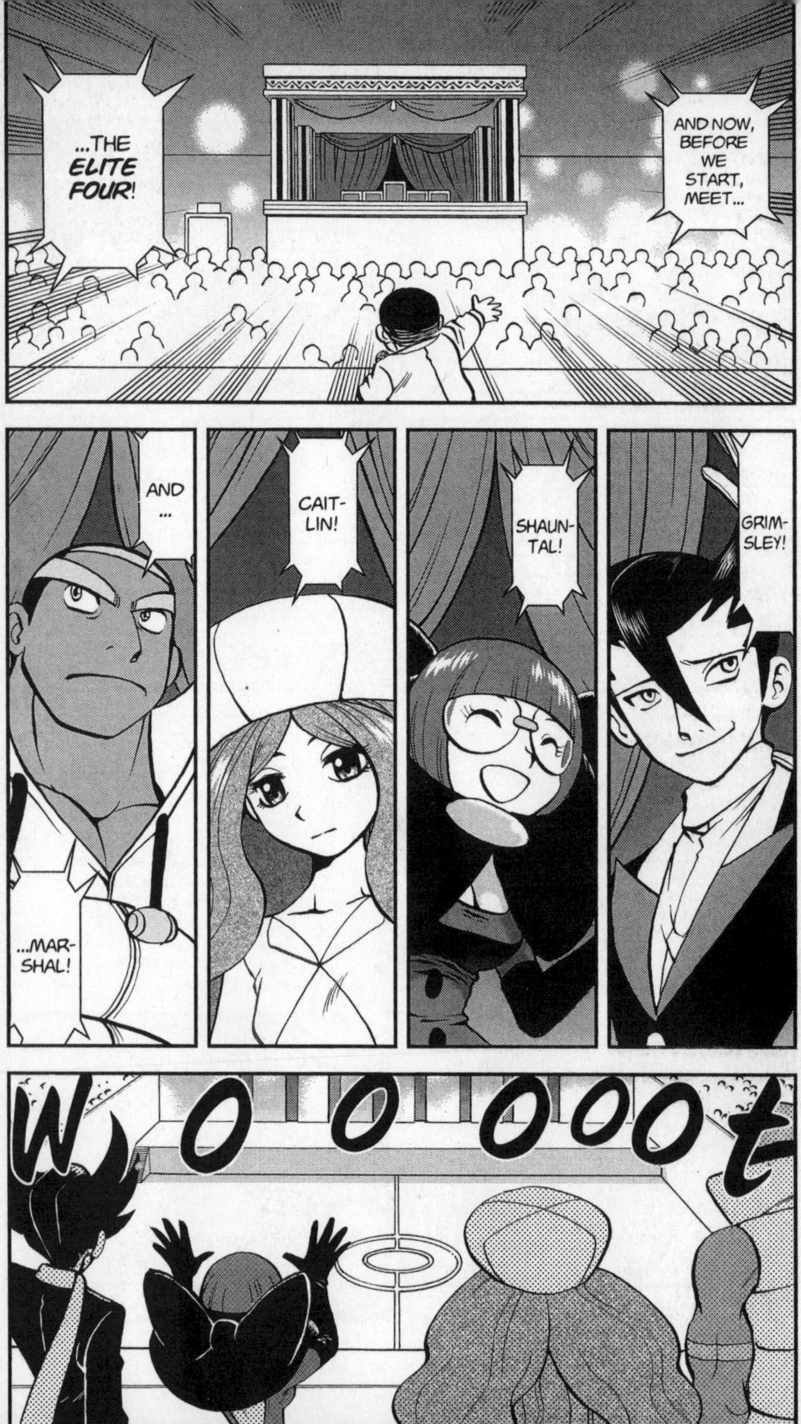
AND NOW, BEFORE WE START, MEET...
...THE *ELITE FOUR*!
GRIM-SLEY!
SHAUN-TAL!
CAIT-LIN!
AND ...
...MAR-SHAL!
WOOOOOt

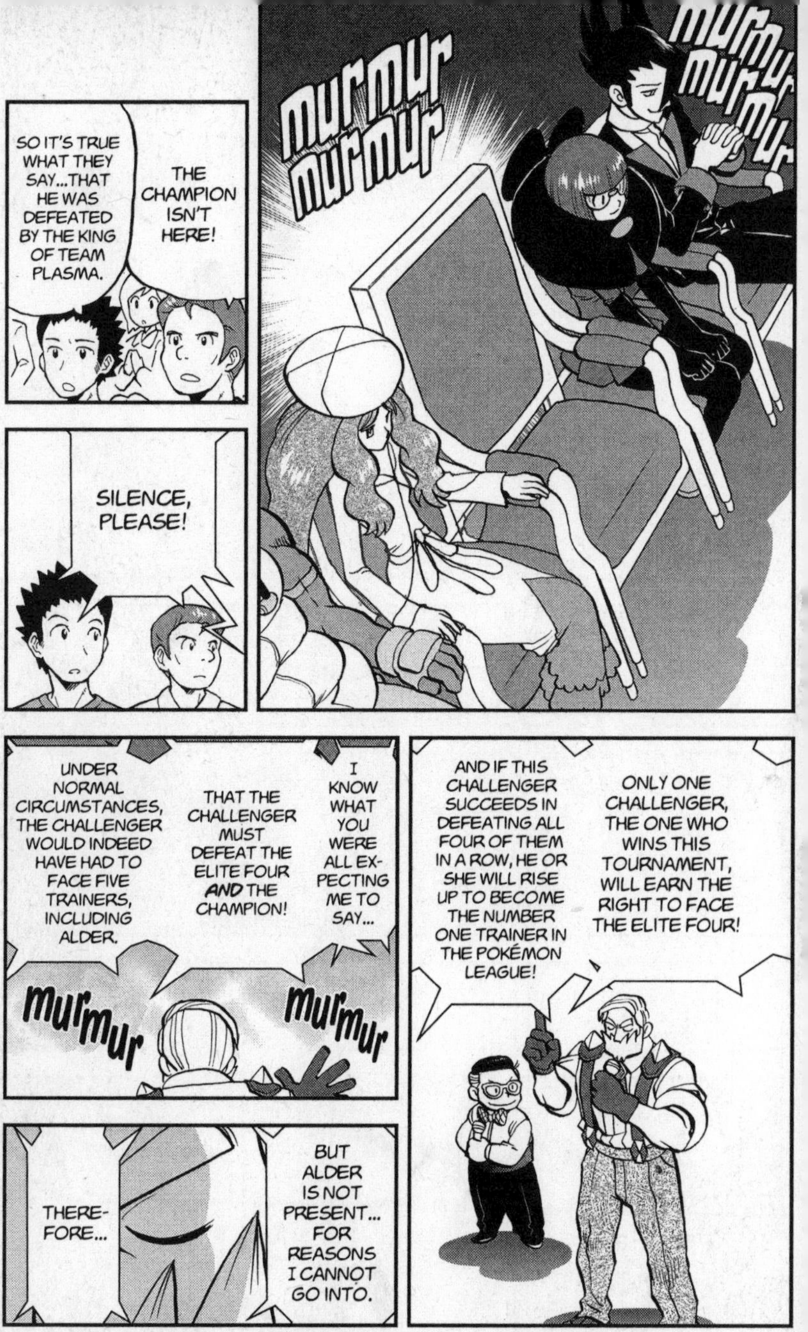
murmur murmur
murmur murmur
THE CHAMPION ISN'T HERE!
SO IT'S TRUE WHAT THEY SAY...THAT HE WAS DEFEATED BY THE KING OF TEAM PLASMA.
SILENCE, PLEASE!
ONLY ONE CHALLENGER, THE ONE WHO WINS THIS TOURNAMENT, WILL EARN THE RIGHT TO FACE THE ELITE FOUR!
AND IF THIS CHALLENGER SUCCEEDS IN DEFEATING ALL FOUR OF THEM IN A ROW, HE OR SHE WILL RISE UP TO BECOME THE NUMBER ONE TRAINER IN THE POKÉMON LEAGUE!
I KNOW WHAT YOU WERE ALL EX-PECTING ME TO SAY...
THAT THE CHALLENGER MUST DEFEAT THE ELITE FOUR *AND* THE CHAMPION!
UNDER NORMAL CIRCUMSTANCES, THE CHALLENGER WOULD INDEED HAVE HAD TO FACE FIVE TRAINERS, INCLUDING ALDER.
murmur
murmur
BUT ALDER IS NOT PRESENT... FOR REASONS I CANNOT GO INTO.
THERE-FORE...

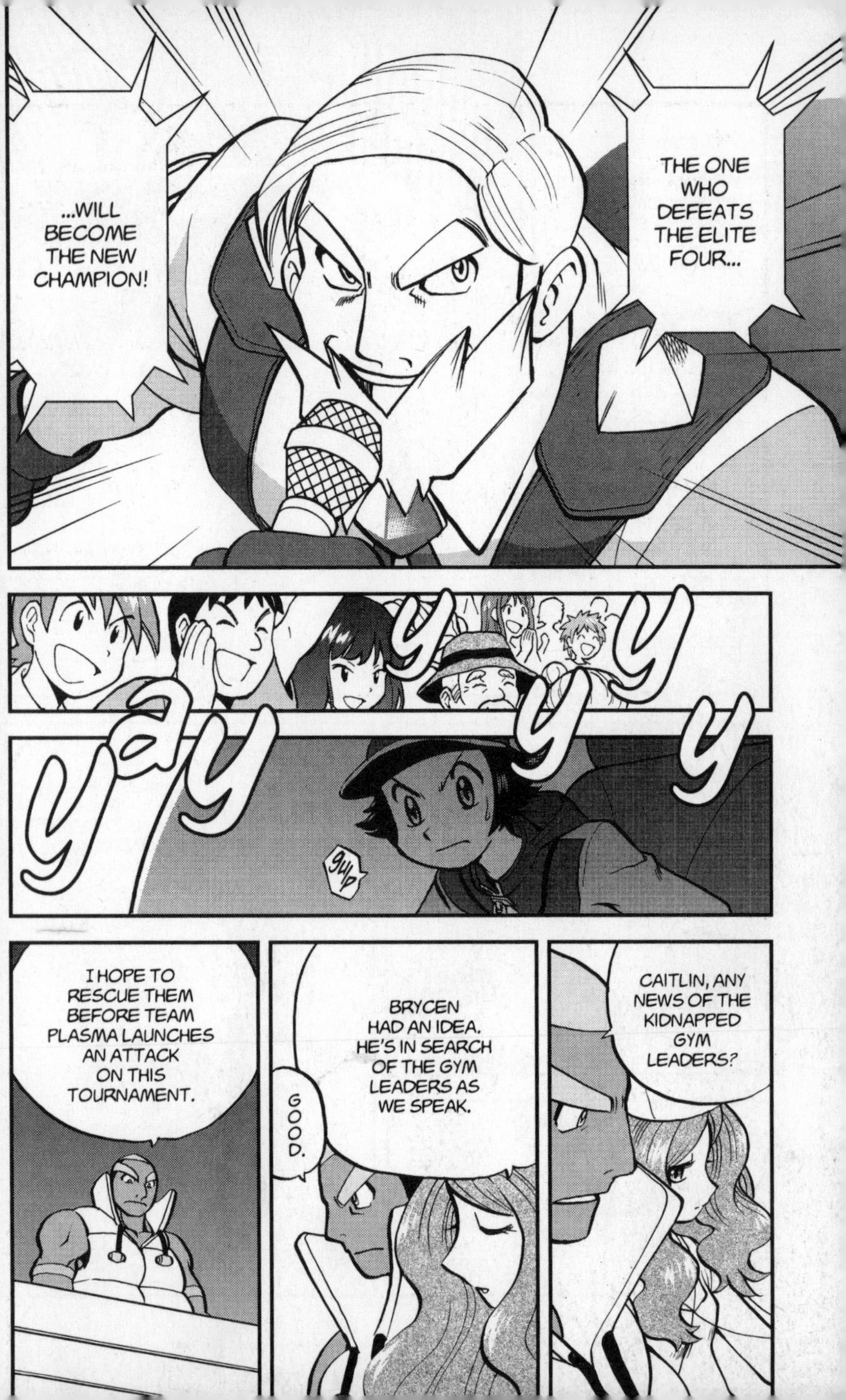
THE ONE WHO DEFEATS THE ELITE FOUR...
...WILL BECOME THE NEW CHAMPION!
yay
gulp
CAITLIN, ANY NEWS OF THE KIDNAPPED GYM LEADERS?
BRYCEN HAD AN IDEA. HE'S IN SEARCH OF THE GYM LEADERS AS WE SPEAK.
GOOD.
I HOPE TO RESCUE THEM BEFORE TEAM PLASMA LAUNCHES AN ATTACK ON THIS TOURNAMENT.

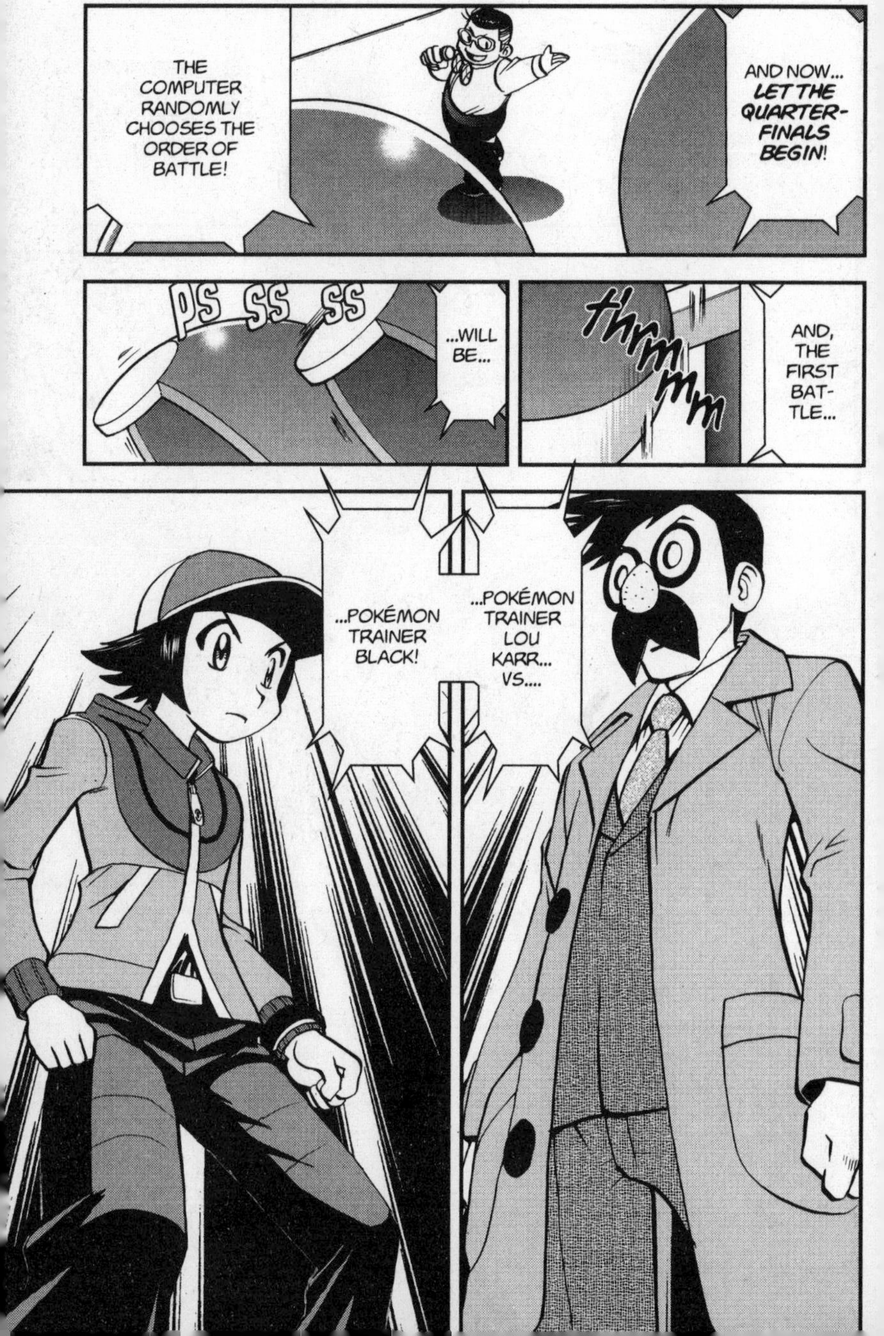
AND NOW... LET THE QUARTER-FINALS BEGIN!
THE COMPUTER RANDOMLY CHOOSES THE ORDER OF BATTLE!
AND, THE FIRST BAT-TLE...
thrmmm
...WILL BE...
ps ss ss
...POKÉMON TRAINER LOU KARR... VS....
...POKÉMON TRAINER BLACK!

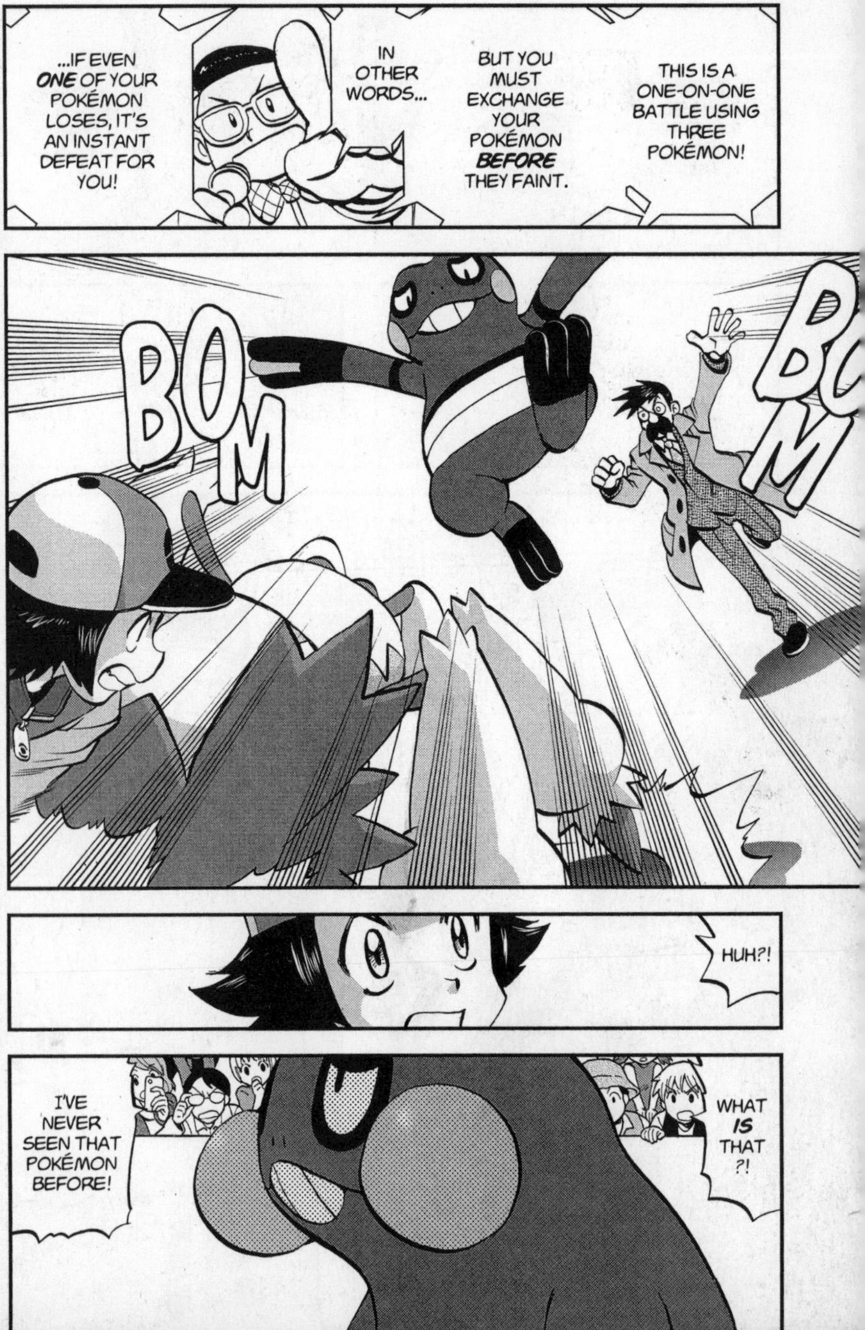
THIS IS A ONE-ON-ONE BATTLE USING THREE POKÉMON!
BUT YOU MUST EXCHANGE YOUR POKÉMON ***BEFORE*** THEY FAINT.
IN OTHER WORDS...
...IF EVEN ***ONE*** OF YOUR POKÉMON LOSES, IT'S AN INSTANT DEFEAT FOR YOU!
BOM
BOM
HUH?!
WHAT ***IS*** THAT?!
I'VE NEVER SEEN THAT POKÉMON BEFORE!

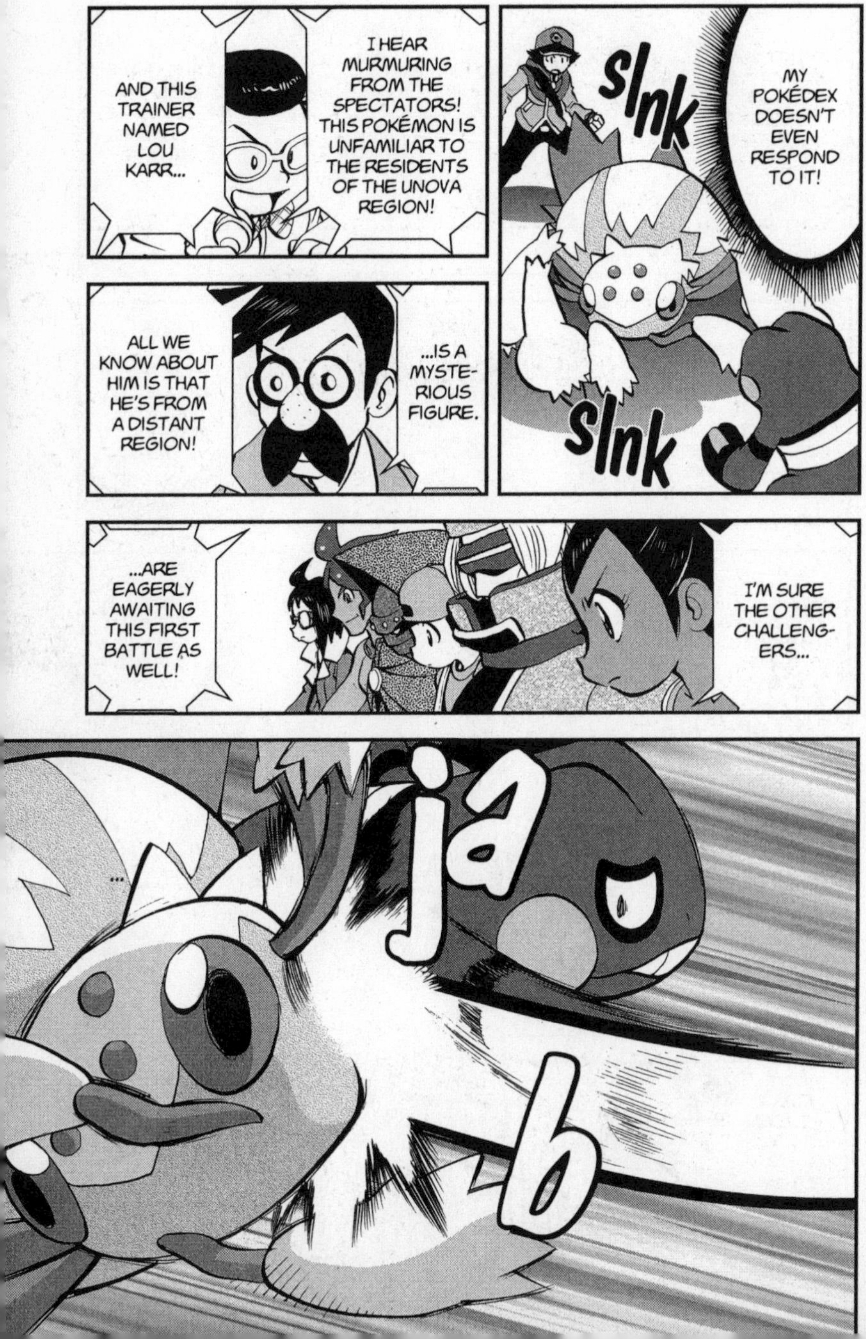
MY POKÉDEX DOESN'T EVEN RESPOND TO IT!
slnk
slnk
I HEAR MURMURING FROM THE SPECTATORS! THIS POKÉMON IS UNFAMILIAR TO THE RESIDENTS OF THE UNOVA REGION!
AND THIS TRAINER NAMED LOU KARR...
...IS A MYSTERIOUS FIGURE.
ALL WE KNOW ABOUT HIM IS THAT HE'S FROM A DISTANT REGION!
I'M SURE THE OTHER CHALLENGERS...
...ARE EAGERLY AWAITING THIS FIRST BATTLE AS WELL!
jab
...

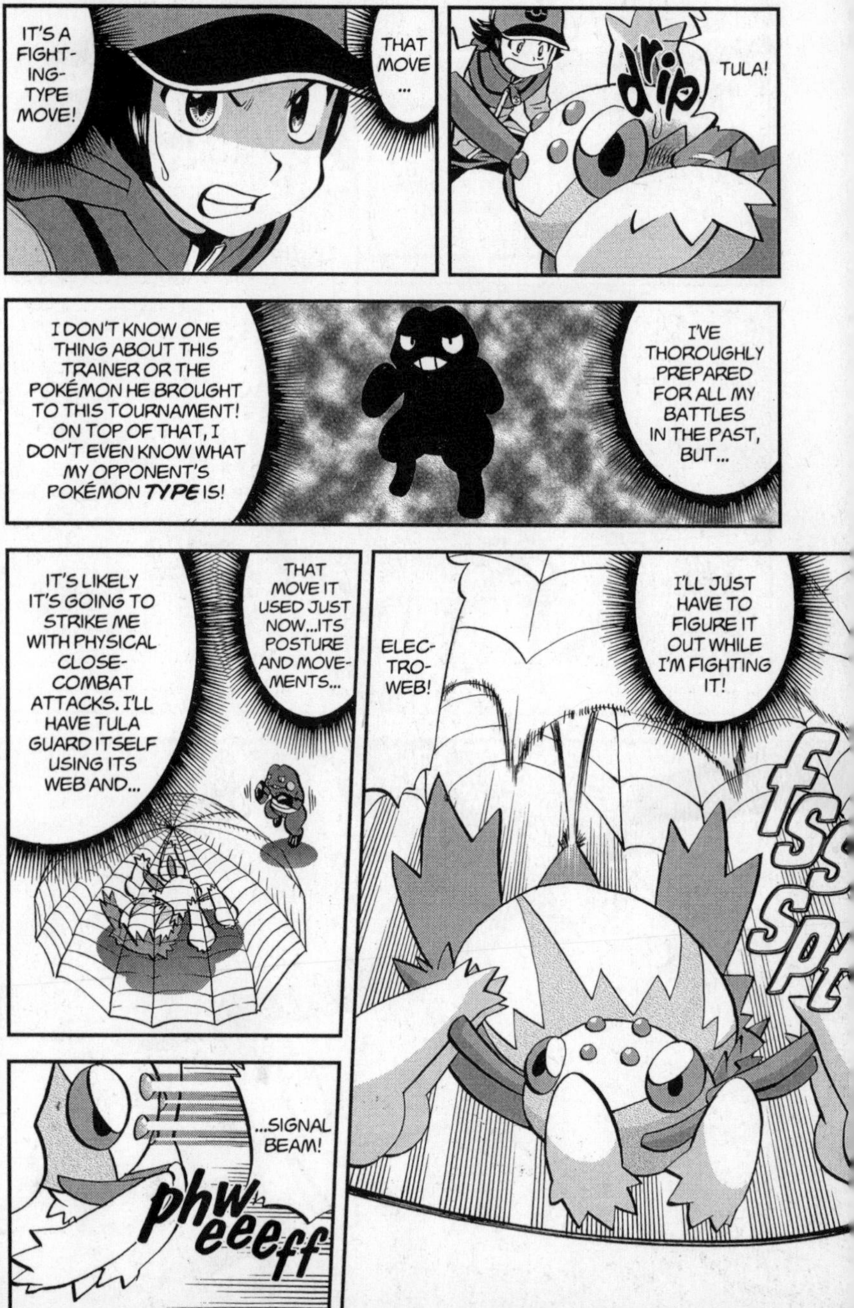
drip
TULA!
THAT MOVE ...
IT'S A FIGHTING-TYPE MOVE!
I'VE THOROUGHLY PREPARED FOR ALL MY BATTLES IN THE PAST, BUT...
I DON'T KNOW ONE THING ABOUT THIS TRAINER OR THE POKÉMON HE BROUGHT TO THIS TOURNAMENT! ON TOP OF THAT, I DON'T EVEN KNOW WHAT MY OPPONENT'S POKÉMON TYPE IS!
I'LL JUST HAVE TO FIGURE IT OUT WHILE I'M FIGHTING IT!
ELECTROWEB!
fsss spt
THAT MOVE IT USED JUST NOW...ITS POSTURE AND MOVEMENTS...
IT'S LIKELY IT'S GOING TO STRIKE ME WITH PHYSICAL CLOSE-COMBAT ATTACKS. I'LL HAVE TULA GUARD ITSELF USING ITS WEB AND...
...SIGNAL BEAM!
phweeeff

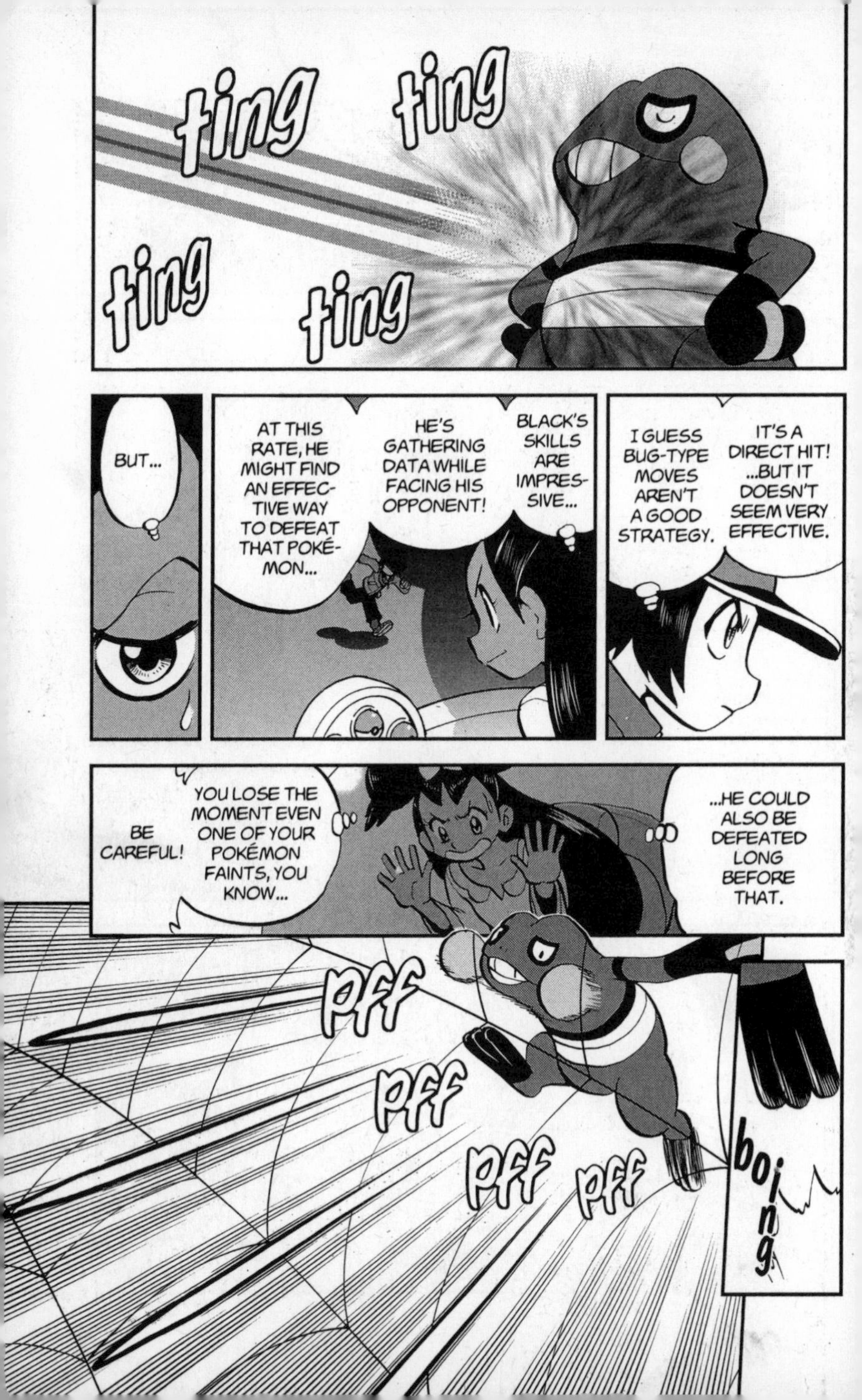
ting
ting
ting
ting
IT'S A DIRECT HIT! ...BUT IT DOESN'T SEEM VERY EFFECTIVE.
I GUESS BUG-TYPE MOVES AREN'T A GOOD STRATEGY.
BLACK'S SKILLS ARE IMPRESSIVE...
HE'S GATHERING DATA WHILE FACING HIS OPPONENT!
AT THIS RATE, HE MIGHT FIND AN EFFECTIVE WAY TO DEFEAT THAT POKÉMON...
BUT...
...HE COULD ALSO BE DEFEATED LONG BEFORE THAT.
YOU LOSE THE MOMENT EVEN ONE OF YOUR POKÉMON FAINTS, YOU KNOW...
BE CAREFUL!
boing
pff
pff
pff
pff

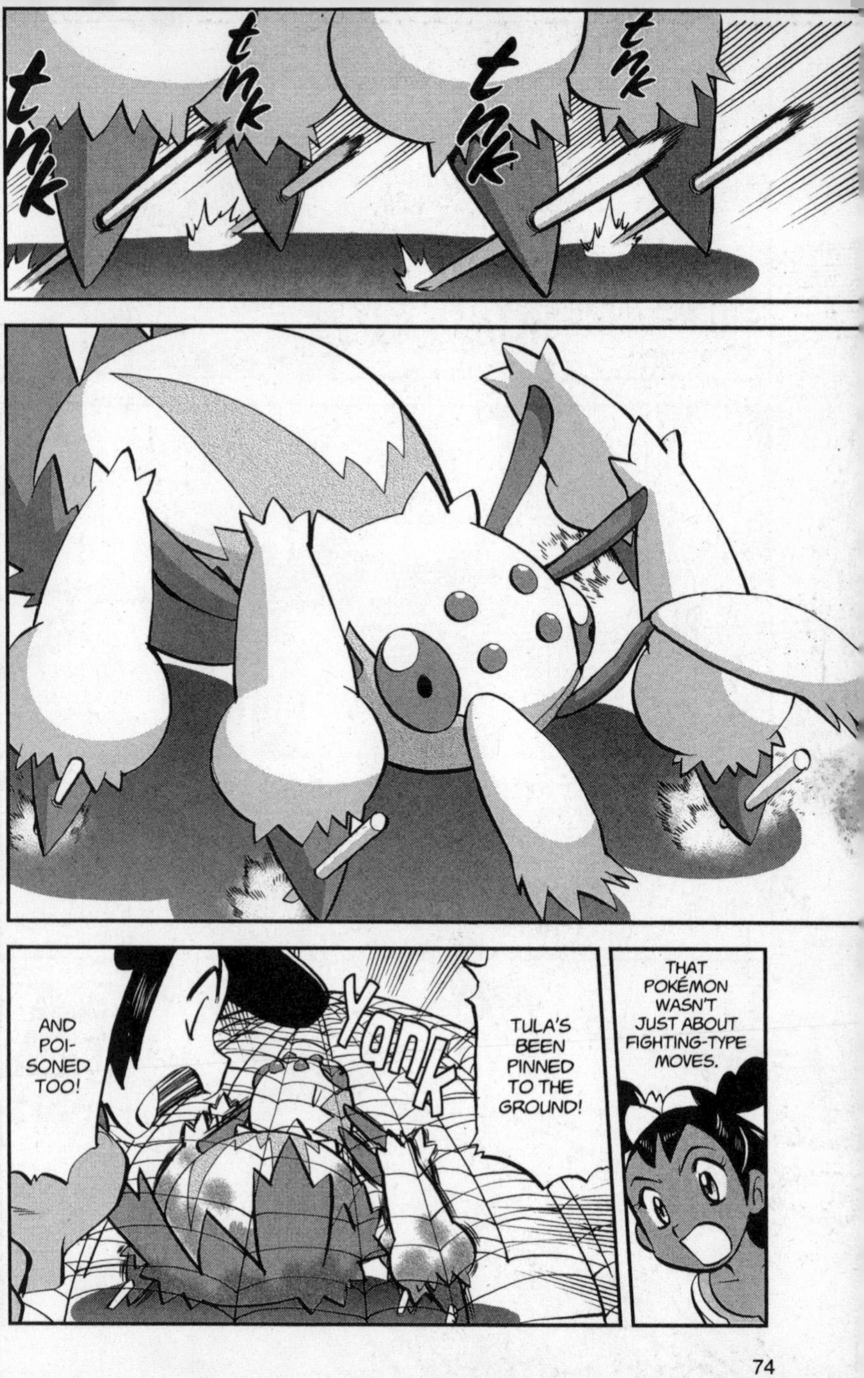
tnk
tnk
tnk
tnk
THAT POKÉMON WASN'T JUST ABOUT FIGHTING-TYPE MOVES.
TULA'S BEEN PINNED TO THE GROUND!
Yank
AND POI-SONED TOO!

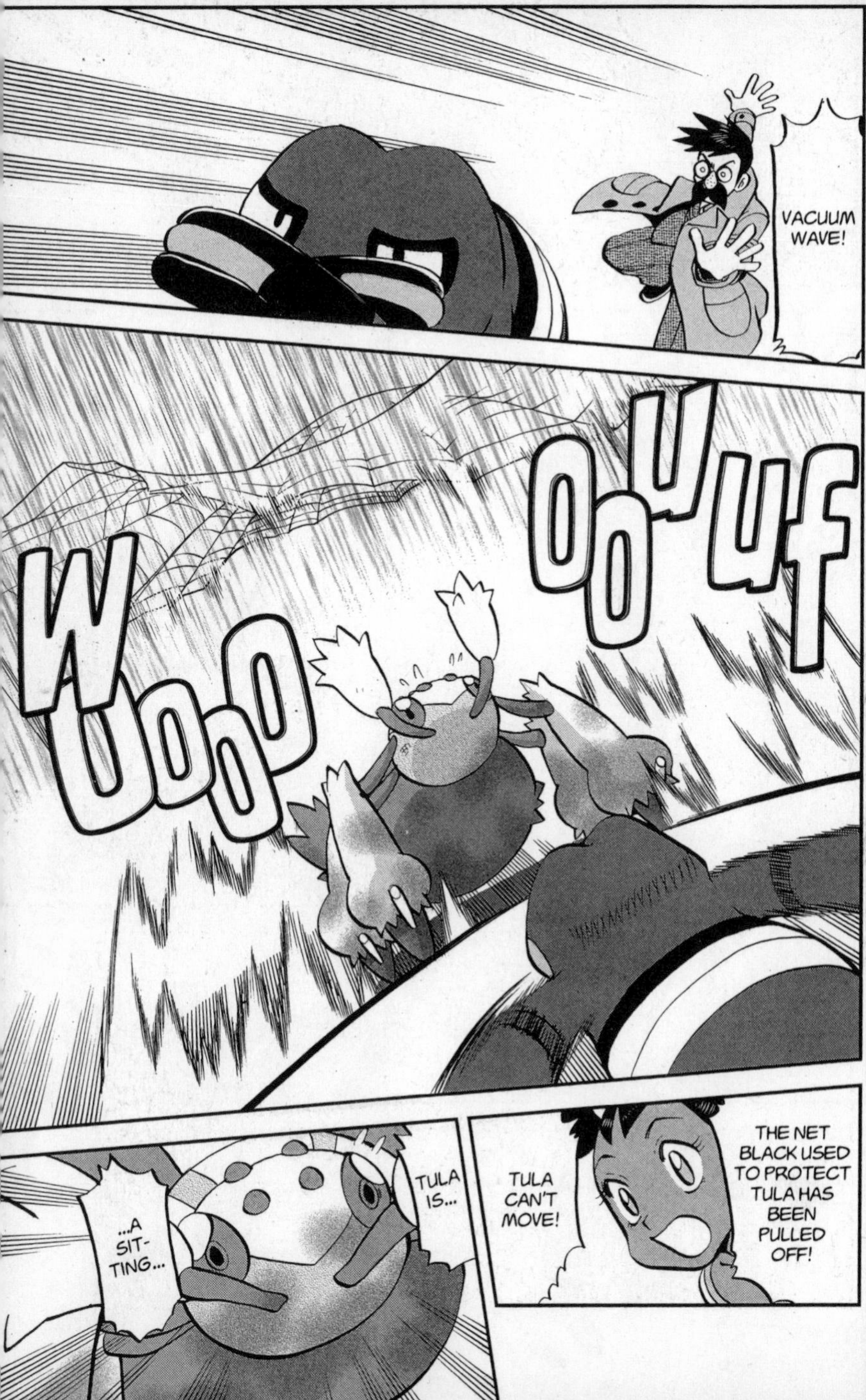
VACUUM WAVE!
WUOOOO
OOUUUF
THE NET BLACK USED TO PROTECT TULA HAS BEEN PULLED OFF!
TULA CAN'T MOVE!
TULA IS...
...A SIT-TING...

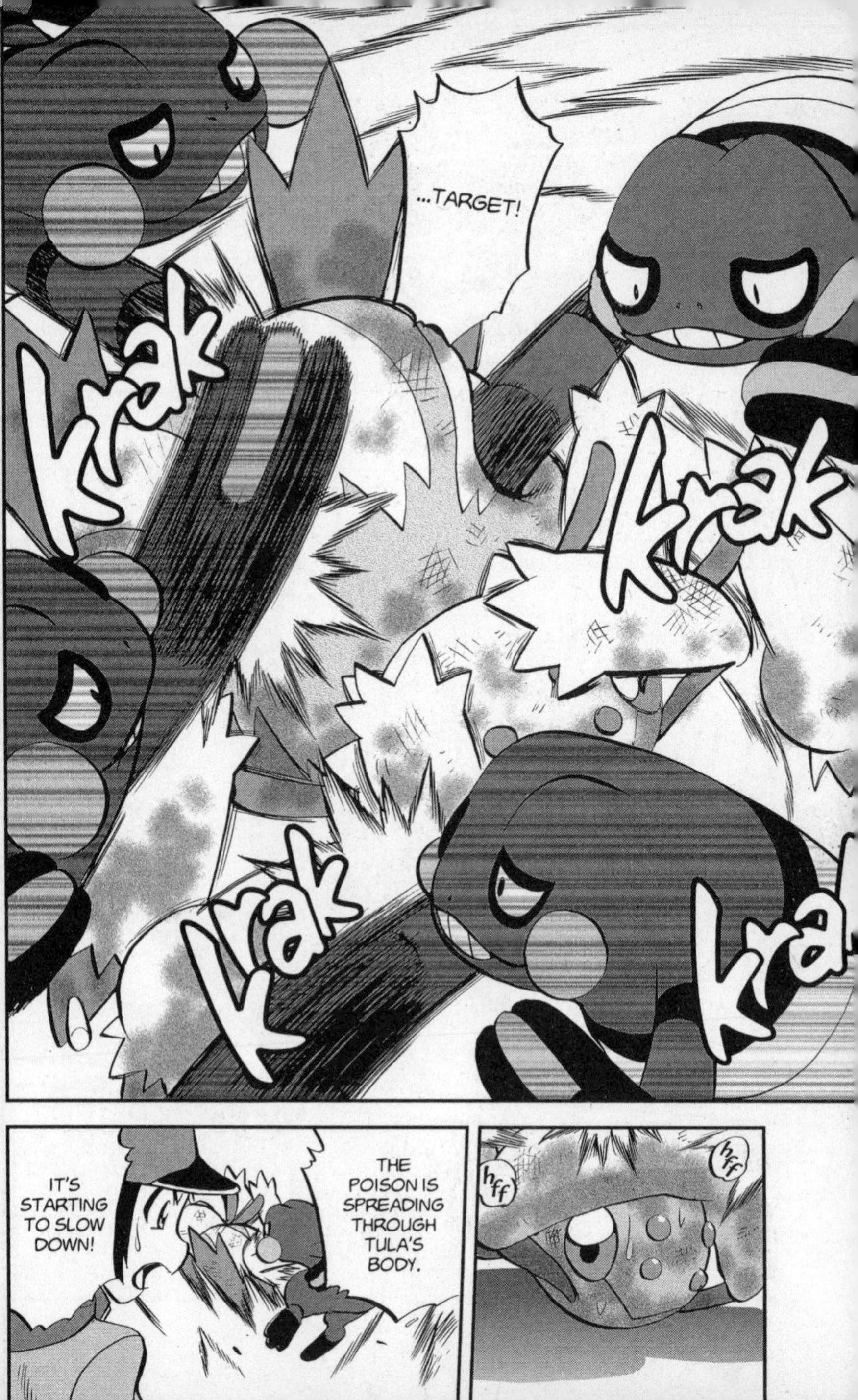
...TARGET!
krak
krak
krak
kra
hff
hff
THE POISON IS SPREADING THROUGH TULA'S BODY.
IT'S STARTING TO SLOW DOWN!

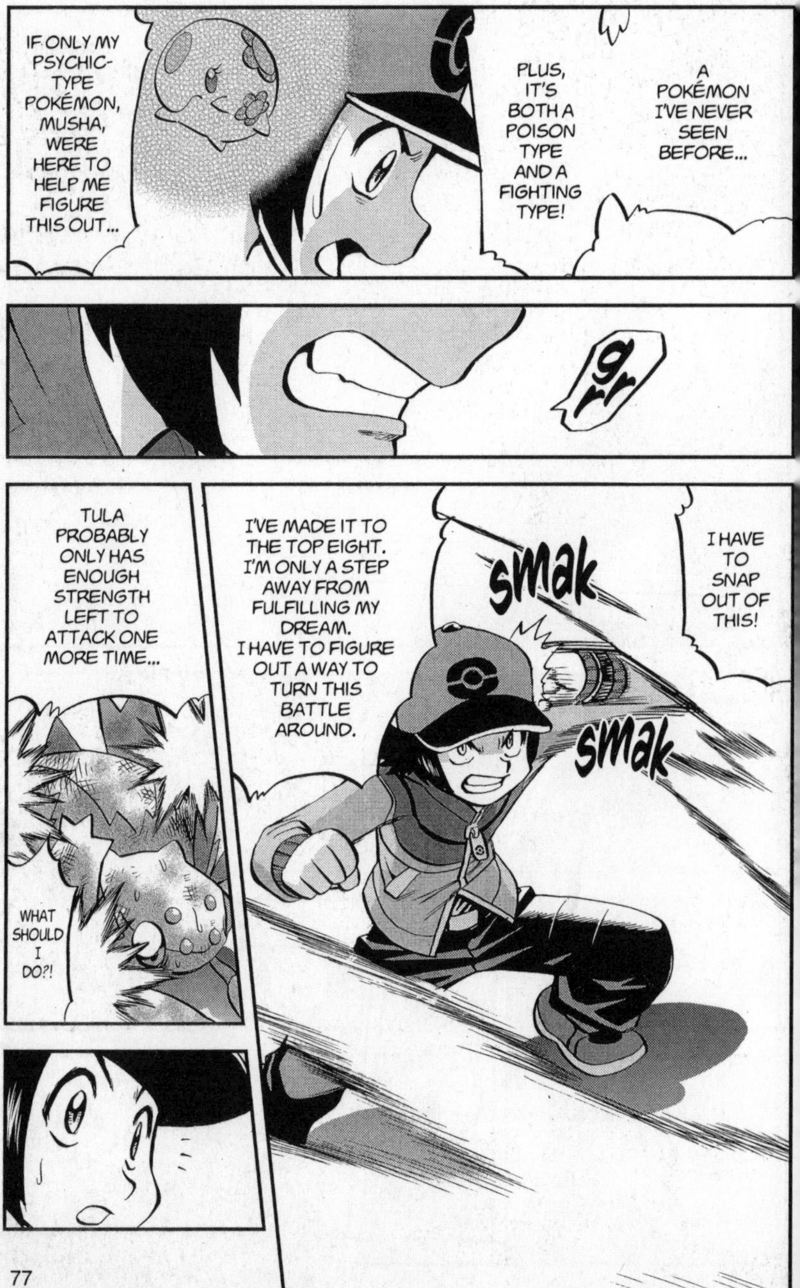
A POKÉMON I'VE NEVER SEEN BEFORE...
PLUS, IT'S BOTH A POISON TYPE AND A FIGHTING TYPE!
IF ONLY MY PSYCHIC-TYPE POKÉMON, MUSHA, WERE HERE TO HELP ME FIGURE THIS OUT...
gr
I HAVE TO SNAP OUT OF THIS!
smak
smak
I'VE MADE IT TO THE TOP EIGHT. I'M ONLY A STEP AWAY FROM FULFILLING MY DREAM. I HAVE TO FIGURE OUT A WAY TO TURN THIS BATTLE AROUND.
TULA PROBABLY ONLY HAS ENOUGH STRENGTH LEFT TO ATTACK ONE MORE TIME...
WHAT SHOULD I DO?!

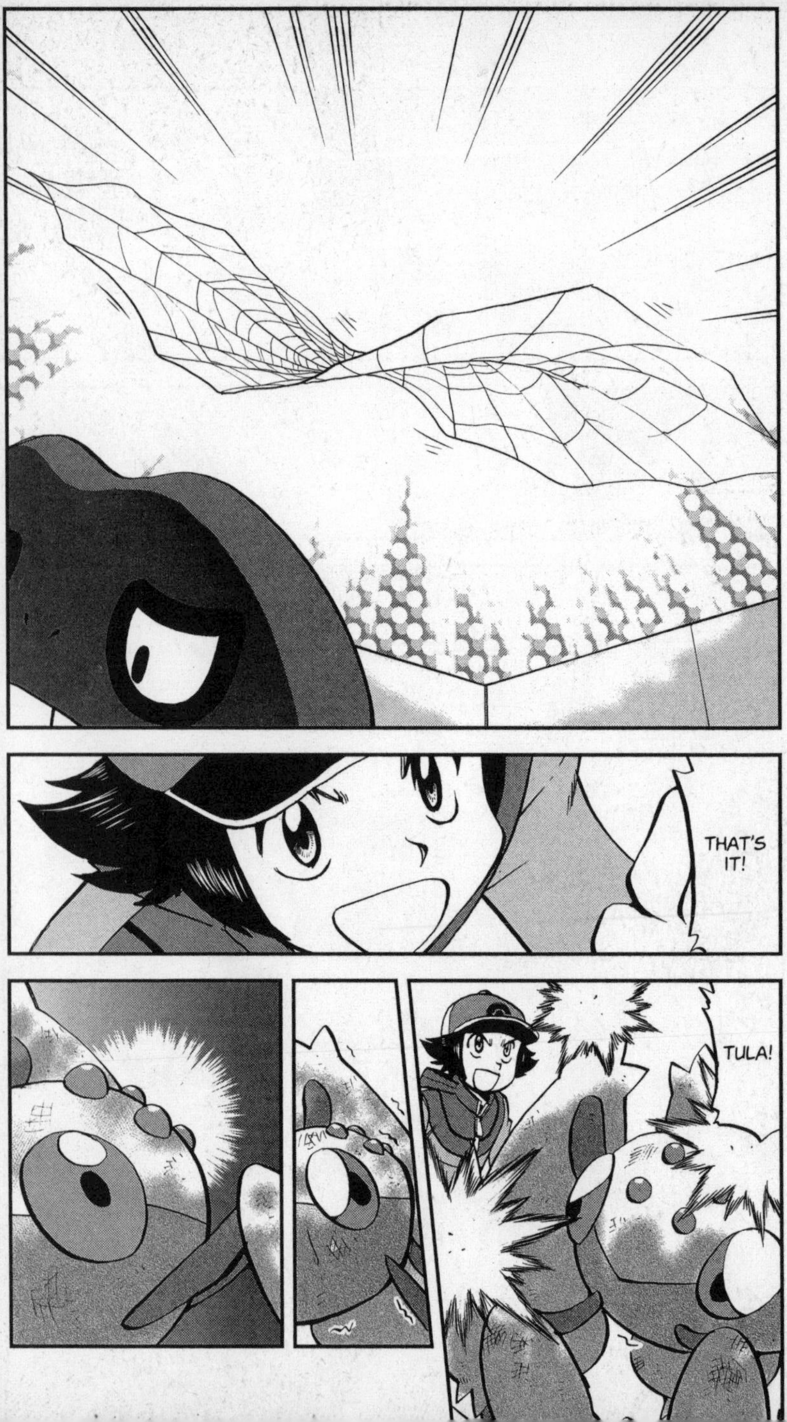
THAT'S IT!
TULA!

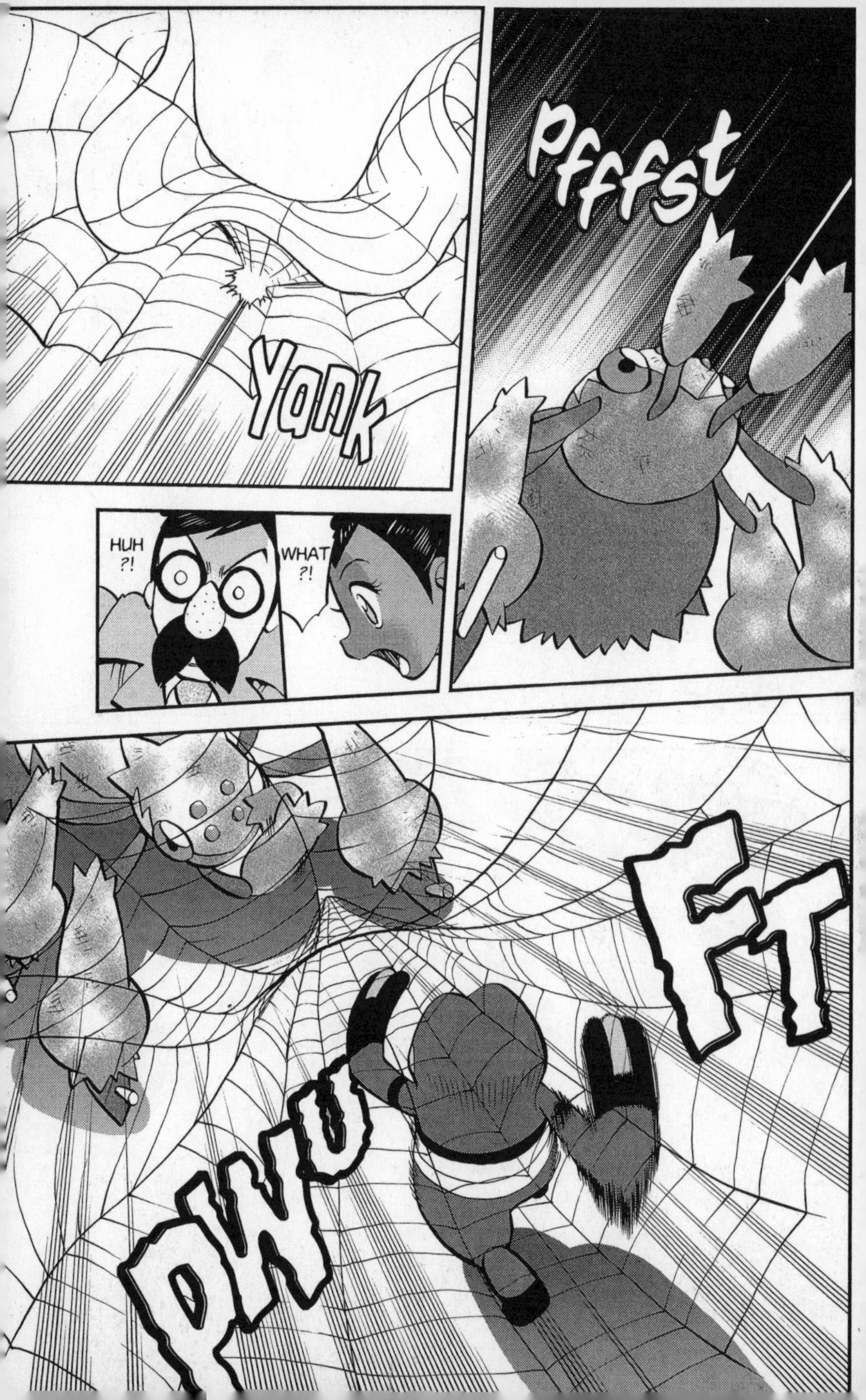
Pffffst
Yank
WHAT ?!
HUH ?!
DKUUFT

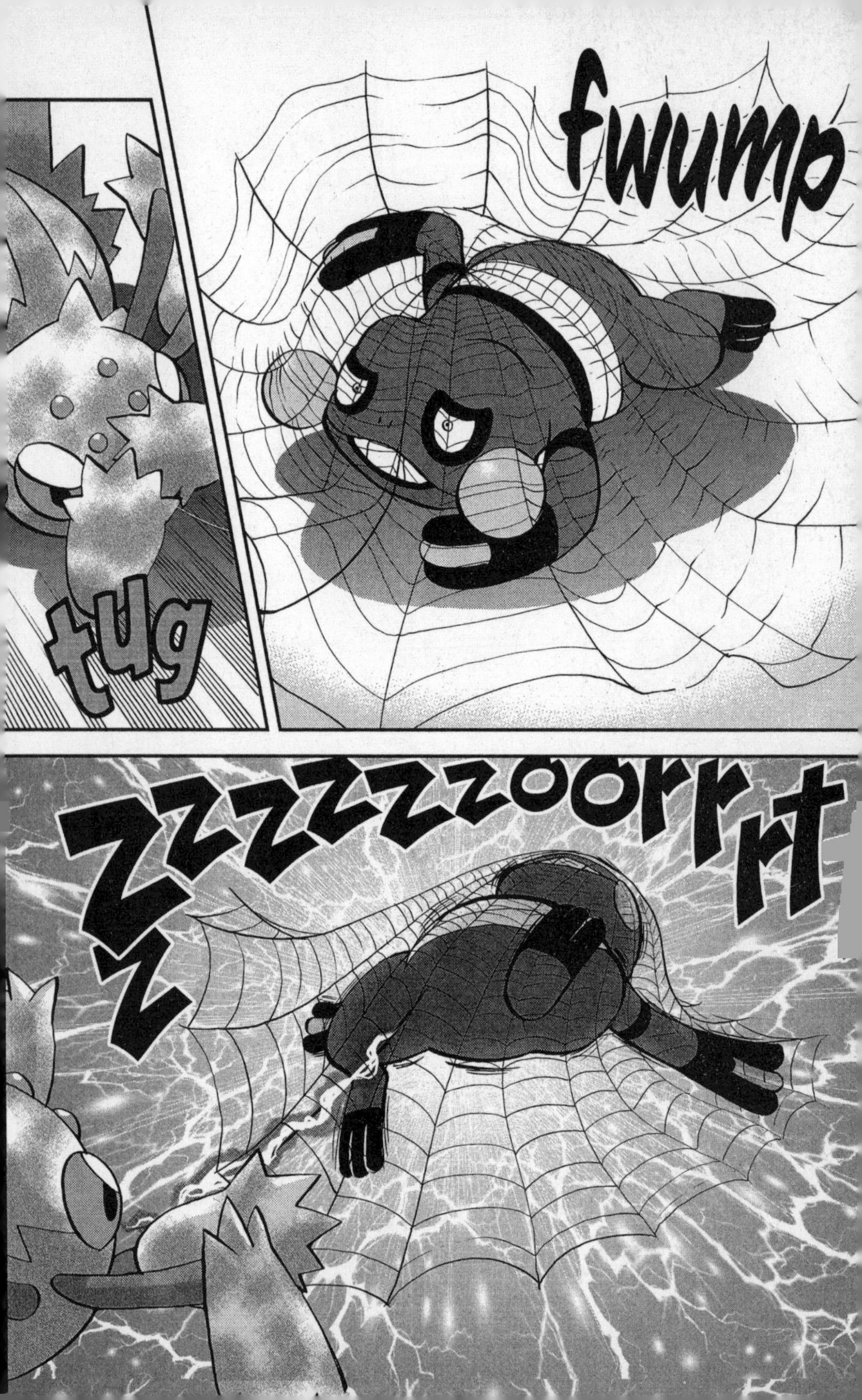
fwump
tug
ZZZZZZZZOOrrrt

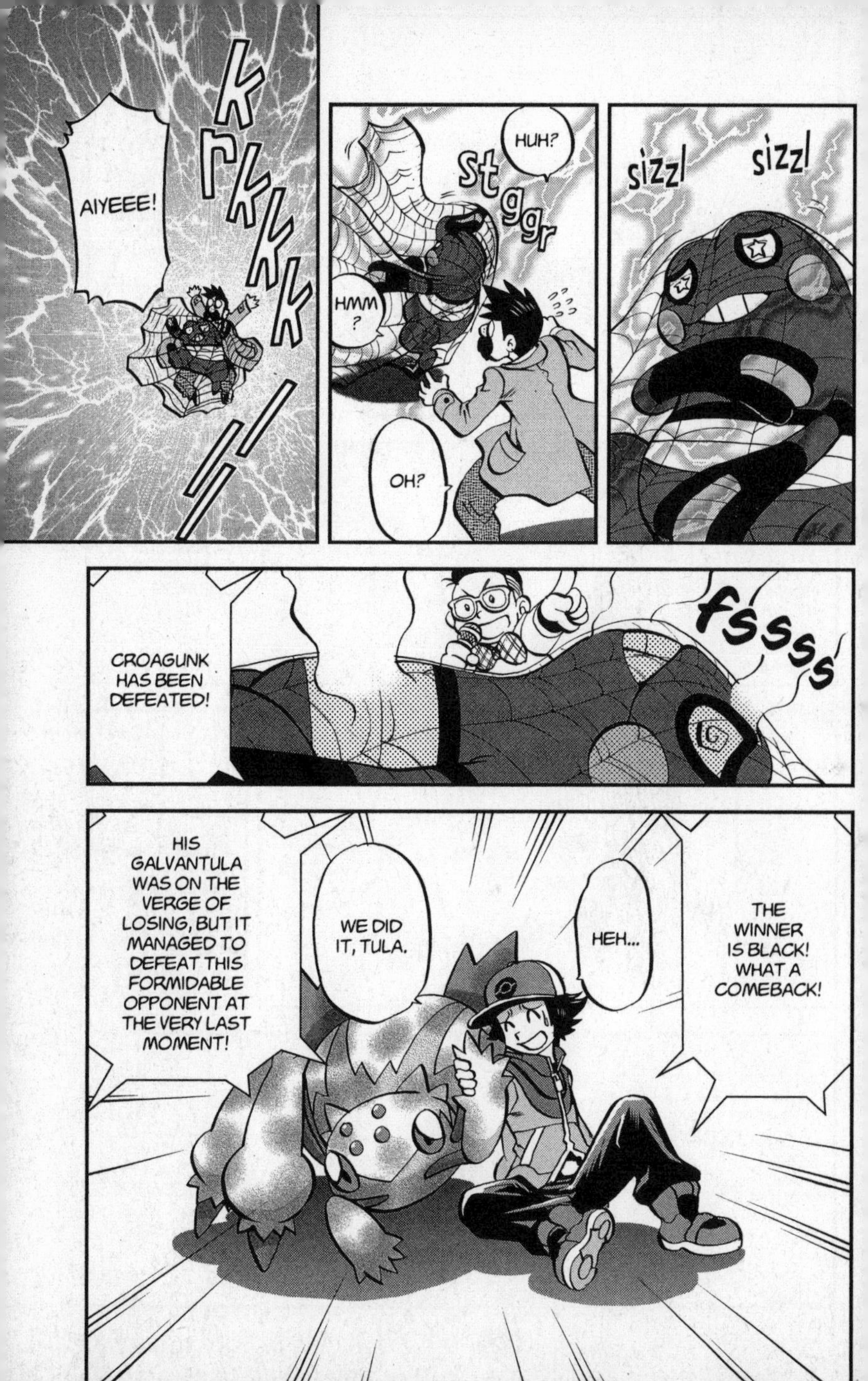
sizzl
sizzl
HUH?
stggr
HMM?
OH?
AIYEEE!
krkkkk
fssss
CROAGUNK HAS BEEN DEFEATED!
THE WINNER IS BLACK! WHAT A COMEBACK!
HEH...
WE DID IT, TULA.
HIS GALVANTULA WAS ON THE VERGE OF LOSING, BUT IT MANAGED TO DEFEAT THIS FORMIDABLE OPPONENT AT THE VERY LAST MOMENT!

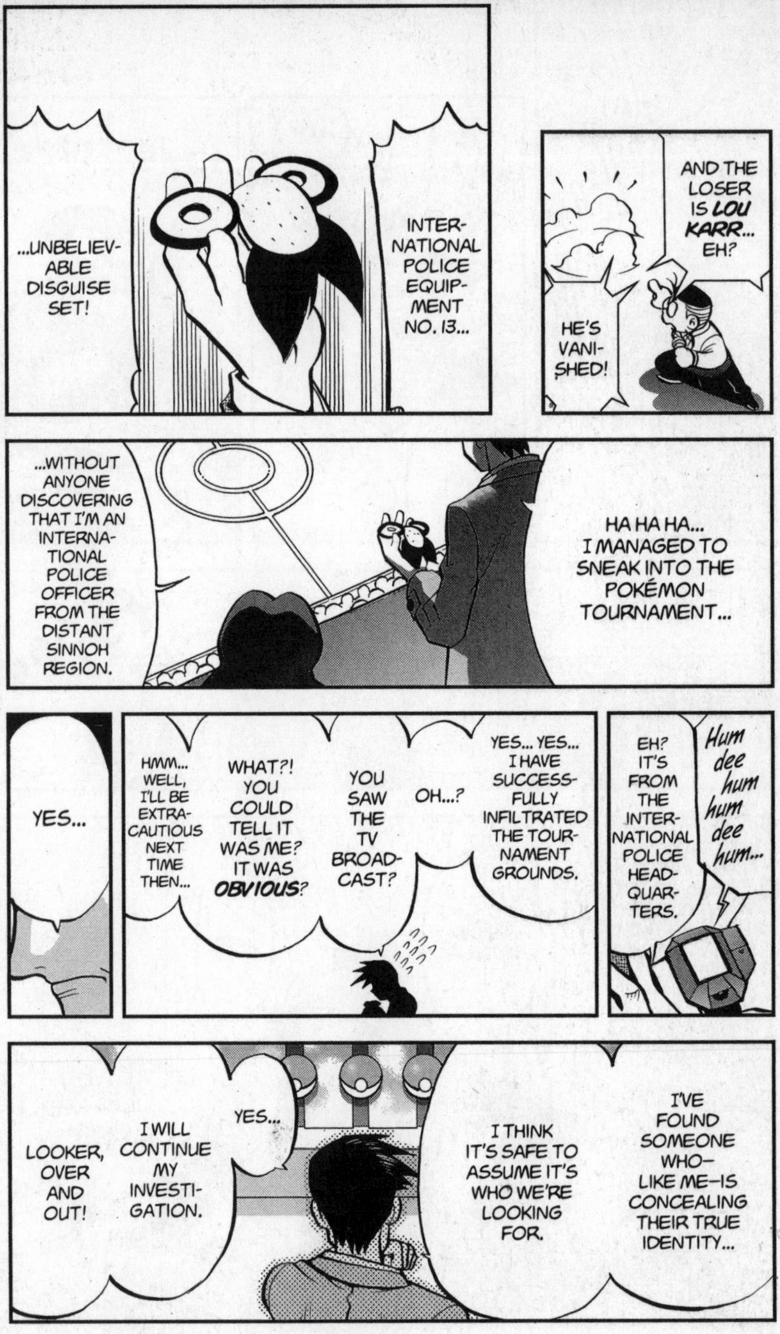
AND THE LOSER IS *LOU KARR*... EH?
HE'S VANISHED!
INTERNATIONAL POLICE EQUIPMENT NO. 13...
...UNBELIEVABLE DISGUISE SET!
HA HA HA... I MANAGED TO SNEAK INTO THE POKÉMON TOURNAMENT...
...WITHOUT ANYONE DISCOVERING THAT I'M AN INTERNATIONAL POLICE OFFICER FROM THE DISTANT SINNOH REGION.
*Hum dee hum hum dee hum...*
EH? IT'S FROM THE INTERNATIONAL POLICE HEADQUARTERS.
YES... YES... I HAVE SUCCESSFULLY INFILTRATED THE TOURNAMENT GROUNDS.
OH...?
YOU SAW THE TV BROADCAST?
WHAT?! YOU COULD TELL IT WAS ME? IT WAS *OBVIOUS*?
HMM... WELL, I'LL BE EXTRA-CAUTIOUS NEXT TIME THEN...
YES...
I'VE FOUND SOMEONE WHO—LIKE ME—IS CONCEALING THEIR TRUE IDENTITY...
I THINK IT'S SAFE TO ASSUME IT'S WHO WE'RE LOOKING FOR.
YES...
I WILL CONTINUE MY INVESTIGATION.
LOOKER, OVER AND OUT!

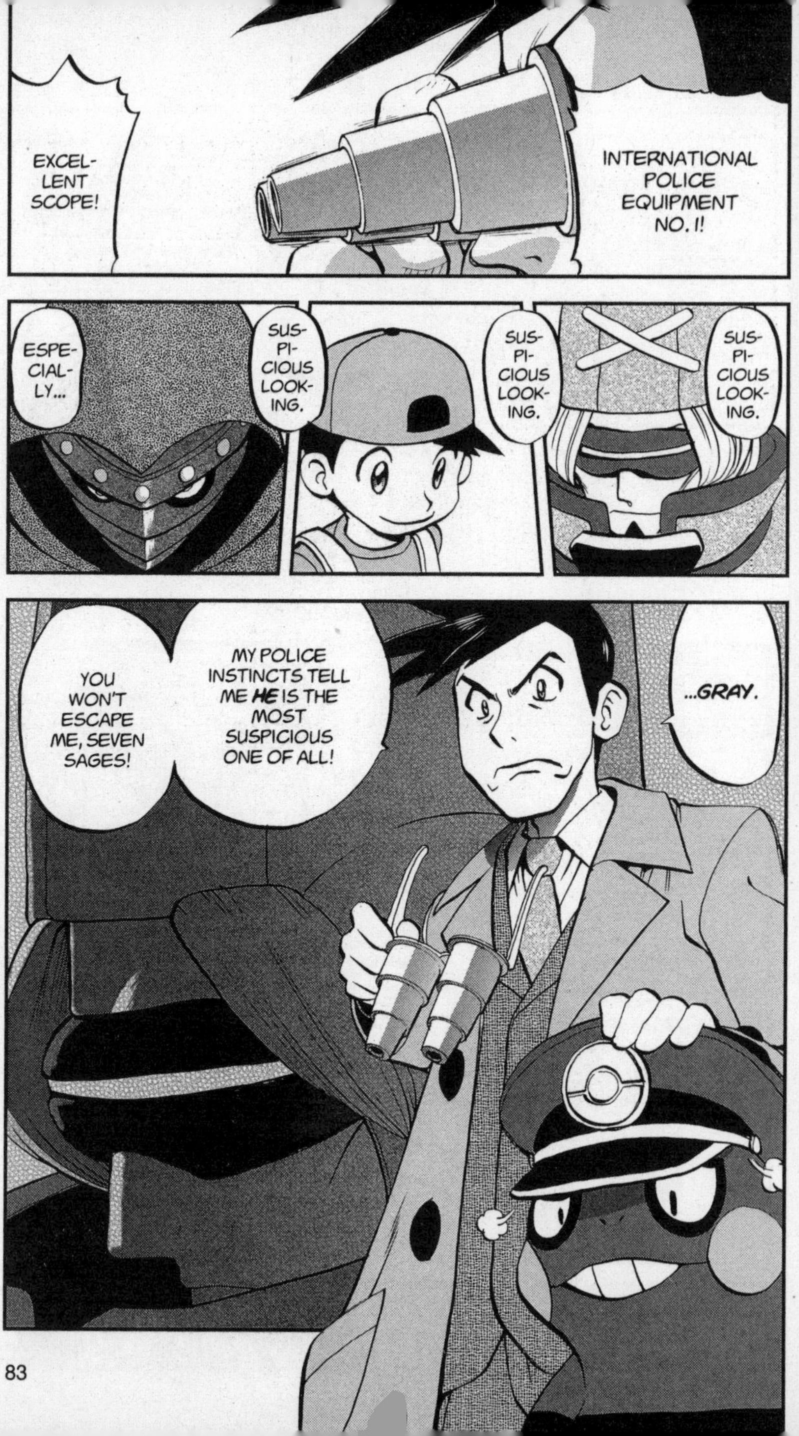
INTERNATIONAL POLICE EQUIPMENT NO. 1!
EXCELLENT SCOPE!
SUSPICIOUS LOOKING.
SUSPICIOUS LOOKING.
SUSPICIOUS LOOKING.
ESPECIALLY...
...GRAY.
MY POLICE INSTINCTS TELL ME **HE** IS THE MOST SUSPICIOUS ONE OF ALL!
YOU WON'T ESCAPE ME, SEVEN SAGES!

# ADVENTURE MAP

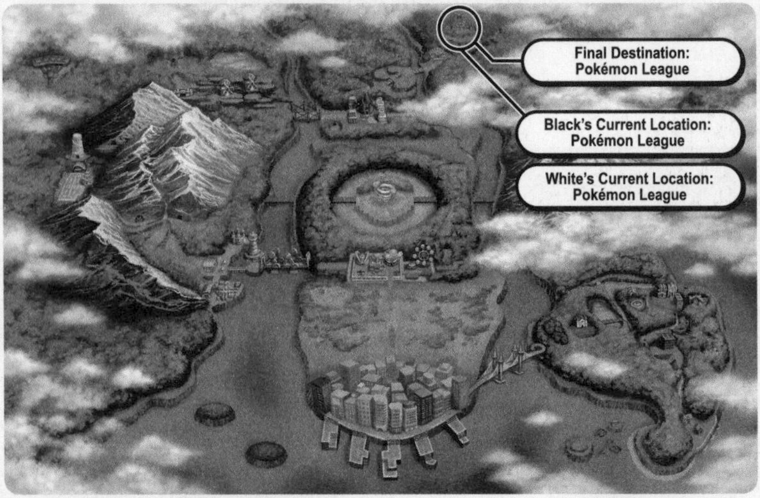

Final Destination: Pokémon League
Black's Current Location: Pokémon League
White's Current Location: Pokémon League


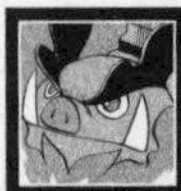
**Bo**
Mega Fire Pig Pokémon
Emboar ♂ Fire Fighting
Lv.48 Ability: Blaze

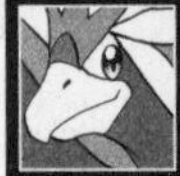
**Brav**
Valiant Pokémon
Braviary ♂ Normal Flying
Lv.58 Ability: Sheer Force

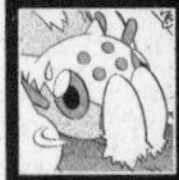
**Tula**
EleSpider Pokémon
Galvantula ♂ Bug Electric
Lv.58 Ability: Unnerve

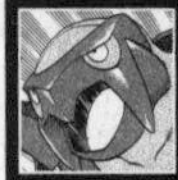
**Costa**
Prototurtle Pokémon
Tirtouga ♂ Water Rock
Lv.42 Ability: Solid Rock

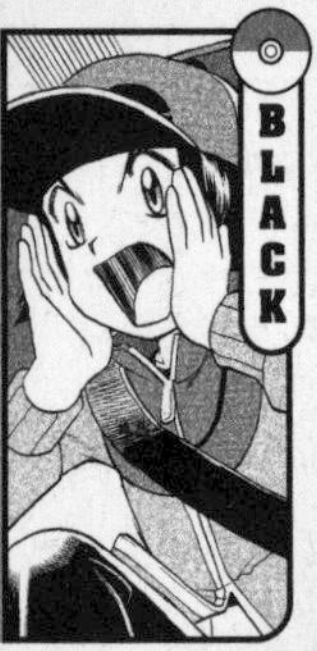

BLACK


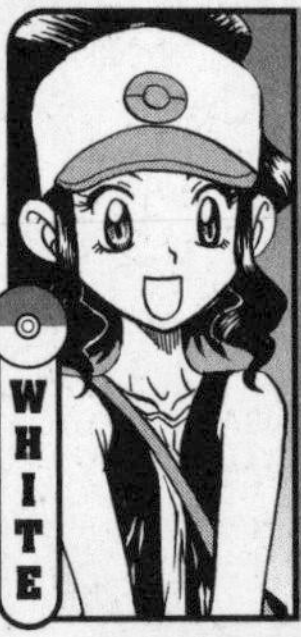

WHITE


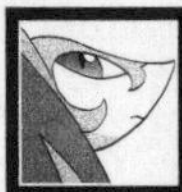
**Amanda**
Grass Snake Pokémon
Servine ♀ Grass
Lv.39 Ability: Overgrow

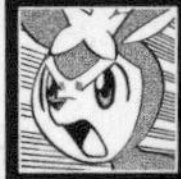
**Darlene**
Season Pokémon
Deerling ♀ Normal Grass
Lv.31 Ability: Chlorophyll

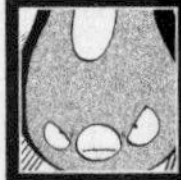
**Dorothy**
Trap Pokémon
Stunfisk ♀ Ground Electric
Lv.34 Ability: Limber

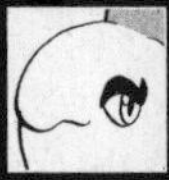
**Nancy**
Caring Pokémon
Alomomola ♀ Water
Lv.35 Ability: Healer

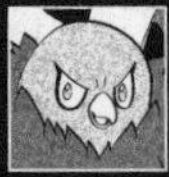
**Barbara**
Diapered Pokémon
Vullaby ♀ Dark Flying
Lv.39 Ability: Big Pecks

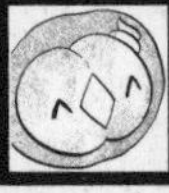
**Solly**
Cell Pokémon
Solosis ♂ Psychic
Lv.29 Ability: Magic Guard

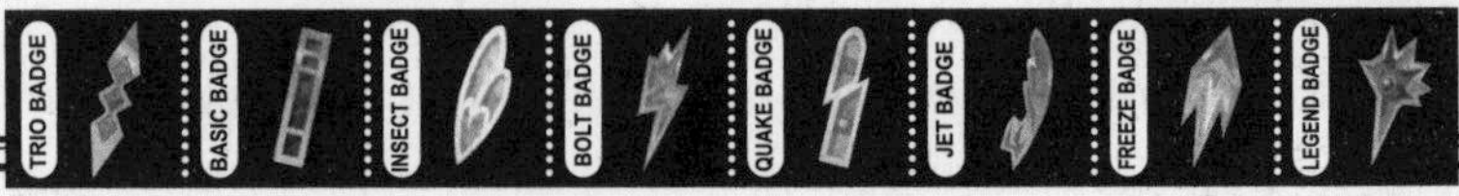

TRIO BADGE
BASIC BADGE
INSECT BADGE
BOLT BADGE
QUAKE BADGE
JET BADGE
FREEZE BADGE
LEGEND BADGE

Pokémon Adventures Black & White

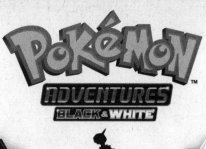

DEINO

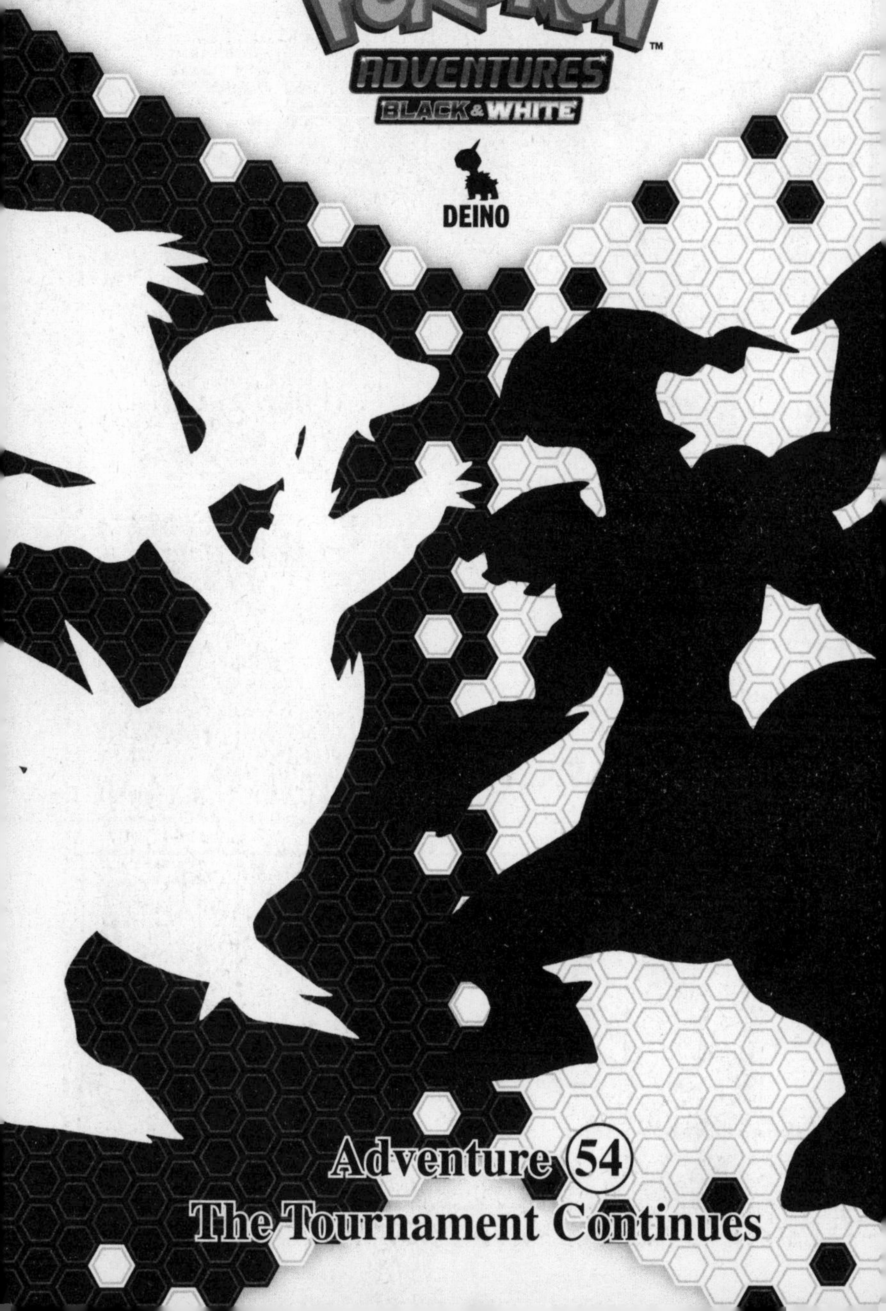

# Adventure 54
## The Tournament Continues

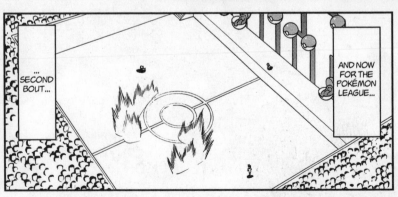

...SECOND BOUT...

AND NOW FOR THE POKÉMON LEAGUE...

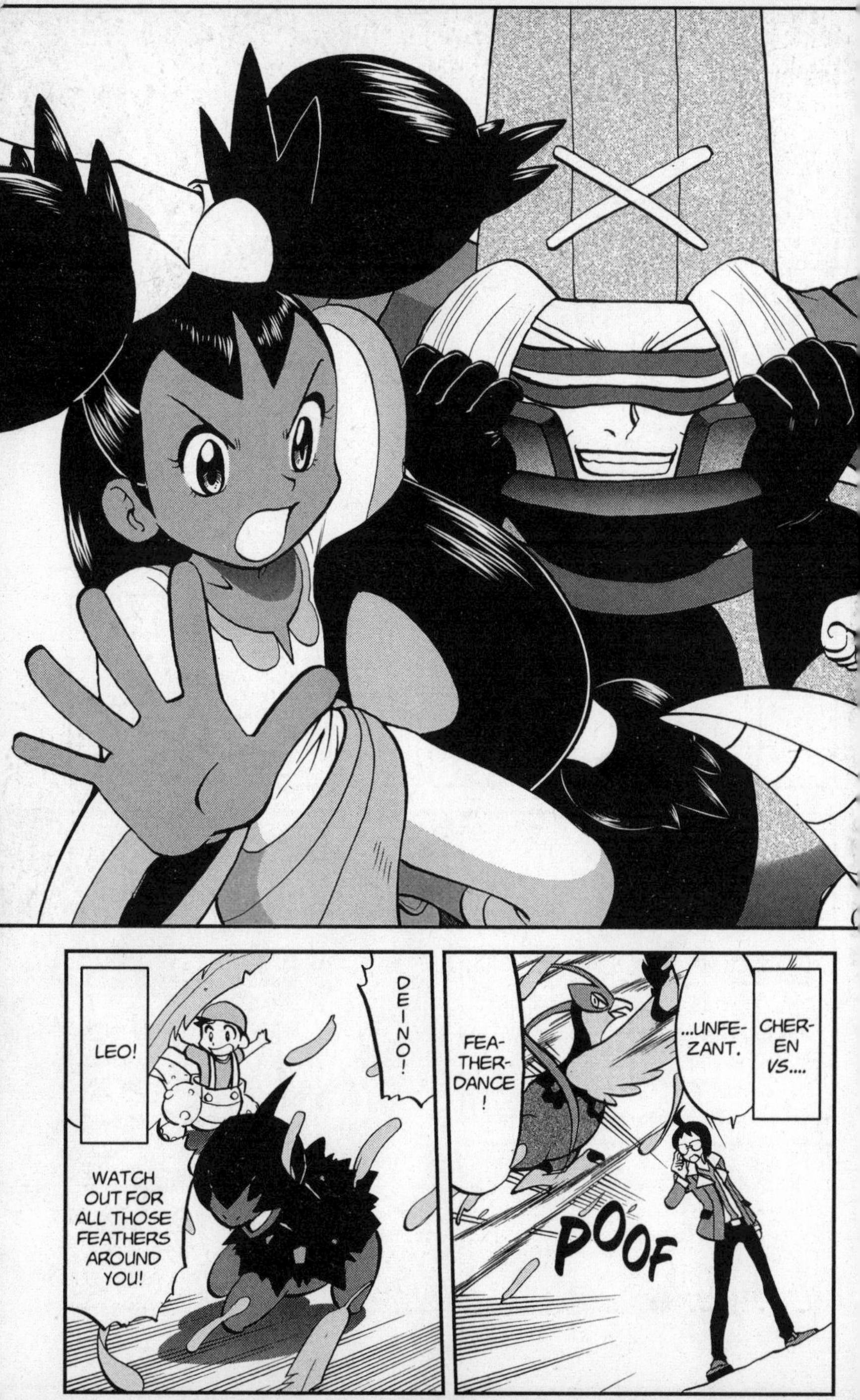
CHEREN VS....
...UNFEZANT.
FEATHER-DANCE!
POOF
DEINO!
LEO!
WATCH OUT FOR ALL THOSE FEATHERS AROUND YOU!

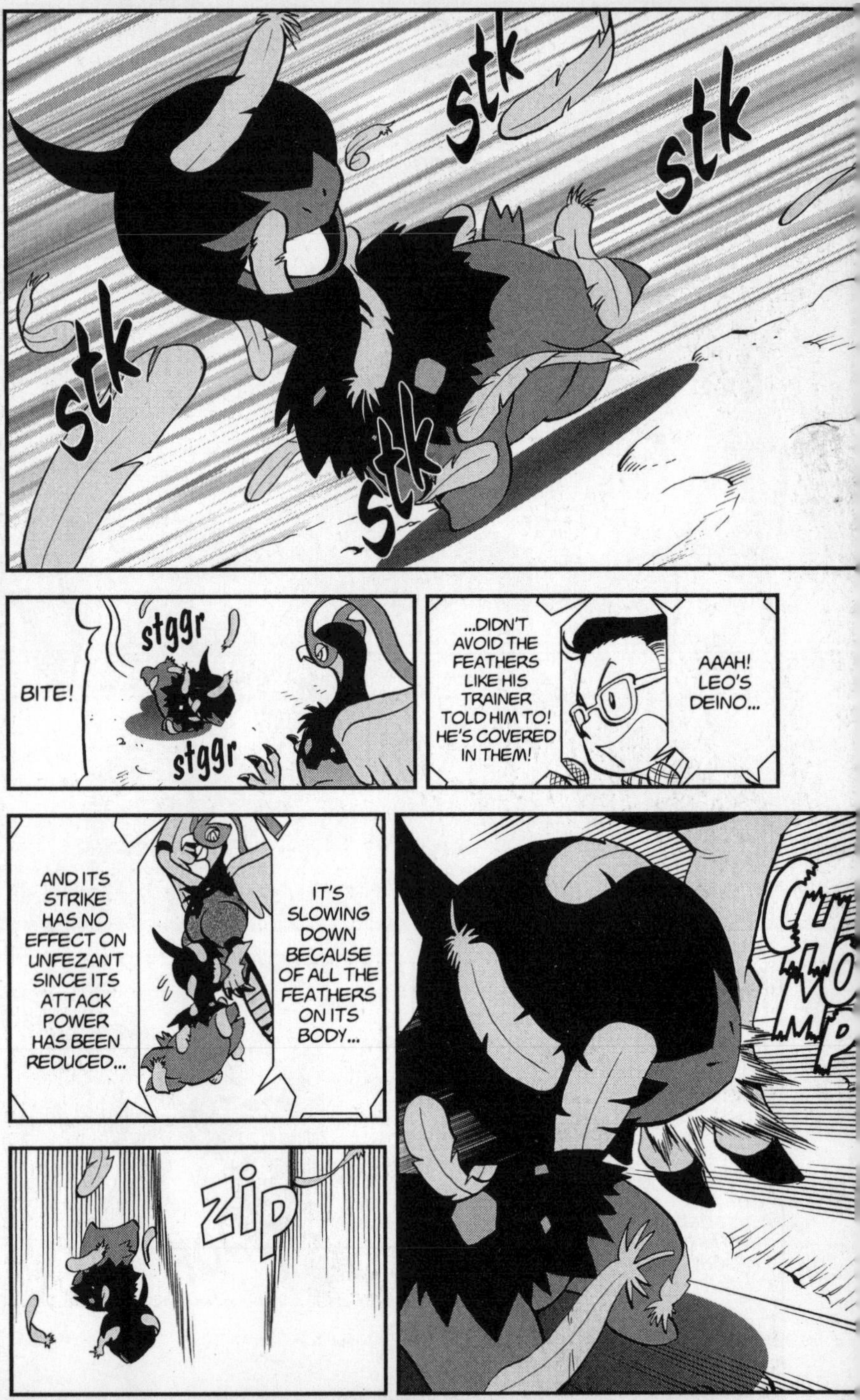
stk
stk
stk
stk
AAAH! LEO'S DEINO...
...DIDN'T AVOID THE FEATHERS LIKE HIS TRAINER TOLD HIM TO! HE'S COVERED IN THEM!
stggr
BITE!
stggr
CHOMP
IT'S SLOWING DOWN BECAUSE OF ALL THE FEATHERS ON ITS BODY...
AND ITS STRIKE HAS NO EFFECT ON UNFEZANT SINCE ITS ATTACK POWER HAS BEEN REDUCED...
zip

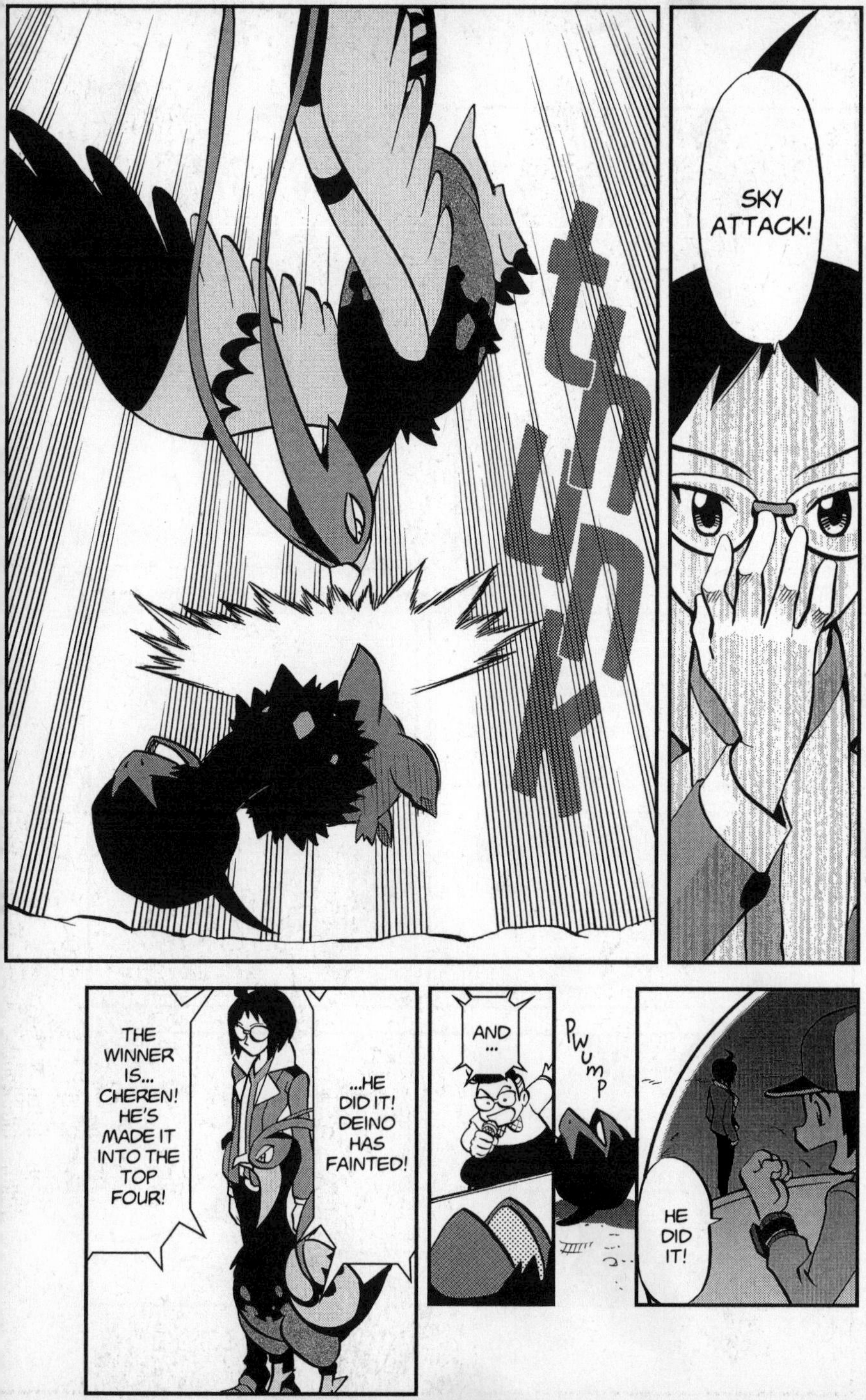
SKY ATTACK!
THUNK
HE DID IT!
AND...
PWUMP
...HE DID IT! DEINO HAS FAINTED!
THE WINNER IS... CHEREN! HE'S MADE IT INTO THE TOP FOUR!

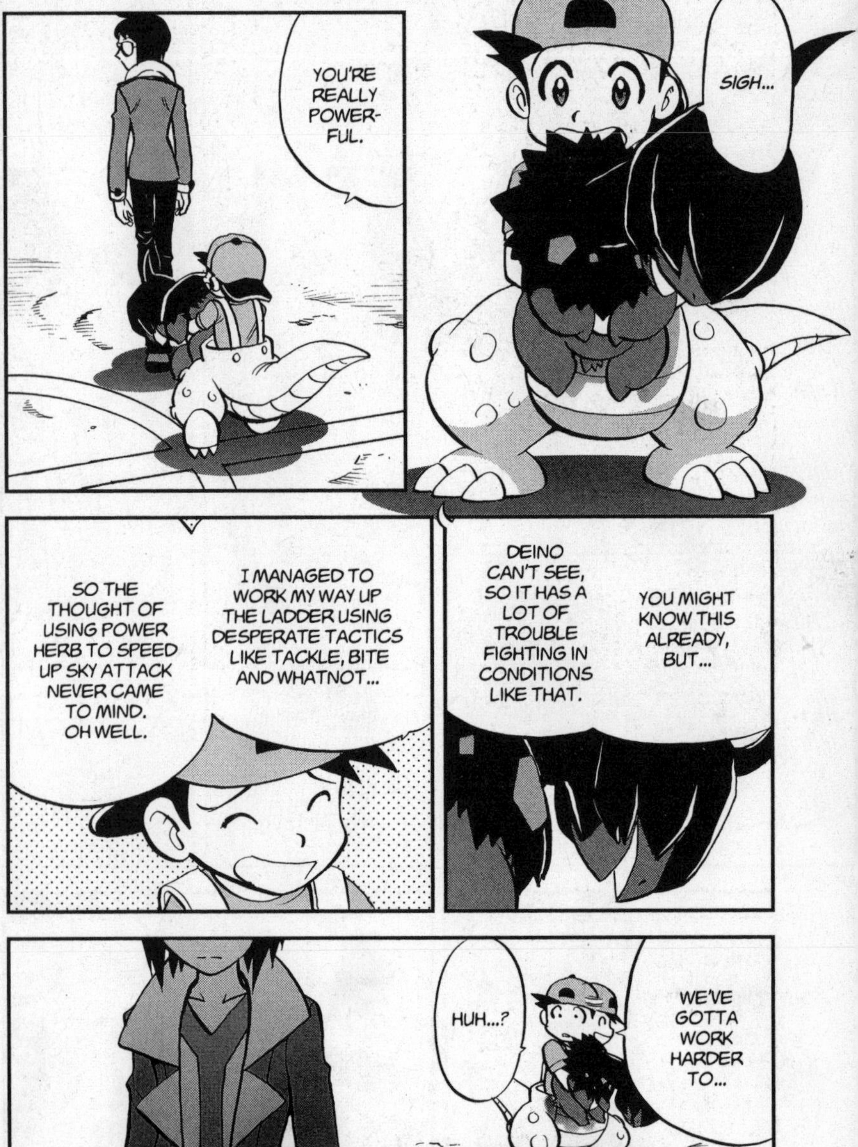
SIGH...
YOU'RE REALLY POWER-FUL.
YOU MIGHT KNOW THIS ALREADY, BUT...
DEINO CAN'T SEE, SO IT HAS A LOT OF TROUBLE FIGHTING IN CONDITIONS LIKE THAT.
I MANAGED TO WORK MY WAY UP THE LADDER USING DESPERATE TACTICS LIKE TACKLE, BITE AND WHATNOT...
SO THE THOUGHT OF USING POWER HERB TO SPEED UP SKY ATTACK NEVER CAME TO MIND. OH WELL.
WE'VE GOTTA WORK HARDER TO...
HUH...?

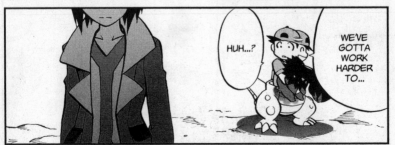

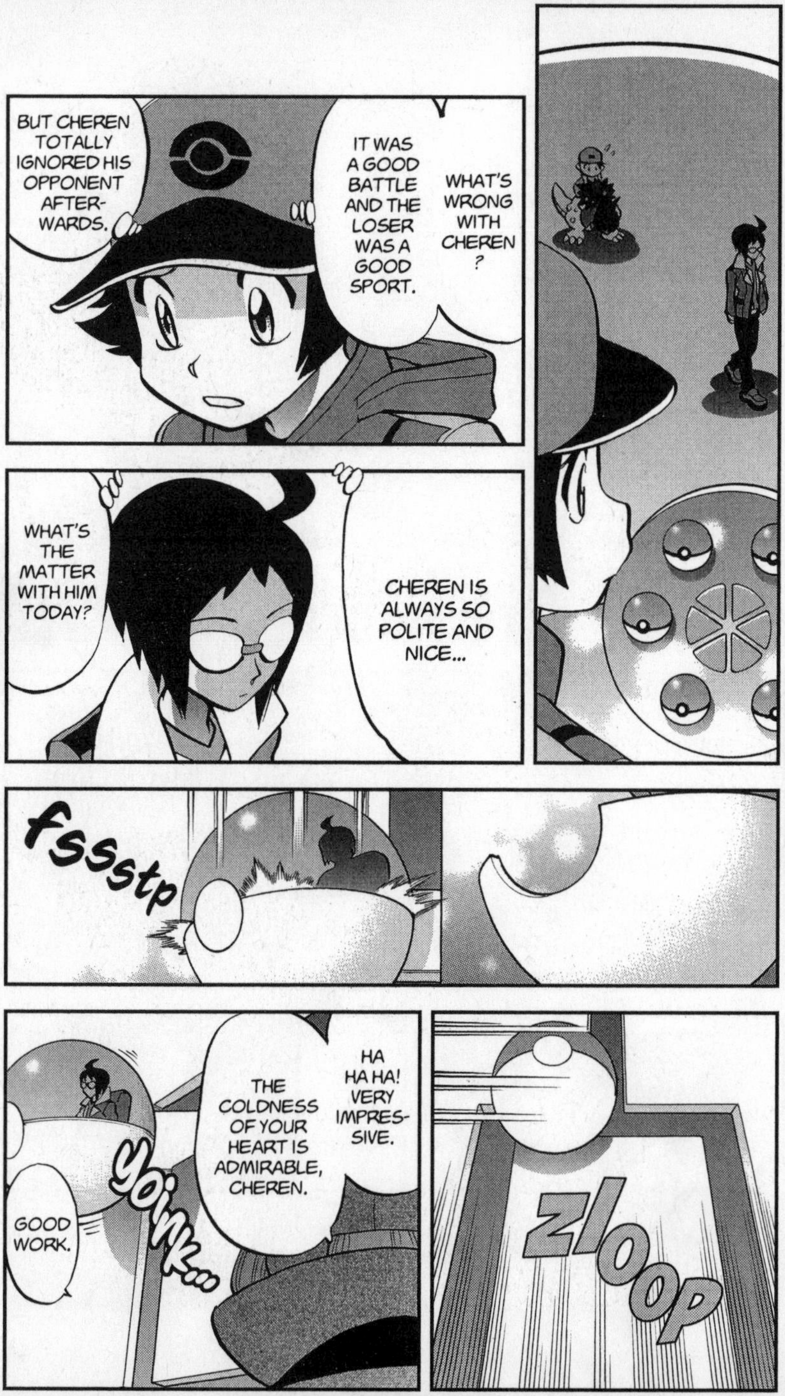
WHAT'S WRONG WITH CHEREN?
IT WAS A GOOD BATTLE AND THE LOSER WAS A GOOD SPORT.
BUT CHEREN TOTALLY IGNORED HIS OPPONENT AFTER-WARDS.
CHEREN IS ALWAYS SO POLITE AND NICE...
WHAT'S THE MATTER WITH HIM TODAY?
fssstp
ZlOOP
HA HA HA! VERY IMPRES-SIVE.
THE COLDNESS OF YOUR HEART IS ADMIRABLE, CHEREN.
yoink...
GOOD WORK.

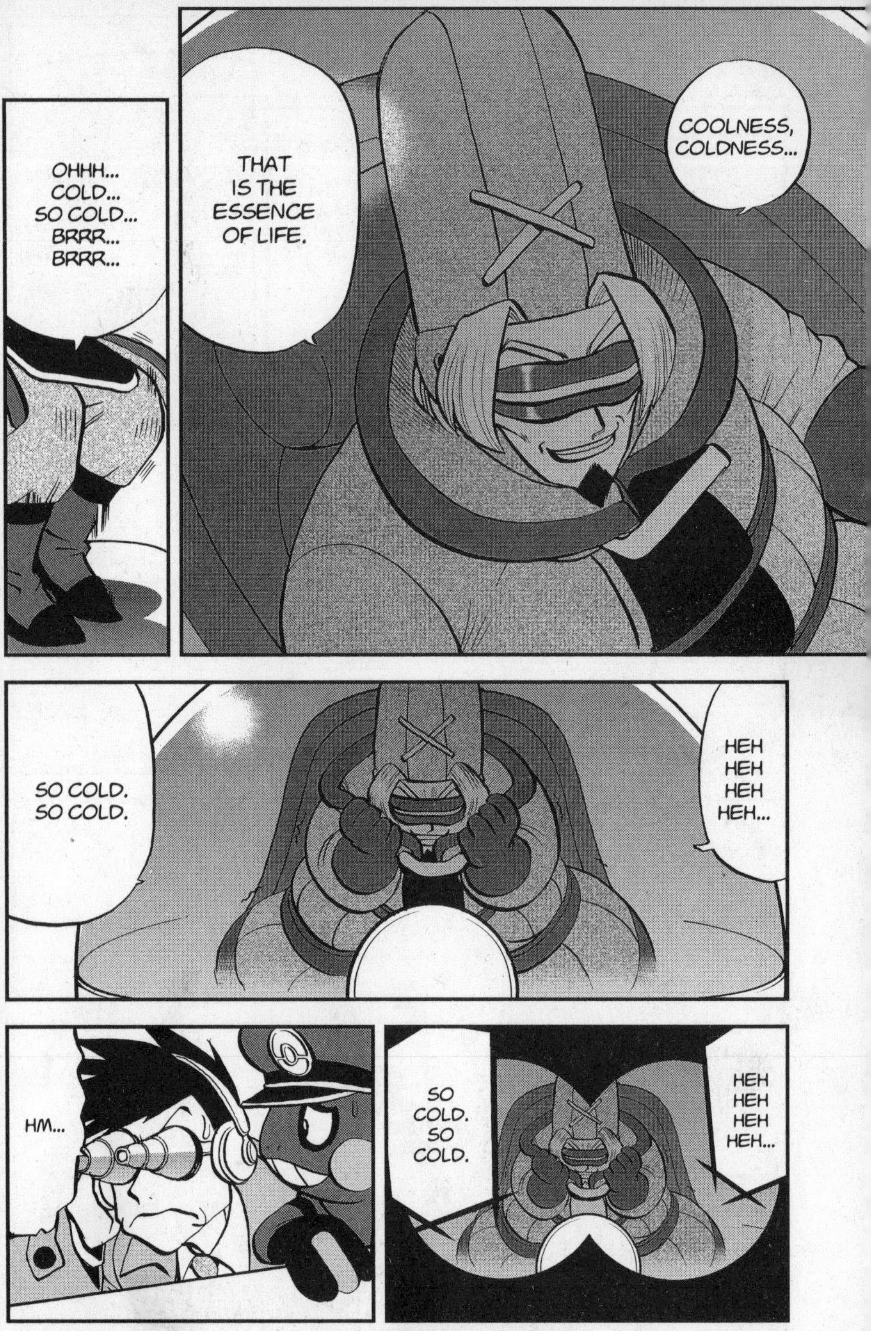

COOLNESS, COLDNESS...
THAT IS THE ESSENCE OF LIFE.
OHHH... COLD... SO COLD... BRRR... BRRR...
HEH HEH HEH HEH...
SO COLD. SO COLD.
HEH HEH HEH HEH...
SO COLD. SO COLD.
HM...

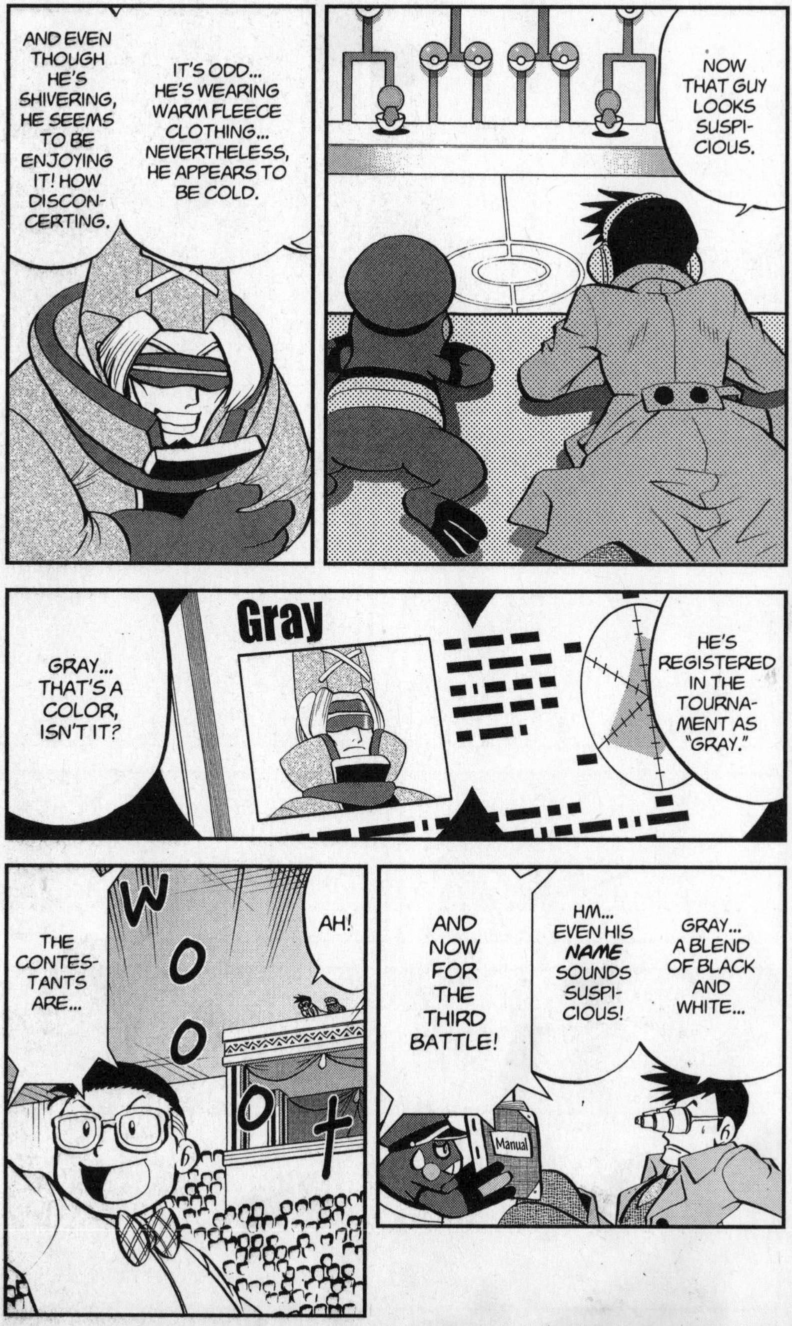
NOW THAT GUY LOOKS SUSPICIOUS.
IT'S ODD... HE'S WEARING WARM FLEECE CLOTHING... NEVERTHELESS, HE APPEARS TO BE COLD.
AND EVEN THOUGH HE'S SHIVERING, HE SEEMS TO BE ENJOYING IT! HOW DISCONCERTING.
HE'S REGISTERED IN THE TOURNAMENT AS "GRAY."
Gray
GRAY... THAT'S A COLOR, ISN'T IT?
GRAY... A BLEND OF BLACK AND WHITE...
HM... EVEN HIS ***NAME*** SOUNDS SUSPICIOUS!
Manual
AND NOW FOR THE THIRD BATTLE!
AH!
THE CONTESTANTS ARE...
WOOOT

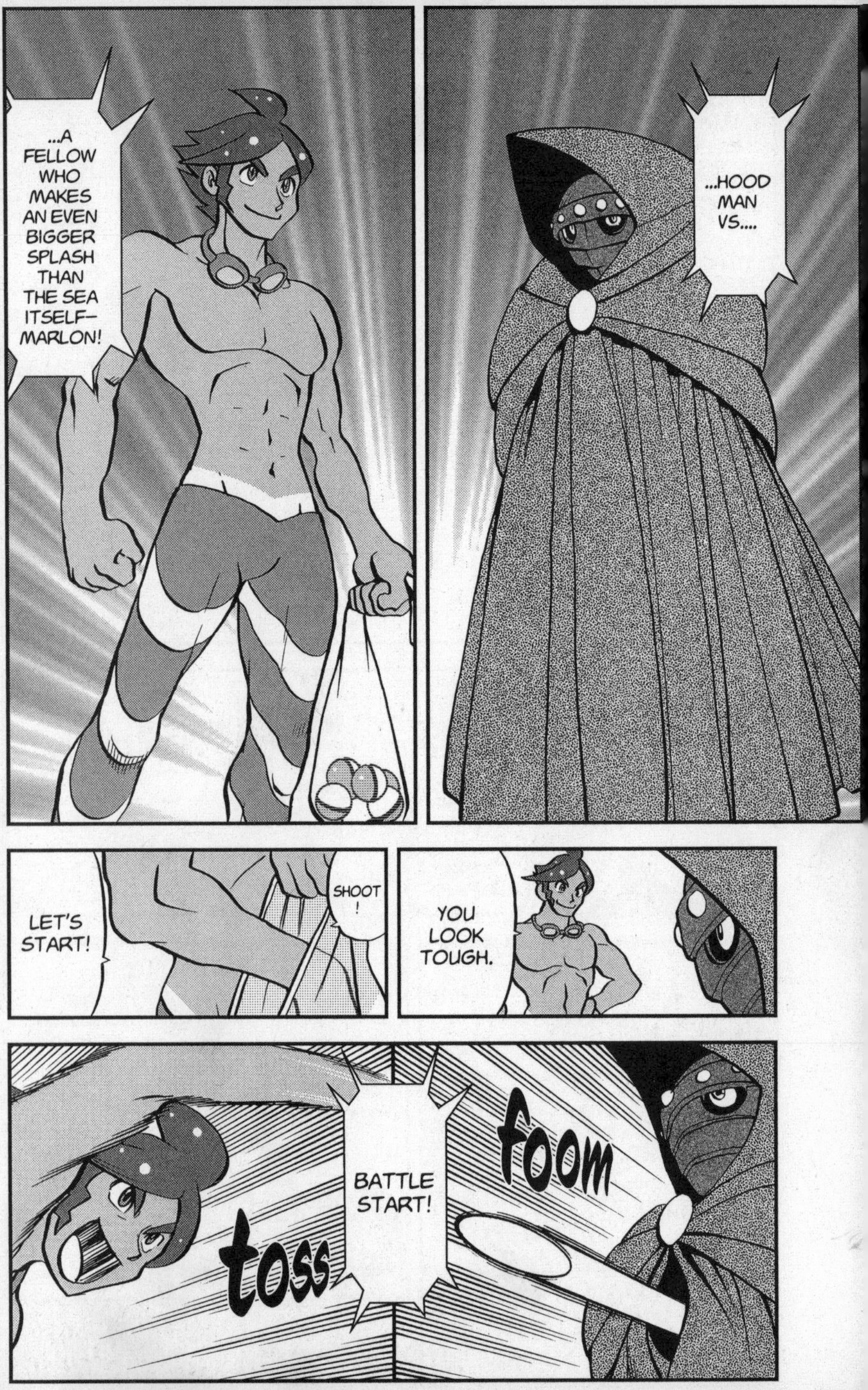
...HOOD MAN VS....
...A FELLOW WHO MAKES AN EVEN BIGGER SPLASH THAN THE SEA ITSELF—MARLON!
YOU LOOK TOUGH.
SHOOT!
LET'S START!
foom
BATTLE START!
toss

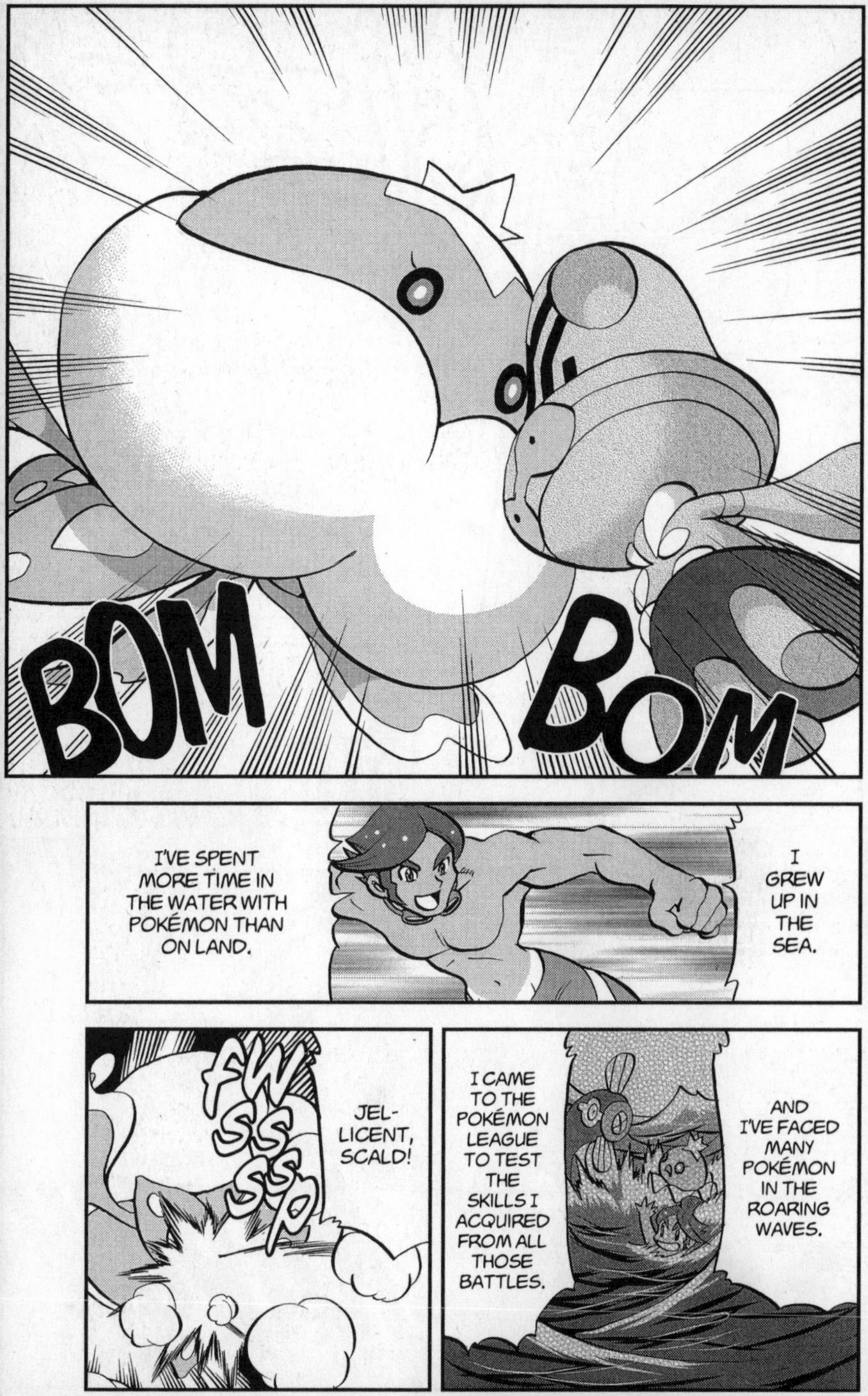
BOM BOM
I GREW UP IN THE SEA.
I'VE SPENT MORE TIME IN THE WATER WITH POKÉMON THAN ON LAND.
AND I'VE FACED MANY POKÉMON IN THE ROARING WAVES.
I CAME TO THE POKÉMON LEAGUE TO TEST THE SKILLS I ACQUIRED FROM ALL THOSE BATTLES.
JEL-LICENT, SCALD!
FWSSSSP

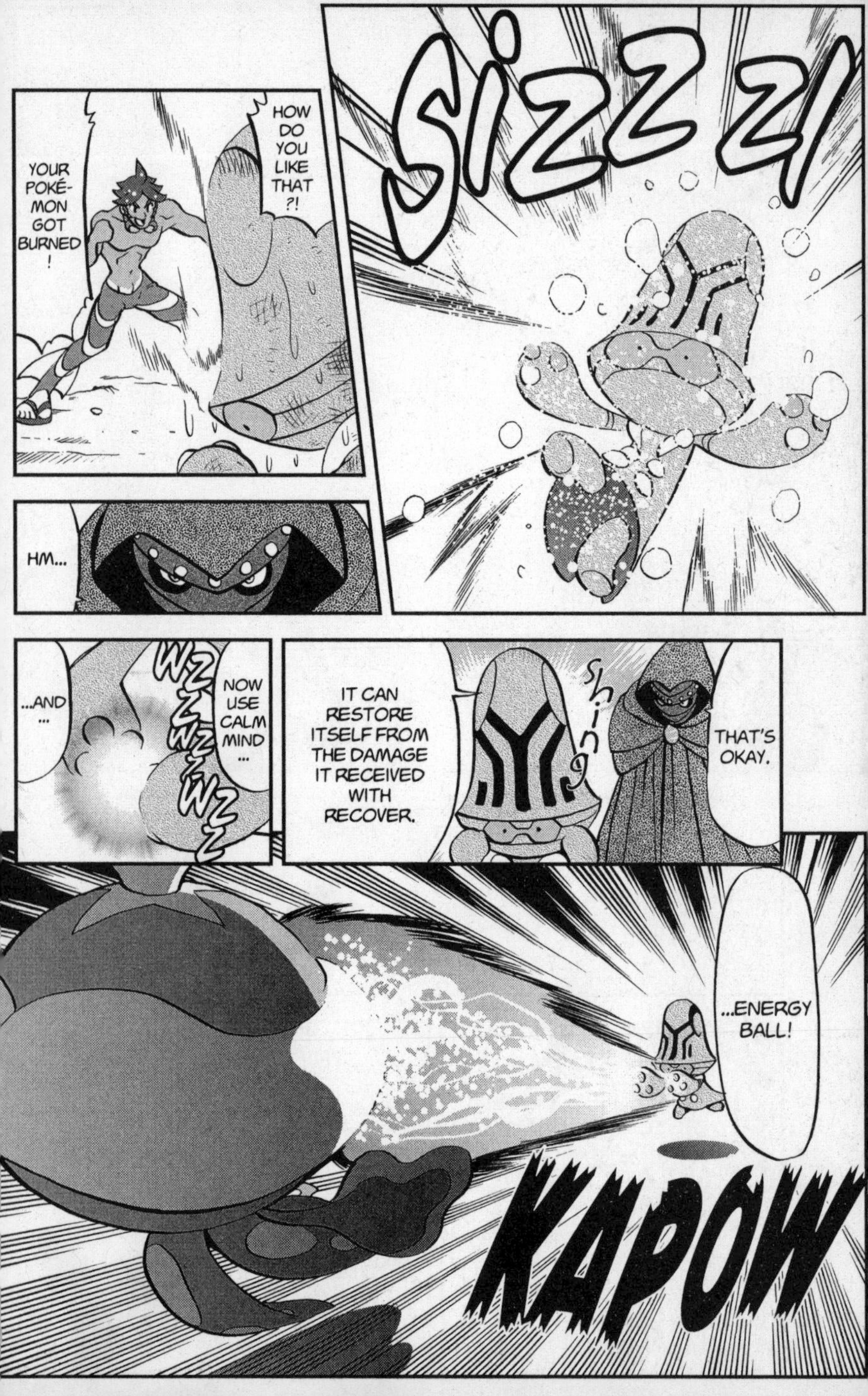
SIZZZ!
HOW DO YOU LIKE THAT?!
YOUR POKÉMON GOT BURNED!
HM...
THAT'S OKAY.
shing
IT CAN RESTORE ITSELF FROM THE DAMAGE IT RECEIVED WITH RECOVER.
NOW USE CALM MIND...
...AND...
...ENERGY BALL!
KAPOW

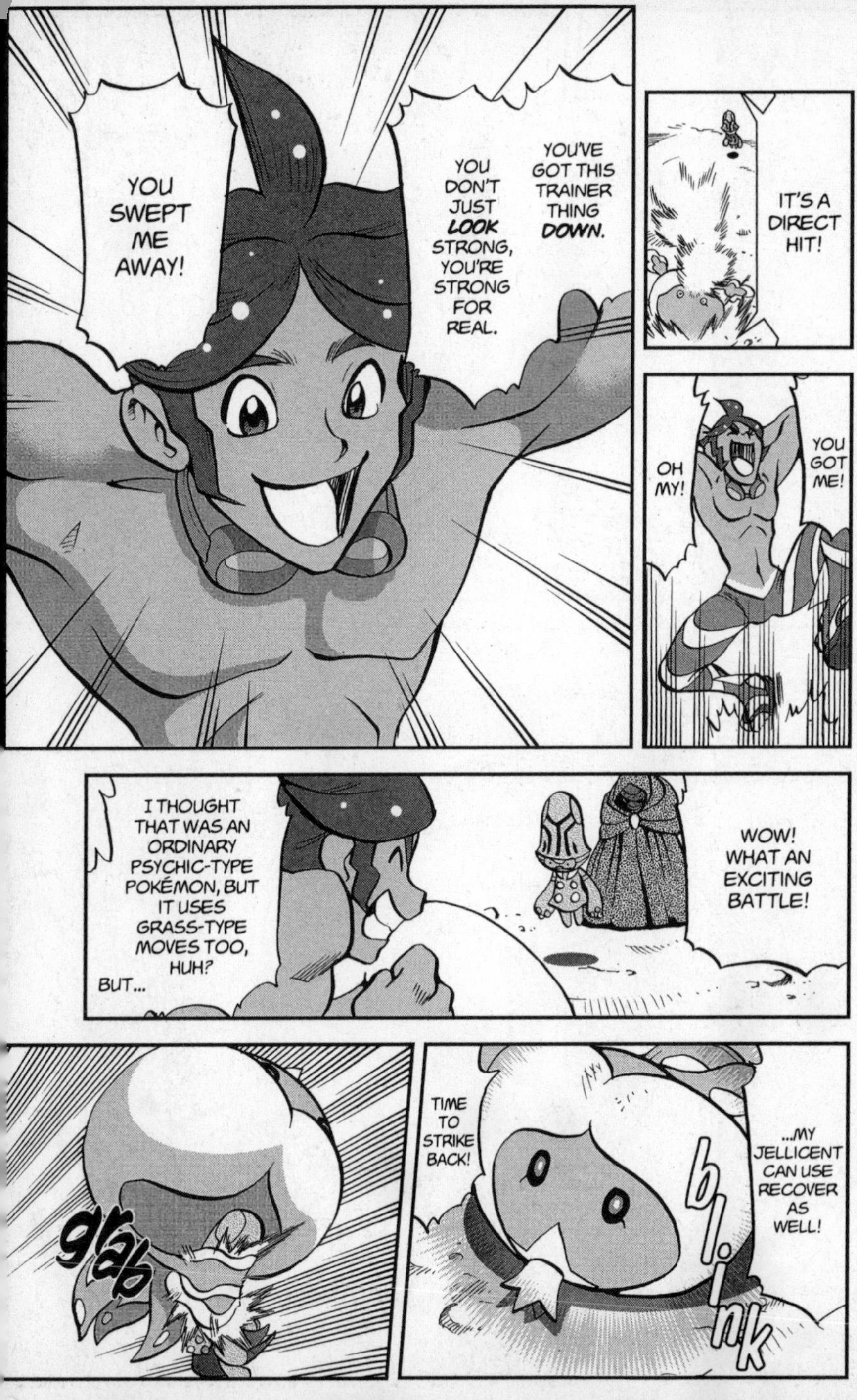
IT'S A DIRECT HIT!
YOU GOT ME!
OH MY!
YOU'VE GOT THIS TRAINER THING DOWN.
YOU DON'T JUST LOOK STRONG, YOU'RE STRONG FOR REAL.
YOU SWEPT ME AWAY!
WOW! WHAT AN EXCITING BATTLE!
I THOUGHT THAT WAS AN ORDINARY PSYCHIC-TYPE POKÉMON, BUT IT USES GRASS-TYPE MOVES TOO, HUH?
BUT...
...MY JELLICENT CAN USE RECOVER AS WELL!
blink
TIME TO STRIKE BACK!
grab

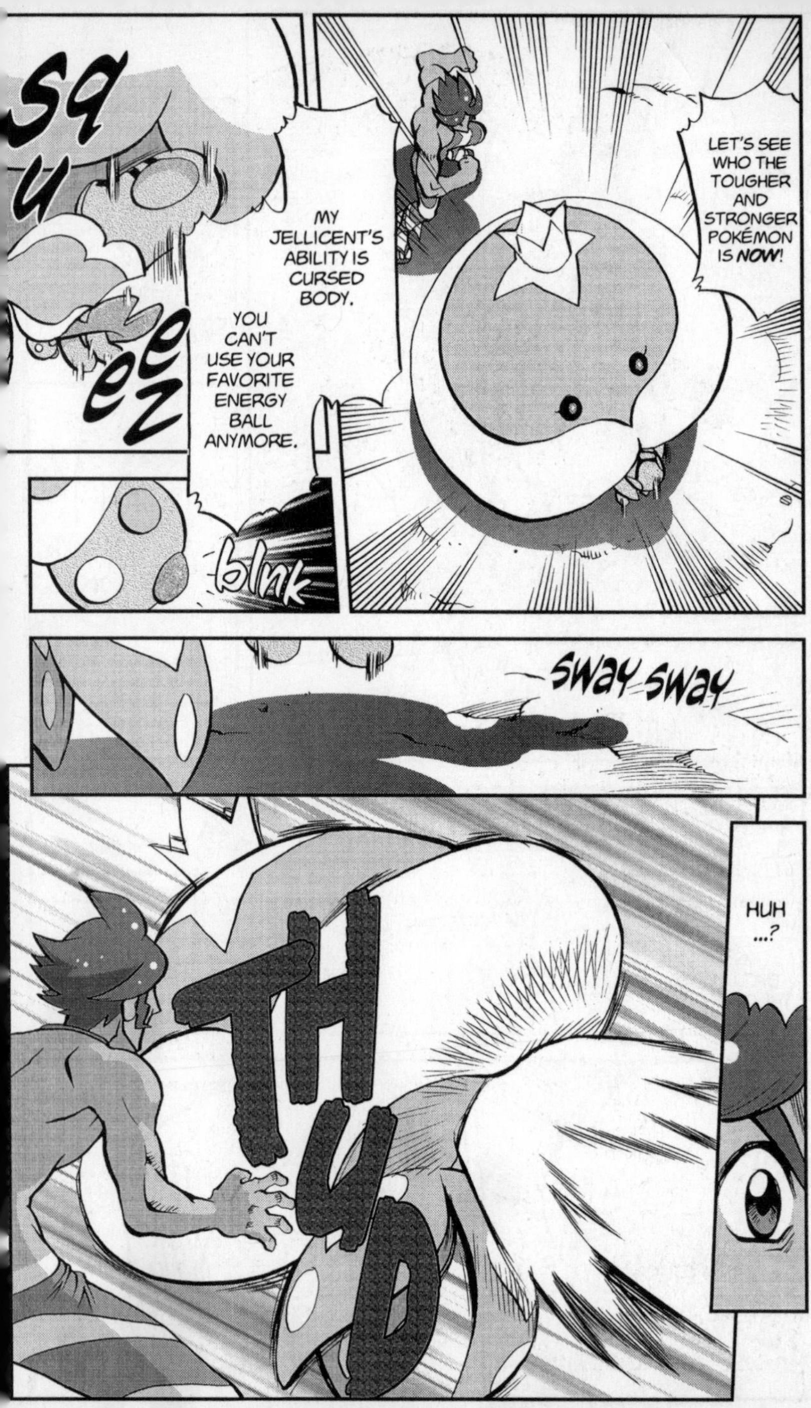
LET'S SEE WHO THE TOUGHER AND STRONGER POKÉMON IS *NOW*!
MY JELLICENT'S ABILITY IS CURSED BODY.
YOU CAN'T USE YOUR FAVORITE ENERGY BALL ANYMORE.
squeeez
blink
sway sway
HUH ...?
THUD

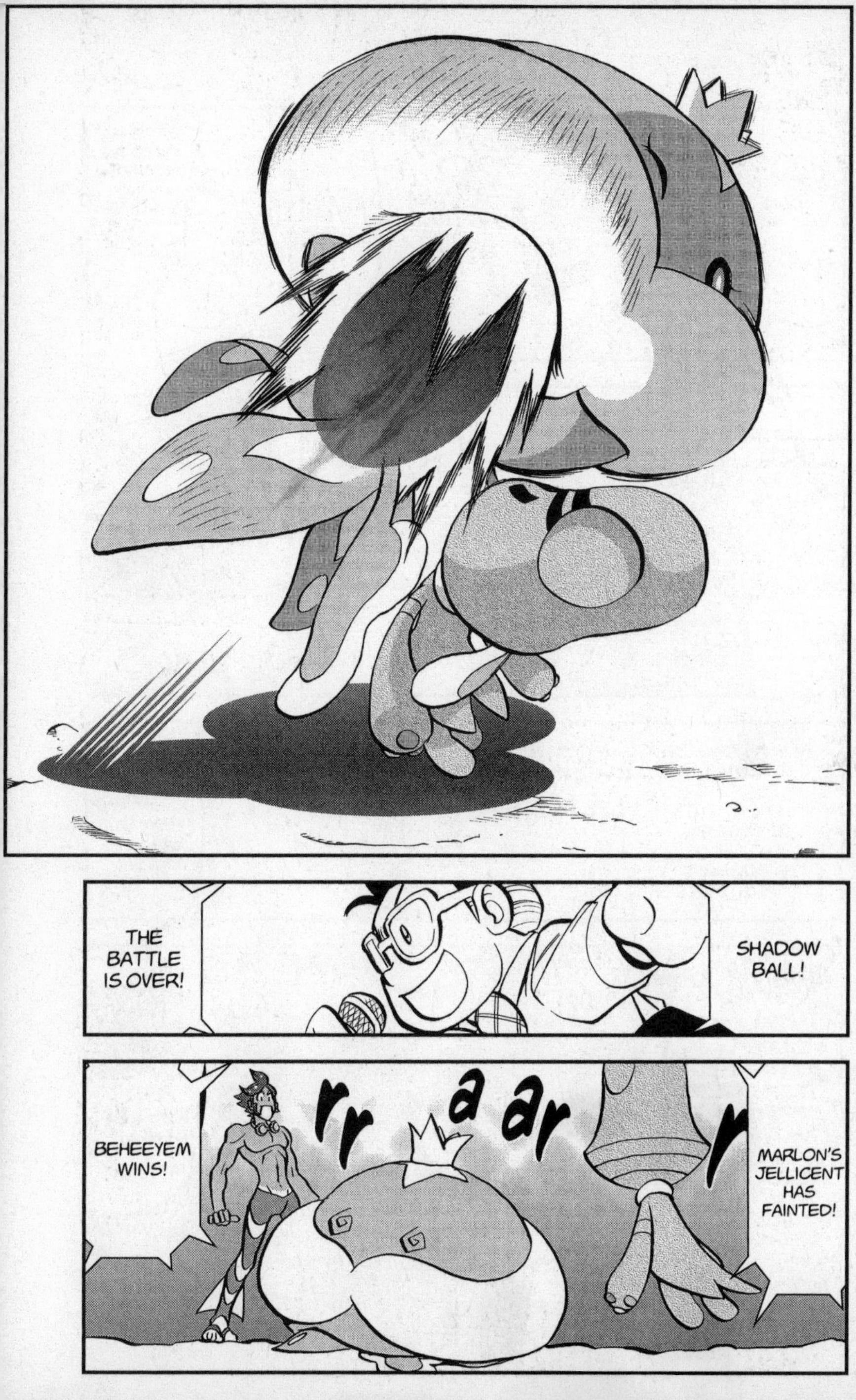
SHADOW BALL!
THE BATTLE IS OVER!
MARLON'S JELLICENT HAS FAINTED!
rr a ar r
BEHEEYEM WINS!

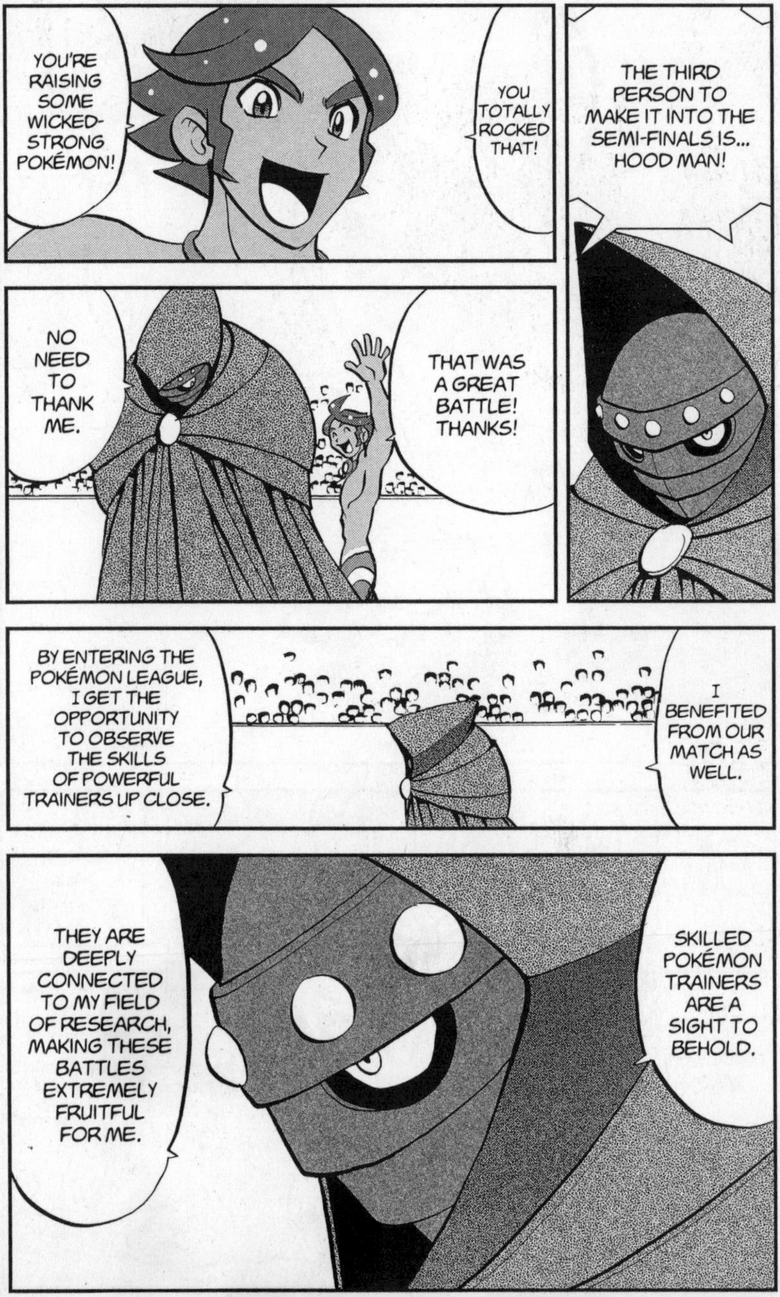
THE THIRD PERSON TO MAKE IT INTO THE SEMI-FINALS IS... HOOD MAN!
YOU TOTALLY ROCKED THAT!
YOU'RE RAISING SOME WICKED-STRONG POKÉMON!
THAT WAS A GREAT BATTLE! THANKS!
NO NEED TO THANK ME.
I BENEFITED FROM OUR MATCH AS WELL.
BY ENTERING THE POKÉMON LEAGUE, I GET THE OPPORTUNITY TO OBSERVE THE SKILLS OF POWERFUL TRAINERS UP CLOSE.
SKILLED POKÉMON TRAINERS ARE A SIGHT TO BEHOLD.
THEY ARE DEEPLY CONNECTED TO MY FIELD OF RESEARCH, MAKING THESE BATTLES EXTREMELY FRUITFUL FOR ME.

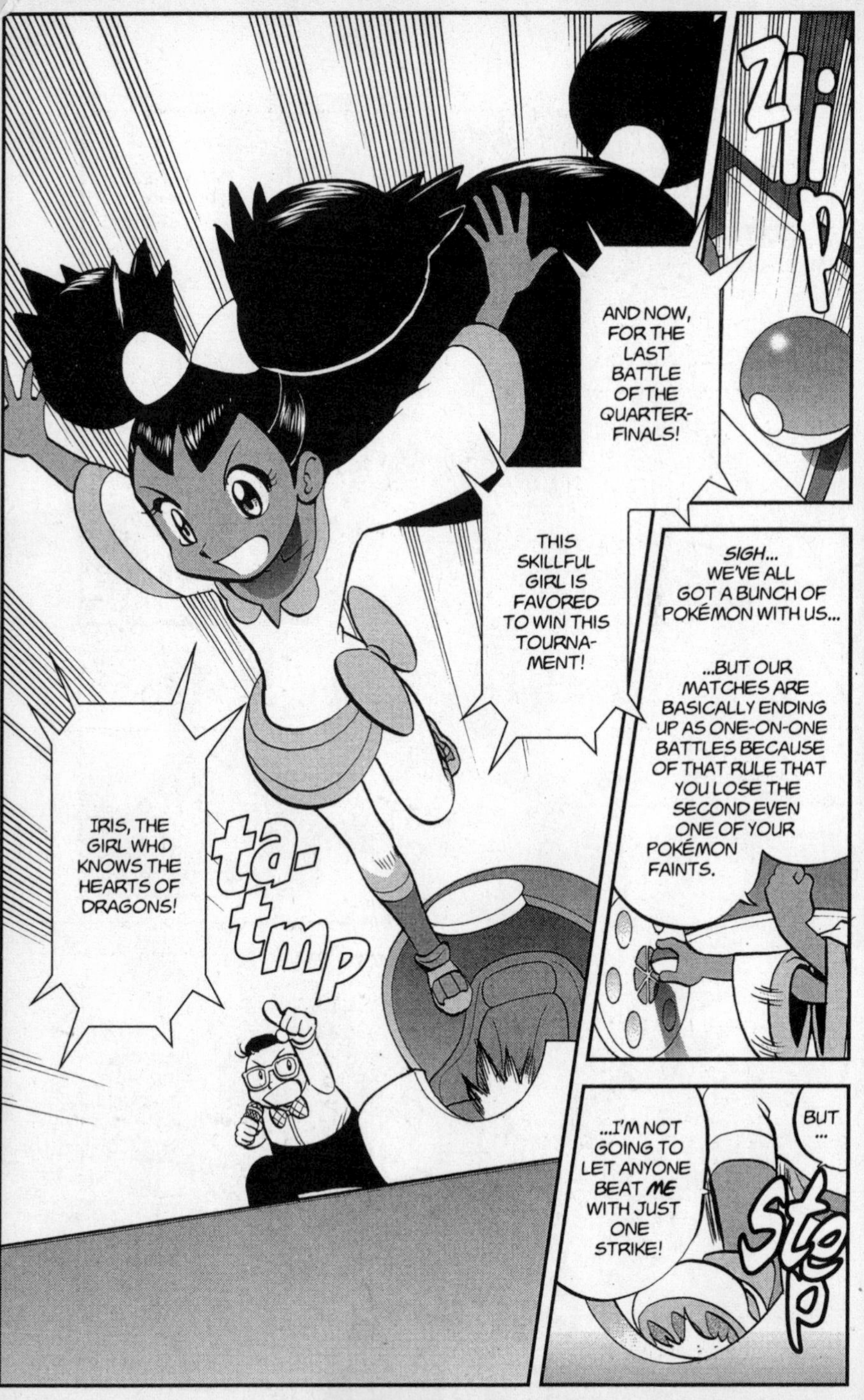

ZIip
AND NOW, FOR THE LAST BATTLE OF THE QUARTER-FINALS!
SIGH... WE'VE ALL GOT A BUNCH OF POKÉMON WITH US...
...BUT OUR MATCHES ARE BASICALLY ENDING UP AS ONE-ON-ONE BATTLES BECAUSE OF THAT RULE THAT YOU LOSE THE SECOND EVEN ONE OF YOUR POKÉMON FAINTS.
BUT ...
Step
...I'M NOT GOING TO LET ANYONE BEAT *ME* WITH JUST ONE STRIKE!
THIS SKILLFUL GIRL IS FAVORED TO WIN THIS TOURNA-MENT!
ta-tmp
IRIS, THE GIRL WHO KNOWS THE HEARTS OF DRAGONS!

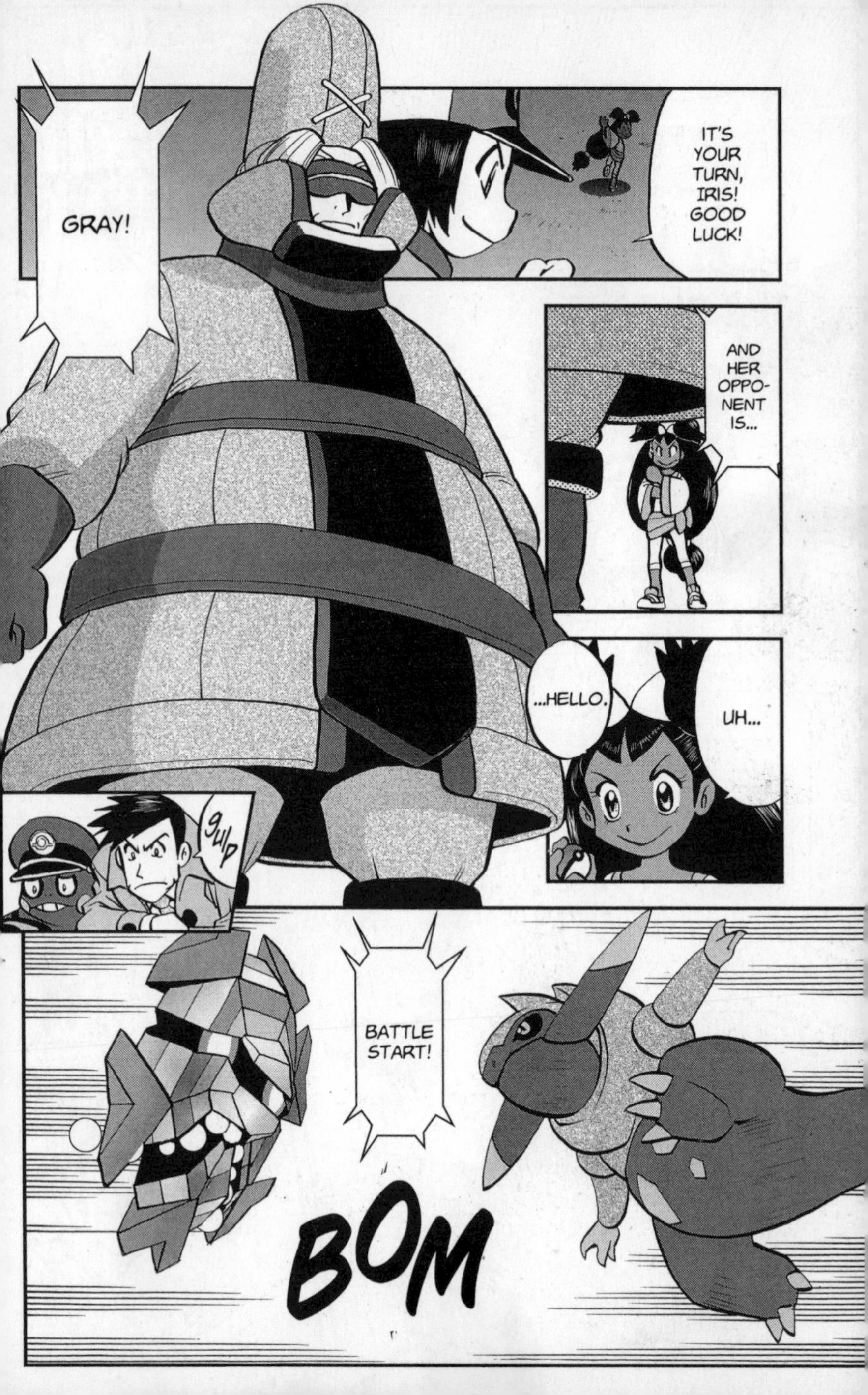
IT'S YOUR TURN, IRIS! GOOD LUCK!
AND HER OPPONENT IS...
UH...
...HELLO.
GRAY!
gulp
BATTLE START!
BOM

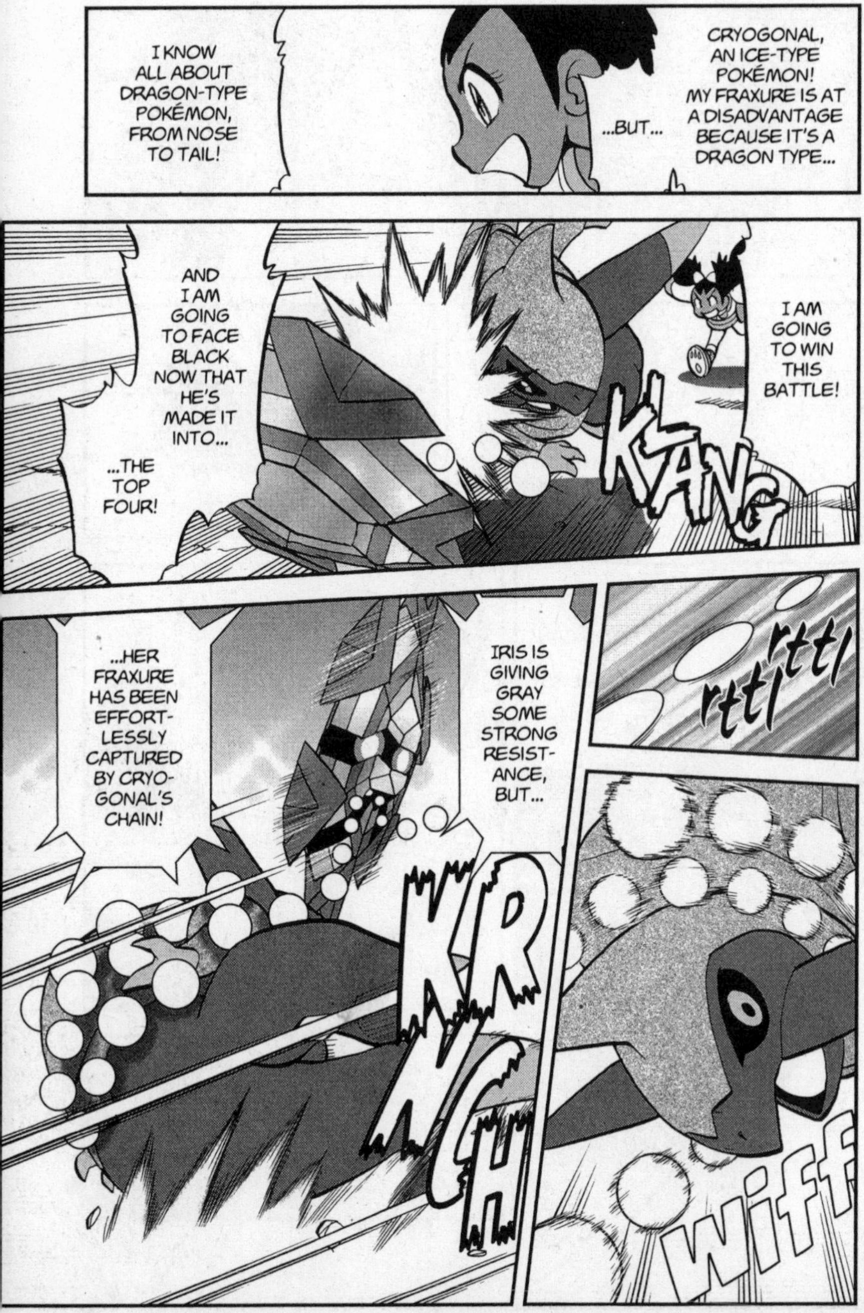
CRYOGONAL, AN ICE-TYPE POKÉMON! MY FRAXURE IS AT A DISADVANTAGE BECAUSE IT'S A DRAGON TYPE...
...BUT...
I KNOW ALL ABOUT DRAGON-TYPE POKÉMON, FROM NOSE TO TAIL!
I AM GOING TO WIN THIS BATTLE!
KLANG
AND I AM GOING TO FACE BLACK NOW THAT HE'S MADE IT INTO...
...THE TOP FOUR!
rttl rttl
wiff
IRIS IS GIVING GRAY SOME STRONG RESISTANCE, BUT...
...HER FRAXURE HAS BEEN EFFORTLESSLY CAPTURED BY CRYOGONAL'S CHAIN!
KRKCH

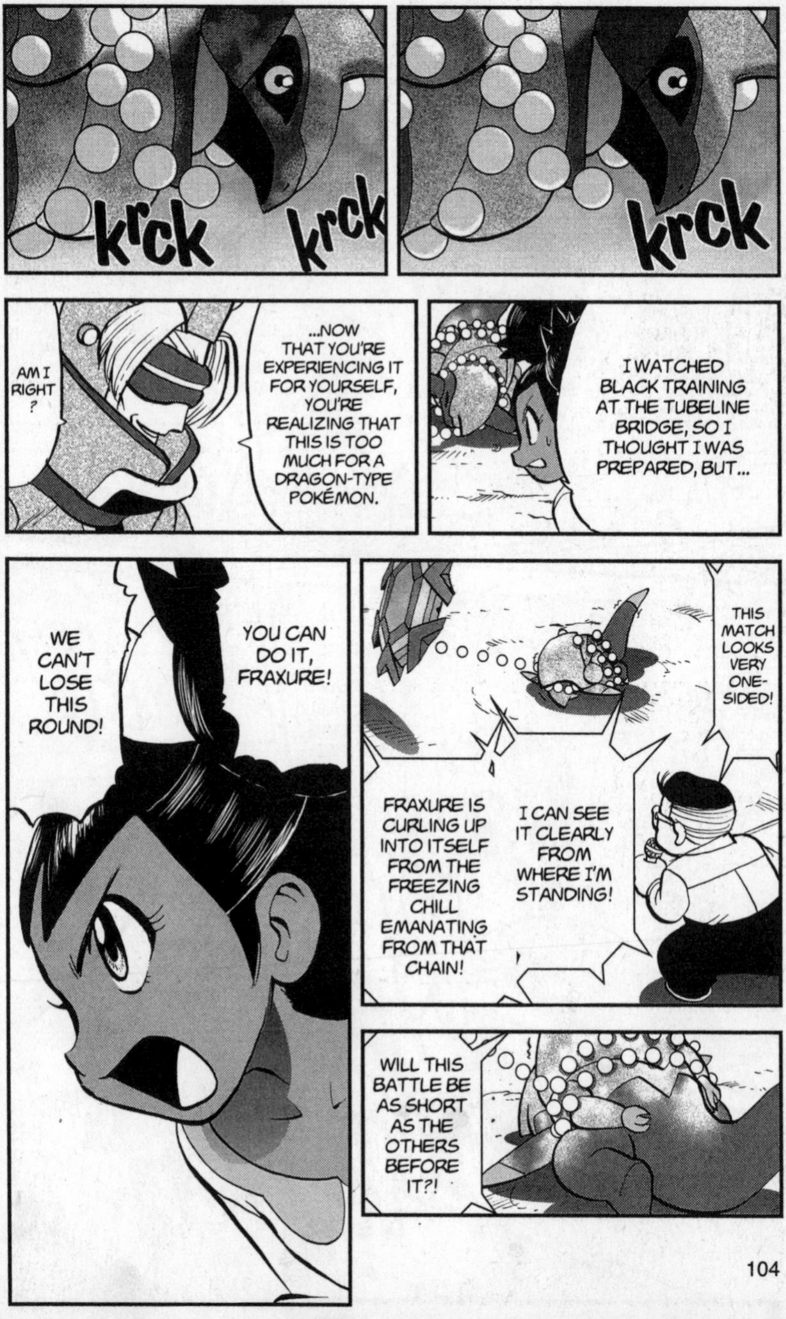
krck
krck
krck
I WATCHED BLACK TRAINING AT THE TUBELINE BRIDGE, SO I THOUGHT I WAS PREPARED, BUT...
...NOW THAT YOU'RE EXPERIENCING IT FOR YOURSELF, YOU'RE REALIZING THAT THIS IS TOO MUCH FOR A DRAGON-TYPE POKÉMON.
AM I RIGHT?
THIS MATCH LOOKS VERY ONE-SIDED!
I CAN SEE IT CLEARLY FROM WHERE I'M STANDING!
FRAXURE IS CURLING UP INTO ITSELF FROM THE FREEZING CHILL EMANATING FROM THAT CHAIN!
WILL THIS BATTLE BE AS SHORT AS THE OTHERS BEFORE IT?!
YOU CAN DO IT, FRAXURE!
WE CAN'T LOSE THIS ROUND!

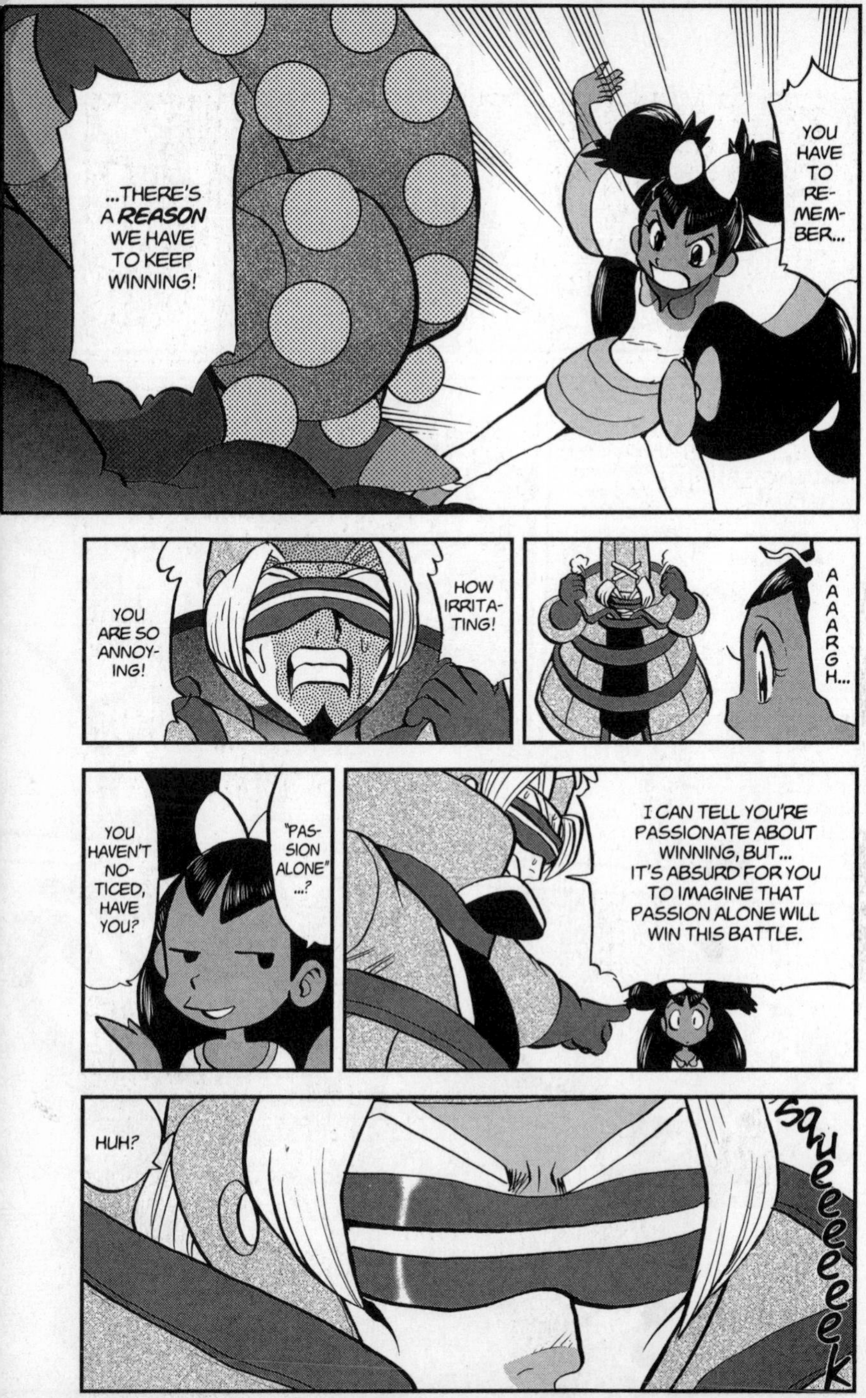
YOU HAVE TO RE-MEM-BER...
...THERE'S A **REASON** WE HAVE TO KEEP WINNING!
AAAAARGH...
HOW IRRITA-TING!
YOU ARE SO ANNOY-ING!
I CAN TELL YOU'RE PASSIONATE ABOUT WINNING, BUT... IT'S ABSURD FOR YOU TO IMAGINE THAT PASSION ALONE WILL WIN THIS BATTLE.
"PAS-SION ALONE" ...?
YOU HAVEN'T NO-TICED, HAVE YOU?
SQUEEEEEEEK
HUH?

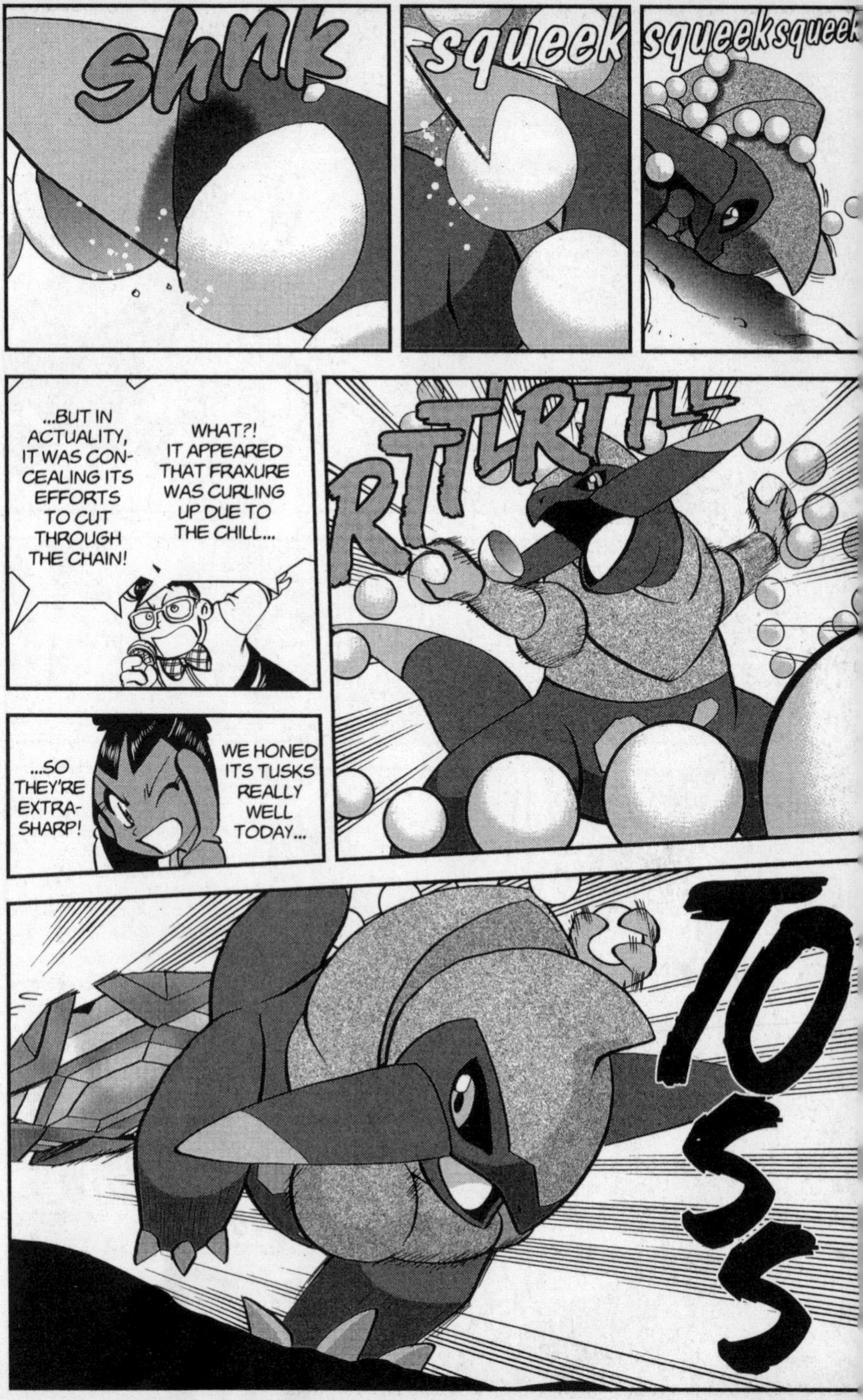
squeeksqueek
squeek
shnk
RTTLRTTLL
WHAT?! IT APPEARED THAT FRAXURE WAS CURLING UP DUE TO THE CHILL...
...BUT IN ACTUALITY, IT WAS CONCEALING ITS EFFORTS TO CUT THROUGH THE CHAIN!
WE HONED ITS TUSKS REALLY WELL TODAY...
...SO THEY'RE EXTRA-SHARP!
TOSS

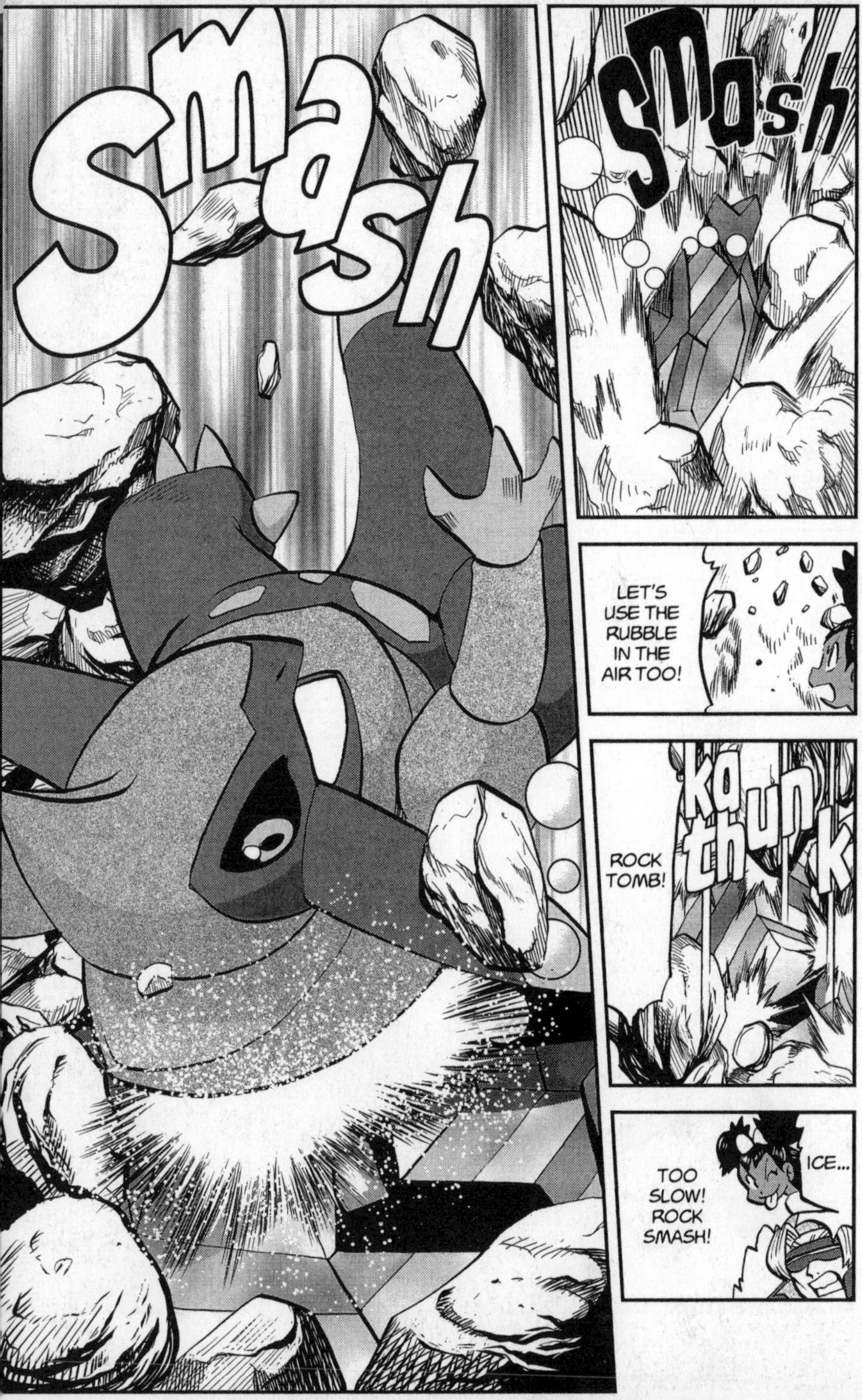
SMASH
LET'S USE THE RUBBLE IN THE AIR TOO!
KA THUNK
ROCK TOMB!
ICE...
TOO SLOW! ROCK SMASH!
SMASH

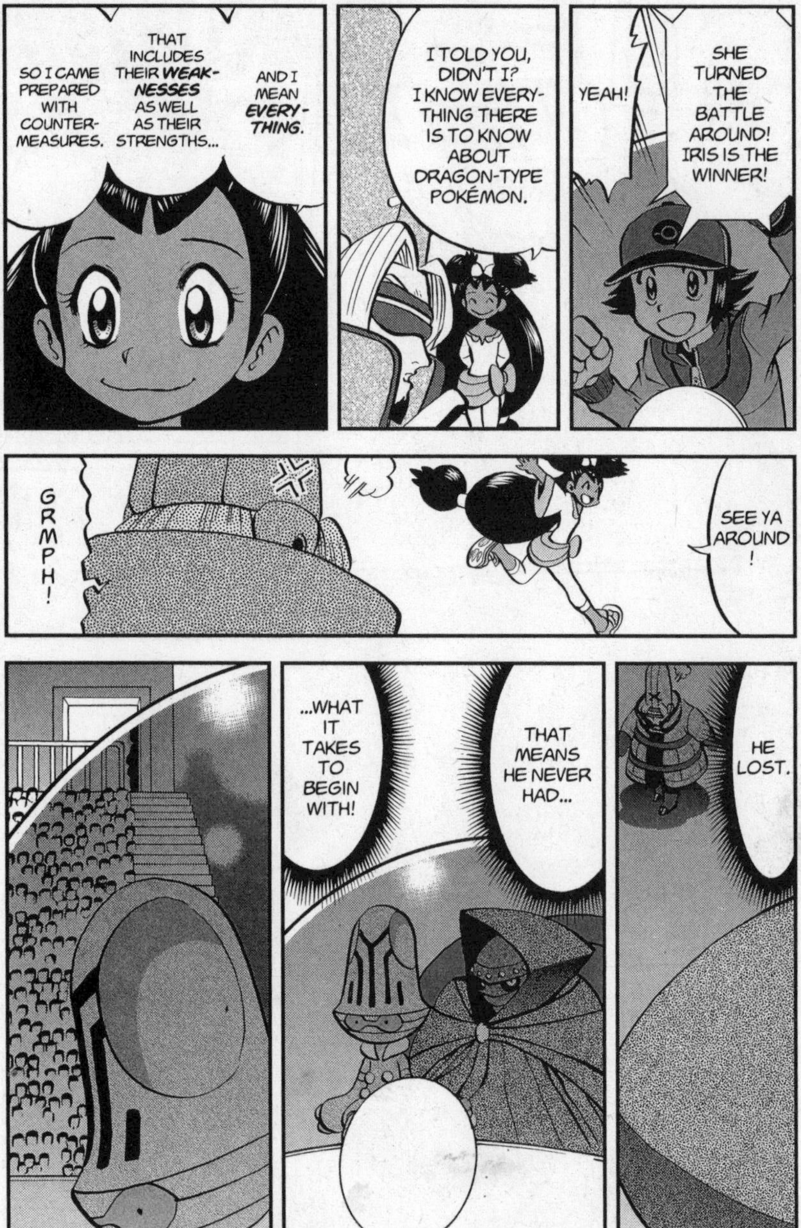

SHE TURNED THE BATTLE AROUND! IRIS IS THE WINNER!
YEAH!
I TOLD YOU, DIDN'T I? I KNOW EVERYTHING THERE IS TO KNOW ABOUT DRAGON-TYPE POKÉMON.
AND I MEAN ***EVERYTHING***.
THAT INCLUDES THEIR ***WEAKNESSES*** AS WELL AS THEIR STRENGTHS...
SO I CAME PREPARED WITH COUNTERMEASURES.
SEE YA AROUND!
GRMPH!
HE LOST.
THAT MEANS HE NEVER HAD...
...WHAT IT TAKES TO BEGIN WITH!

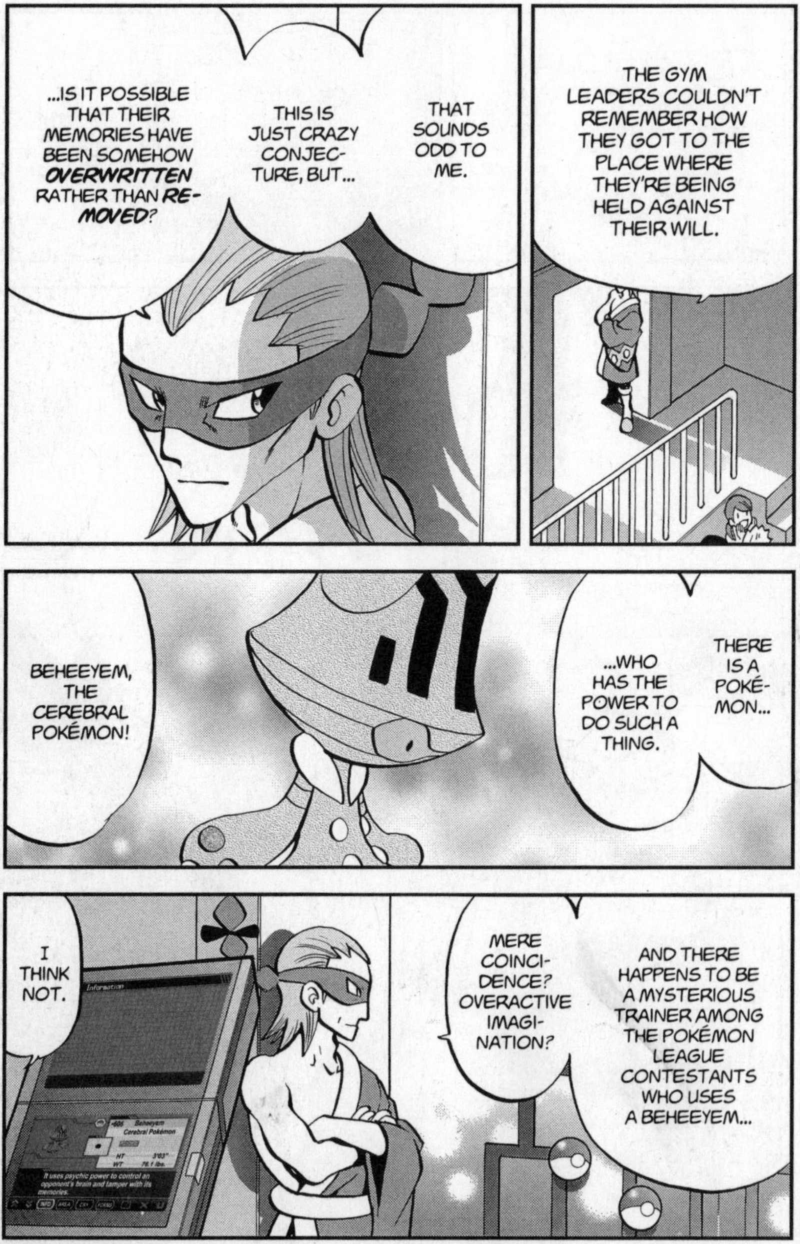
THE GYM LEADERS COULDN'T REMEMBER HOW THEY GOT TO THE PLACE WHERE THEY'RE BEING HELD AGAINST THEIR WILL.
THAT SOUNDS ODD TO ME.
THIS IS JUST CRAZY CONJECTURE, BUT...
...IS IT POSSIBLE THAT THEIR MEMORIES HAVE BEEN SOMEHOW *OVERWRITTEN* RATHER THAN *REMOVED*?
THERE IS A POKÉMON...
...WHO HAS THE POWER TO DO SUCH A THING.
BEHEEYEM, THE CEREBRAL POKÉMON!
AND THERE HAPPENS TO BE A MYSTERIOUS TRAINER AMONG THE POKÉMON LEAGUE CONTESTANTS WHO USES A BEHEEYEM...
MERE COINCIDENCE? OVERACTIVE IMAGINATION?
I THINK NOT.
Information
Beheeyem
Cerebral Pokémon
HT 3'03"
WT 76.1 lbs.
It uses psychic power to control an opponent's brain and tamper with its memories.

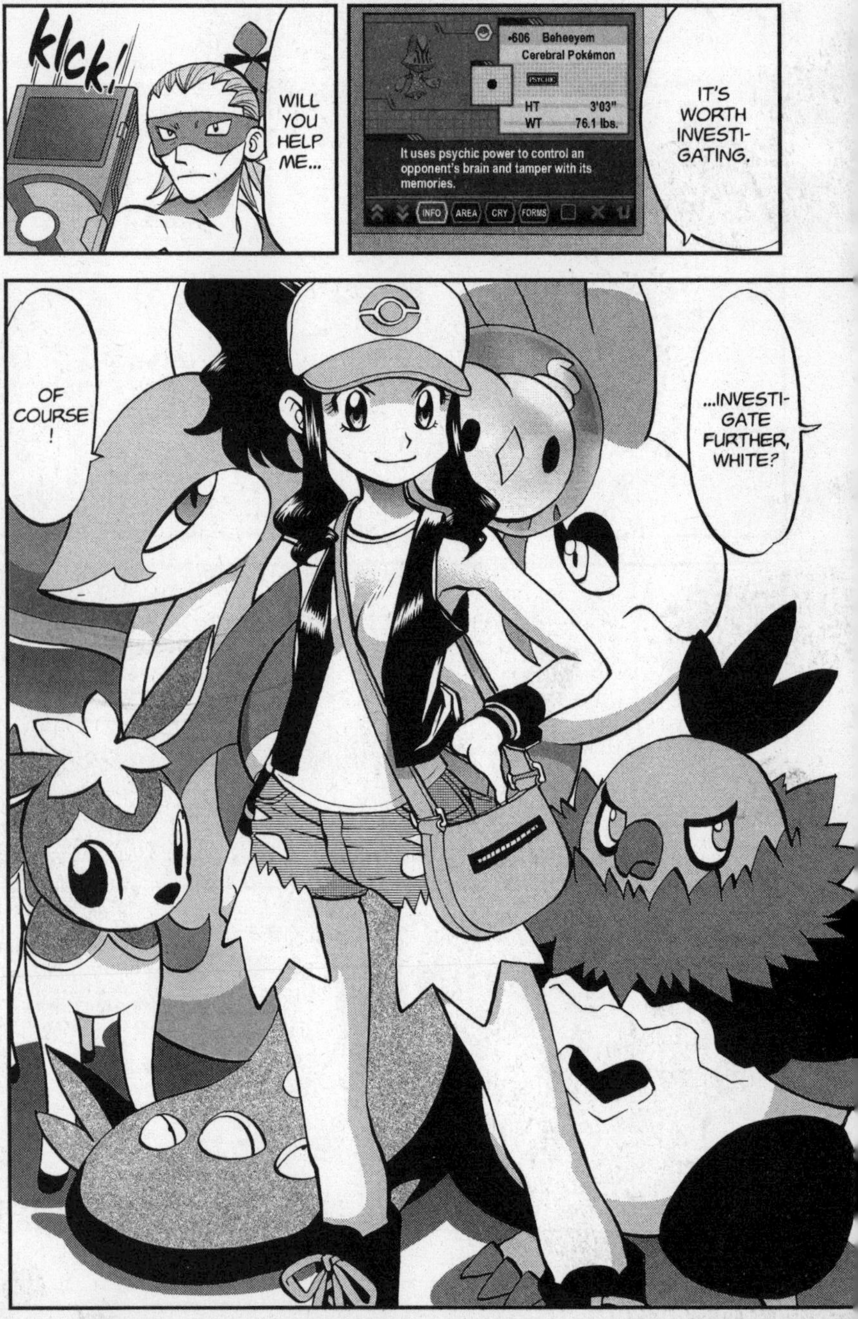
•606 Beheeyem
Cerebral Pokémon
PSYCHIC
HT 3'03"
WT 76.1 lbs.
It uses psychic power to control an opponent's brain and tamper with its memories.
INFO
AREA
CRY
FORMS
IT'S WORTH INVESTIGATING.
klick!
WILL YOU HELP ME...
...INVESTIGATE FURTHER, WHITE?
OF COURSE!

Pokémon™ Adventures Black & White

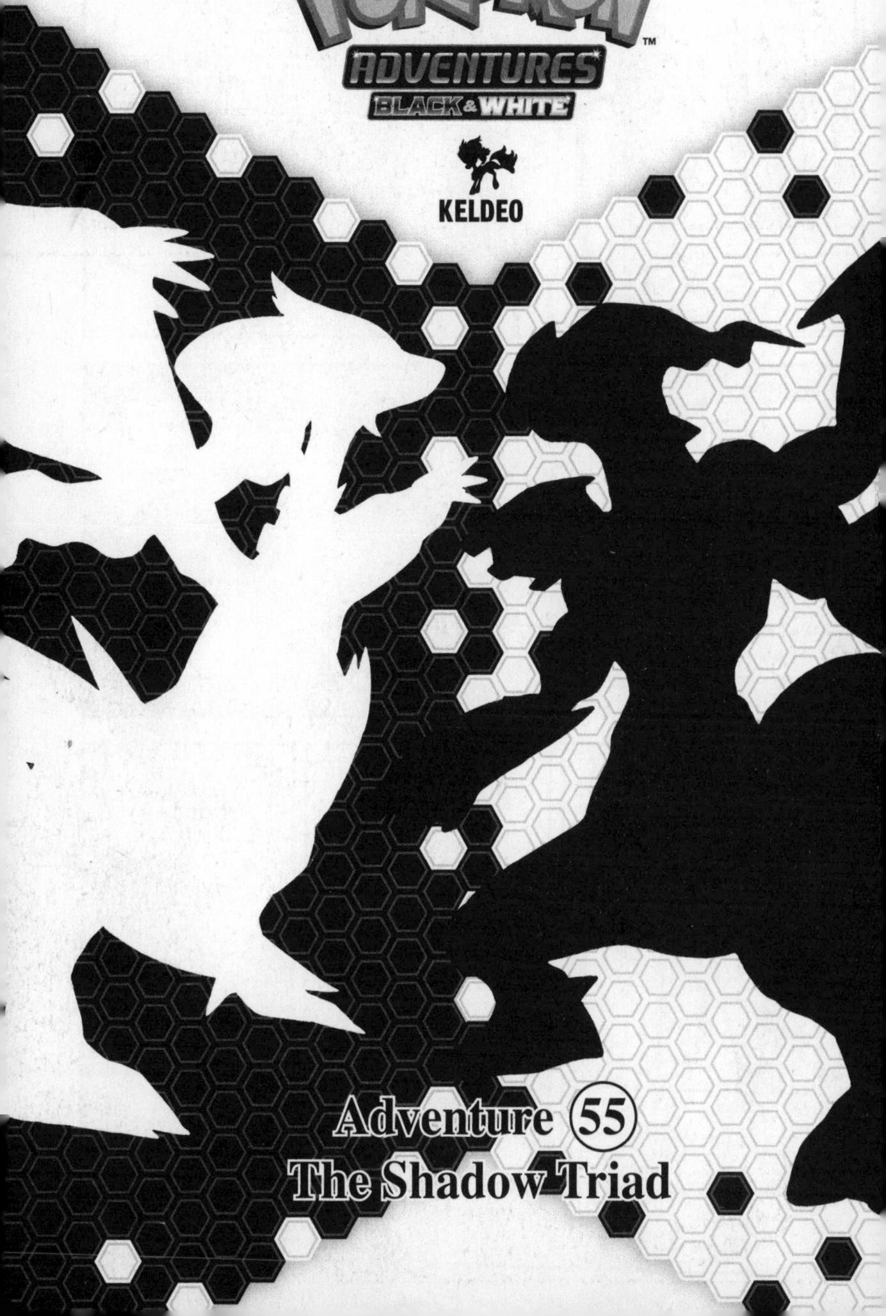
KELDEO

# Adventure 55
# The Shadow Triad

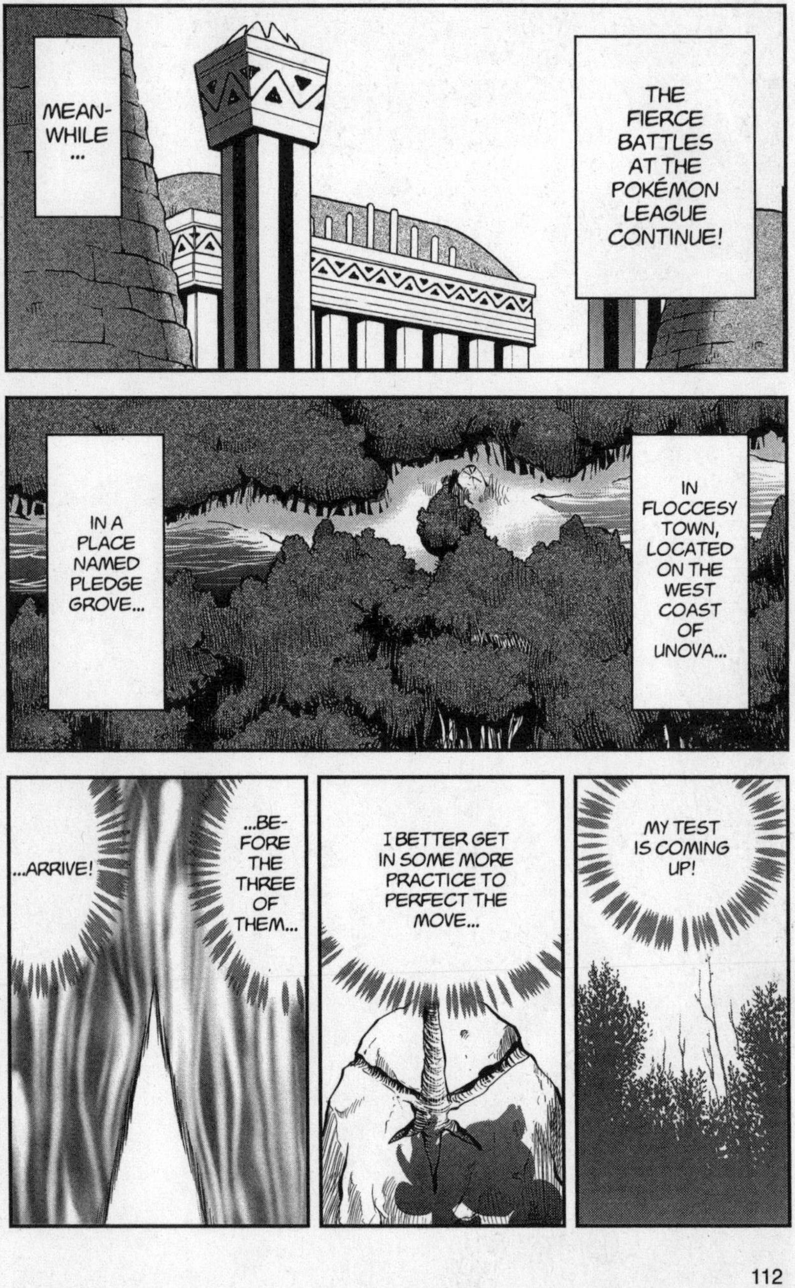
THE FIERCE BATTLES AT THE POKÉMON LEAGUE CONTINUE!
MEAN-WHILE ...
IN FLOCCESY TOWN, LOCATED ON THE WEST COAST OF UNOVA...
IN A PLACE NAMED PLEDGE GROVE...
MY TEST IS COMING UP!
I BETTER GET IN SOME MORE PRACTICE TO PERFECT THE MOVE...
...BE-FORE THE THREE OF THEM...
...ARRIVE!

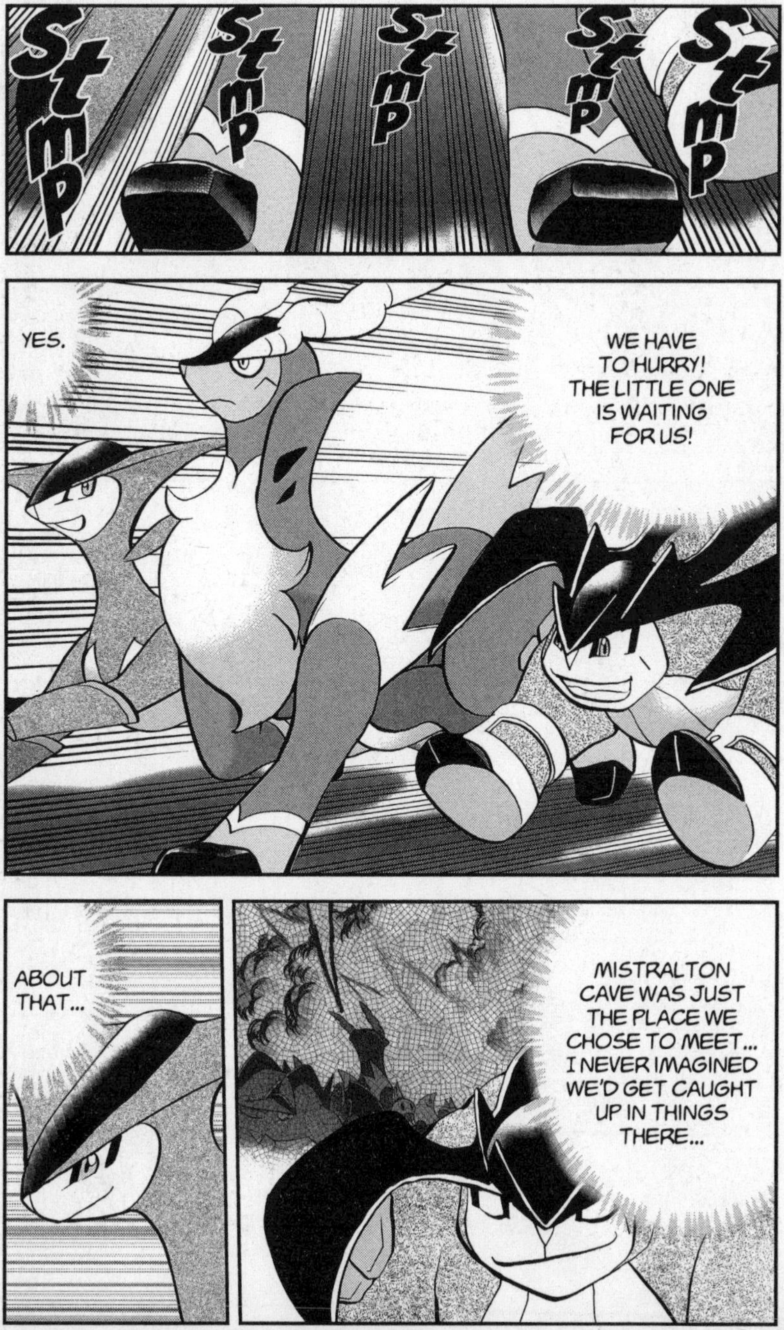
Stmp
Stmp
Stmp
Stmp
Stmp
WE HAVE TO HURRY! THE LITTLE ONE IS WAITING FOR US!
YES.
MISTRALTON CAVE WAS JUST THE PLACE WE CHOSE TO MEET... I NEVER IMAGINED WE'D GET CAUGHT UP IN THINGS THERE...
ABOUT THAT...

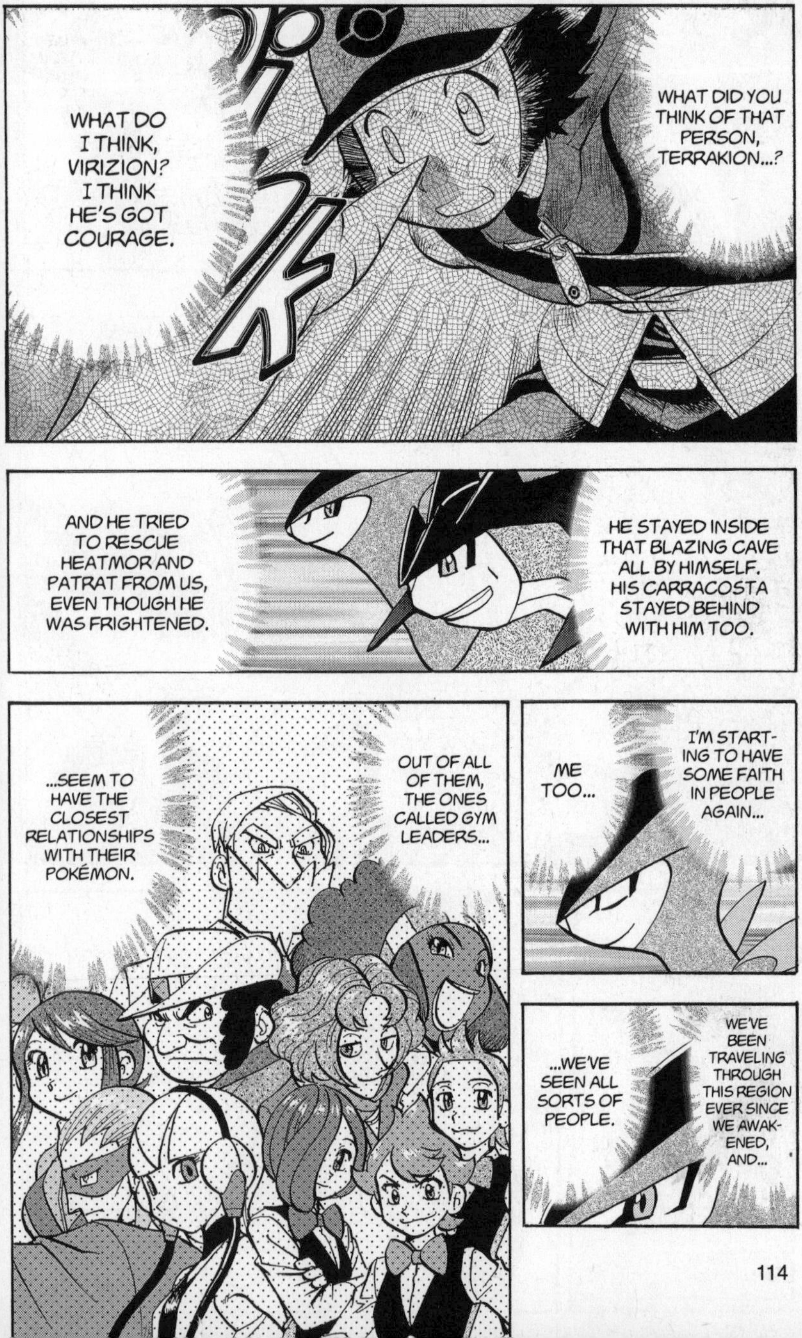
WHAT DID YOU THINK OF THAT PERSON, TERRAKION...?
WHAT DO I THINK, VIRIZION? I THINK HE'S GOT COURAGE.
HE STAYED INSIDE THAT BLAZING CAVE ALL BY HIMSELF. HIS CARRACOSTA STAYED BEHIND WITH HIM TOO.
AND HE TRIED TO RESCUE HEATMOR AND PATRAT FROM US, EVEN THOUGH HE WAS FRIGHTENED.
I'M STARTING TO HAVE SOME FAITH IN PEOPLE AGAIN...
ME TOO...
WE'VE BEEN TRAVELING THROUGH THIS REGION EVER SINCE WE AWAKENED, AND...
...WE'VE SEEN ALL SORTS OF PEOPLE.
OUT OF ALL OF THEM, THE ONES CALLED GYM LEADERS...
...SEEM TO HAVE THE CLOSEST RELATIONSHIPS WITH THEIR POKÉMON.

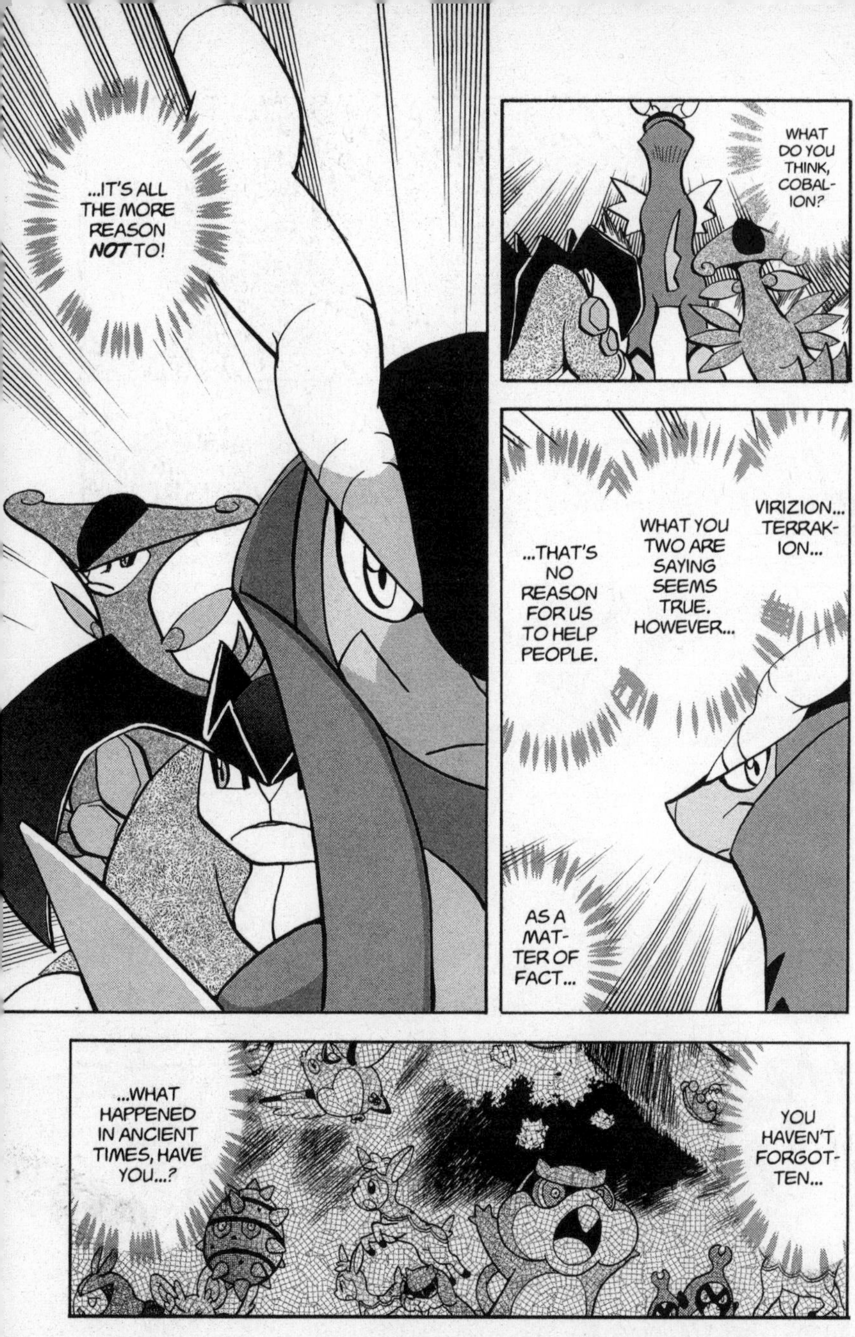
WHAT DO YOU THINK, COBALION?
VIRIZION... TERRAKION...
WHAT YOU TWO ARE SAYING SEEMS TRUE. HOWEVER...
...THAT'S NO REASON FOR US TO HELP PEOPLE.
AS A MATTER OF FACT...
...IT'S ALL THE MORE REASON **NOT** TO!
YOU HAVEN'T FORGOTTEN...
...WHAT HAPPENED IN ANCIENT TIMES, HAVE YOU...?

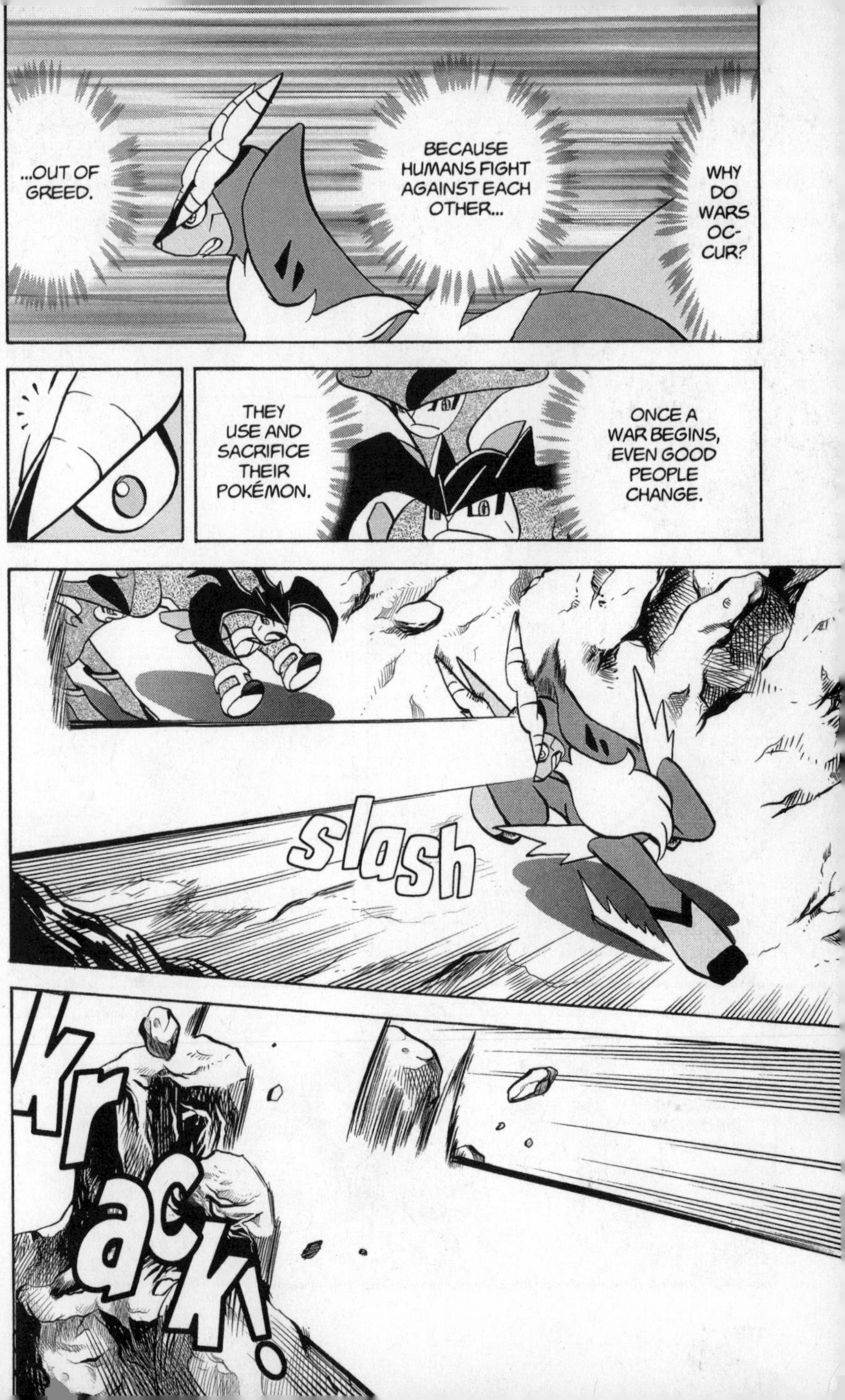
WHY DO WARS OC-CUR?
BECAUSE HUMANS FIGHT AGAINST EACH OTHER...
...OUT OF GREED.
ONCE A WAR BEGINS, EVEN GOOD PEOPLE CHANGE.
THEY USE AND SACRIFICE THEIR POKÉMON.
slash
Krack!

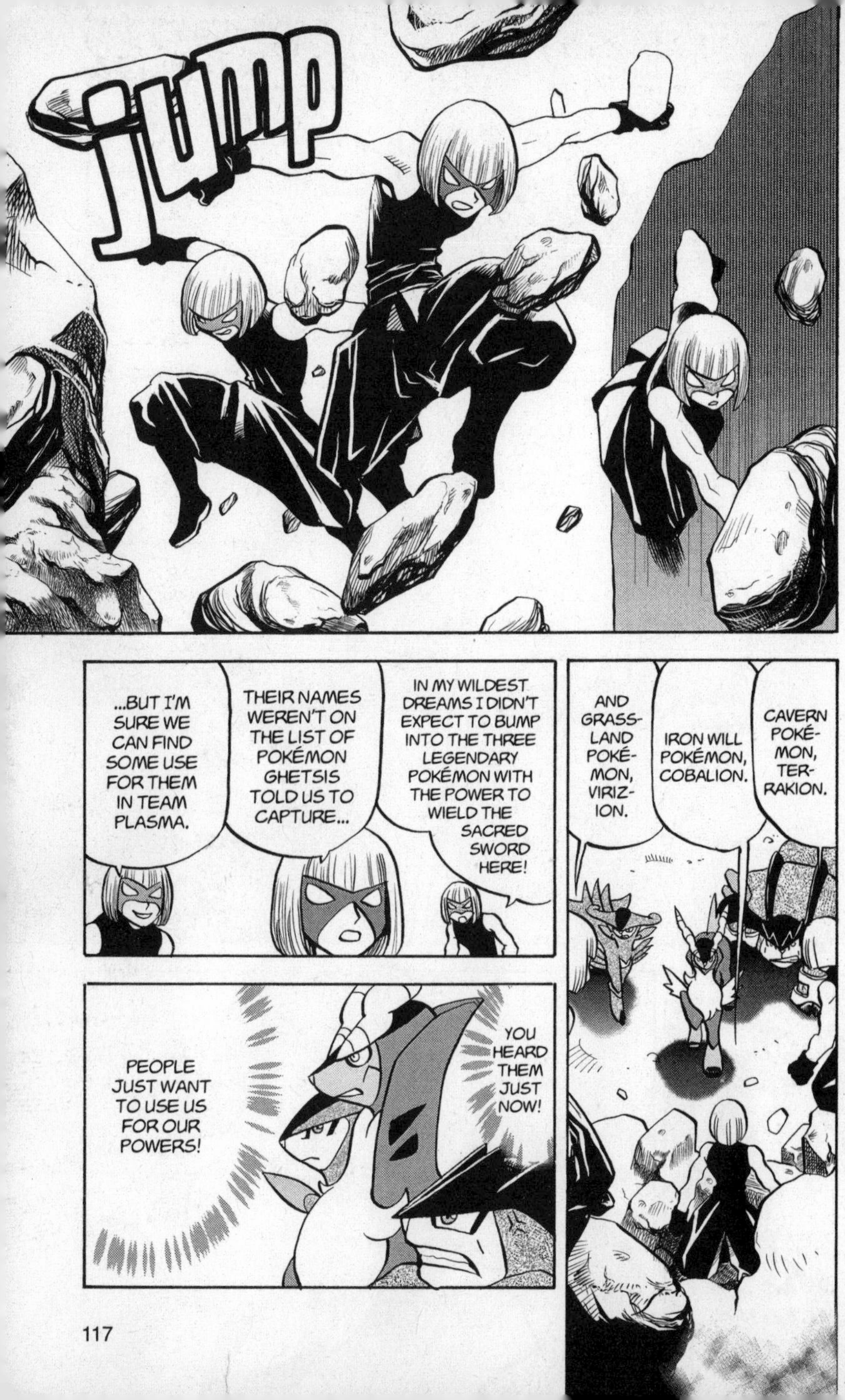
JUMP
CAVERN POKÉMON, TERRAKION.
IRON WILL POKÉMON, COBALION.
AND GRASSLAND POKÉMON, VIRIZION.
IN MY WILDEST DREAMS I DIDN'T EXPECT TO BUMP INTO THE THREE LEGENDARY POKÉMON WITH THE POWER TO WIELD THE SACRED SWORD HERE!
THEIR NAMES WEREN'T ON THE LIST OF POKÉMON GHETSIS TOLD US TO CAPTURE...
...BUT I'M SURE WE CAN FIND SOME USE FOR THEM IN TEAM PLASMA.
YOU HEARD THEM JUST NOW!
PEOPLE JUST WANT TO USE US FOR OUR POWERS!

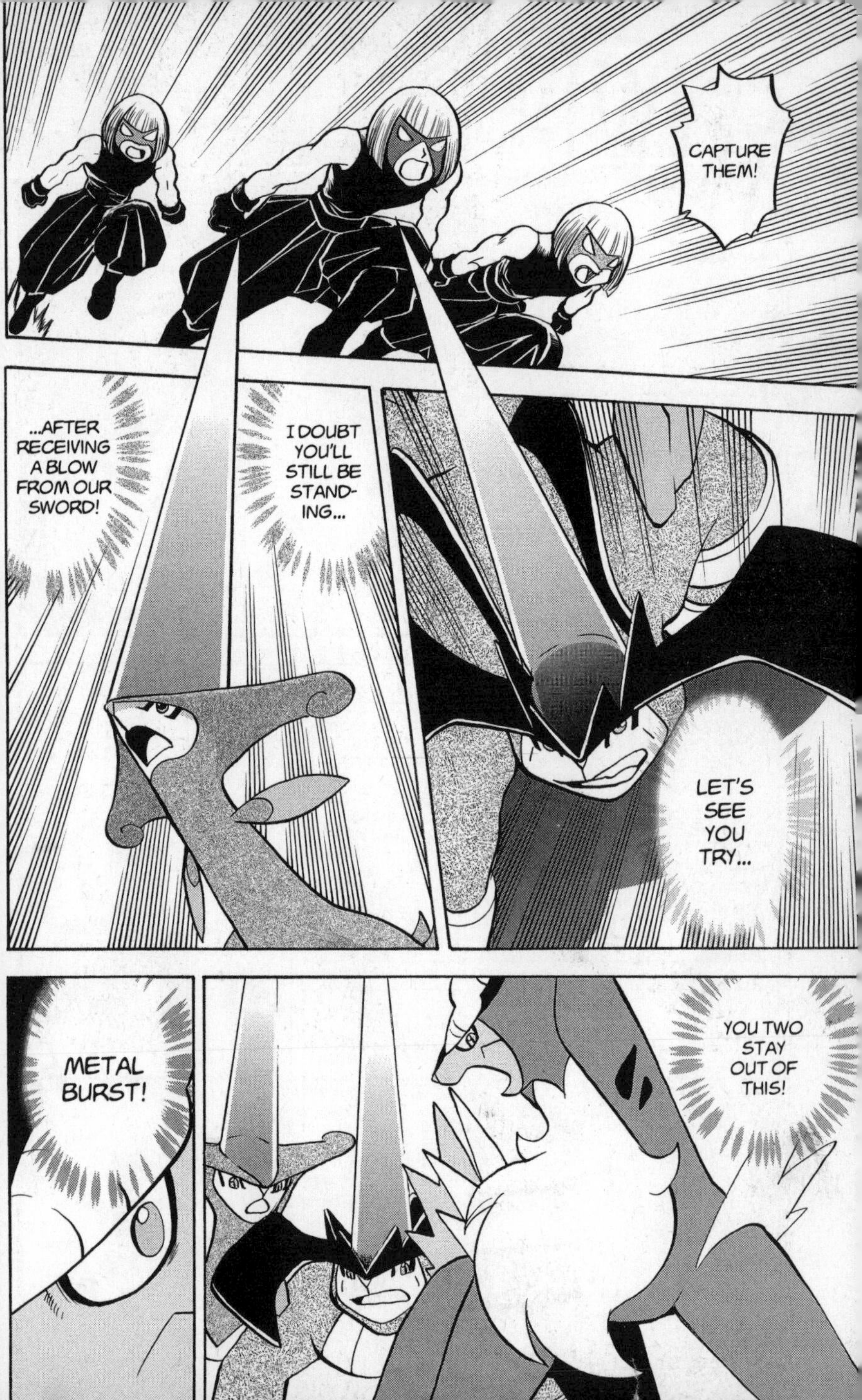
CAPTURE THEM!
LET'S SEE YOU TRY...
I DOUBT YOU'LL STILL BE STANDING...
...AFTER RECEIVING A BLOW FROM OUR SWORD!
YOU TWO STAY OUT OF THIS!
METAL BURST!

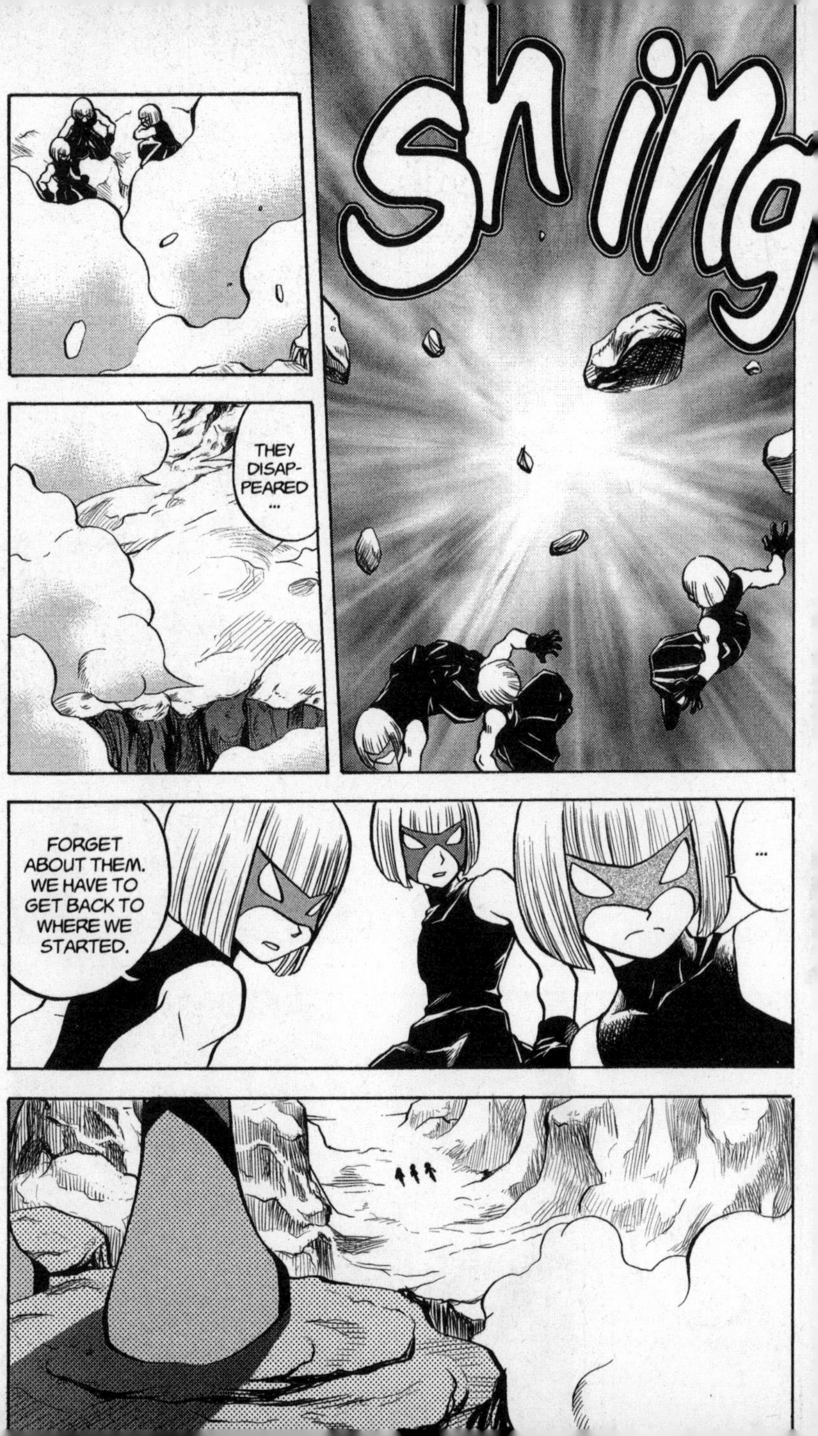
Shing
THEY DISAP-PEARED ...
...
FORGET ABOUT THEM. WE HAVE TO GET BACK TO WHERE WE STARTED.

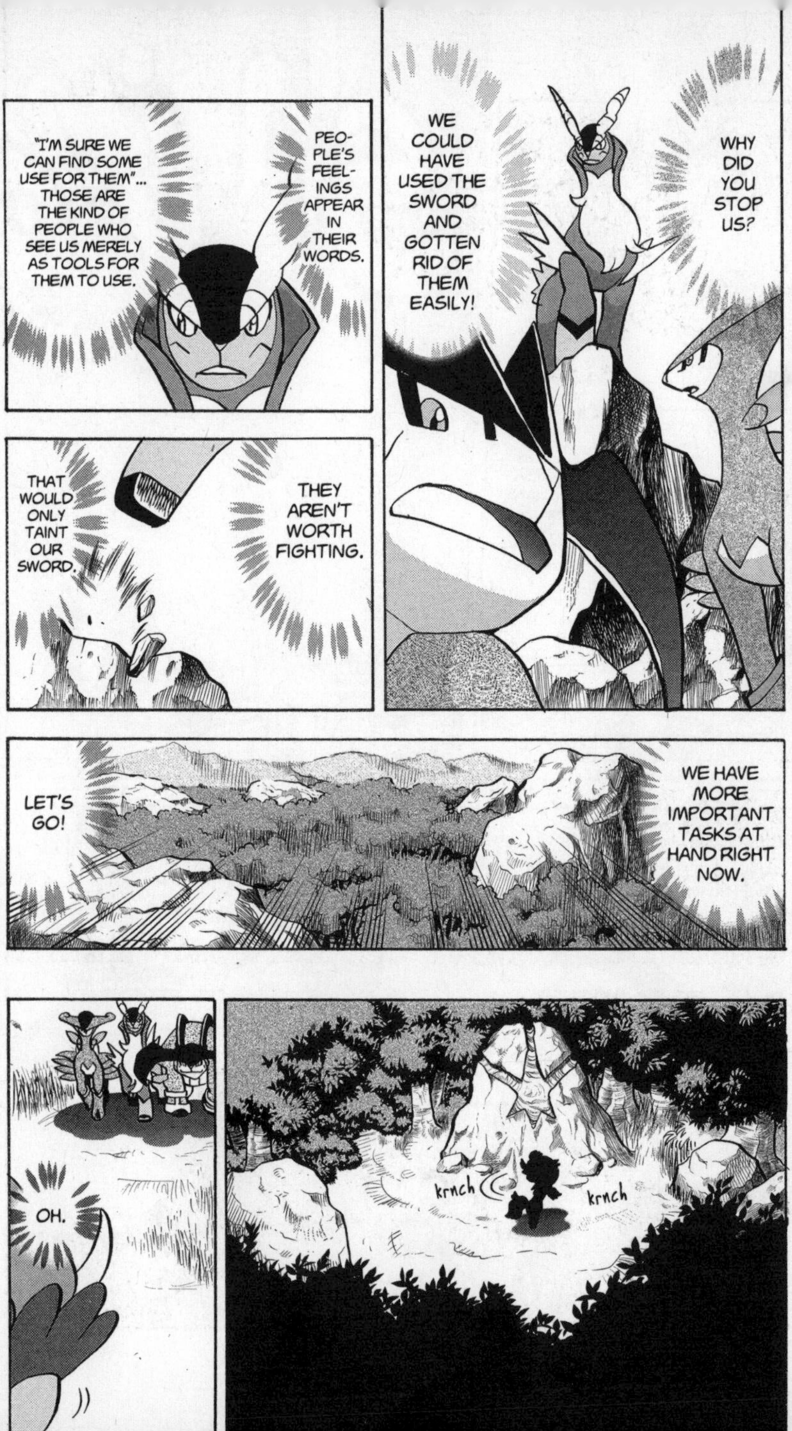
WHY DID YOU STOP US?
WE COULD HAVE USED THE SWORD AND GOTTEN RID OF THEM EASILY!
PEO-PLE'S FEEL-INGS APPEAR IN THEIR WORDS.
"I'M SURE WE CAN FIND SOME USE FOR THEM"... THOSE ARE THE KIND OF PEOPLE WHO SEE US MERELY AS TOOLS FOR THEM TO USE.
THEY AREN'T WORTH FIGHTING.
THAT WOULD ONLY TAINT OUR SWORD.
WE HAVE MORE IMPORTANT TASKS AT HAND RIGHT NOW.
LET'S GO!
krnch
krnch
OH.

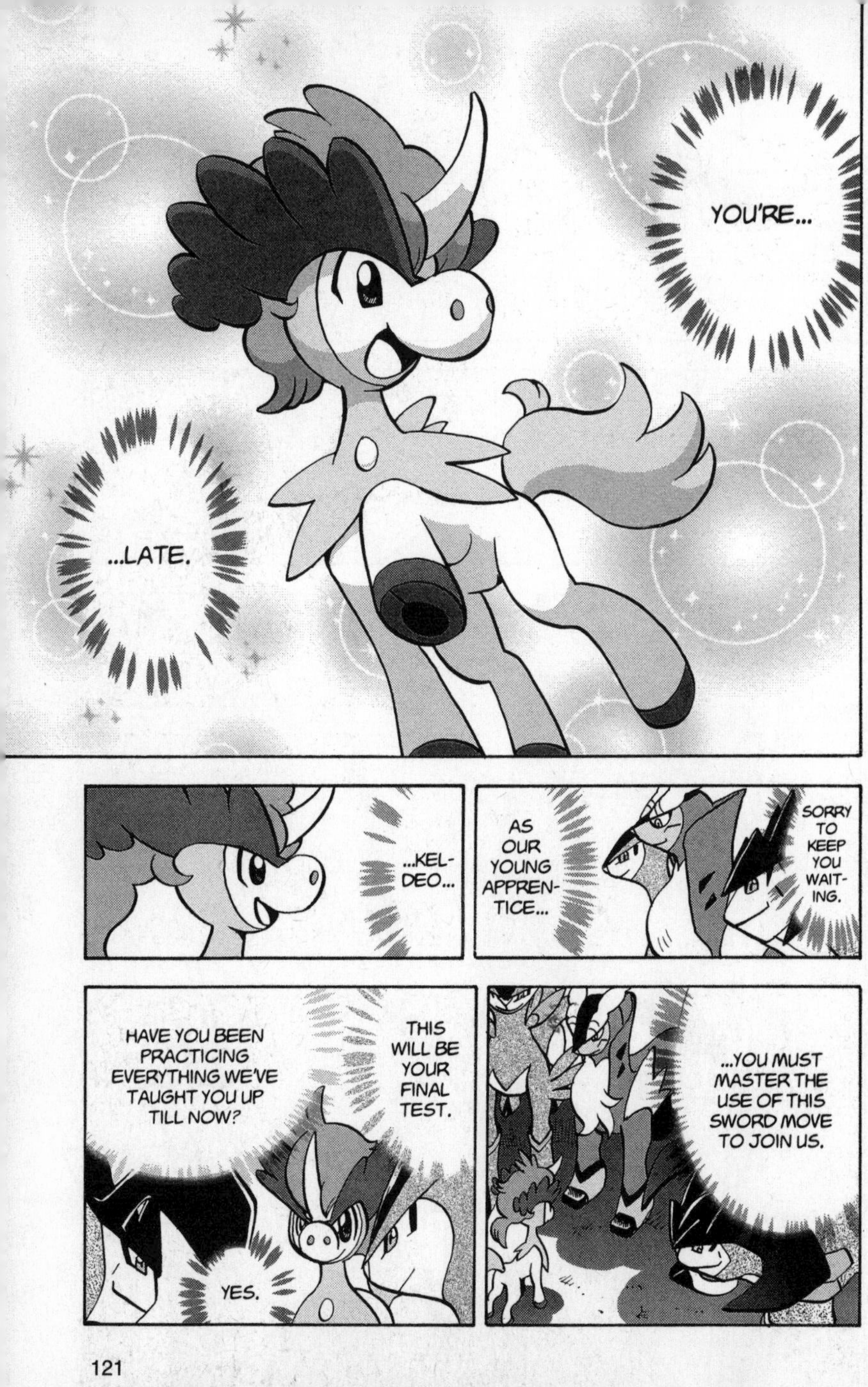
YOU'RE...
...LATE.
SORRY TO KEEP YOU WAIT-ING.
AS OUR YOUNG APPREN-TICE...
...KEL-DEO...
...YOU MUST MASTER THE USE OF THIS SWORD MOVE TO JOIN US.
THIS WILL BE YOUR FINAL TEST.
HAVE YOU BEEN PRACTICING EVERYTHING WE'VE TAUGHT YOU UP TILL NOW?
YES.

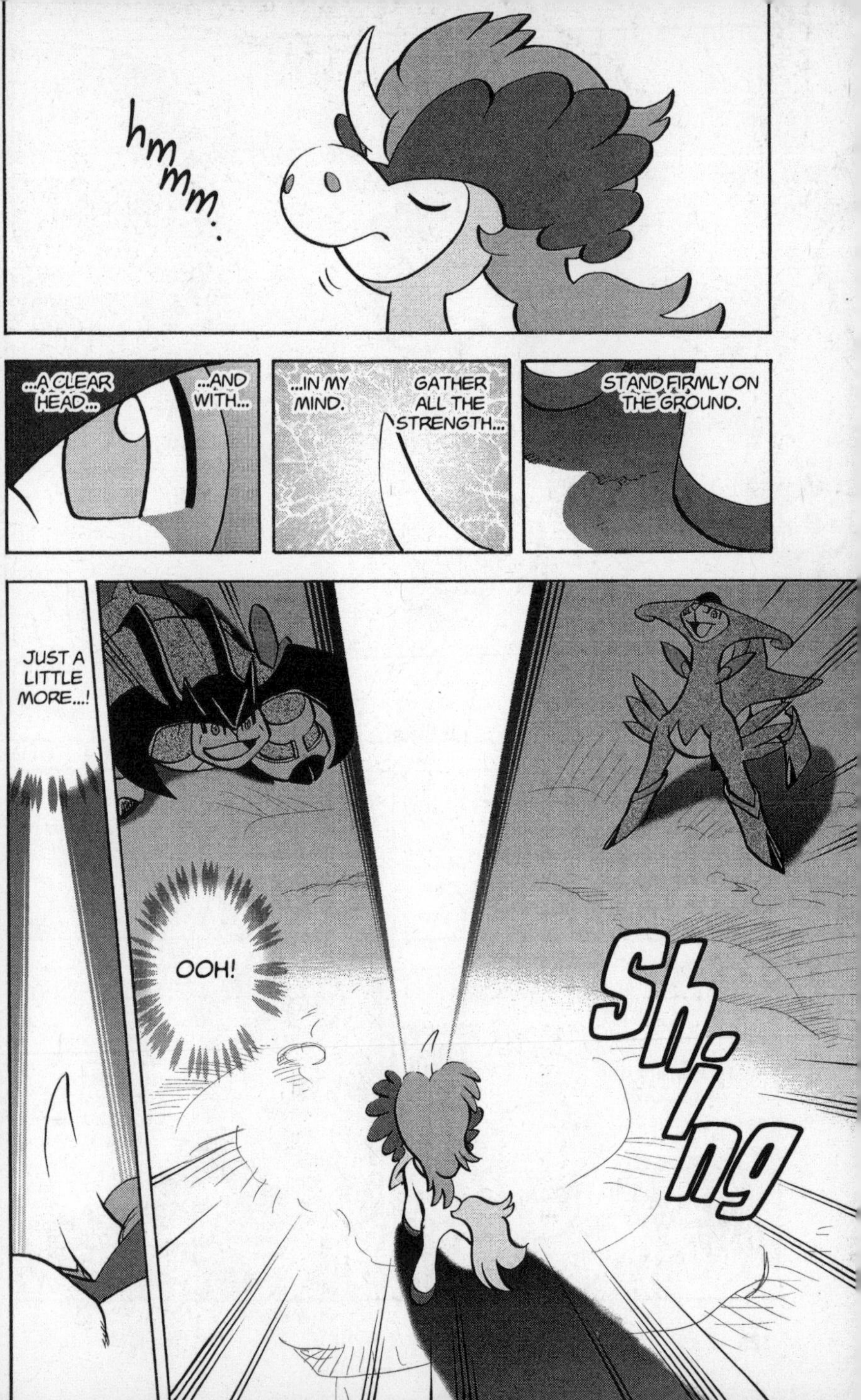
hmmm...
STAND FIRMLY ON THE GROUND.
GATHER ALL THE STRENGTH...
...IN MY MIND.
...AND WITH...
...A CLEAR HEAD...
JUST A LITTLE MORE...!
Shing
OOH!

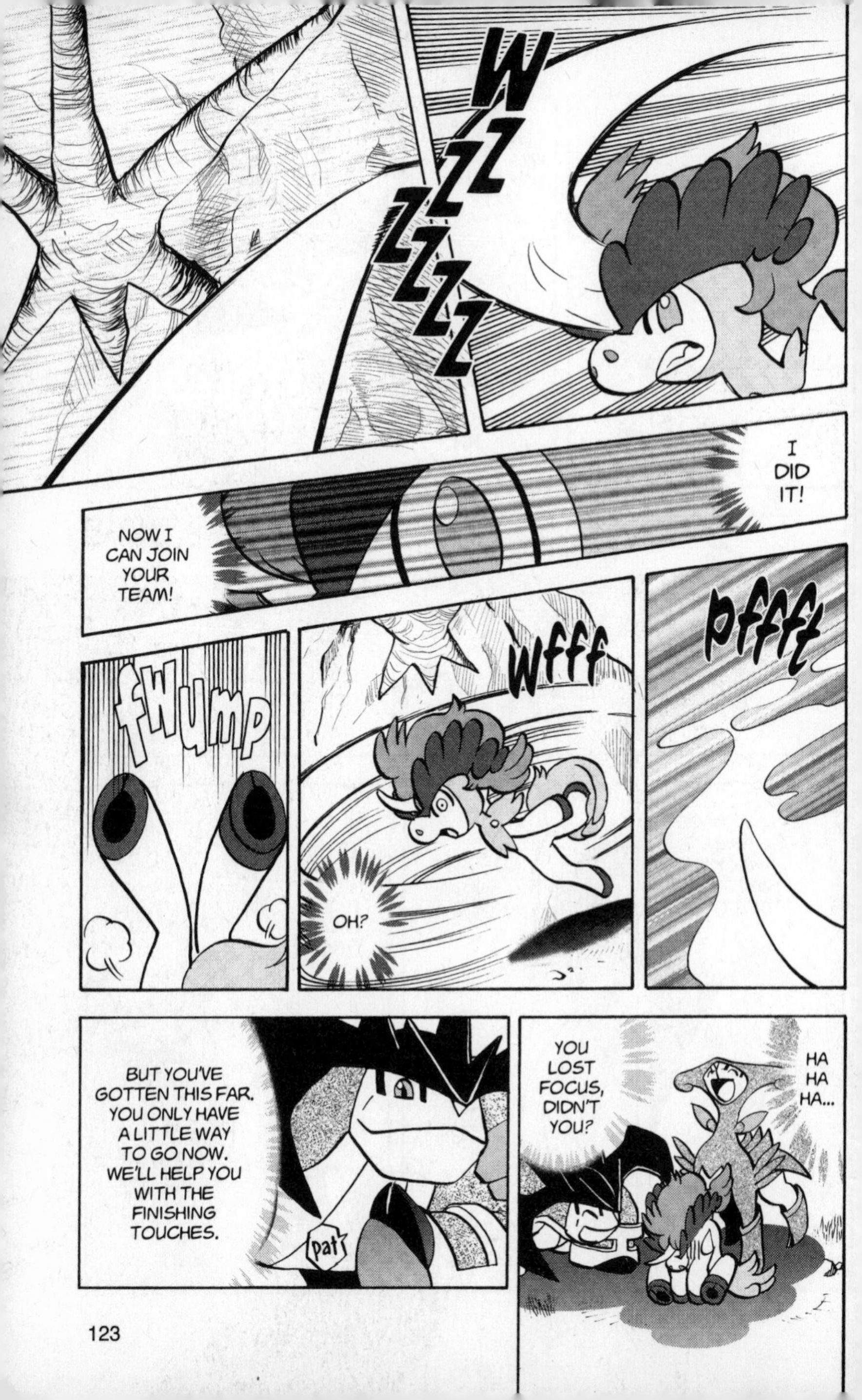
WZZZZZZ
I DID IT!
NOW I CAN JOIN YOUR TEAM!
pffft
wfff
OH?
fWUMP
YOU LOST FOCUS, DIDN'T YOU?
HA HA HA...
BUT YOU'VE GOTTEN THIS FAR. YOU ONLY HAVE A LITTLE WAY TO GO NOW. WE'LL HELP YOU WITH THE FINISHING TOUCHES.
pat

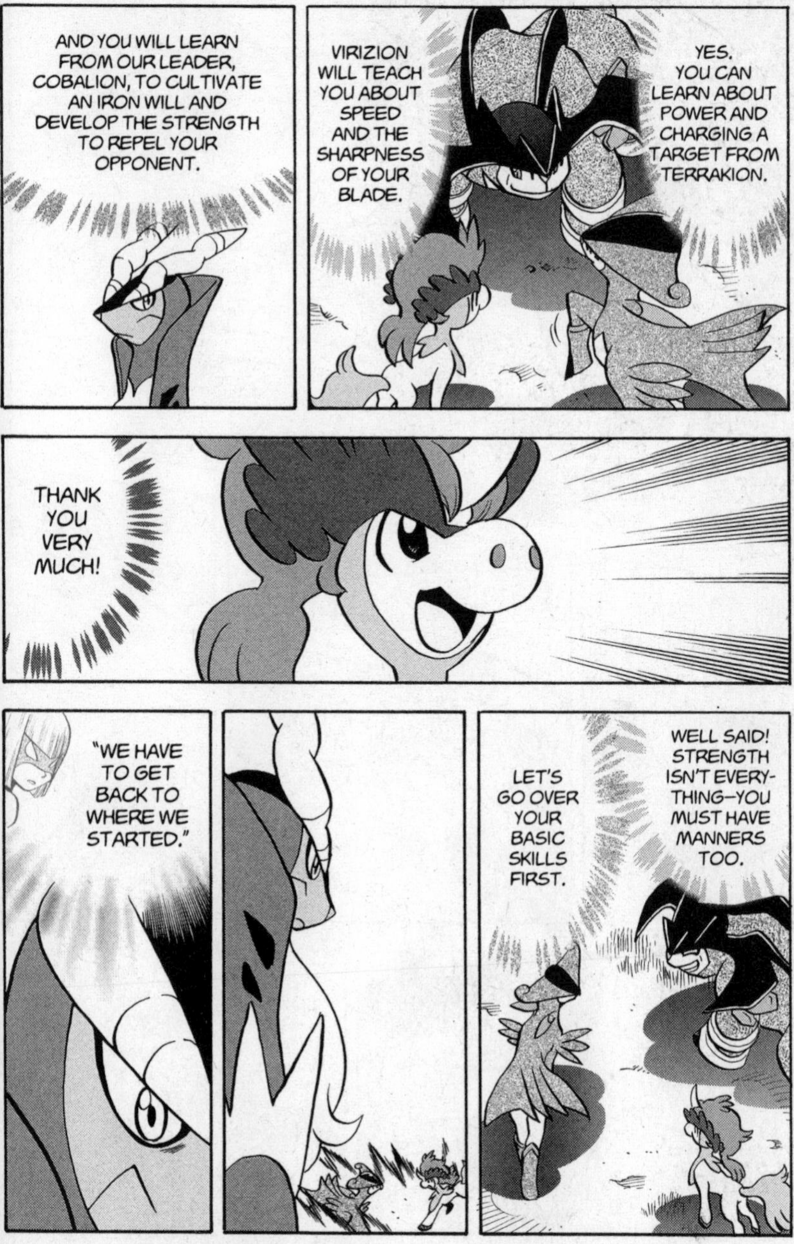
YES. YOU CAN LEARN ABOUT POWER AND CHARGING A TARGET FROM TERRAKION.
VIRIZION WILL TEACH YOU ABOUT SPEED AND THE SHARPNESS OF YOUR BLADE.
AND YOU WILL LEARN FROM OUR LEADER, COBALION, TO CULTIVATE AN IRON WILL AND DEVELOP THE STRENGTH TO REPEL YOUR OPPONENT.
THANK YOU VERY MUCH!
WELL SAID! STRENGTH ISN'T EVERY-THING—YOU MUST HAVE MANNERS TOO.
LET'S GO OVER YOUR BASIC SKILLS FIRST.
"WE HAVE TO GET BACK TO WHERE WE STARTED."

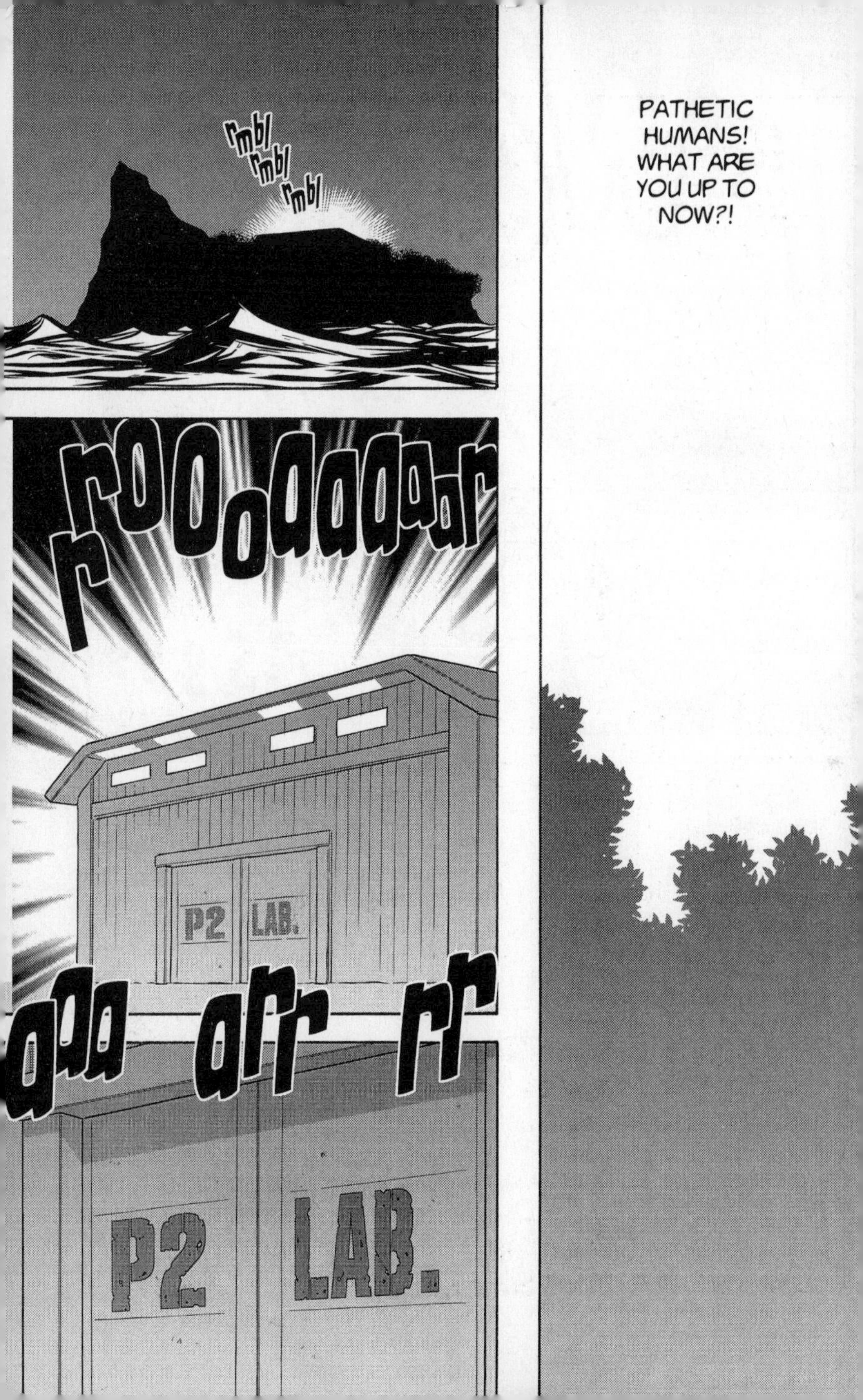
PATHETIC HUMANS! WHAT ARE YOU UP TO NOW?!
rmbl rmbl rmbl
rOOoaaaaar
P2 LAB.
aaa arr rr
P2 LAB.

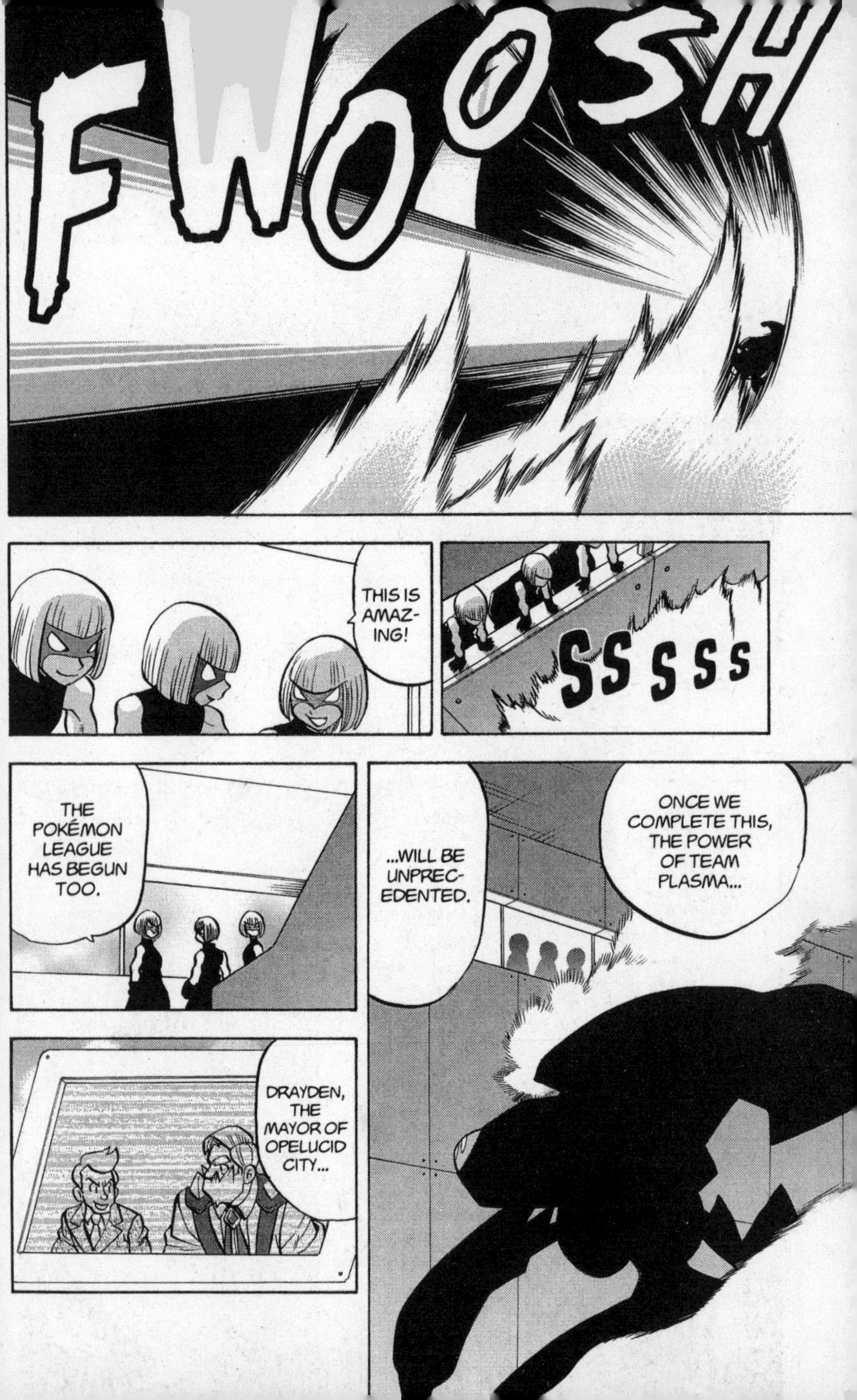
FWOOSH
SSSSS
THIS IS AMAZ-ING!
ONCE WE COMPLETE THIS, THE POWER OF TEAM PLASMA...
...WILL BE UNPREC-EDENTED.
THE POKÉMON LEAGUE HAS BEGUN TOO.
DRAYDEN, THE MAYOR OF OPELUCID CITY...

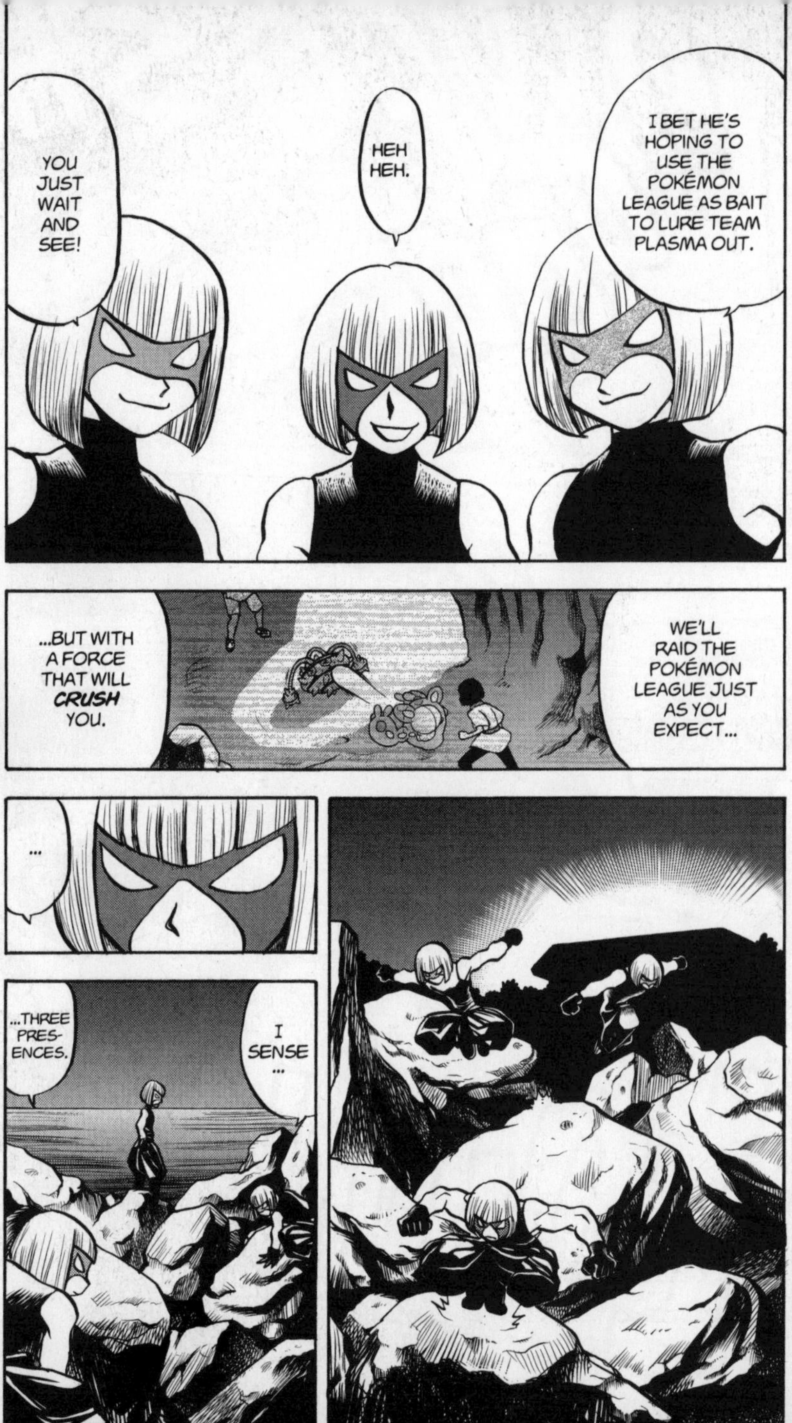
I BET HE'S HOPING TO USE THE POKÉMON LEAGUE AS BAIT TO LURE TEAM PLASMA OUT.
HEH HEH.
YOU JUST WAIT AND SEE!
WE'LL RAID THE POKÉMON LEAGUE JUST AS YOU EXPECT...
...BUT WITH A FORCE THAT WILL CRUSH YOU.
...
I SENSE...
...THREE PRES-ENCES.

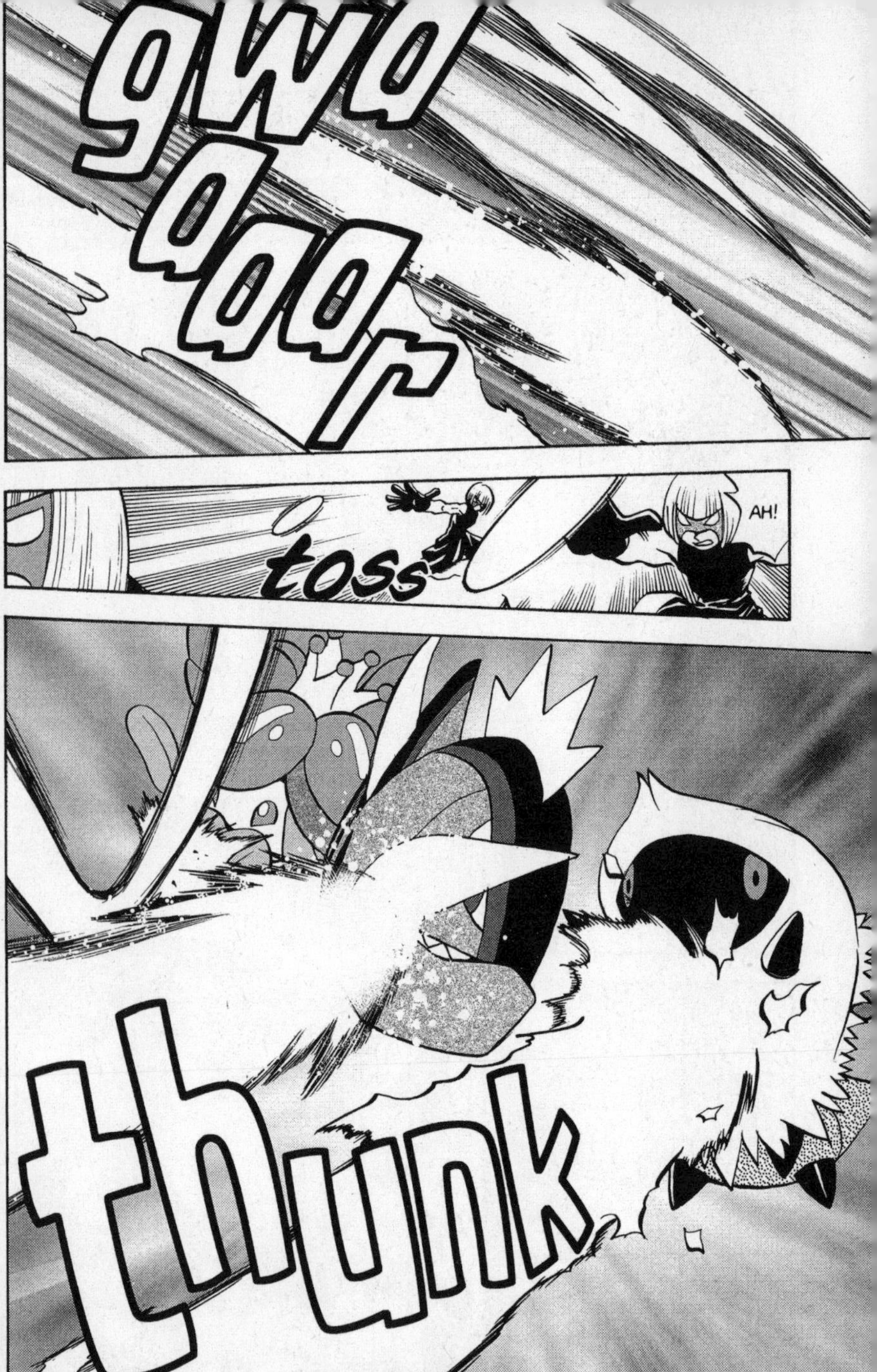
gwoooar
AH!
toss
thunk

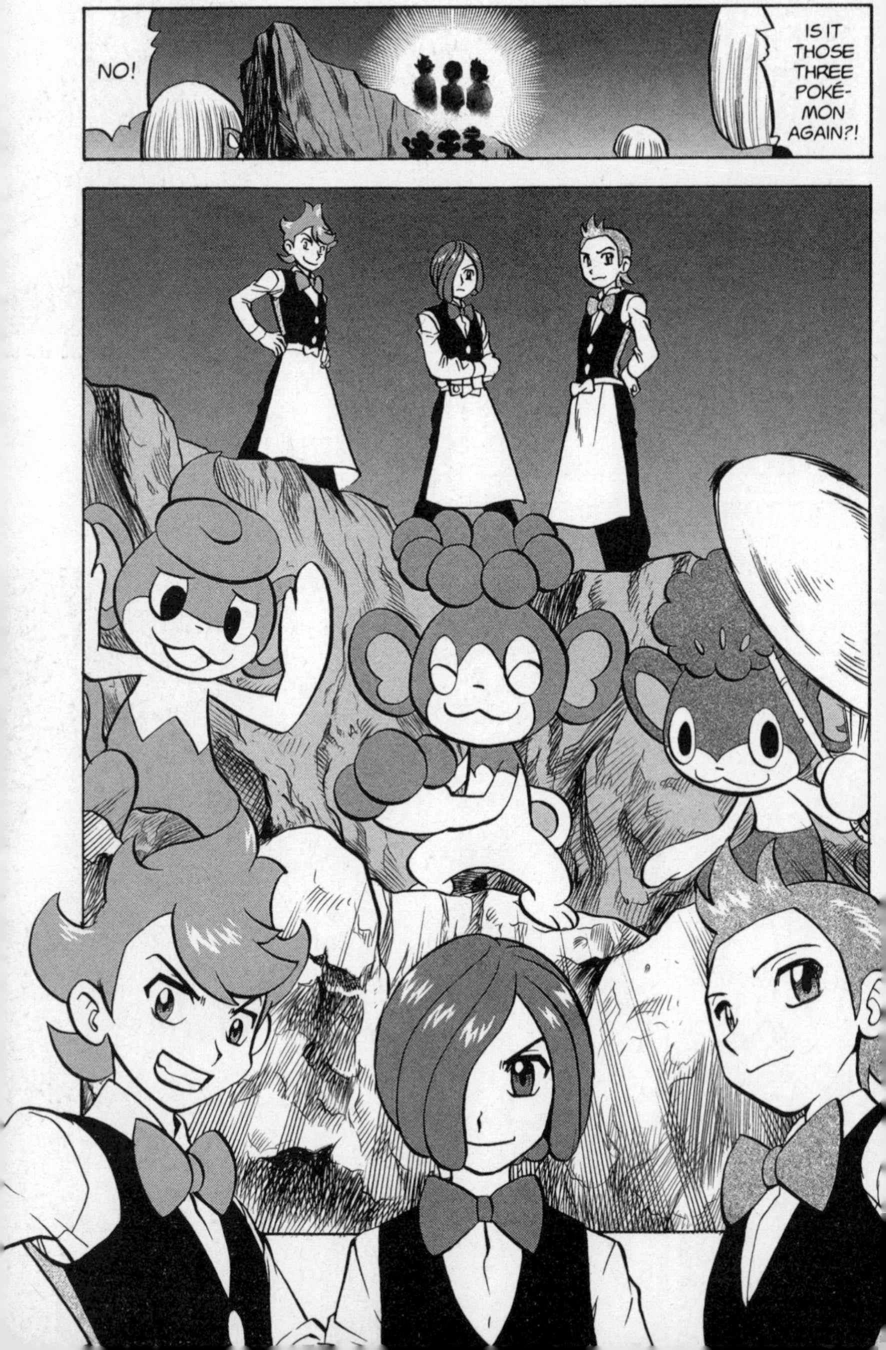
IS IT THOSE THREE POKÉ-MON AGAIN?!
NO!

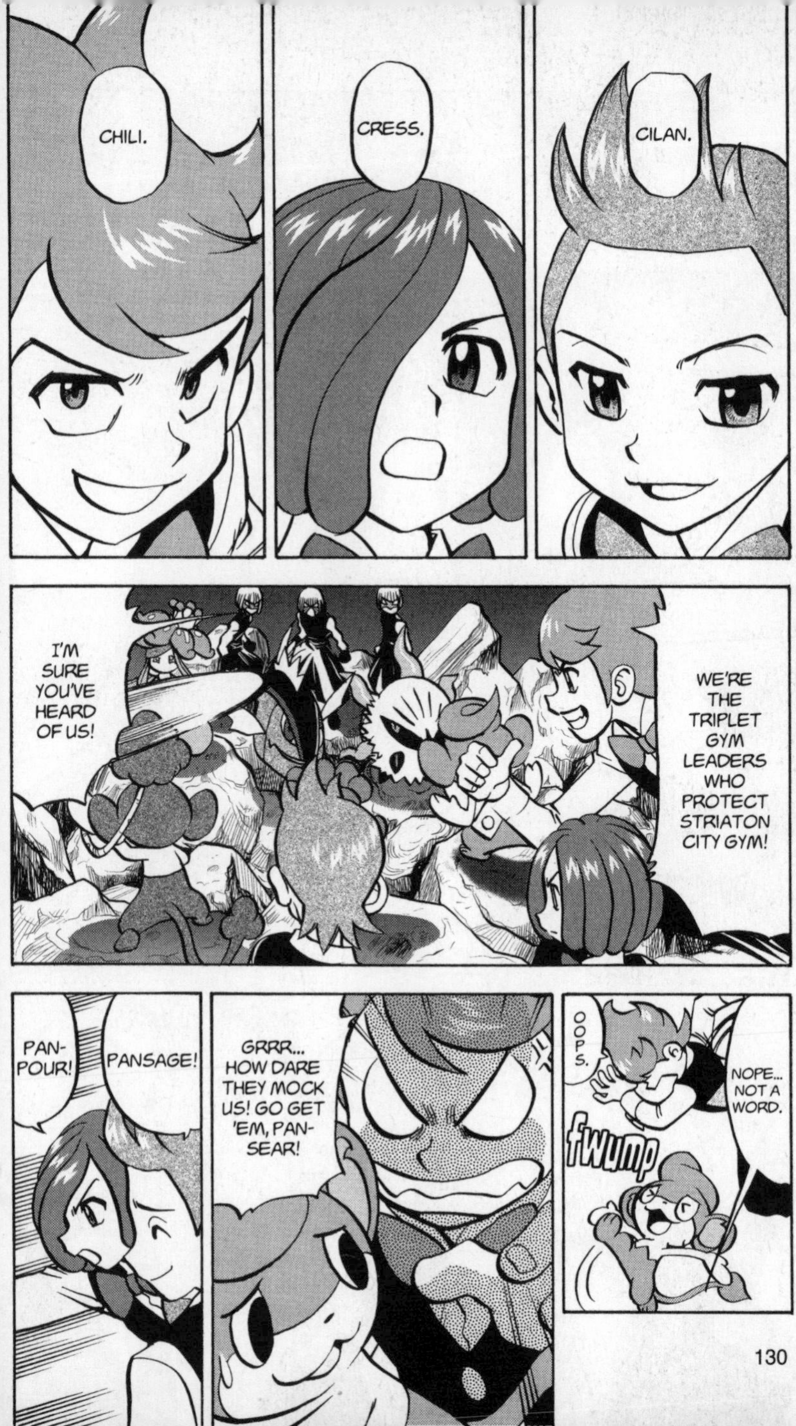
CILAN.
CRESS.
CHILI.
WE'RE THE TRIPLET GYM LEADERS WHO PROTECT STRIATON CITY GYM!
I'M SURE YOU'VE HEARD OF US!
OOPS.
NOPE... NOT A WORD.
fwump
GRRR... HOW DARE THEY MOCK US! GO GET 'EM, PAN-SEAR!
PANSAGE!
PAN-POUR!

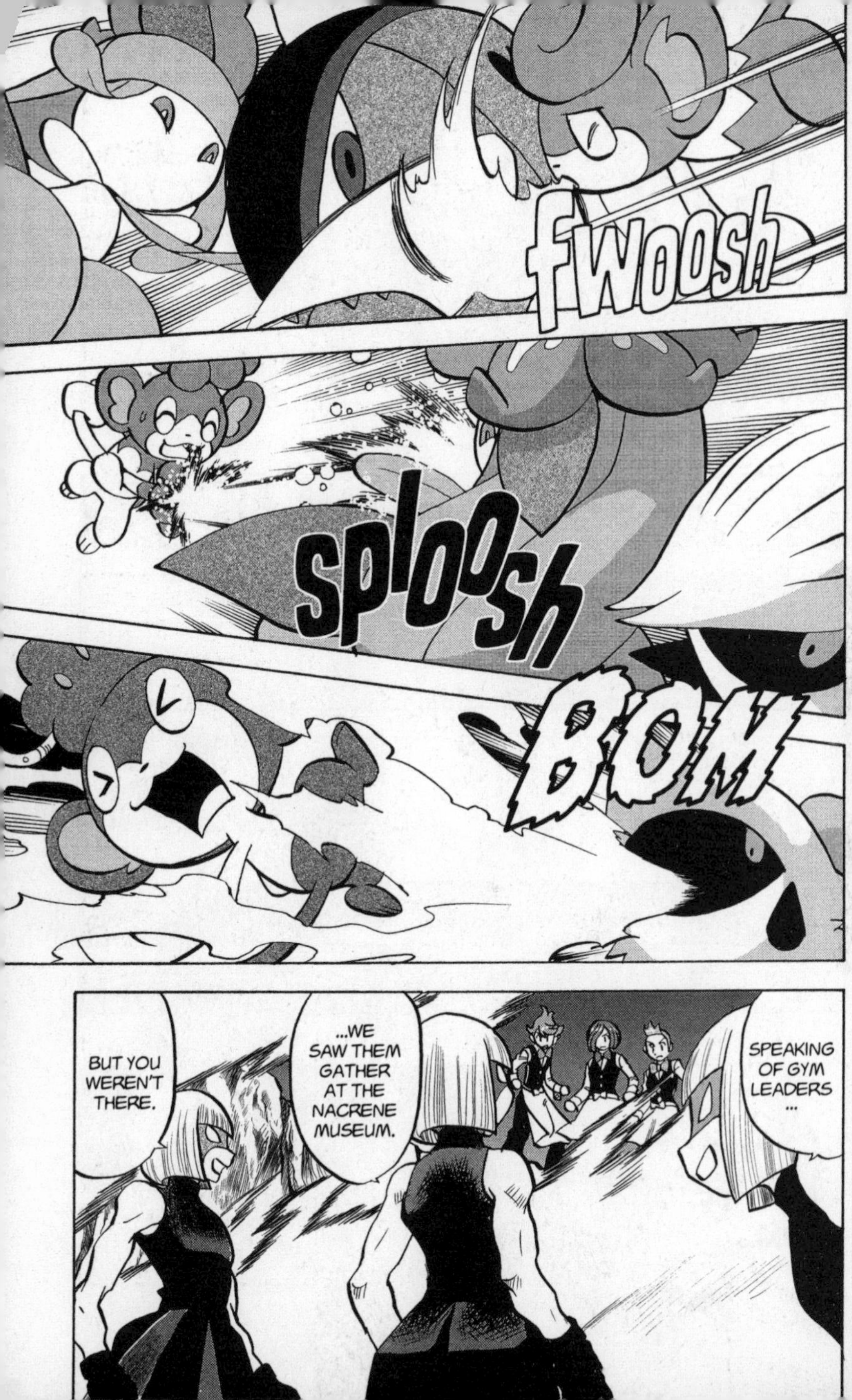
fwoosh
sploosh
BOM
SPEAKING OF GYM LEADERS ...
...WE SAW THEM GATHER AT THE NACRENE MUSEUM.
BUT YOU WEREN'T THERE.

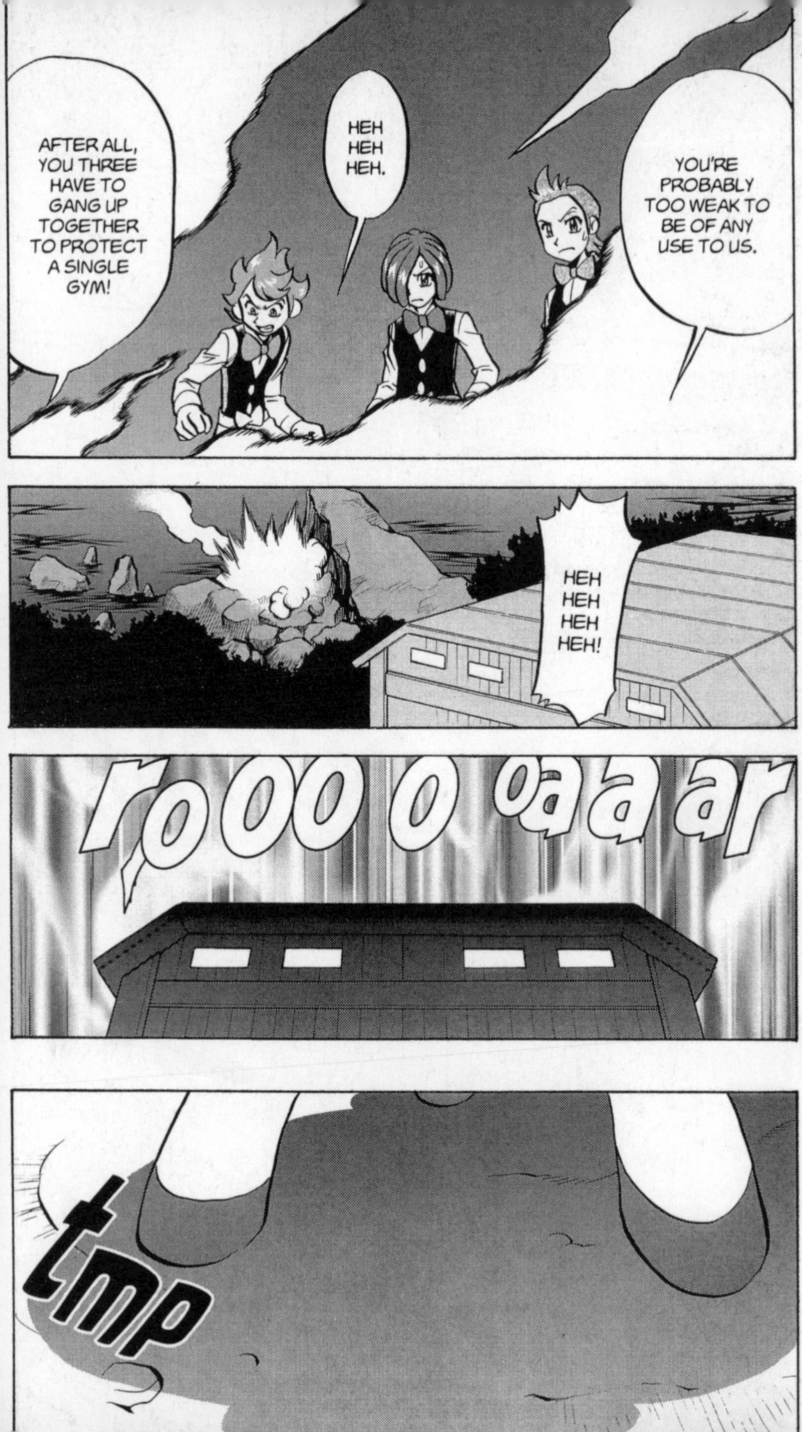
YOU'RE PROBABLY TOO WEAK TO BE OF ANY USE TO US.
HEH HEH HEH.
AFTER ALL, YOU THREE HAVE TO GANG UP TOGETHER TO PROTECT A SINGLE GYM!
HEH HEH HEH HEH!
roooo oaaar
tmp

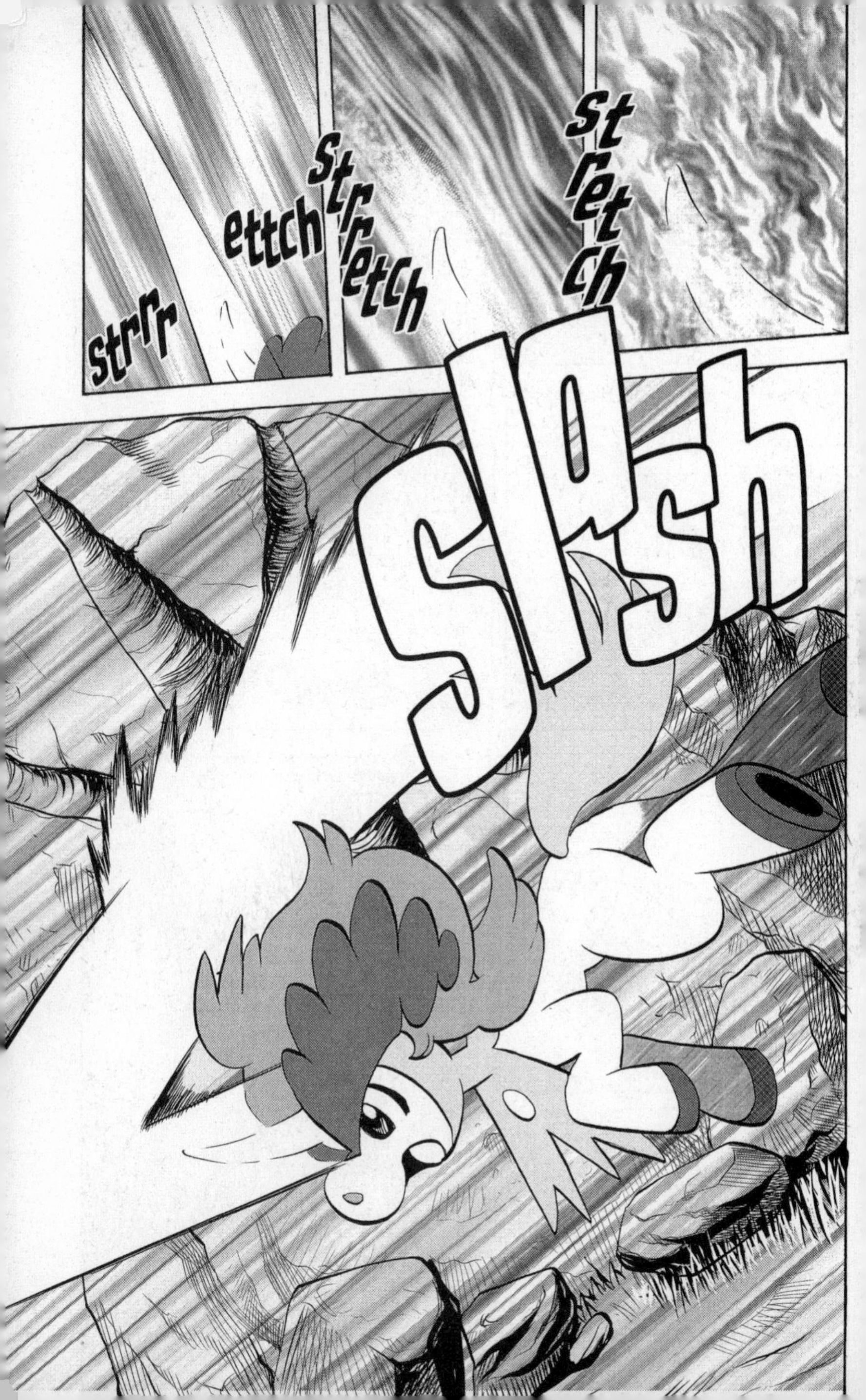
Stretch
Strretch
ettch
strrr
Slash

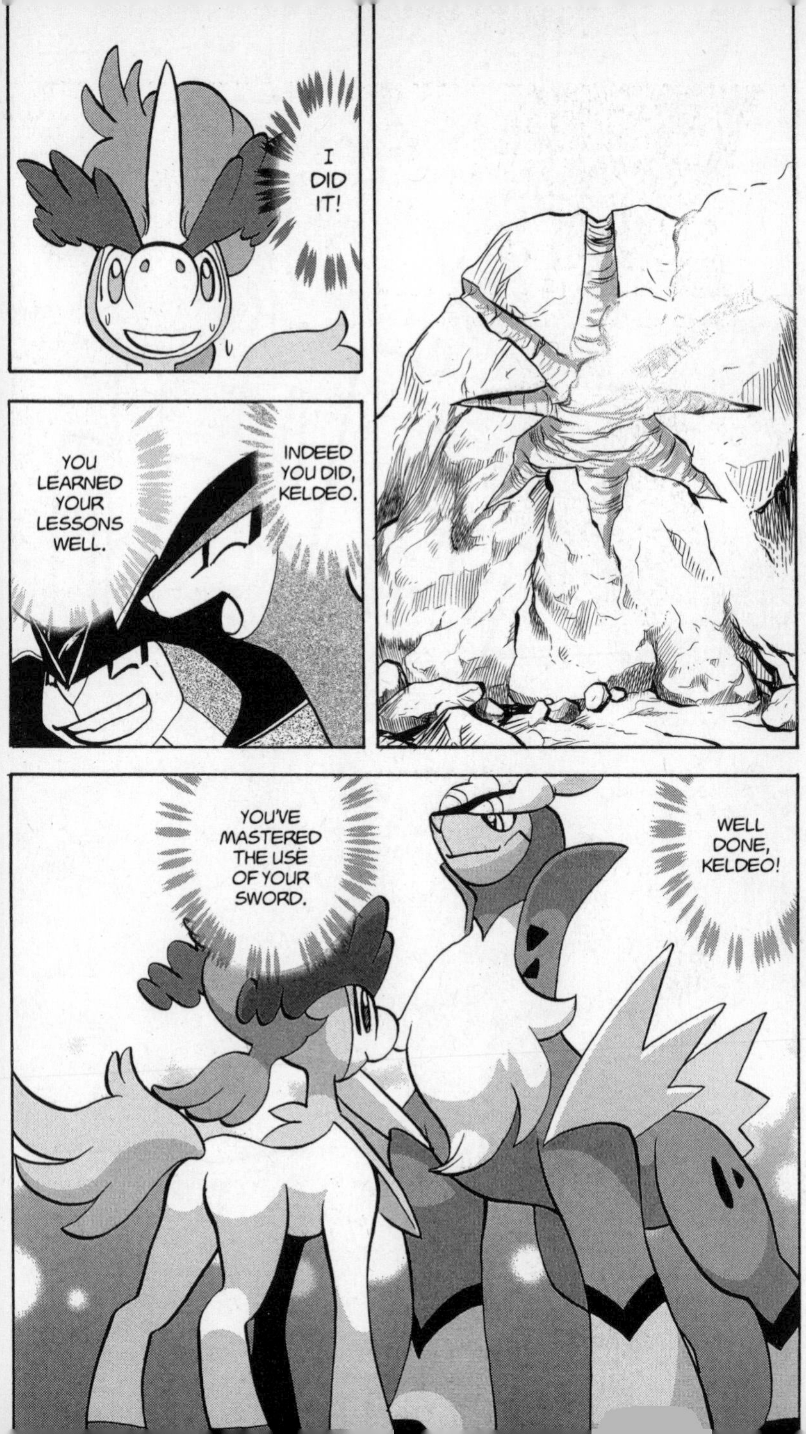
I DID IT!
INDEED YOU DID, KELDEO.
YOU LEARNED YOUR LESSONS WELL.
WELL DONE, KELDEO!
YOU'VE MASTERED THE USE OF YOUR SWORD.

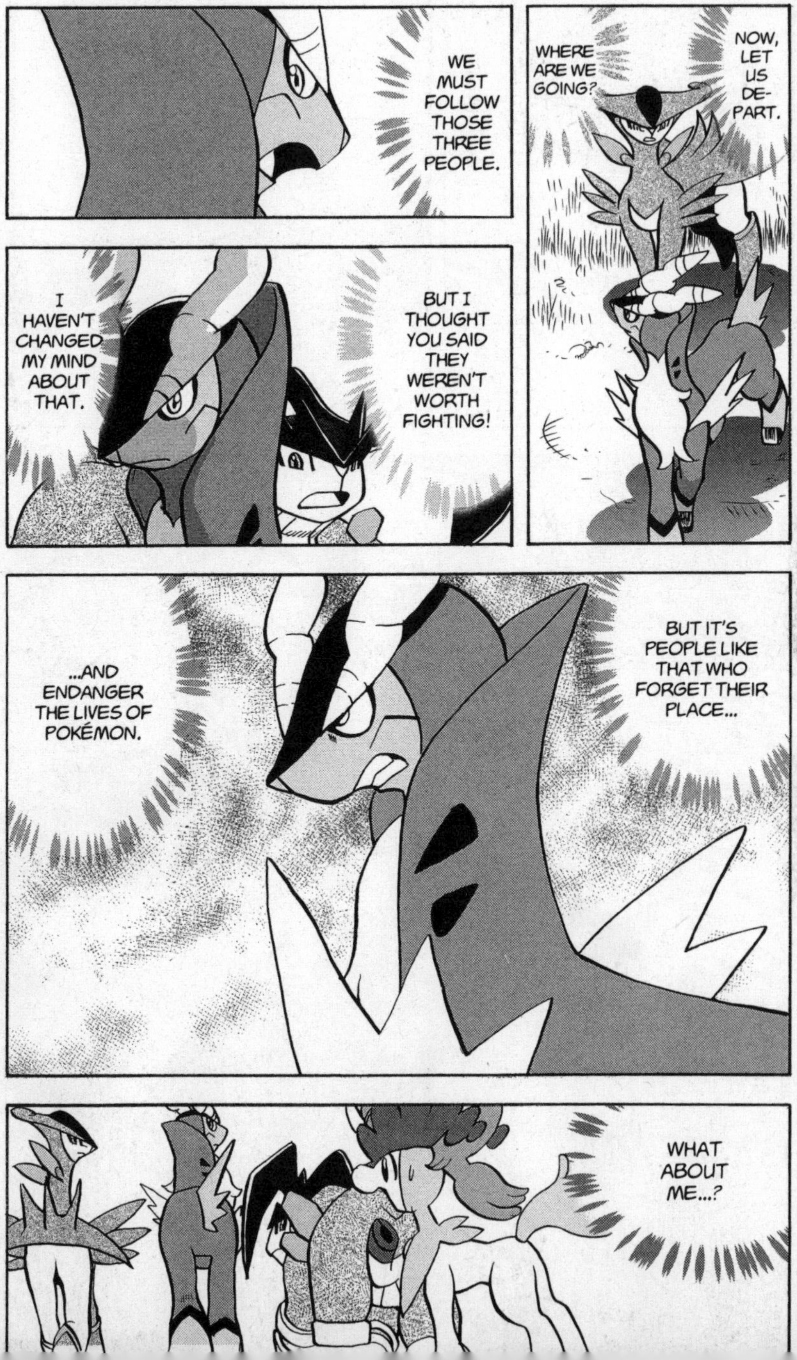
NOW, LET US DE-PART.
WHERE ARE WE GOING?
WE MUST FOLLOW THOSE THREE PEOPLE.
BUT I THOUGHT YOU SAID THEY WEREN'T WORTH FIGHTING!
I HAVEN'T CHANGED MY MIND ABOUT THAT.
BUT IT'S PEOPLE LIKE THAT WHO FORGET THEIR PLACE...
...AND ENDANGER THE LIVES OF POKÉMON.
WHAT ABOUT ME...?

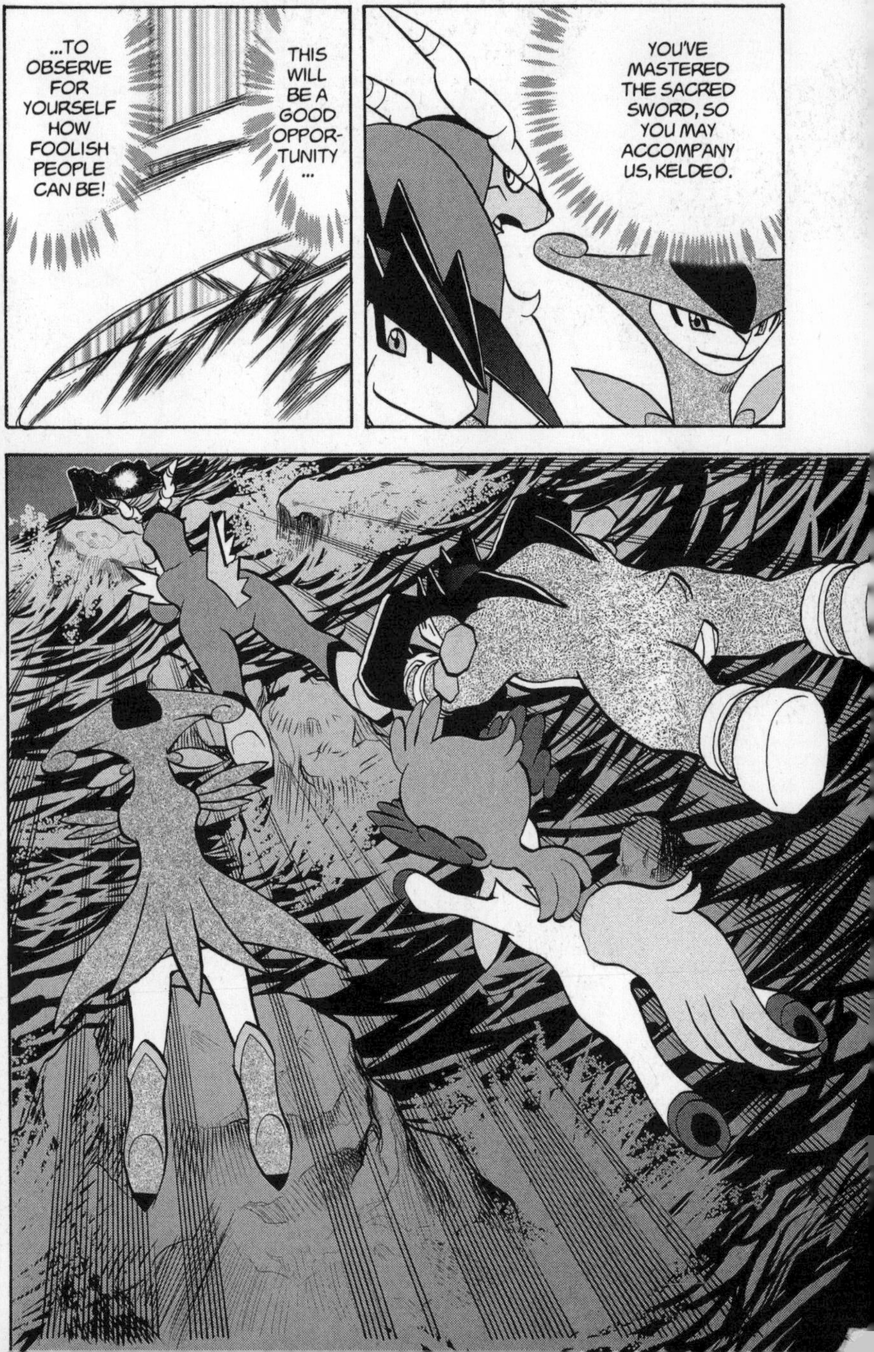
YOU'VE MASTERED THE SACRED SWORD, SO YOU MAY ACCOMPANY US, KELDEO.
THIS WILL BE A GOOD OPPORTUNITY...
...TO OBSERVE FOR YOURSELF HOW FOOLISH PEOPLE CAN BE!

Pokémon™ Adventures Black & White

FRAXURE

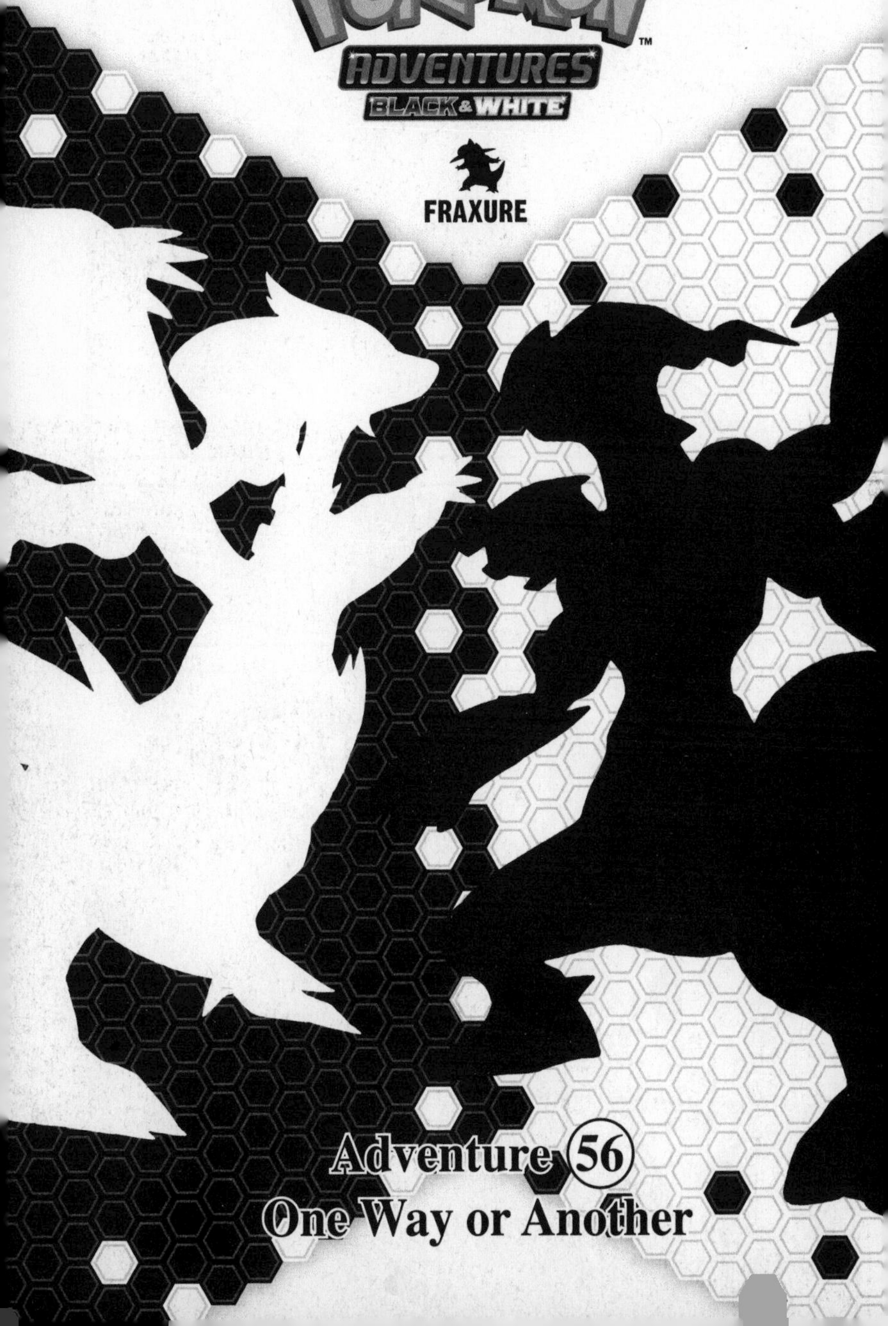

# Adventure 56
## One Way or Another

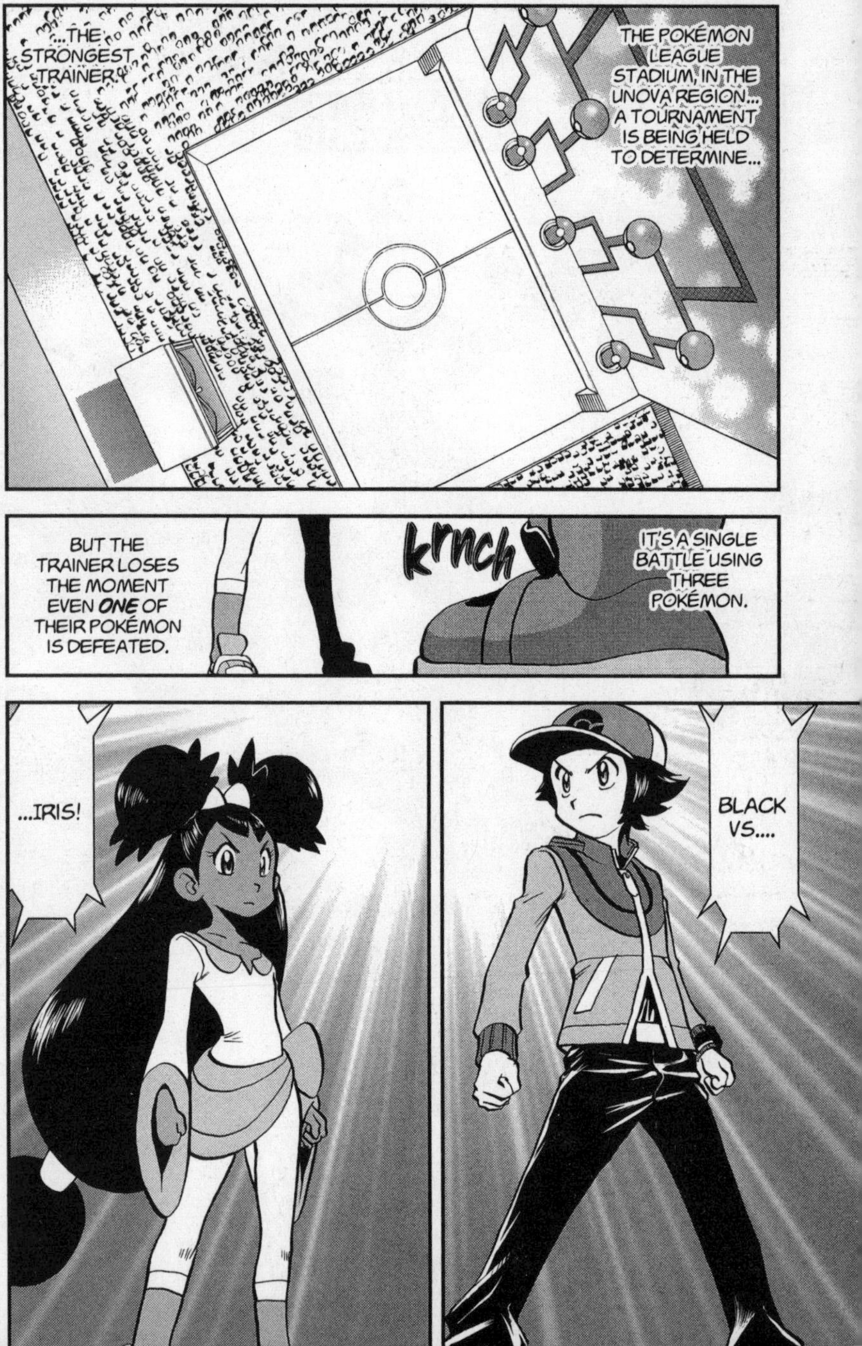
THE POKÉMON LEAGUE STADIUM, IN THE UNOVA REGION... A TOURNAMENT IS BEING HELD TO DETERMINE...
...THE STRONGEST TRAINER!
IT'S A SINGLE BATTLE USING THREE POKÉMON.
krnch
BUT THE TRAINER LOSES THE MOMENT EVEN ONE OF THEIR POKÉMON IS DEFEATED.
BLACK VS....
...IRIS!

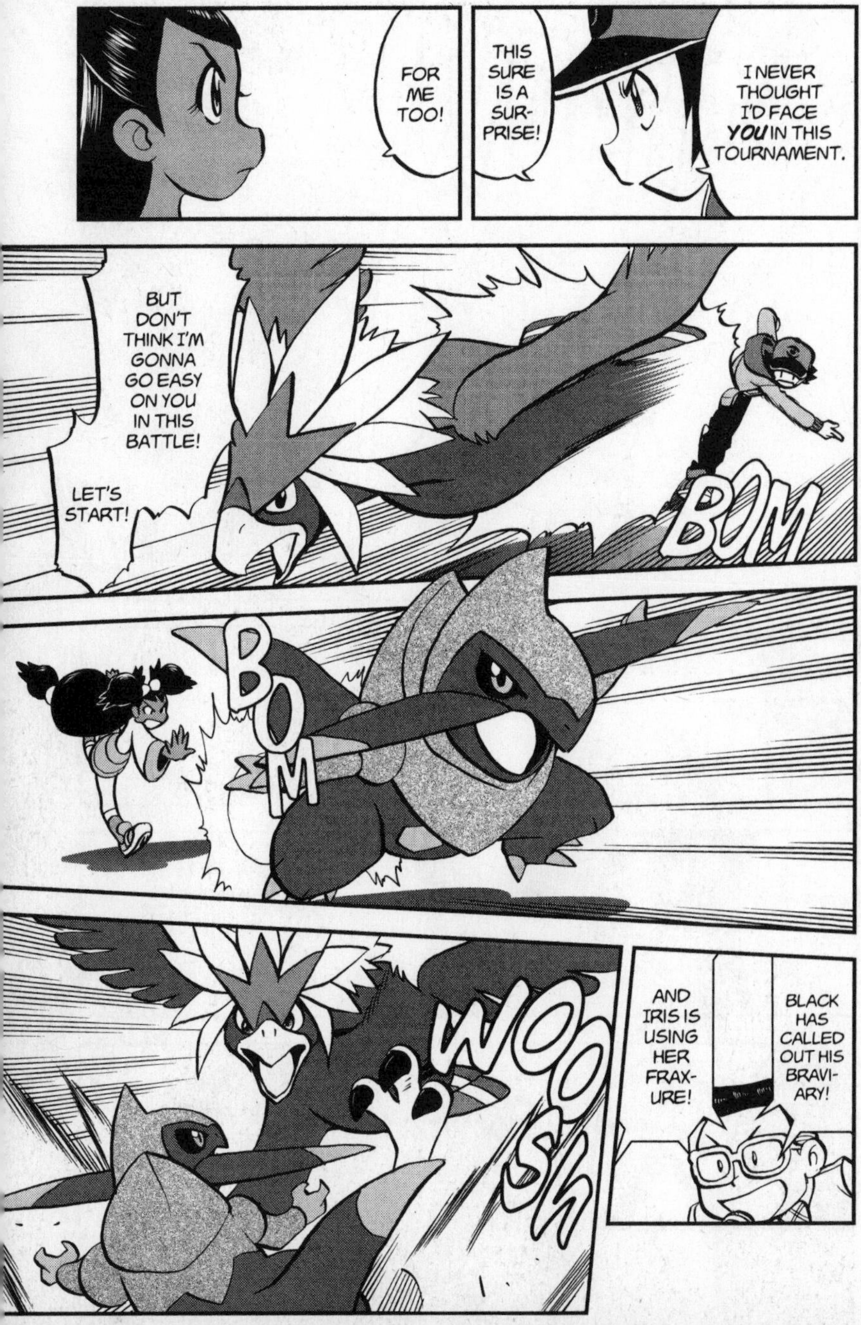

I NEVER THOUGHT I'D FACE ***YOU*** IN THIS TOURNAMENT.
THIS SURE IS A SUR-PRISE!
FOR ME TOO!
BUT DON'T THINK I'M GONNA GO EASY ON YOU IN THIS BATTLE!
LET'S START!
BOM
BOM
BLACK HAS CALLED OUT HIS BRAVI-ARY!
AND IRIS IS USING HER FRAX-URE!
WOOOSH

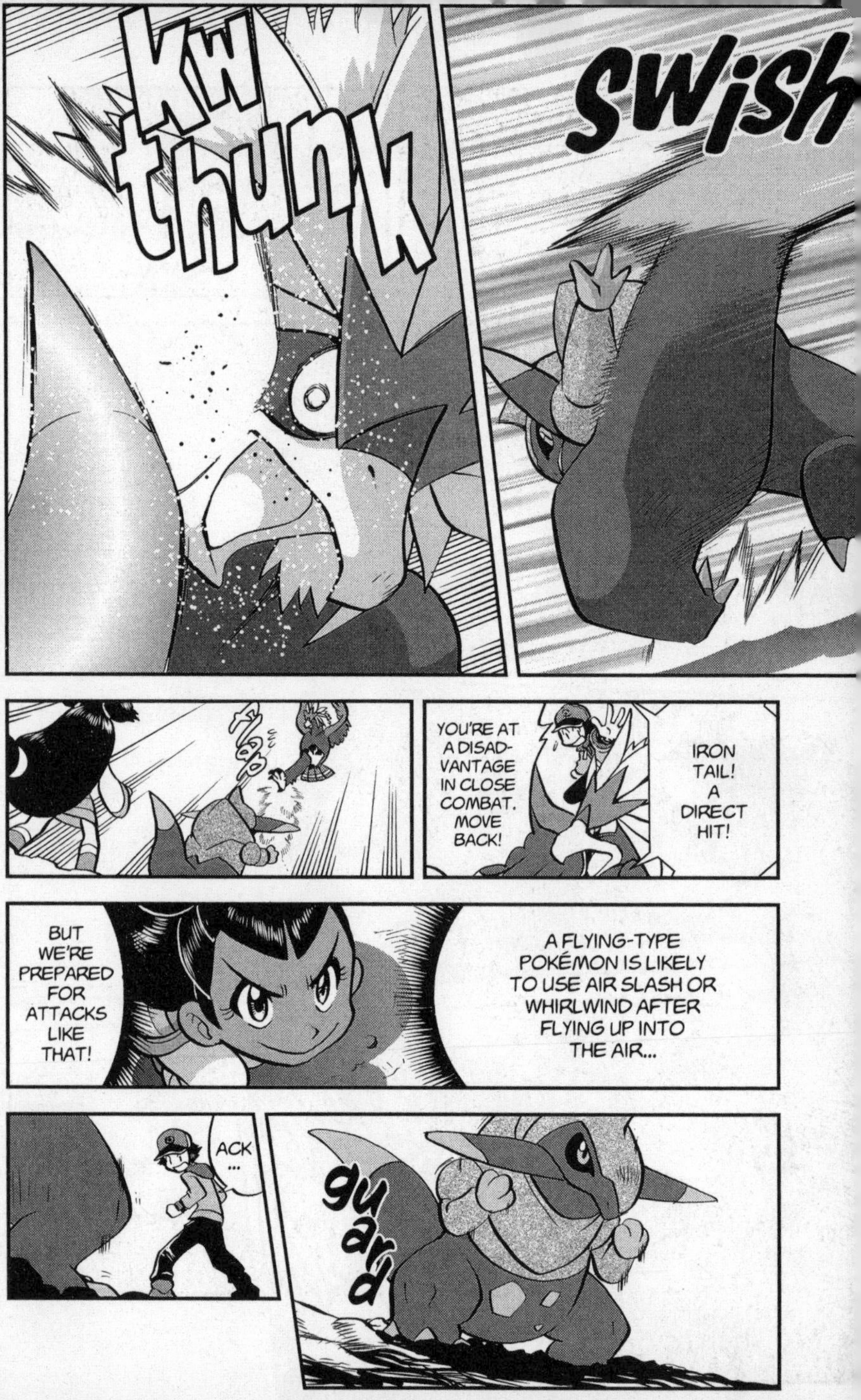
SWISH
KW
THUNK
IRON TAIL! A DIRECT HIT!
YOU'RE AT A DISAD-VANTAGE IN CLOSE COMBAT. MOVE BACK!
flap
A FLYING-TYPE POKÉMON IS LIKELY TO USE AIR SLASH OR WHIRLWIND AFTER FLYING UP INTO THE AIR...
BUT WE'RE PREPARED FOR ATTACKS LIKE THAT!
guard
ACK ...

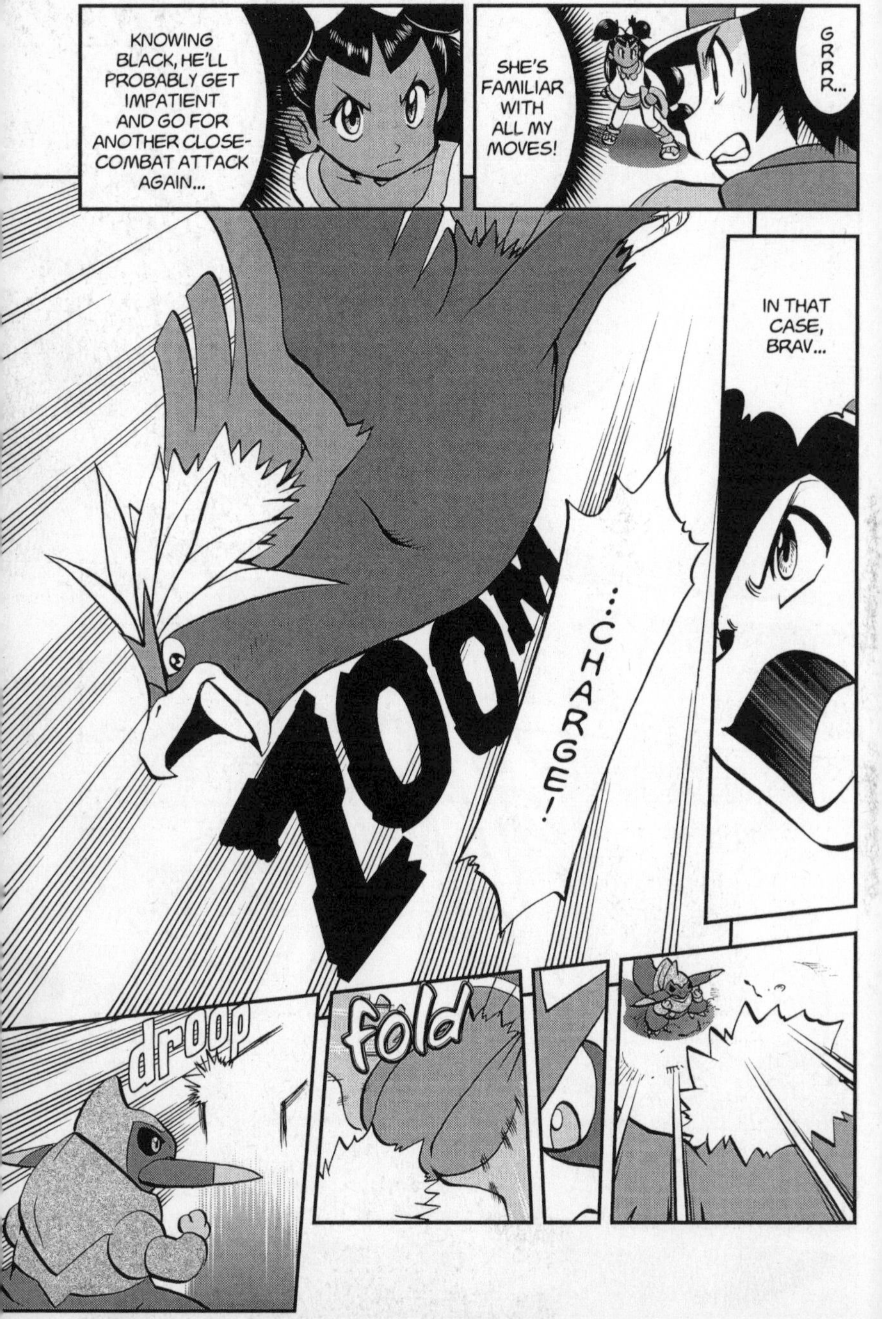
GRRR...
SHE'S FAMILIAR WITH ALL MY MOVES!
KNOWING BLACK, HE'LL PROBABLY GET IMPATIENT AND GO FOR ANOTHER CLOSE-COMBAT ATTACK AGAIN...
IN THAT CASE, BRAV...
...CHARGE!
ZOOM
fold
droop

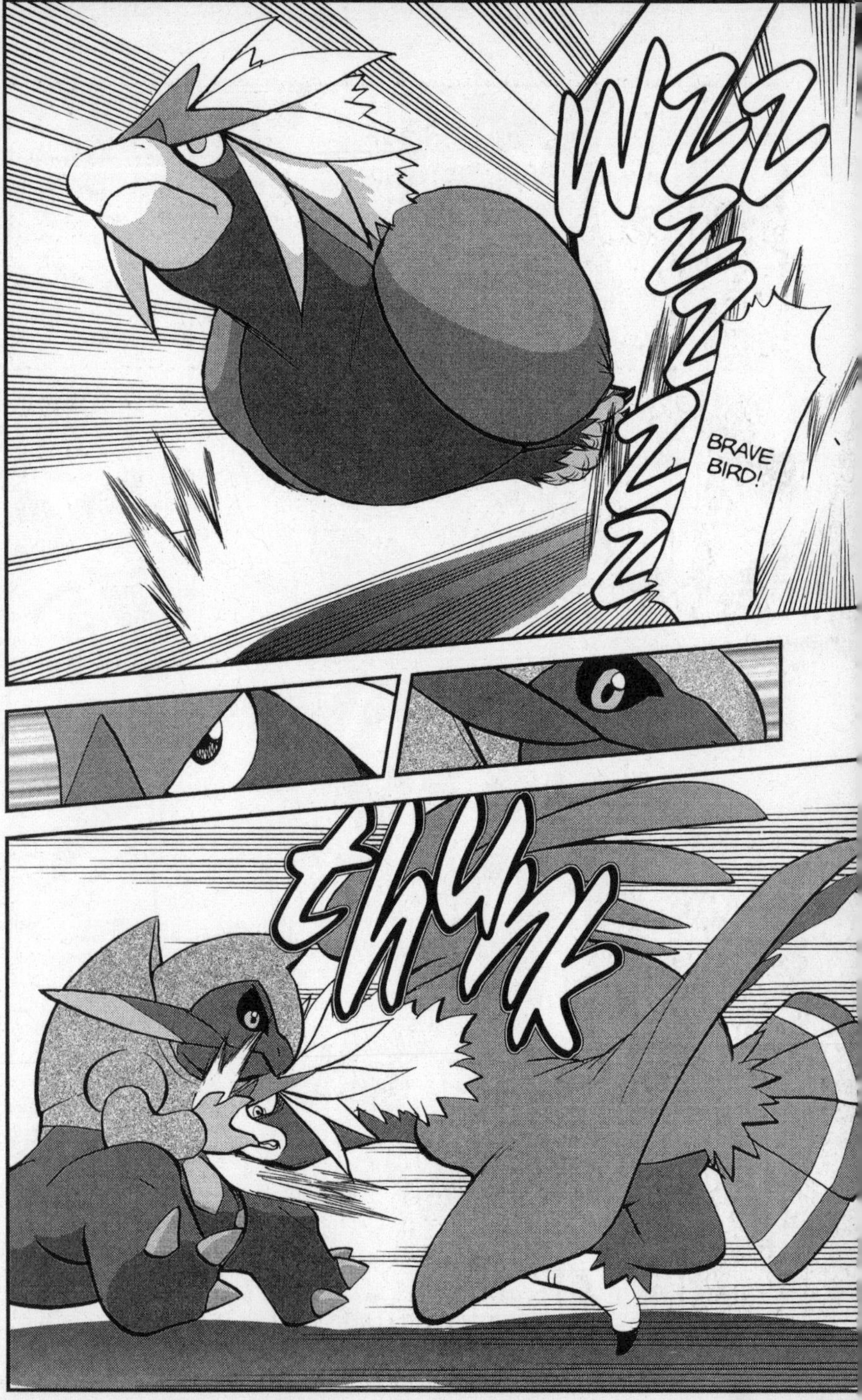
BRAVE BIRD!
WZZZZZZZ
thuk

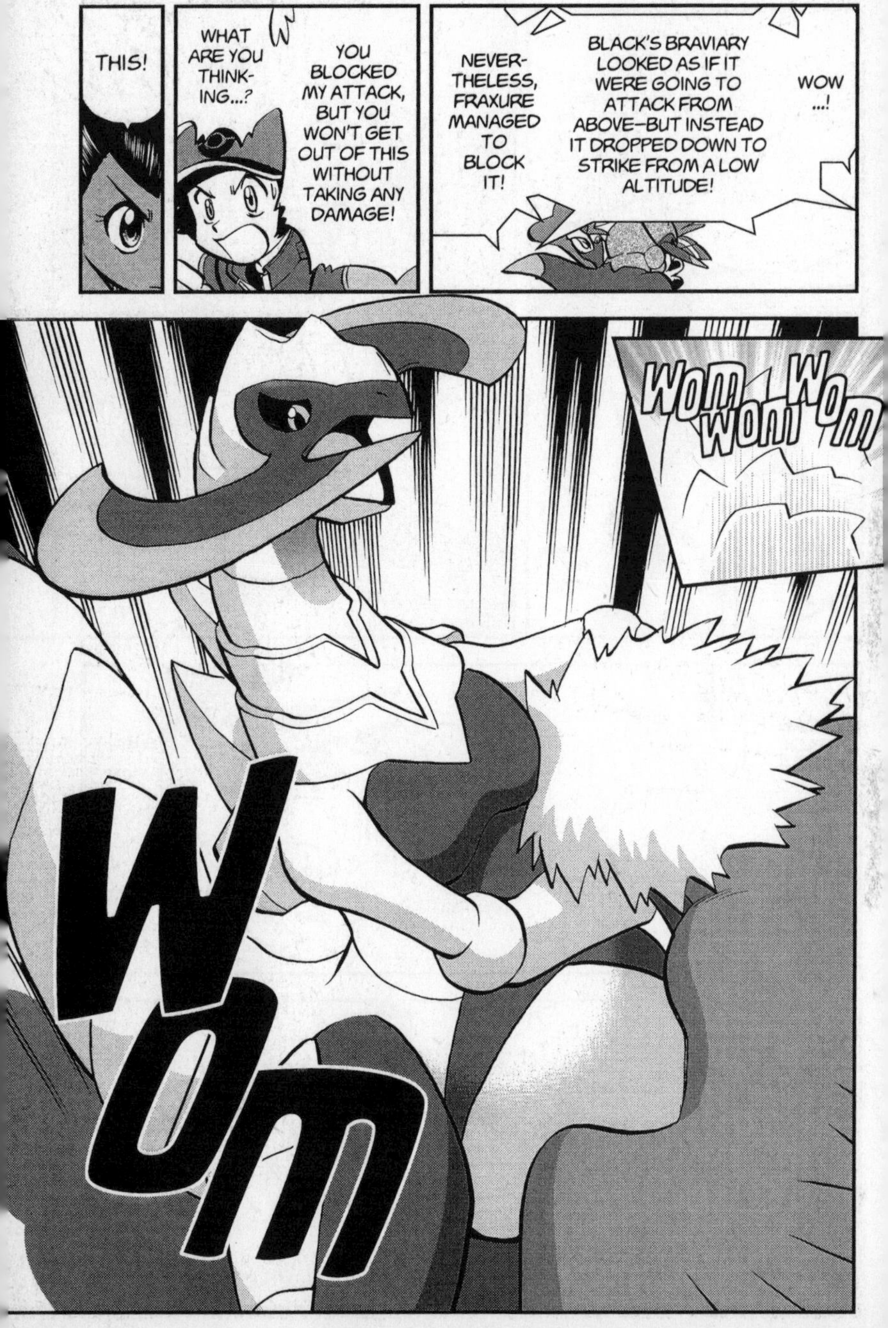
WOW ...!
BLACK'S BRAVIARY LOOKED AS IF IT WERE GOING TO ATTACK FROM ABOVE—BUT INSTEAD IT DROPPED DOWN TO STRIKE FROM A LOW ALTITUDE!
NEVER-THELESS, FRAXURE MANAGED TO BLOCK IT!
YOU BLOCKED MY ATTACK, BUT YOU WON'T GET OUT OF THIS WITHOUT TAKING ANY DAMAGE!
WHAT ARE YOU THINKING...?
THIS!
WOM WOM WOM WOM
WOM

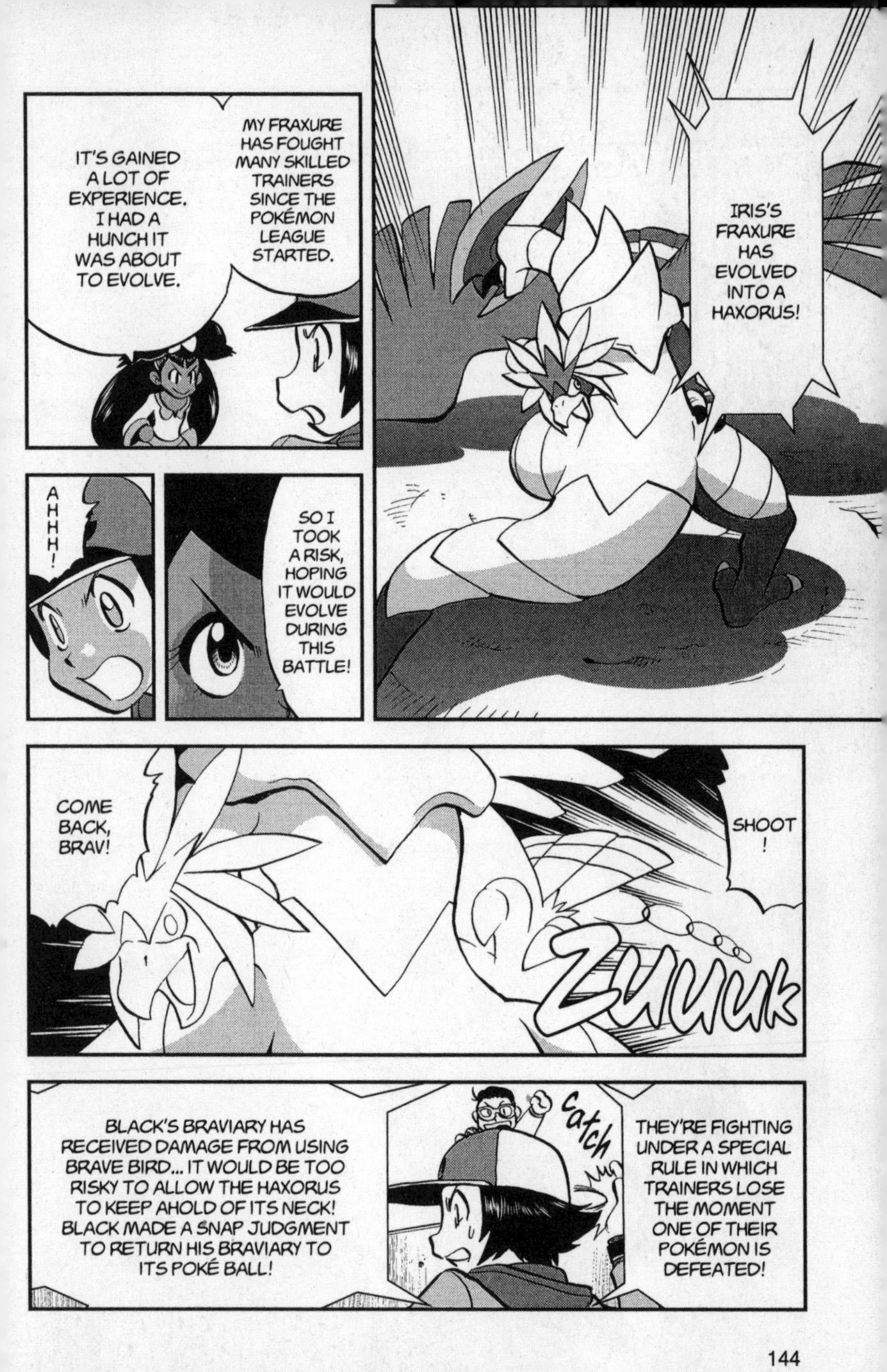
IRIS'S FRAXURE HAS EVOLVED INTO A HAXORUS!
MY FRAXURE HAS FOUGHT MANY SKILLED TRAINERS SINCE THE POKÉMON LEAGUE STARTED.
IT'S GAINED A LOT OF EXPERIENCE. I HAD A HUNCH IT WAS ABOUT TO EVOLVE.
SO I TOOK A RISK, HOPING IT WOULD EVOLVE DURING THIS BATTLE!
AHHH!
SHOOT!
COME BACK, BRAV!
ZUUUK
THEY'RE FIGHTING UNDER A SPECIAL RULE IN WHICH TRAINERS LOSE THE MOMENT ONE OF THEIR POKÉMON IS DEFEATED!
catch
BLACK'S BRAVIARY HAS RECEIVED DAMAGE FROM USING BRAVE BIRD... IT WOULD BE TOO RISKY TO ALLOW THE HAXORUS TO KEEP AHOLD OF ITS NECK! BLACK MADE A SNAP JUDGMENT TO RETURN HIS BRAVIARY TO ITS POKÉ BALL!

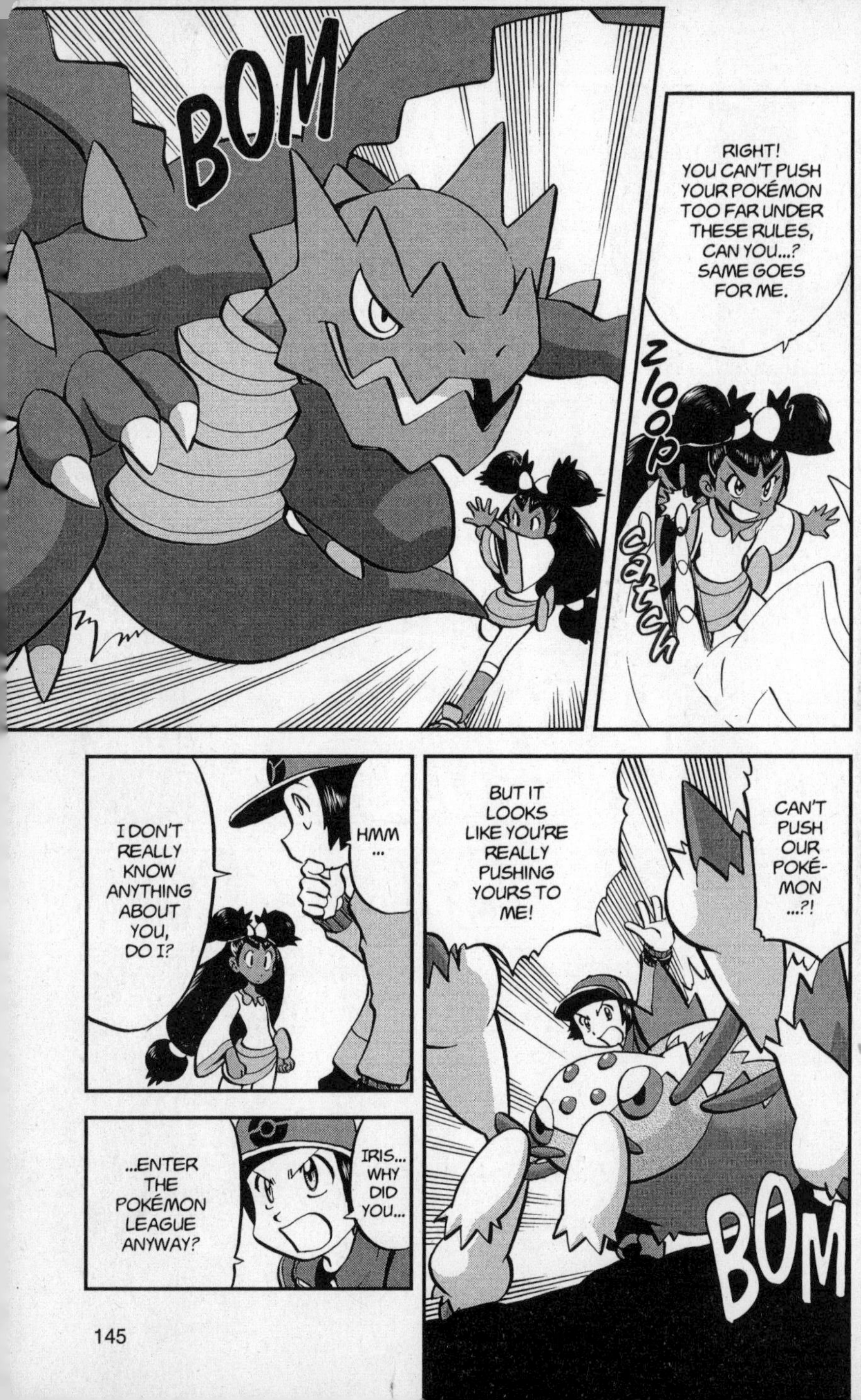
RIGHT! YOU CAN'T PUSH YOUR POKÉMON TOO FAR UNDER THESE RULES, CAN YOU...? SAME GOES FOR ME.
ZLOOP
CATCH
BOM
CAN'T PUSH OUR POKÉ-MON ...?!
BUT IT LOOKS LIKE YOU'RE REALLY PUSHING YOURS TO ME!
BOM
HMM ...
I DON'T REALLY KNOW ANYTHING ABOUT YOU, DO I?
IRIS... WHY DID YOU...
...ENTER THE POKÉMON LEAGUE ANYWAY?

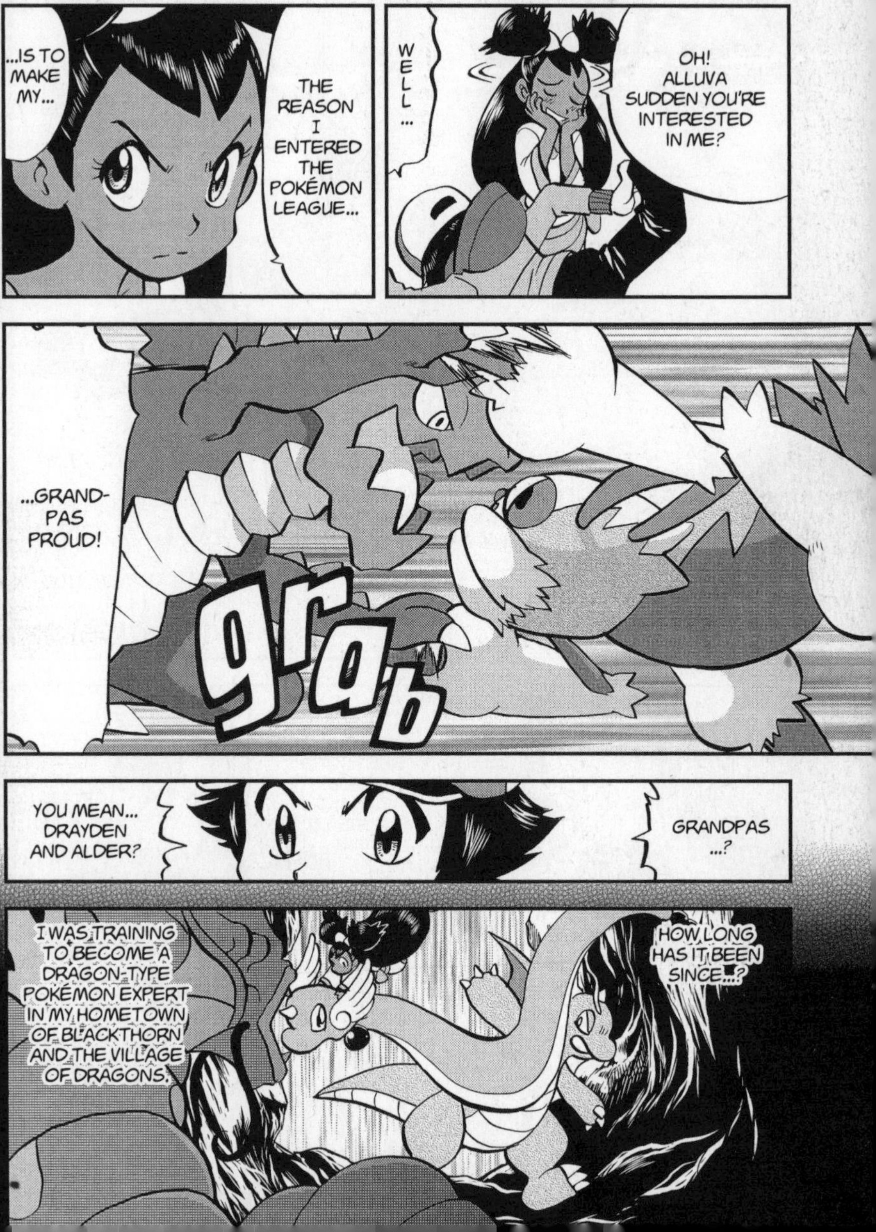
OH! ALLUVA SUDDEN YOU'RE INTERESTED IN ME?
WELL...
THE REASON I ENTERED THE POKÉMON LEAGUE...
...IS TO MAKE MY...
...GRAND-PAS PROUD!
grab
GRANDPAS ...?
YOU MEAN... DRAYDEN AND ALDER?
HOW LONG HAS IT BEEN SINCE...?
I WAS TRAINING TO BECOME A DRAGON-TYPE POKÉMON EXPERT IN MY HOMETOWN OF BLACKTHORN AND THE VILLAGE OF DRAGONS.

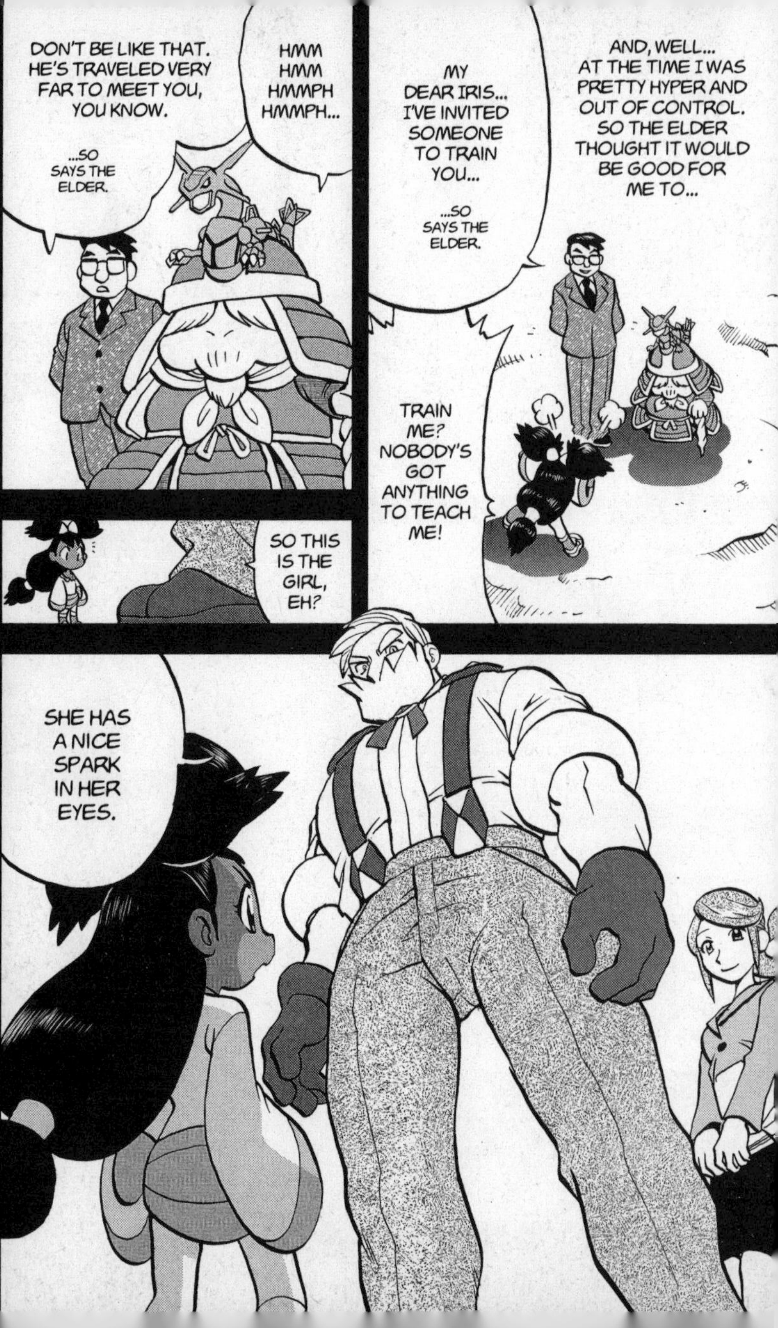
AND, WELL... AT THE TIME I WAS PRETTY HYPER AND OUT OF CONTROL. SO THE ELDER THOUGHT IT WOULD BE GOOD FOR ME TO...
MY DEAR IRIS... I'VE INVITED SOMEONE TO TRAIN YOU...
...SO SAYS THE ELDER.
TRAIN ME? NOBODY'S GOT ANYTHING TO TEACH ME!
HMM HMM HMMPH HMMPH...
DON'T BE LIKE THAT. HE'S TRAVELED VERY FAR TO MEET YOU, YOU KNOW.
...SO SAYS THE ELDER.
SO THIS IS THE GIRL, EH?
SHE HAS A NICE SPARK IN HER EYES.

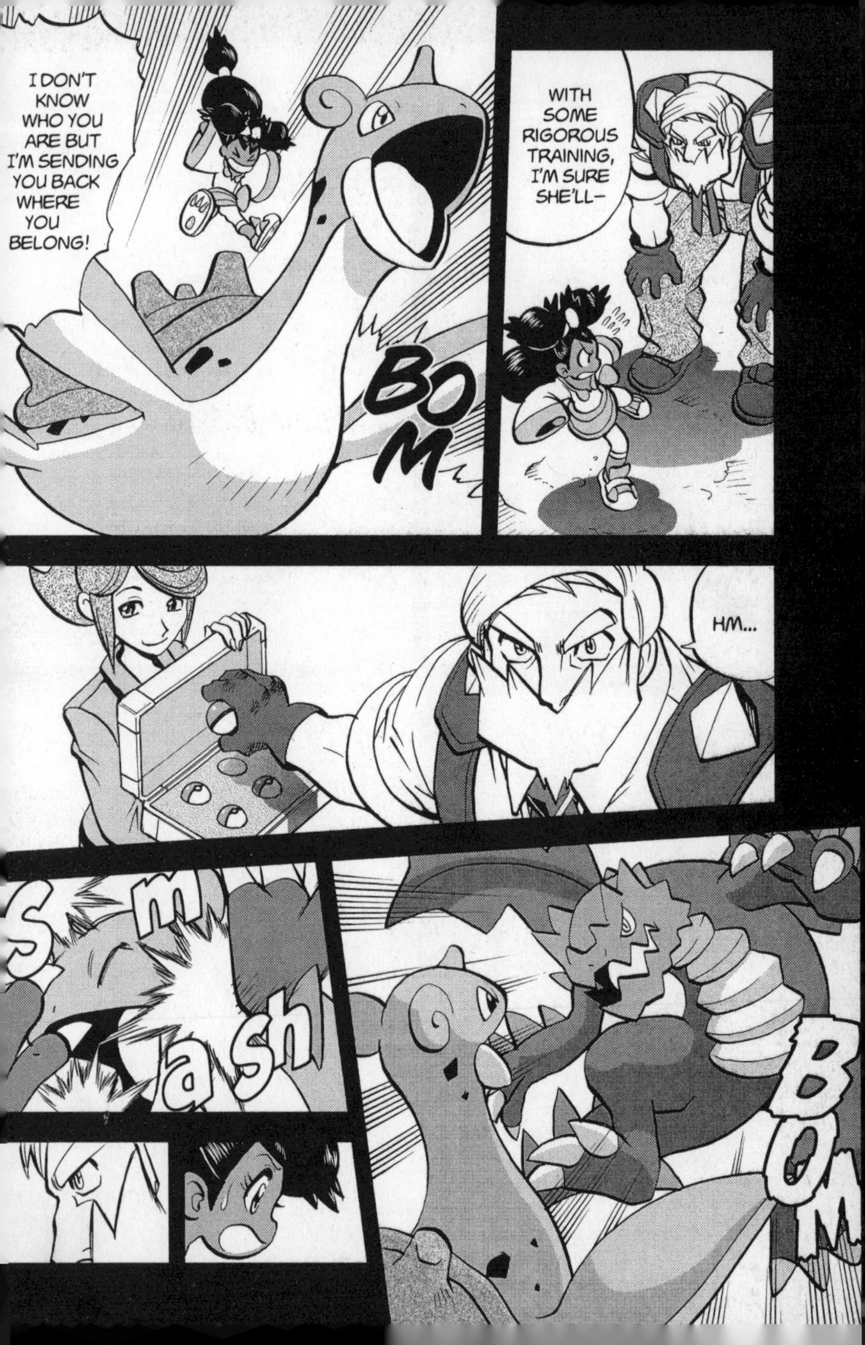
WITH SOME RIGOROUS TRAINING, I'M SURE SHE'LL—
I DON'T KNOW WHO YOU ARE BUT I'M SENDING YOU BACK WHERE YOU BELONG!
BOOM
HM...
BOOM
Smash

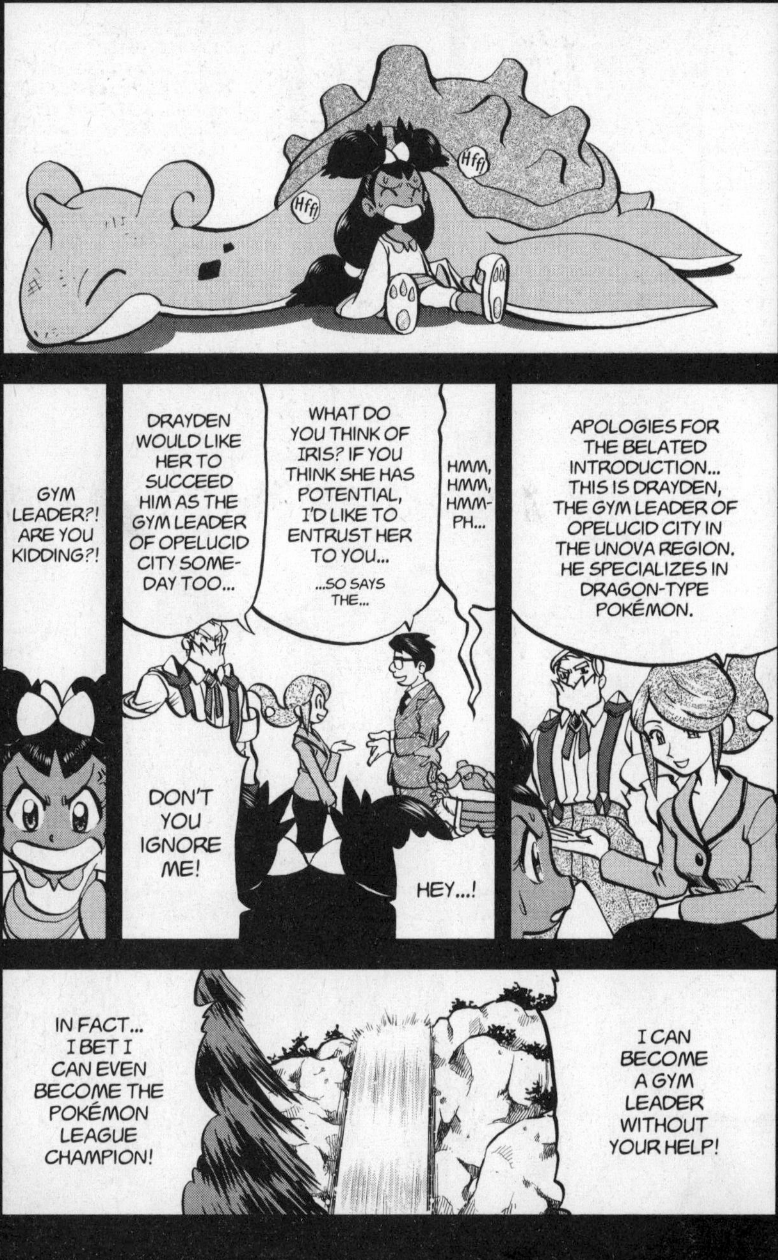
Hffi
Hffi
APOLOGIES FOR THE BELATED INTRODUCTION... THIS IS DRAYDEN, THE GYM LEADER OF OPELUCID CITY IN THE UNOVA REGION. HE SPECIALIZES IN DRAGON-TYPE POKÉMON.
HMM, HMM, HMM-PH...
WHAT DO YOU THINK OF IRIS? IF YOU THINK SHE HAS POTENTIAL, I'D LIKE TO ENTRUST HER TO YOU...
...SO SAYS THE...
DRAYDEN WOULD LIKE HER TO SUCCEED HIM AS THE GYM LEADER OF OPELUCID CITY SOME-DAY TOO...
HEY...!
DON'T YOU IGNORE ME!
GYM LEADER?! ARE YOU KIDDING?!
I CAN BECOME A GYM LEADER WITHOUT YOUR HELP!
IN FACT... I BET I CAN EVEN BECOME THE POKÉMON LEAGUE CHAMPION!

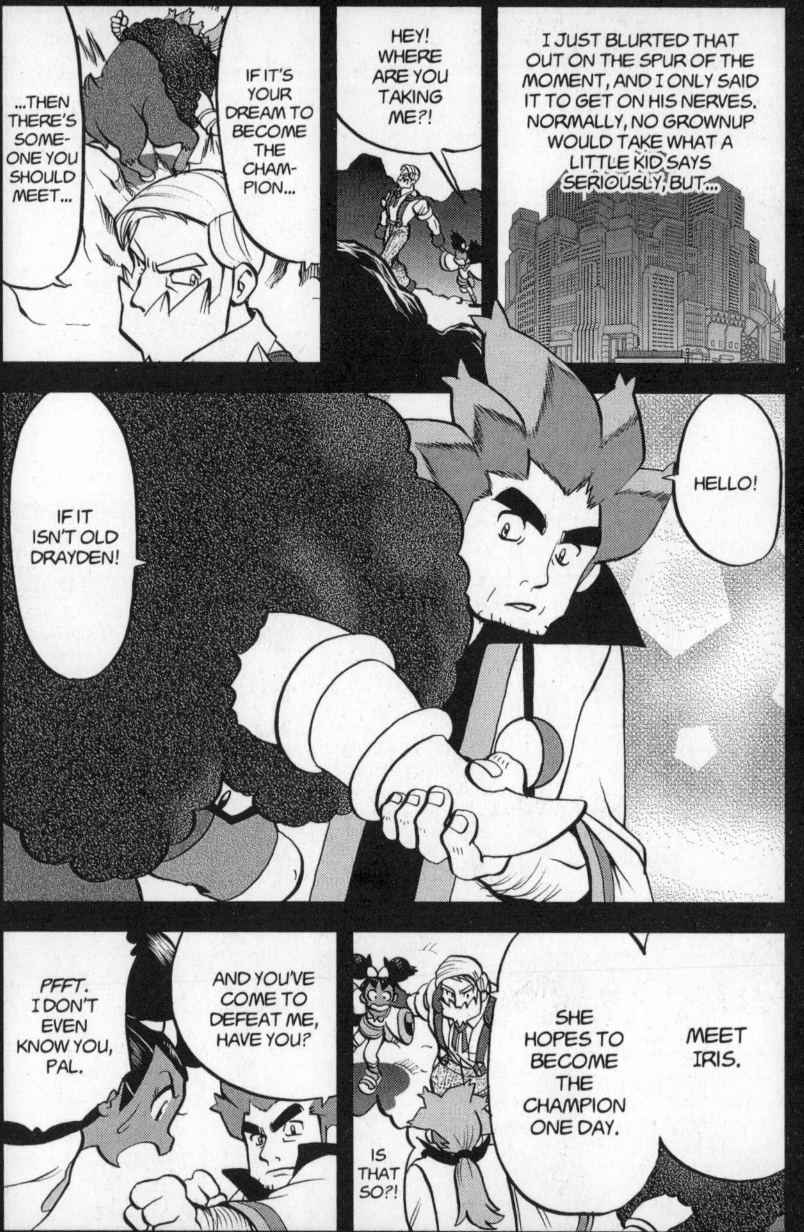
I JUST BLURTED THAT OUT ON THE SPUR OF THE MOMENT, AND I ONLY SAID IT TO GET ON HIS NERVES. NORMALLY, NO GROWNUP WOULD TAKE WHAT A LITTLE KID SAYS SERIOUSLY, BUT...
HEY! WHERE ARE YOU TAKING ME?!
IF IT'S YOUR DREAM TO BECOME THE CHAMPION...
...THEN THERE'S SOMEONE YOU SHOULD MEET...
HELLO!
IF IT ISN'T OLD DRAYDEN!
MEET IRIS.
SHE HOPES TO BECOME THE CHAMPION ONE DAY.
IS THAT SO?!
AND YOU'VE COME TO DEFEAT ME, HAVE YOU?
PFFT. I DON'T EVEN KNOW YOU, PAL.

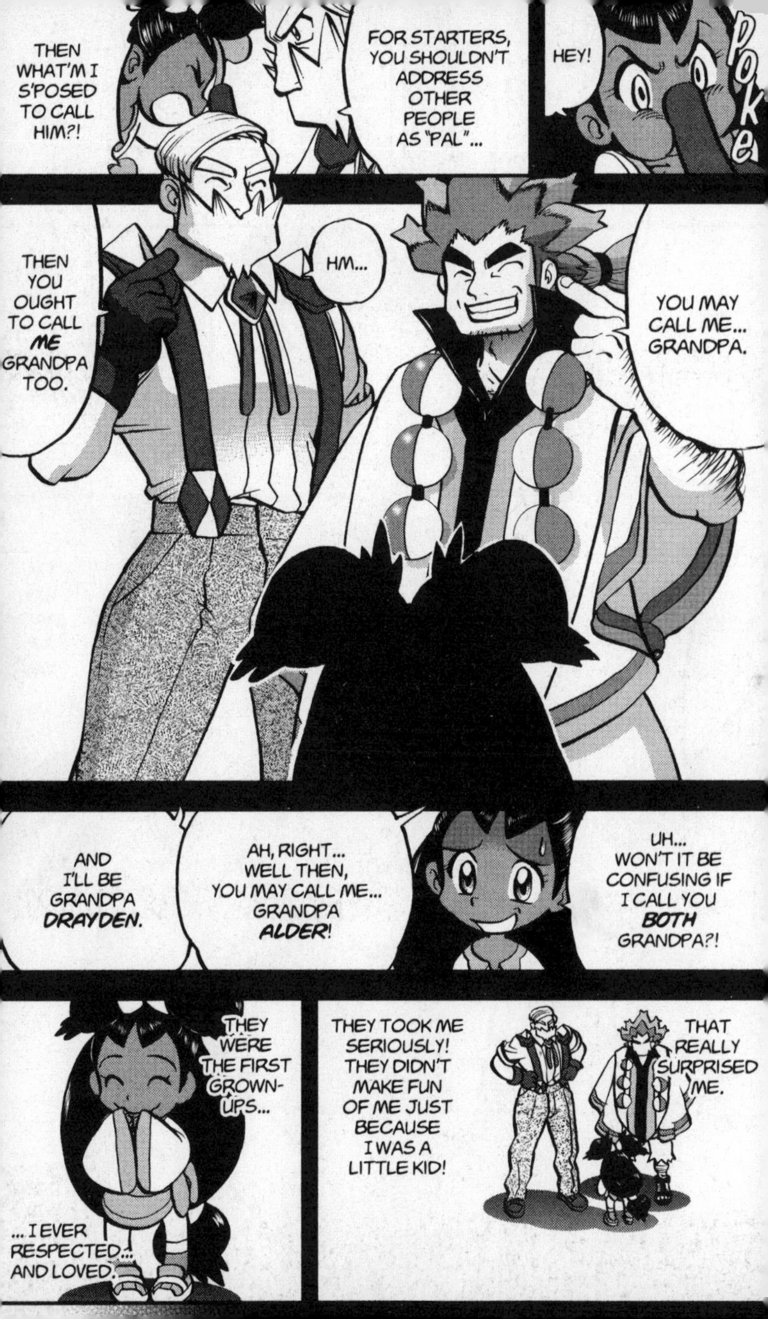
HEY!
POKE
FOR STARTERS, YOU SHOULDN'T ADDRESS OTHER PEOPLE AS "PAL"...
THEN WHAT'M I S'POSED TO CALL HIM?!
YOU MAY CALL ME... GRANDPA.
HM...
THEN YOU OUGHT TO CALL *ME* GRANDPA TOO.
UH... WON'T IT BE CONFUSING IF I CALL YOU ***BOTH*** GRANDPA?!
AH, RIGHT... WELL THEN, YOU MAY CALL ME... GRANDPA ***ALDER***!
AND I'LL BE GRANDPA ***DRAYDEN***.
THAT REALLY SURPRISED ME.
THEY TOOK ME SERIOUSLY! THEY DIDN'T MAKE FUN OF ME JUST BECAUSE I WAS A LITTLE KID!
THEY WERE THE FIRST GROWN-UPS...
...I EVER RESPECTED... AND LOVED.

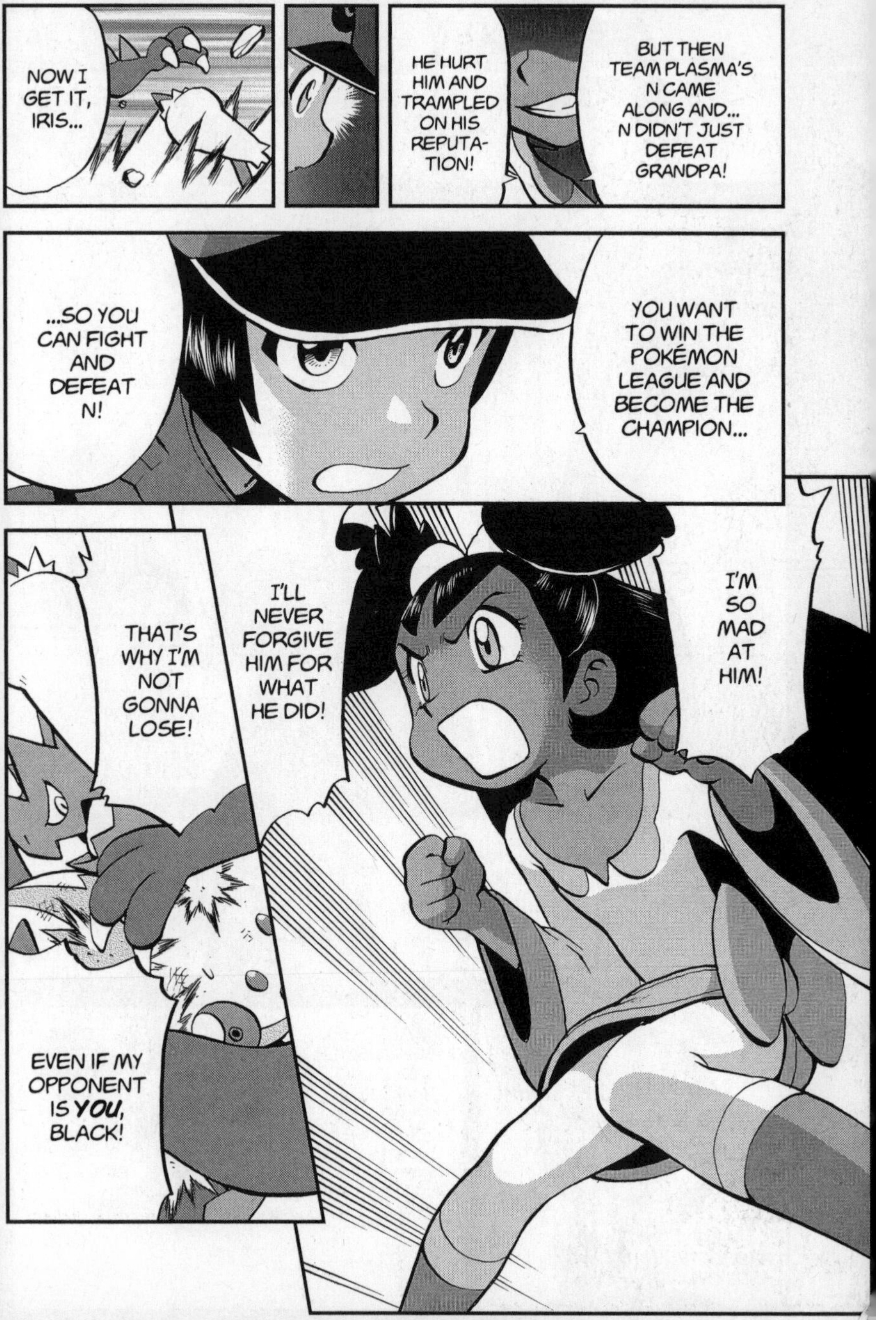
BUT THEN TEAM PLASMA'S N CAME ALONG AND... N DIDN'T JUST DEFEAT GRANDPA!
HE HURT HIM AND TRAMPLED ON HIS REPUTA-TION!
NOW I GET IT, IRIS...
YOU WANT TO WIN THE POKÉMON LEAGUE AND BECOME THE CHAMPION...
...SO YOU CAN FIGHT AND DEFEAT N!
I'M SO MAD AT HIM!
I'LL NEVER FORGIVE HIM FOR WHAT HE DID!
THAT'S WHY I'M NOT GONNA LOSE!
EVEN IF MY OPPONENT IS ***YOU***, BLACK!

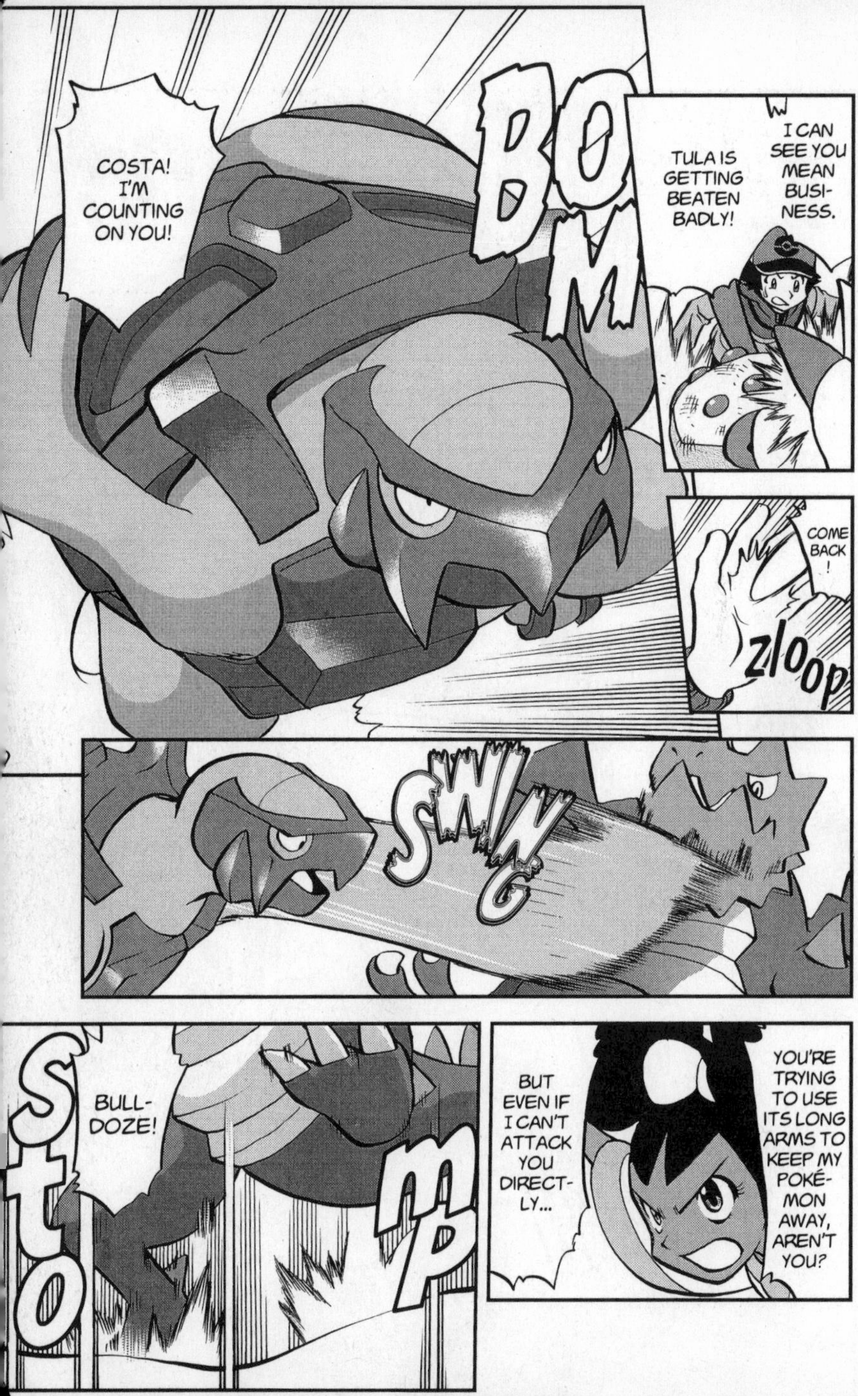
I CAN SEE YOU MEAN BUSI- NESS.
TULA IS GETTING BEATEN BADLY!
COME BACK!
ZLOOP
BOOM
COSTA! I'M COUNTING ON YOU!
SWING
YOU'RE TRYING TO USE ITS LONG ARMS TO KEEP MY POKÉ- MON AWAY, AREN'T YOU?
BUT EVEN IF I CAN'T ATTACK YOU DIRECT- LY...
Stomp
BULL- DOZE!

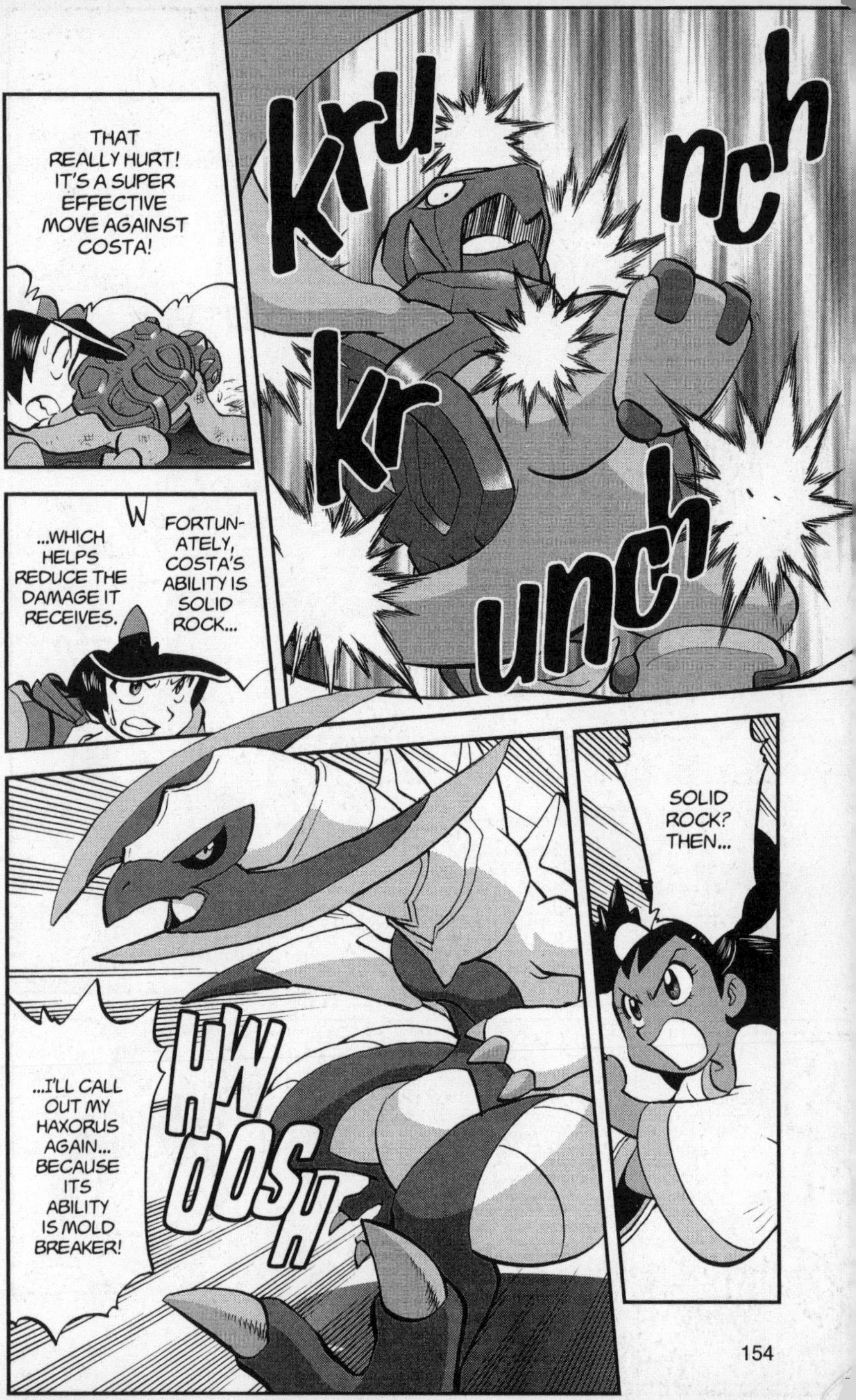
KRUNCH
KRUNCH
THAT REALLY HURT! IT'S A SUPER EFFECTIVE MOVE AGAINST COSTA!
FORTUN-ATELY, COSTA'S ABILITY IS SOLID ROCK...
...WHICH HELPS REDUCE THE DAMAGE IT RECEIVES.
SOLID ROCK? THEN...
...I'LL CALL OUT MY HAXORUS AGAIN... BECAUSE ITS ABILITY IS MOLD BREAKER!
HWOOSH

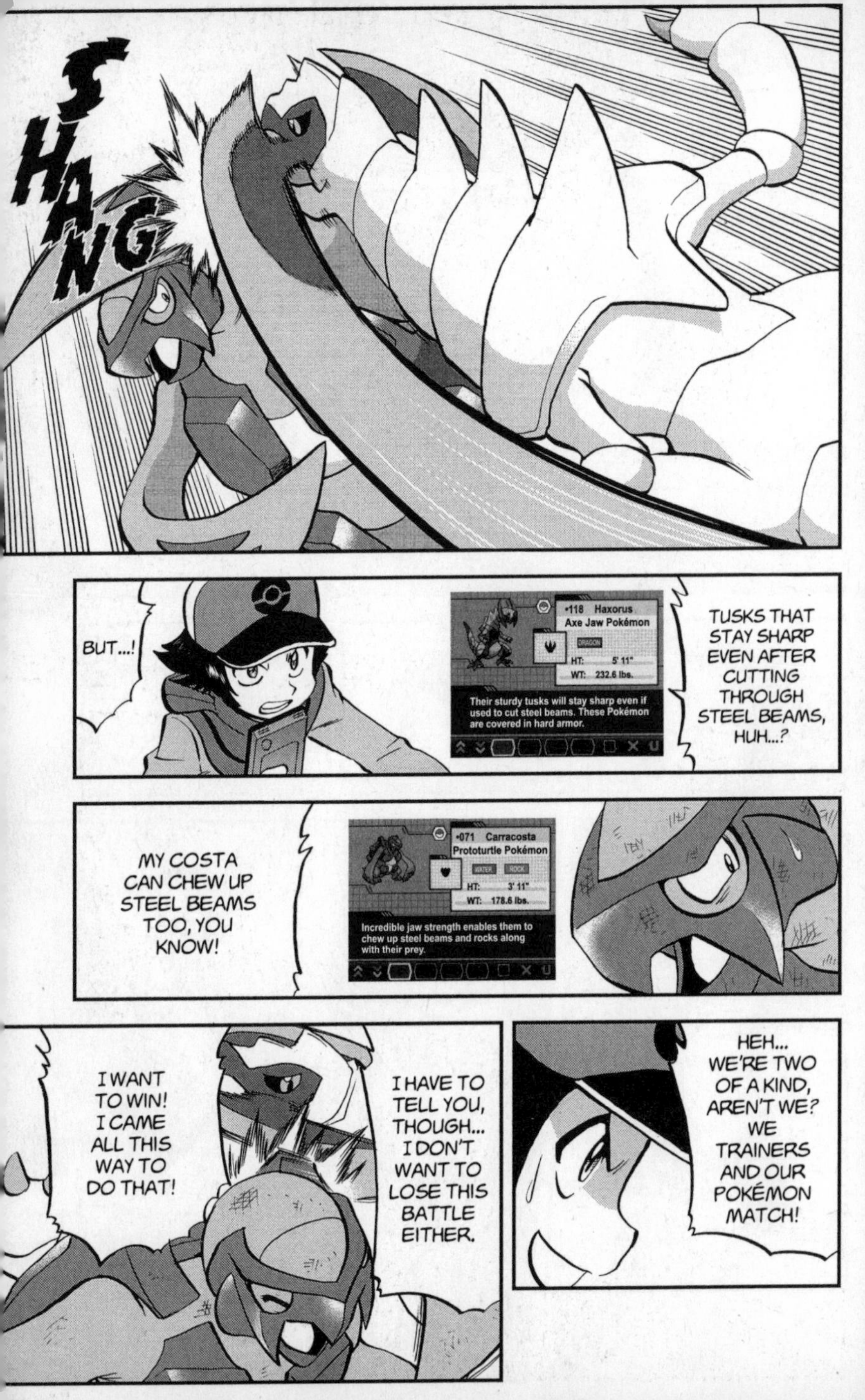
SHANG
TUSKS THAT STAY SHARP EVEN AFTER CUTTING THROUGH STEEL BEAMS, HUH...?
•118 Haxorus
Axe Jaw Pokémon
DRAGON
HT: 5' 11"
WT: 232.6 lbs.
Their sturdy tusks will stay sharp even if used to cut steel beams. These Pokémon are covered in hard armor.
BUT...!
•071 Carracosta
Prototurtle Pokémon
WATER
ROCK
HT: 3' 11"
WT: 178.6 lbs.
Incredible jaw strength enables them to chew up steel beams and rocks along with their prey.
MY COSTA CAN CHEW UP STEEL BEAMS TOO, YOU KNOW!
HEH... WE'RE TWO OF A KIND, AREN'T WE? WE TRAINERS AND OUR POKÉMON MATCH!
I HAVE TO TELL YOU, THOUGH... I DON'T WANT TO LOSE THIS BATTLE EITHER.
I WANT TO WIN! I CAME ALL THIS WAY TO DO THAT!

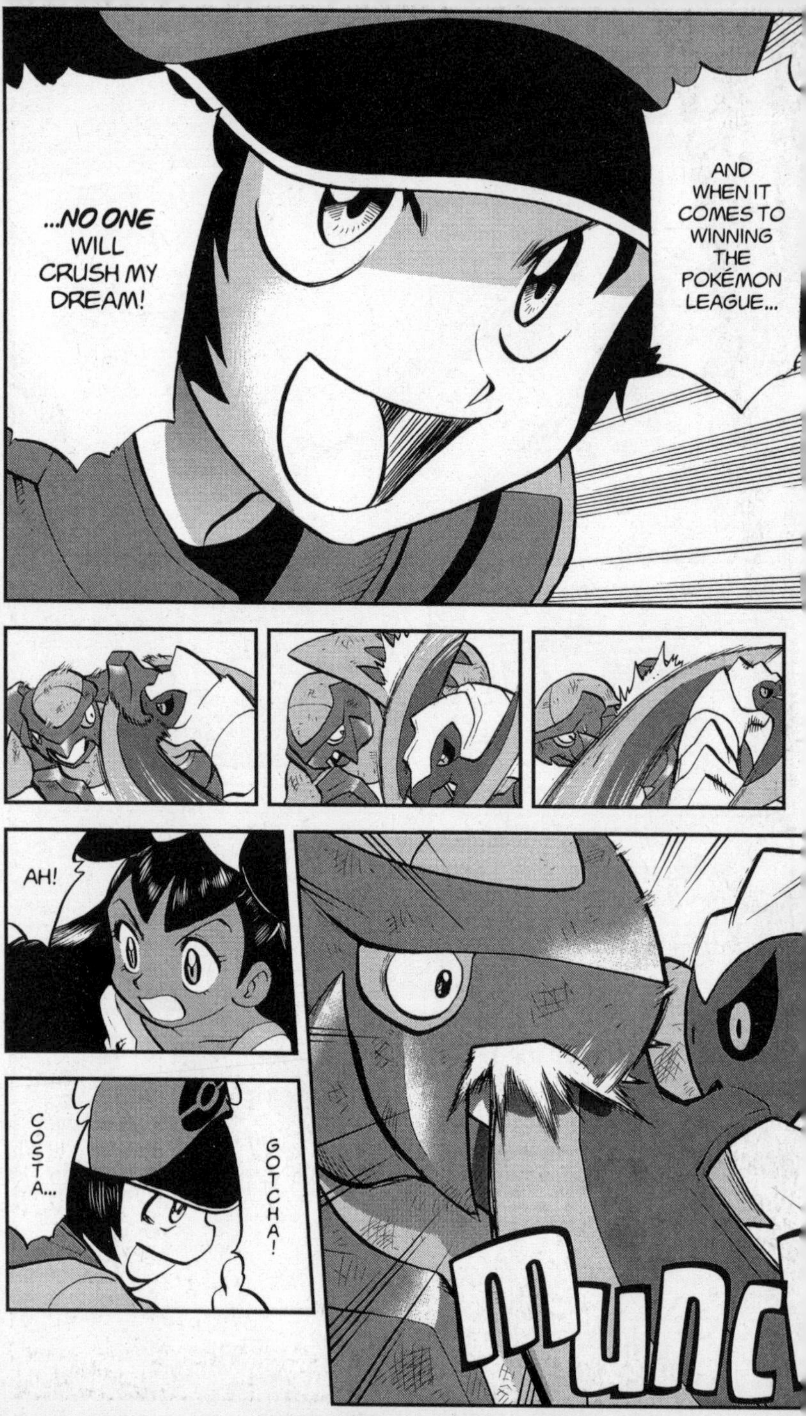
AND WHEN IT COMES TO WINNING THE POKÉMON LEAGUE...
...NO ONE WILL CRUSH MY DREAM!
MUNC
AH!
GOTCHA!
COSTA...

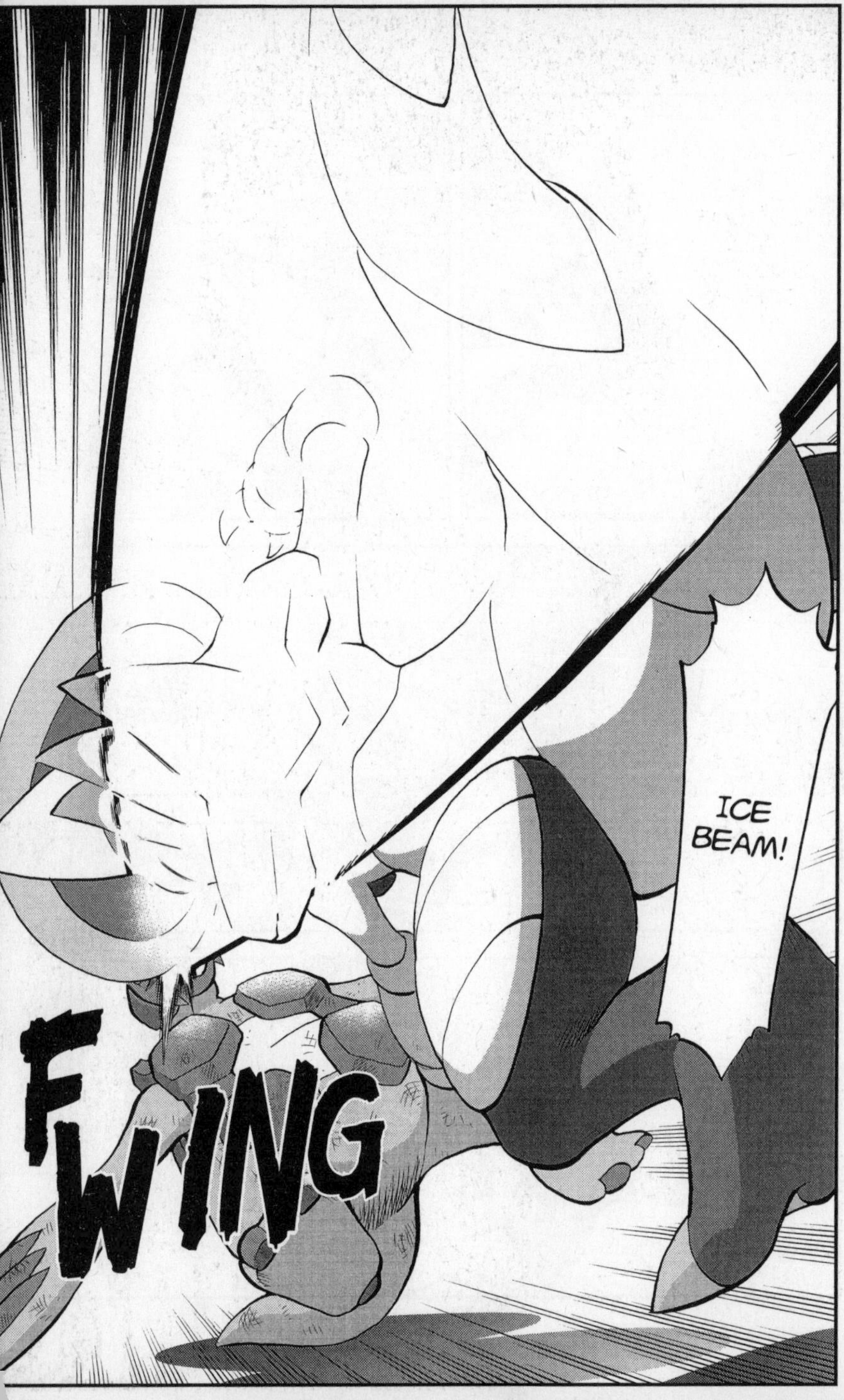
ICE BEAM!
FWING

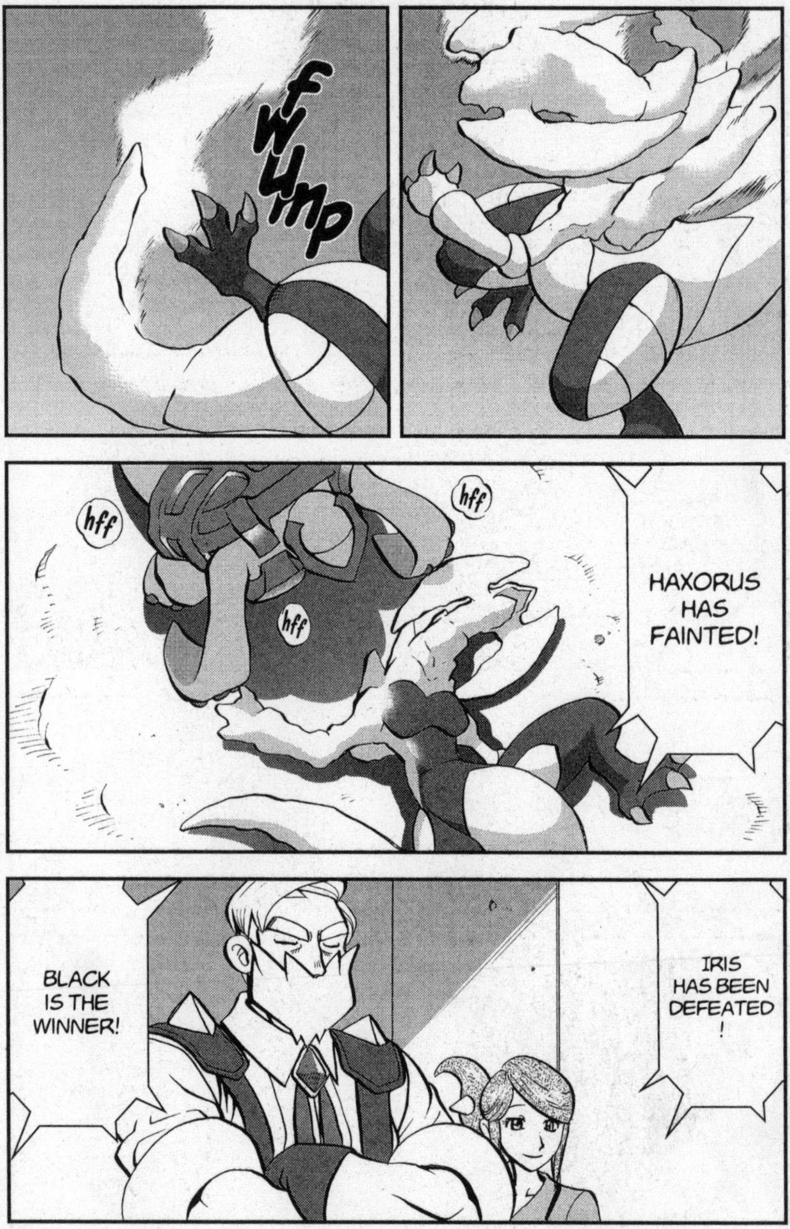
fwump
hff
hff
hff
HAXORUS HAS FAINTED!
IRIS HAS BEEN DEFEATED!
BLACK IS THE WINNER!

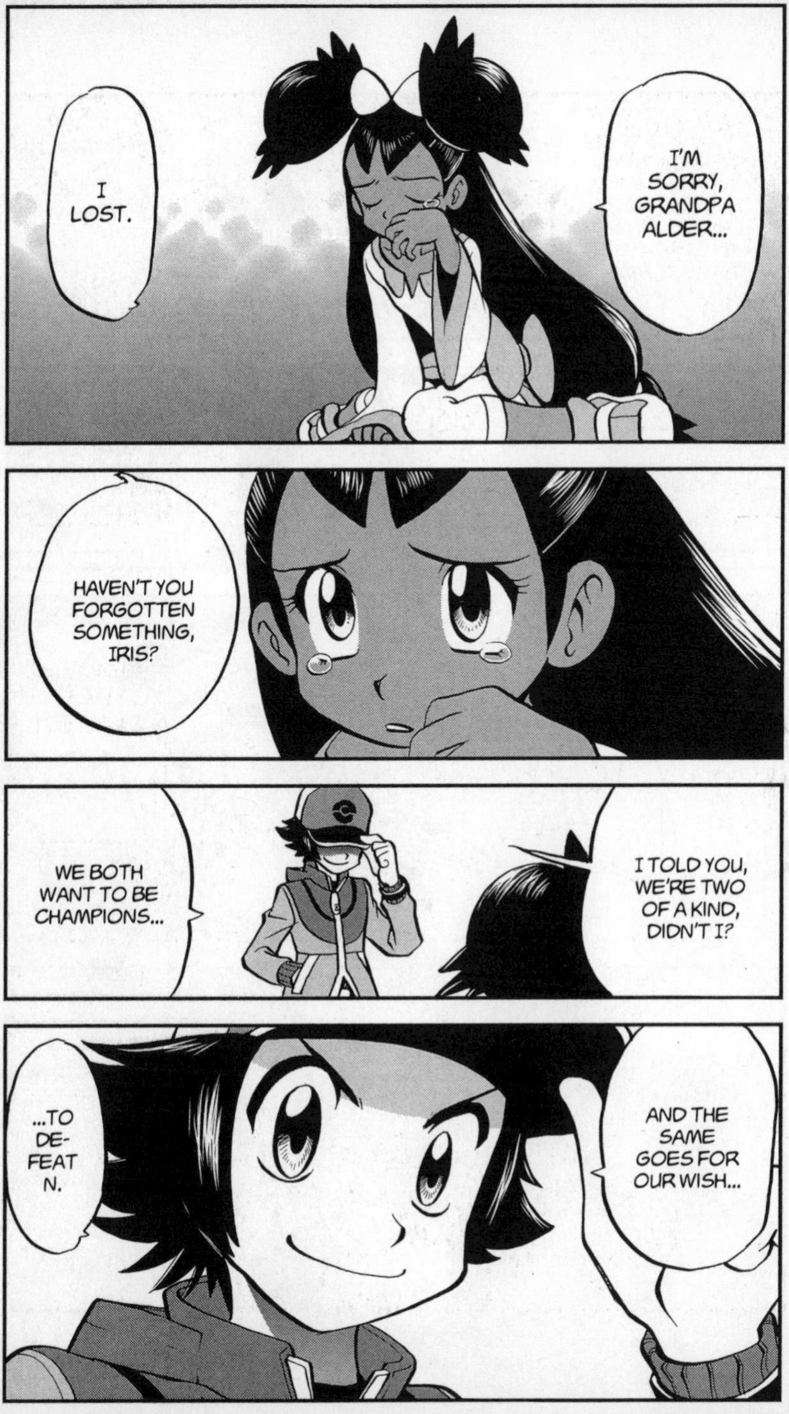
I'M SORRY, GRANDPA ALDER...
I LOST.
HAVEN'T YOU FORGOTTEN SOMETHING, IRIS?
I TOLD YOU, WE'RE TWO OF A KIND, DIDN'T I?
WE BOTH WANT TO BE CHAMPIONS...
AND THE SAME GOES FOR OUR WISH...
...TO DE-FEAT N.

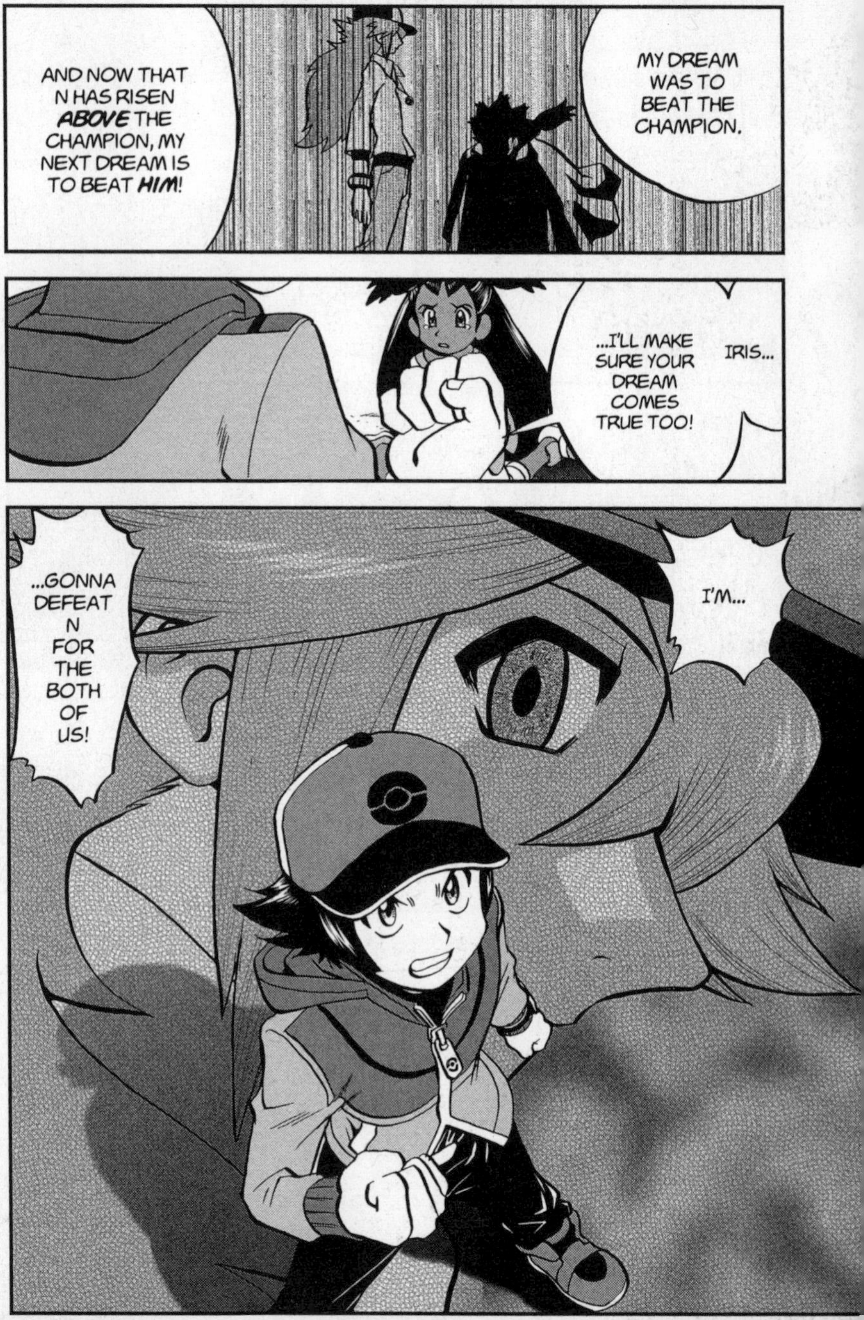
MY DREAM WAS TO BEAT THE CHAMPION.
AND NOW THAT N HAS RISEN ABOVE THE CHAMPION, MY NEXT DREAM IS TO BEAT HIM!
IRIS...
...I'LL MAKE SURE YOUR DREAM COMES TRUE TOO!
I'M...
...GONNA DEFEAT N FOR THE BOTH OF US!

Pokémon™ Adventures Black & White

BEHEEYEM

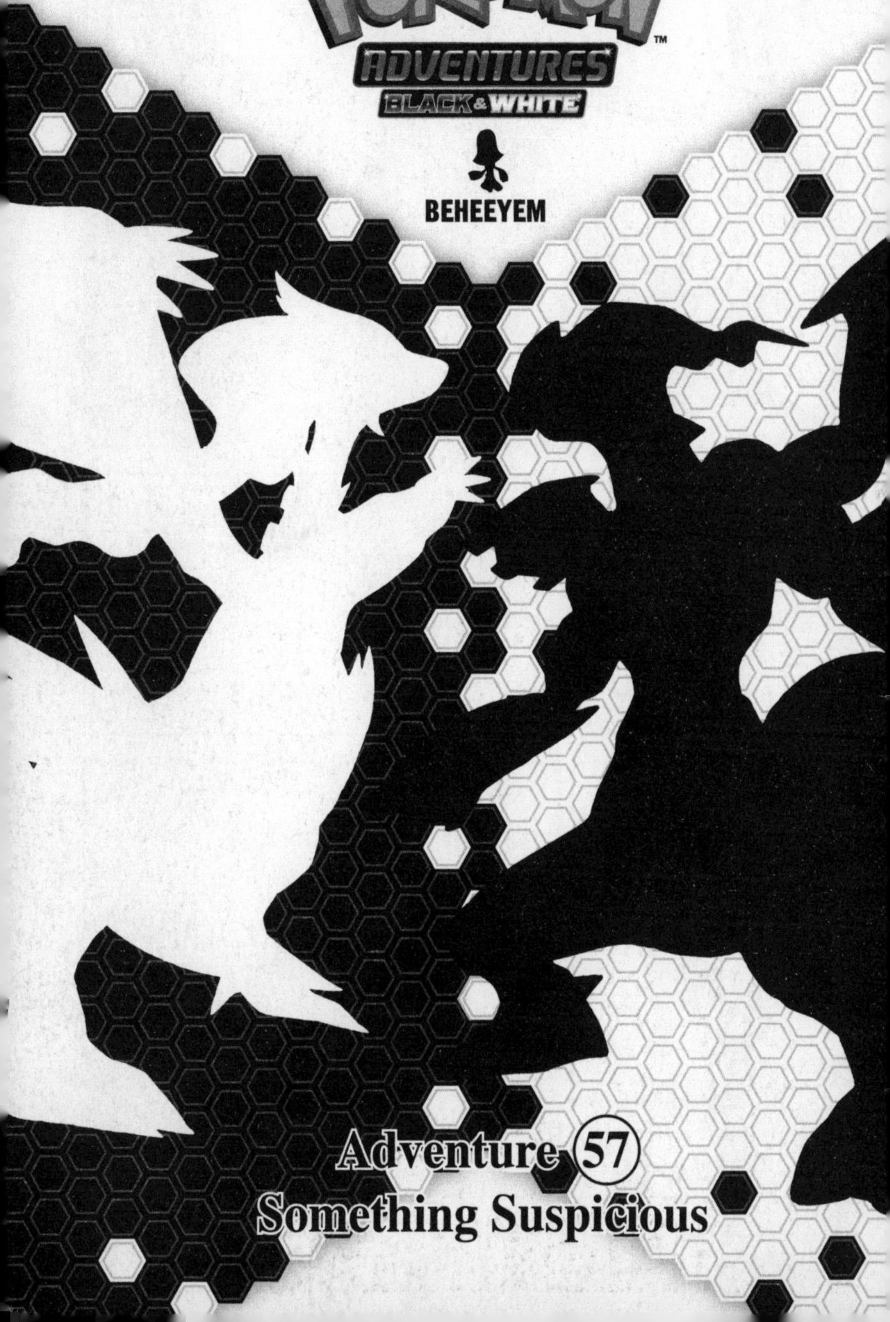

# Adventure 57
# Something Suspicious

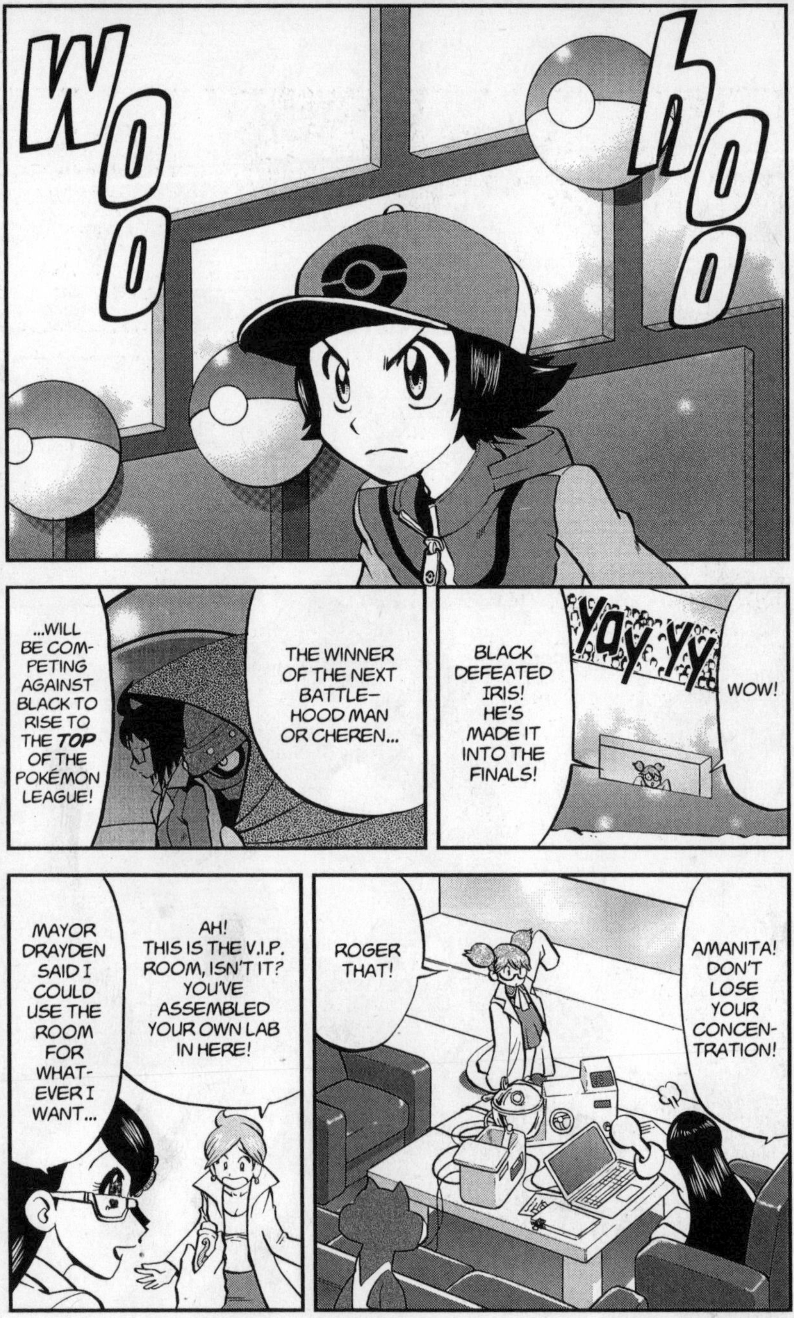
Woo hoo
WOW!
Yay yy
BLACK DEFEATED IRIS! HE'S MADE IT INTO THE FINALS!
THE WINNER OF THE NEXT BATTLE—HOOD MAN OR CHEREN...
...WILL BE COMPETING AGAINST BLACK TO RISE TO THE *TOP* OF THE POKÉMON LEAGUE!
AMANITA! DON'T LOSE YOUR CONCENTRATION!
ROGER THAT!
AH! THIS IS THE V.I.P. ROOM, ISN'T IT? YOU'VE ASSEMBLED YOUR OWN LAB IN HERE!
MAYOR DRAYDEN SAID I COULD USE THE ROOM FOR WHATEVER I WANT...

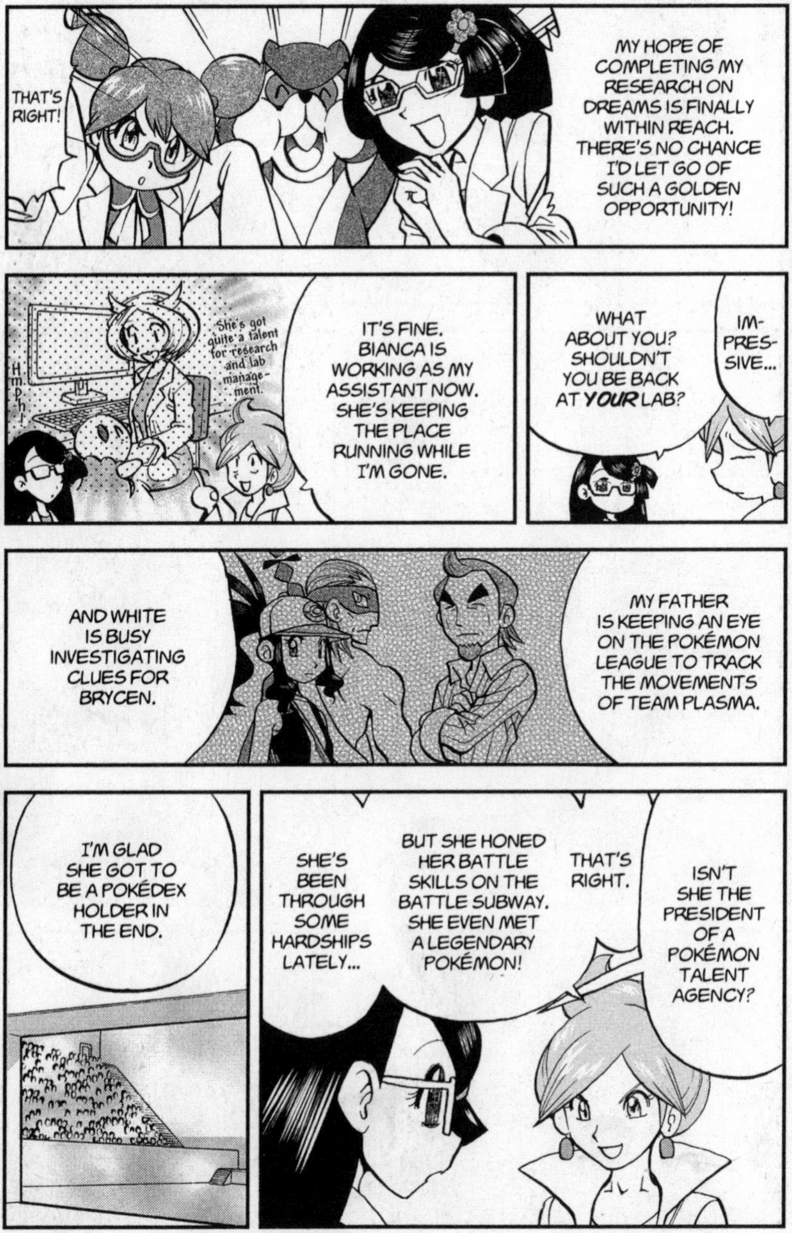
MY HOPE OF COMPLETING MY RESEARCH ON DREAMS IS FINALLY WITHIN REACH. THERE'S NO CHANCE I'D LET GO OF SUCH A GOLDEN OPPORTUNITY!
THAT'S RIGHT!
IM-PRES-SIVE...
WHAT ABOUT YOU? SHOULDN'T YOU BE BACK AT ***YOUR*** LAB?
IT'S FINE. BIANCA IS WORKING AS MY ASSISTANT NOW. SHE'S KEEPING THE PLACE RUNNING WHILE I'M GONE.
She's got quite a talent for research and lab manage-ment.
Hmph!
MY FATHER IS KEEPING AN EYE ON THE POKÉMON LEAGUE TO TRACK THE MOVEMENTS OF TEAM PLASMA.
AND WHITE IS BUSY INVESTIGATING CLUES FOR BRYCEN.
ISN'T SHE THE PRESIDENT OF A POKÉMON TALENT AGENCY?
THAT'S RIGHT.
BUT SHE HONED HER BATTLE SKILLS ON THE BATTLE SUBWAY. SHE EVEN MET A LEGENDARY POKÉMON!
SHE'S BEEN THROUGH SOME HARDSHIPS LATELY...
I'M GLAD SHE GOT TO BE A POKÉDEX HOLDER IN THE END.

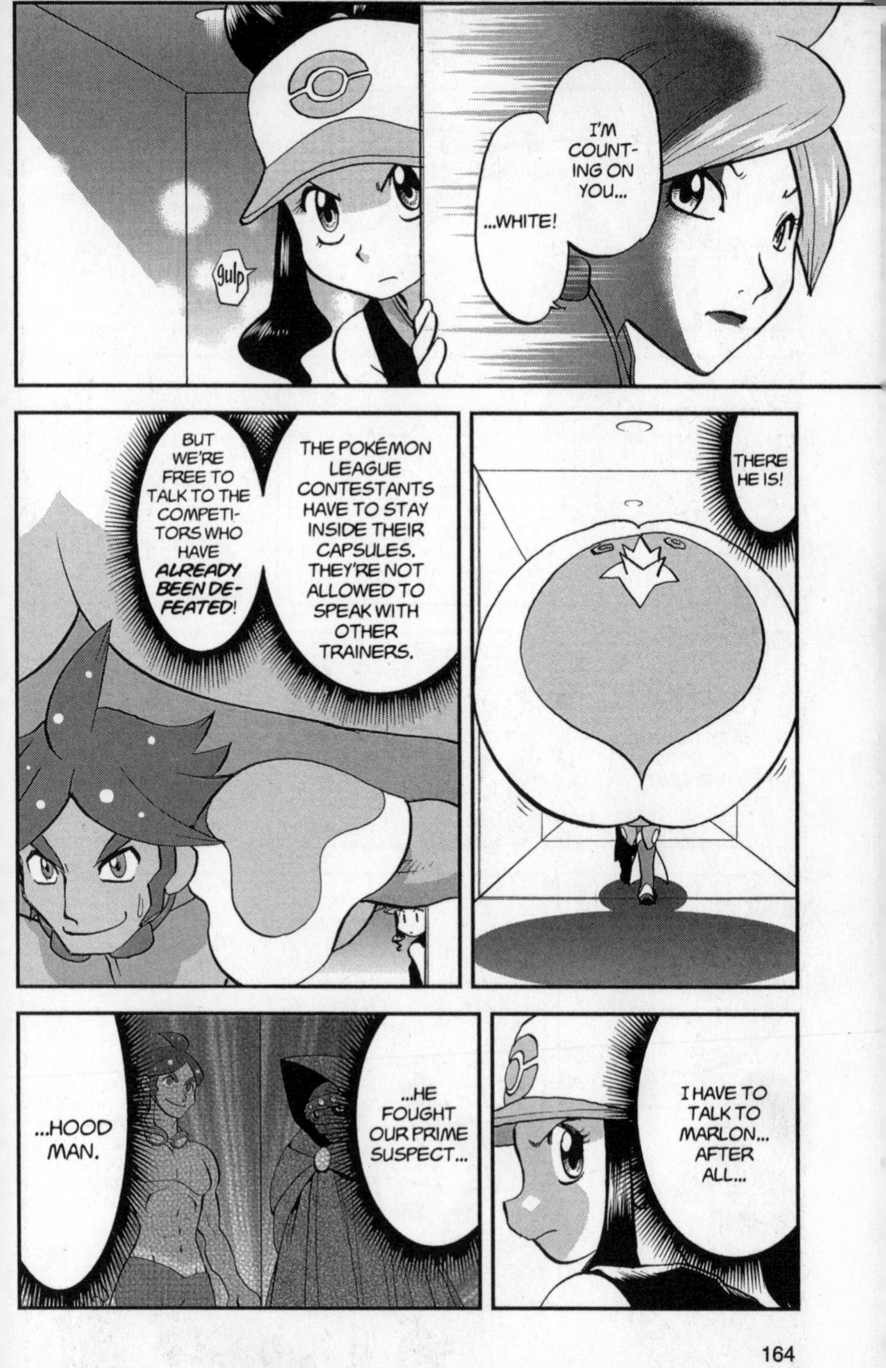
I'M COUNTING ON YOU...
...WHITE!
gulp
THERE HE IS!
THE POKÉMON LEAGUE CONTESTANTS HAVE TO STAY INSIDE THEIR CAPSULES. THEY'RE NOT ALLOWED TO SPEAK WITH OTHER TRAINERS.
BUT WE'RE FREE TO TALK TO THE COMPETITORS WHO HAVE ALREADY BEEN DEFEATED!
I HAVE TO TALK TO MARLON... AFTER ALL...
...HE FOUGHT OUR PRIME SUSPECT...
...HOOD MAN.

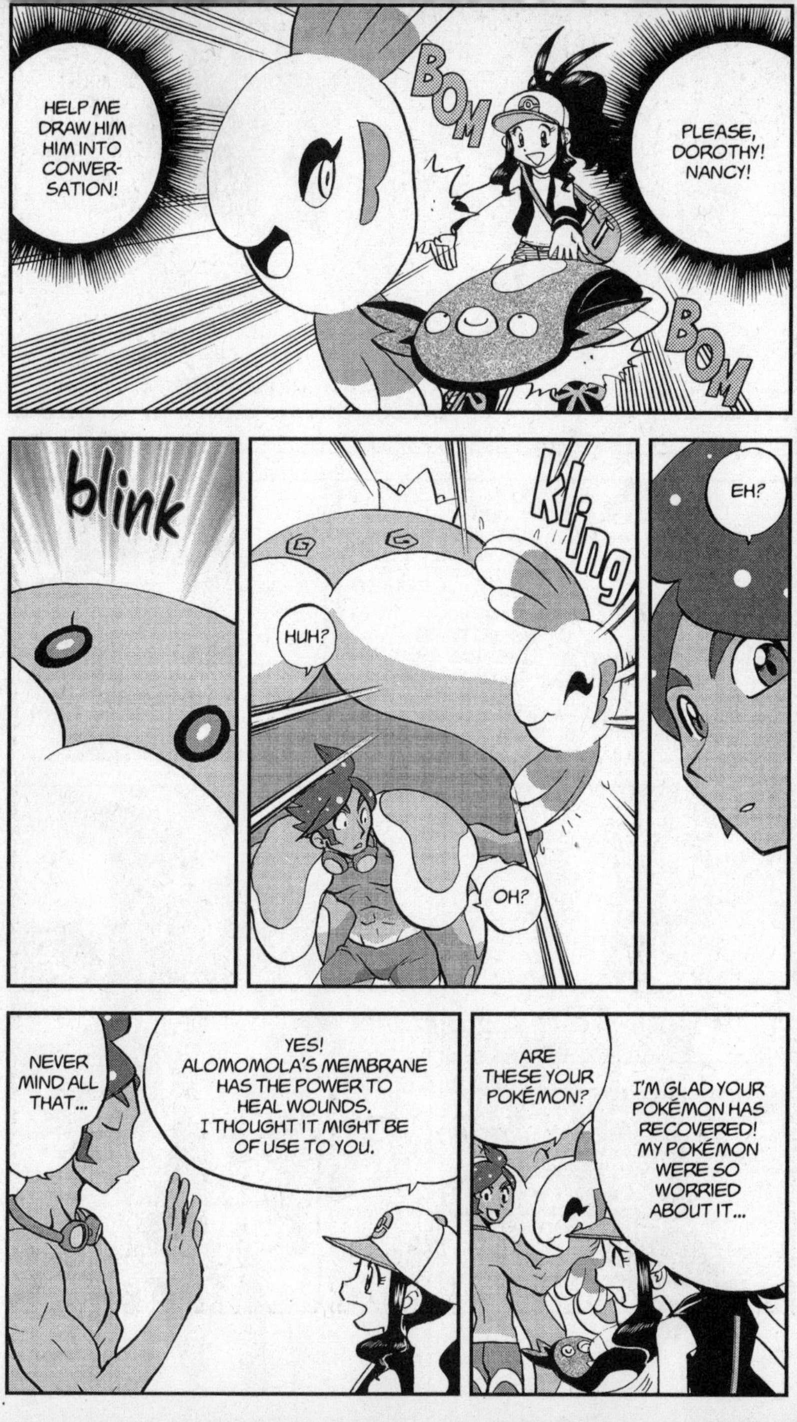
PLEASE, DOROTHY! NANCY!
BOM
HELP ME DRAW HIM HIM INTO CONVER-SATION!
BOM
EH?
Kling
HUH?
OH?
blink
I'M GLAD YOUR POKÉMON HAS RECOVERED! MY POKÉMON WERE SO WORRIED ABOUT IT...
ARE THESE YOUR POKÉMON?
YES! ALOMOMOLA'S MEMBRANE HAS THE POWER TO HEAL WOUNDS. I THOUGHT IT MIGHT BE OF USE TO YOU.
NEVER MIND ALL THAT...

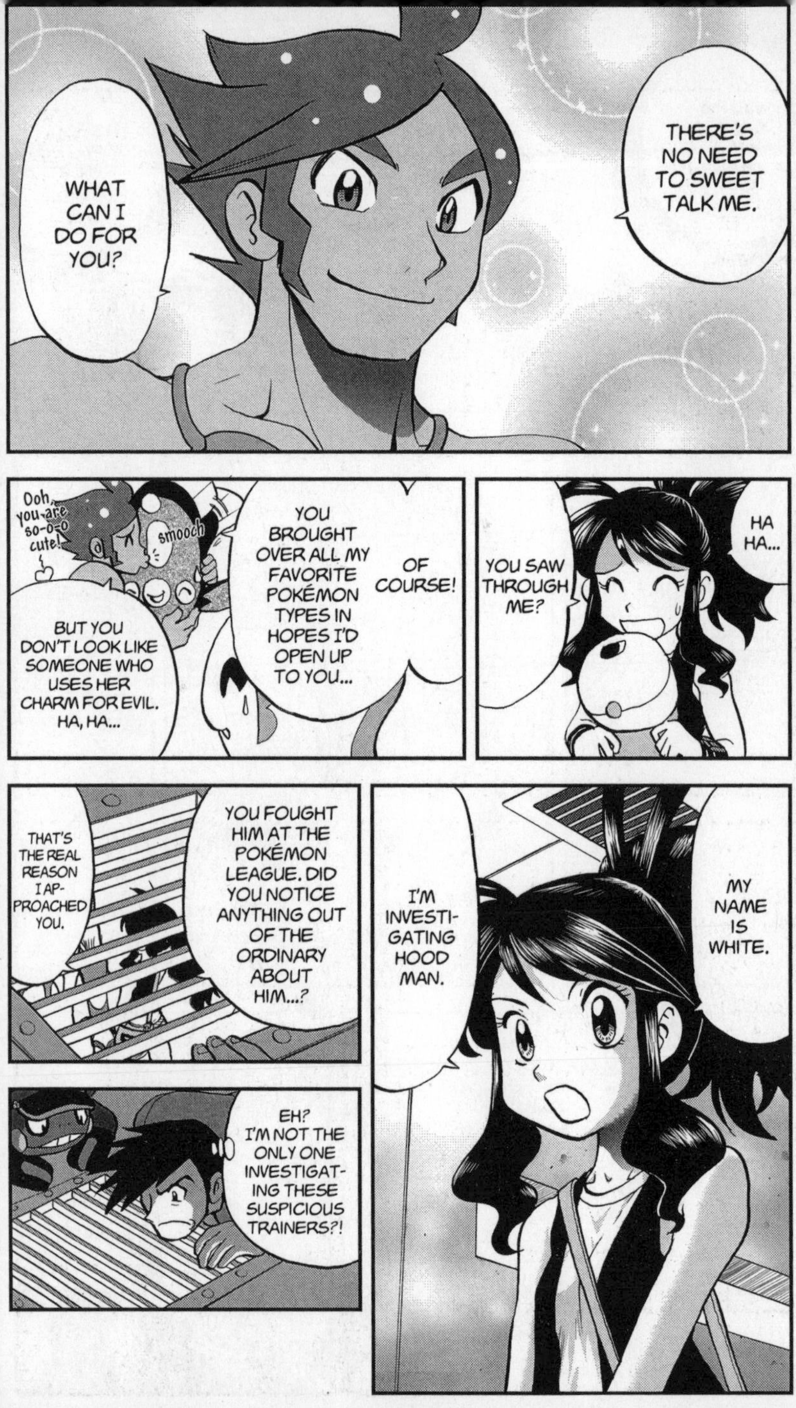
THERE'S NO NEED TO SWEET TALK ME.
WHAT CAN I DO FOR YOU?
HA HA...
YOU SAW THROUGH ME?
OF COURSE!
YOU BROUGHT OVER ALL MY FAVORITE POKÉMON TYPES IN HOPES I'D OPEN UP TO YOU...
Ooh, you are so-o-o cute!
smooch
BUT YOU DON'T LOOK LIKE SOMEONE WHO USES HER CHARM FOR EVIL. HA, HA...
MY NAME IS WHITE.
I'M INVESTI-GATING HOOD MAN.
YOU FOUGHT HIM AT THE POKÉMON LEAGUE. DID YOU NOTICE ANYTHING OUT OF THE ORDINARY ABOUT HIM...?
THAT'S THE REAL REASON I AP-PROACHED YOU.
EH? I'M NOT THE ONLY ONE INVESTIGAT-ING THESE SUSPICIOUS TRAINERS?!

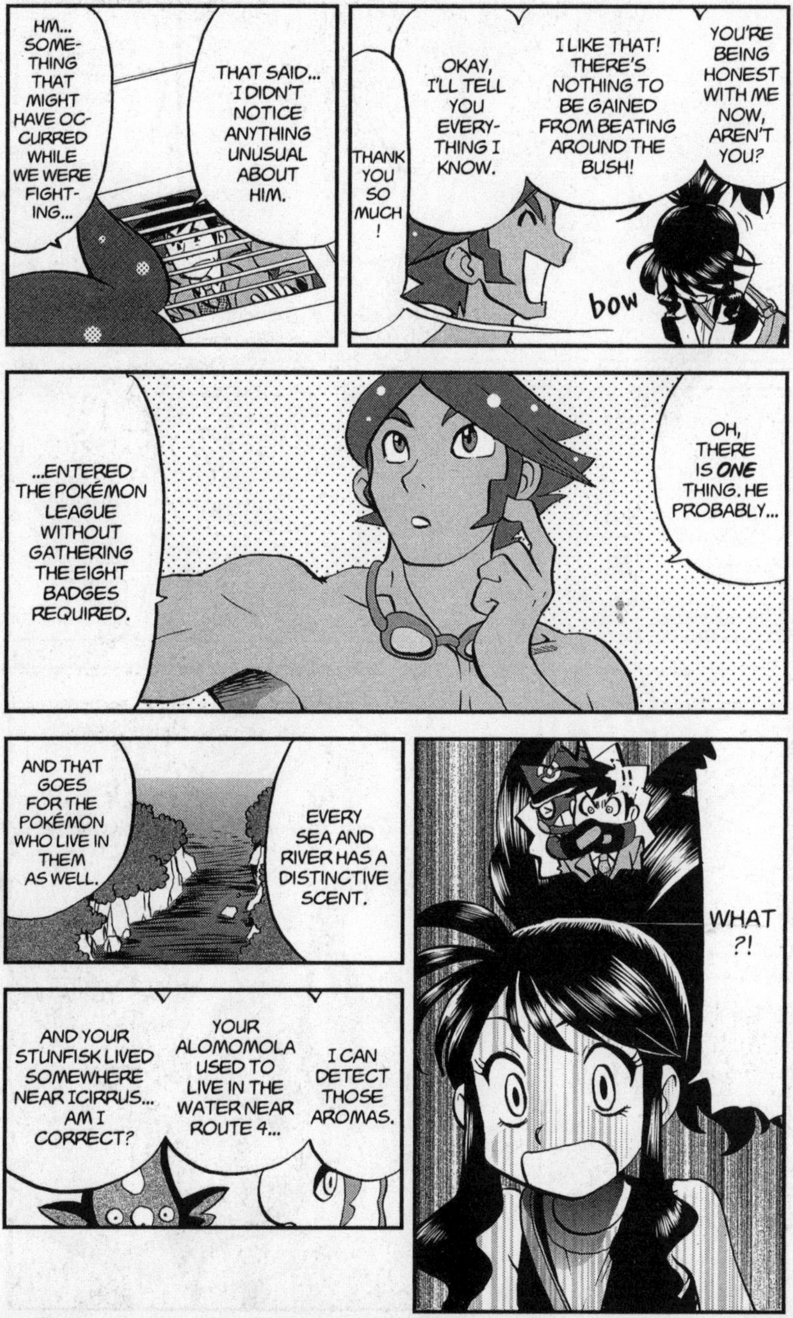
YOU'RE BEING HONEST WITH ME NOW, AREN'T YOU?
I LIKE THAT! THERE'S NOTHING TO BE GAINED FROM BEATING AROUND THE BUSH!
OKAY, I'LL TELL YOU EVERYTHING I KNOW.
THANK YOU SO MUCH!
bow
THAT SAID... I DIDN'T NOTICE ANYTHING UNUSUAL ABOUT HIM.
HM... SOMETHING THAT MIGHT HAVE OCCURRED WHILE WE WERE FIGHTING...
OH, THERE IS *ONE* THING. HE PROBABLY...
...ENTERED THE POKÉMON LEAGUE WITHOUT GATHERING THE EIGHT BADGES REQUIRED.
!!
WHAT?!
EVERY SEA AND RIVER HAS A DISTINCTIVE SCENT.
AND THAT GOES FOR THE POKÉMON WHO LIVE IN THEM AS WELL.
I CAN DETECT THOSE AROMAS.
YOUR ALOMOMOLA USED TO LIVE IN THE WATER NEAR ROUTE 4...
AND YOUR STUNFISK LIVED SOMEWHERE NEAR ICIRRUS... AM I CORRECT?

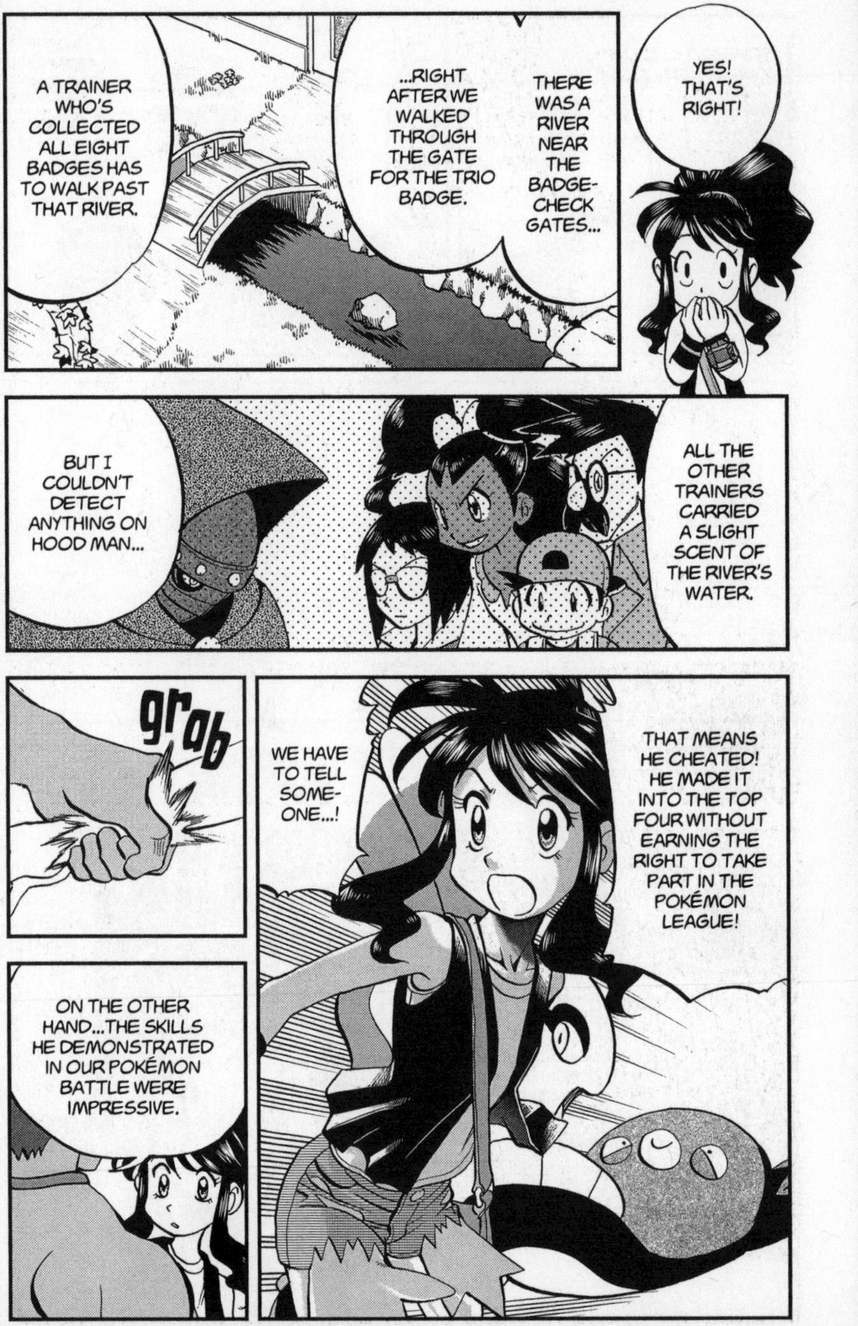
YES! THAT'S RIGHT!
THERE WAS A RIVER NEAR THE BADGE-CHECK GATES...
...RIGHT AFTER WE WALKED THROUGH THE GATE FOR THE TRIO BADGE.
A TRAINER WHO'S COLLECTED ALL EIGHT BADGES HAS TO WALK PAST THAT RIVER.
ALL THE OTHER TRAINERS CARRIED A SLIGHT SCENT OF THE RIVER'S WATER.
BUT I COULDN'T DETECT ANYTHING ON HOOD MAN...
THAT MEANS HE CHEATED! HE MADE IT INTO THE TOP FOUR WITHOUT EARNING THE RIGHT TO TAKE PART IN THE POKÉMON LEAGUE!
WE HAVE TO TELL SOME-ONE...!
grab
ON THE OTHER HAND...THE SKILLS HE DEMONSTRATED IN OUR POKÉMON BATTLE WERE IMPRESSIVE.

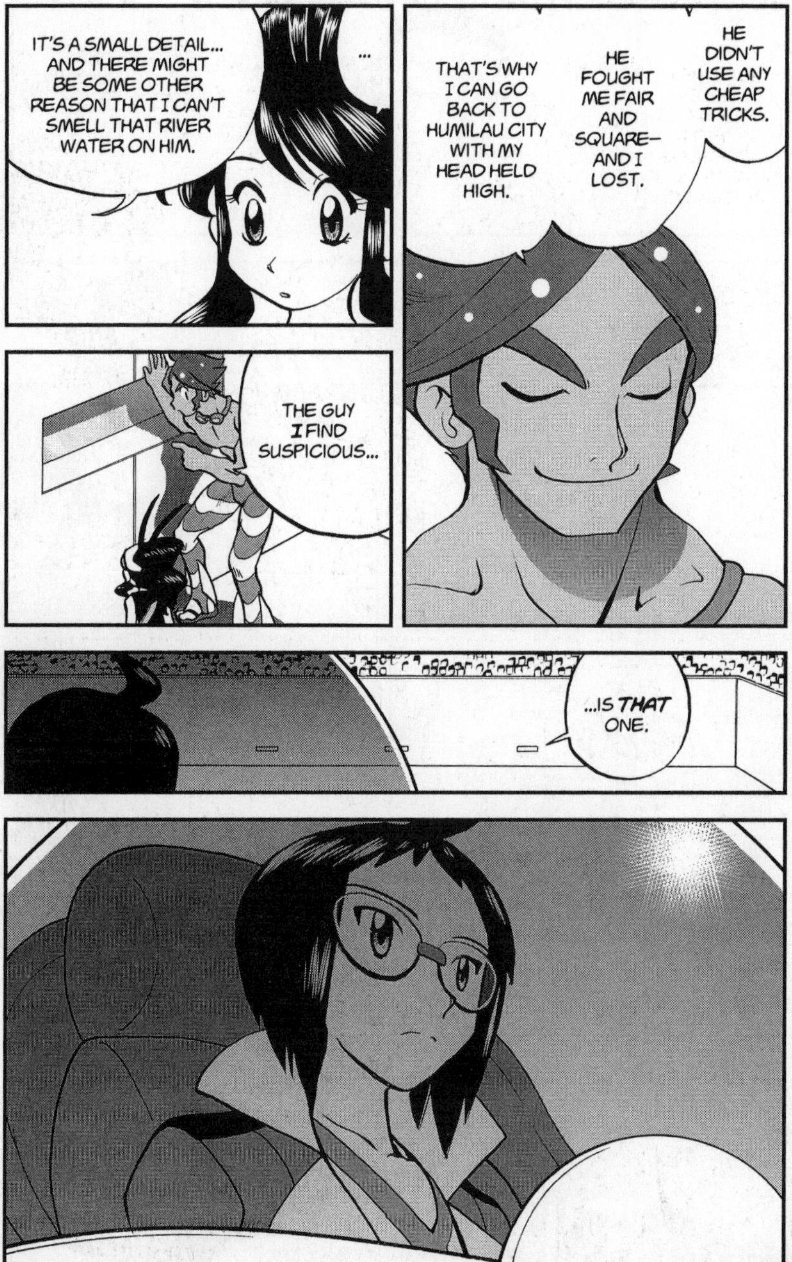
HE DIDN'T USE ANY CHEAP TRICKS.
HE FOUGHT ME FAIR AND SQUARE—AND I LOST.
THAT'S WHY I CAN GO BACK TO HUMILAU CITY WITH MY HEAD HELD HIGH.
...
IT'S A SMALL DETAIL... AND THERE MIGHT BE SOME OTHER REASON THAT I CAN'T SMELL THAT RIVER WATER ON HIM.
THE GUY *I* FIND SUSPICIOUS...
...IS *THAT* ONE.

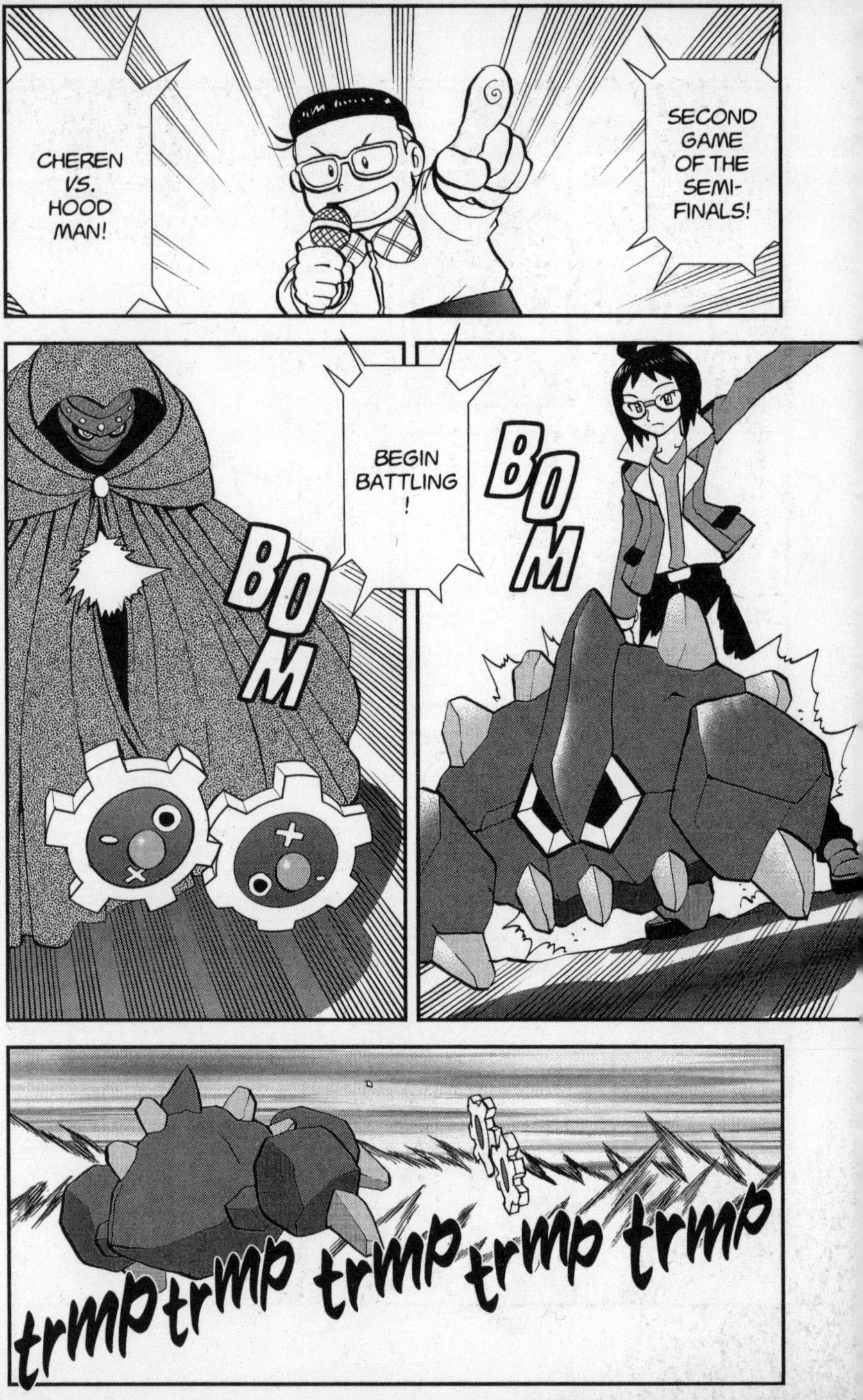
SECOND GAME OF THE SEMI-FINALS!
CHEREN VS. HOOD MAN!
BOOM
BEGIN BATTLING!
BOOM
trmp trmp trmp trmp trmp

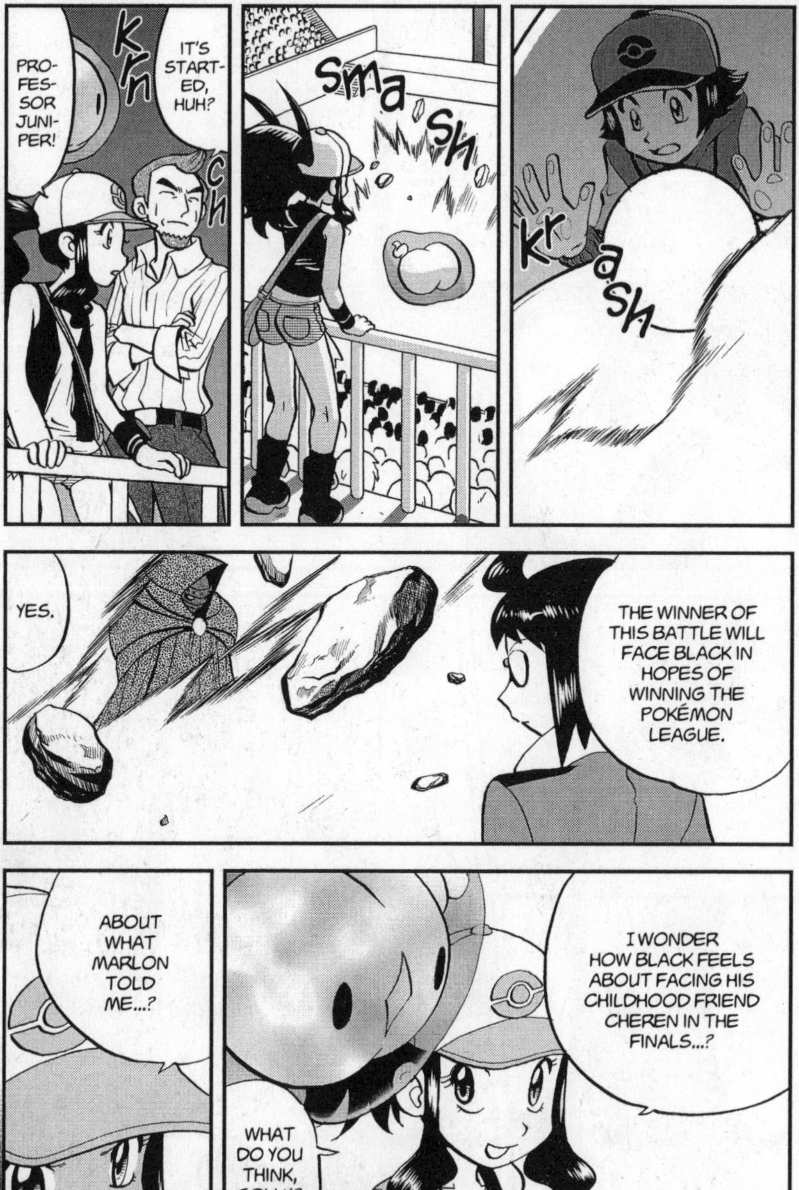
kr
ash
smash
IT'S STARTED, HUH?
krn
PROFESSOR JUNIPER!
ch
THE WINNER OF THIS BATTLE WILL FACE BLACK IN HOPES OF WINNING THE POKÉMON LEAGUE.
YES.
I WONDER HOW BLACK FEELS ABOUT FACING HIS CHILDHOOD FRIEND CHEREN IN THE FINALS...?
WHAT DO YOU THINK, SOLLY?
ABOUT WHAT MARLON TOLD ME...?

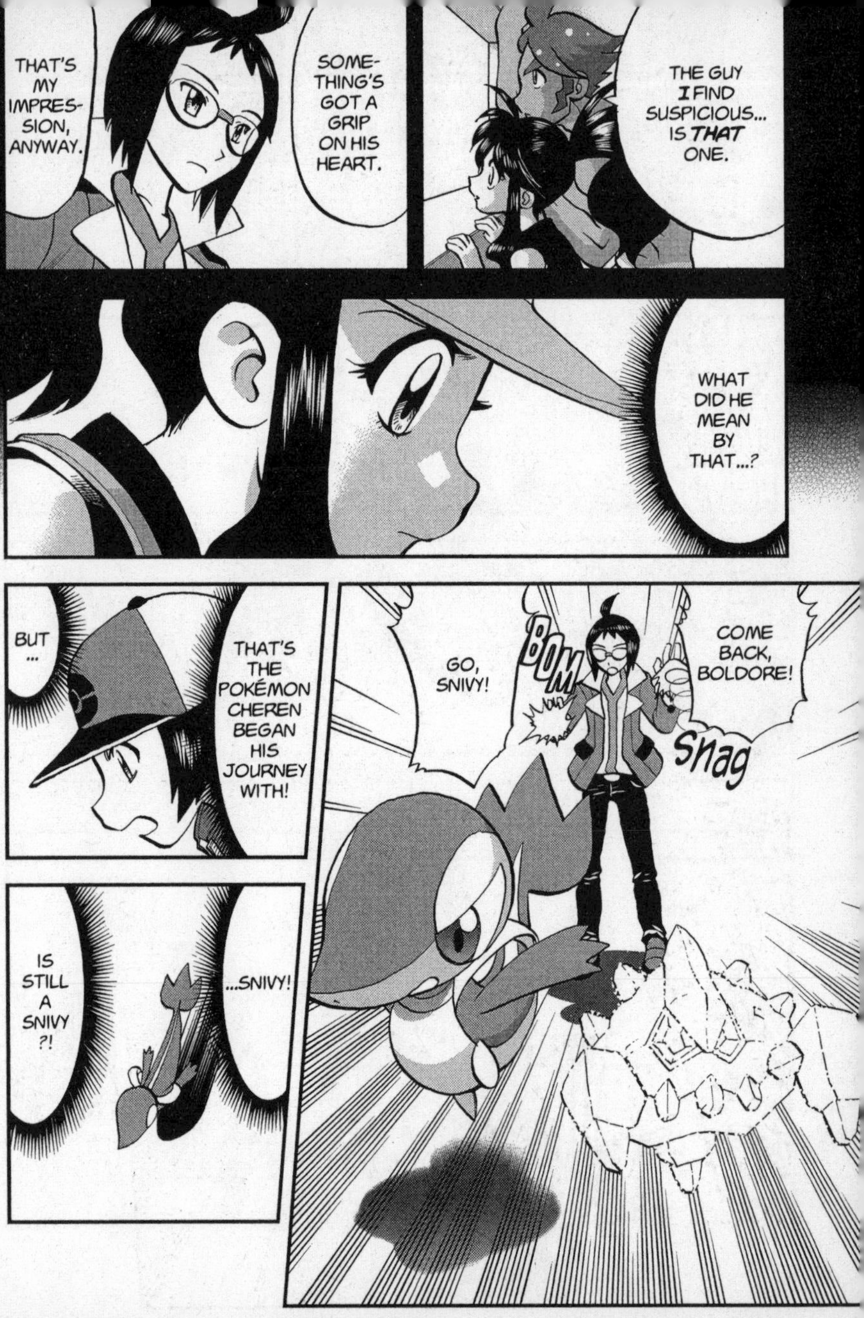
THE GUY I FIND SUSPICIOUS... IS THAT ONE.
SOME-THING'S GOT A GRIP ON HIS HEART.
THAT'S MY IMPRES-SION, ANYWAY.
WHAT DID HE MEAN BY THAT...?
COME BACK, BOLDORE!
Snag
BOM
GO, SNIVY!
THAT'S THE POKÉMON CHEREN BEGAN HIS JOURNEY WITH!
BUT ...
...SNIVY!
IS STILL A SNIVY ?!

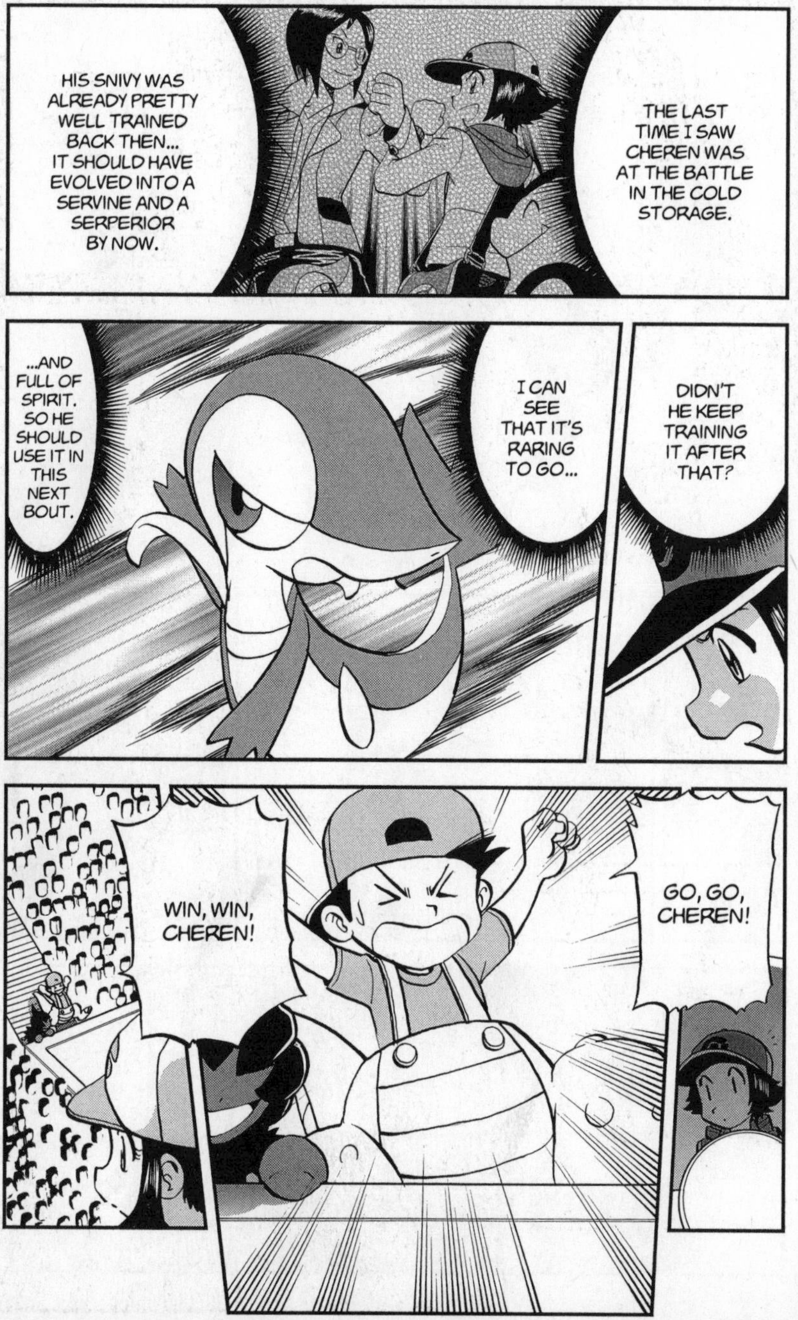
THE LAST TIME I SAW CHEREN WAS AT THE BATTLE IN THE COLD STORAGE.
HIS SNIVY WAS ALREADY PRETTY WELL TRAINED BACK THEN... IT SHOULD HAVE EVOLVED INTO A SERVINE AND A SERPERIOR BY NOW.
DIDN'T HE KEEP TRAINING IT AFTER THAT?
I CAN SEE THAT IT'S RARING TO GO...
...AND FULL OF SPIRIT. SO HE SHOULD USE IT IN THIS NEXT BOUT.
GO, GO, CHEREN!
WIN, WIN, CHEREN!

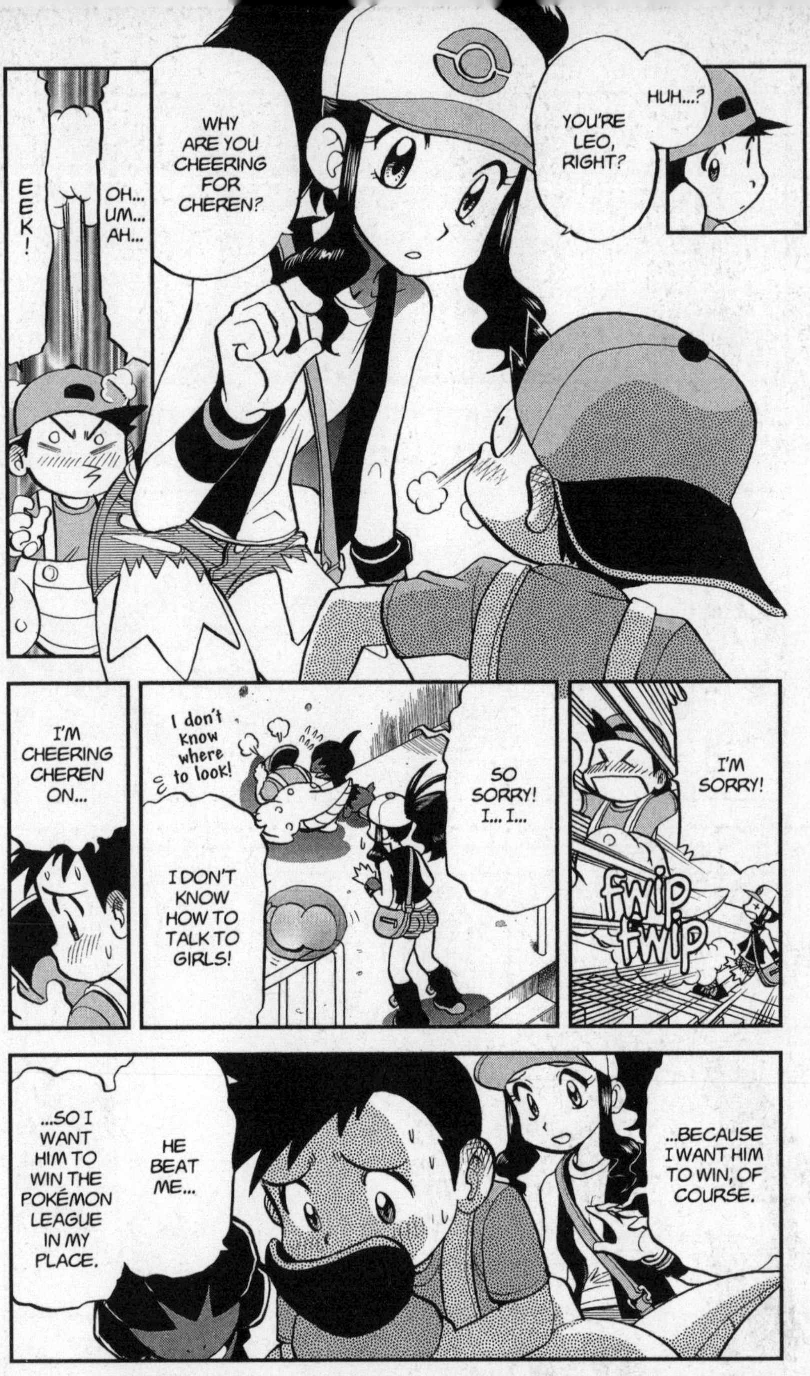
HUH...?
YOU'RE LEO, RIGHT?
WHY ARE YOU CHEERING FOR CHEREN?
OH... UM... AH...
EEK!
I'M SORRY!
fwip fwip
SO SORRY! I... I...
I don't know where to look!
I DON'T KNOW HOW TO TALK TO GIRLS!
I'M CHEERING CHEREN ON...
...BECAUSE I WANT HIM TO WIN, OF COURSE.
HE BEAT ME...
...SO I WANT HIM TO WIN THE POKÉMON LEAGUE IN MY PLACE.

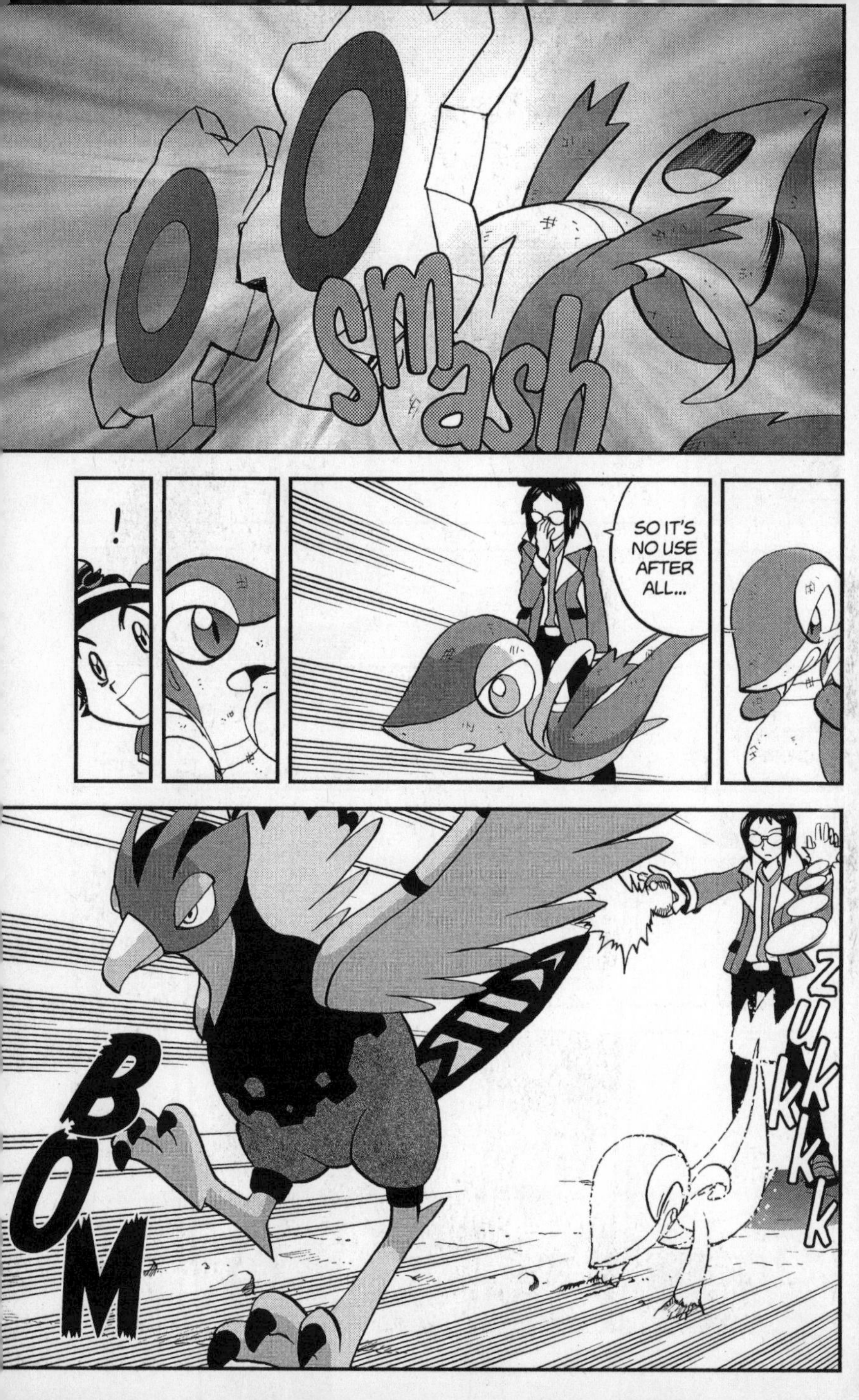
smash
SO IT'S NO USE AFTER ALL...
!
zukkkk
BOOM

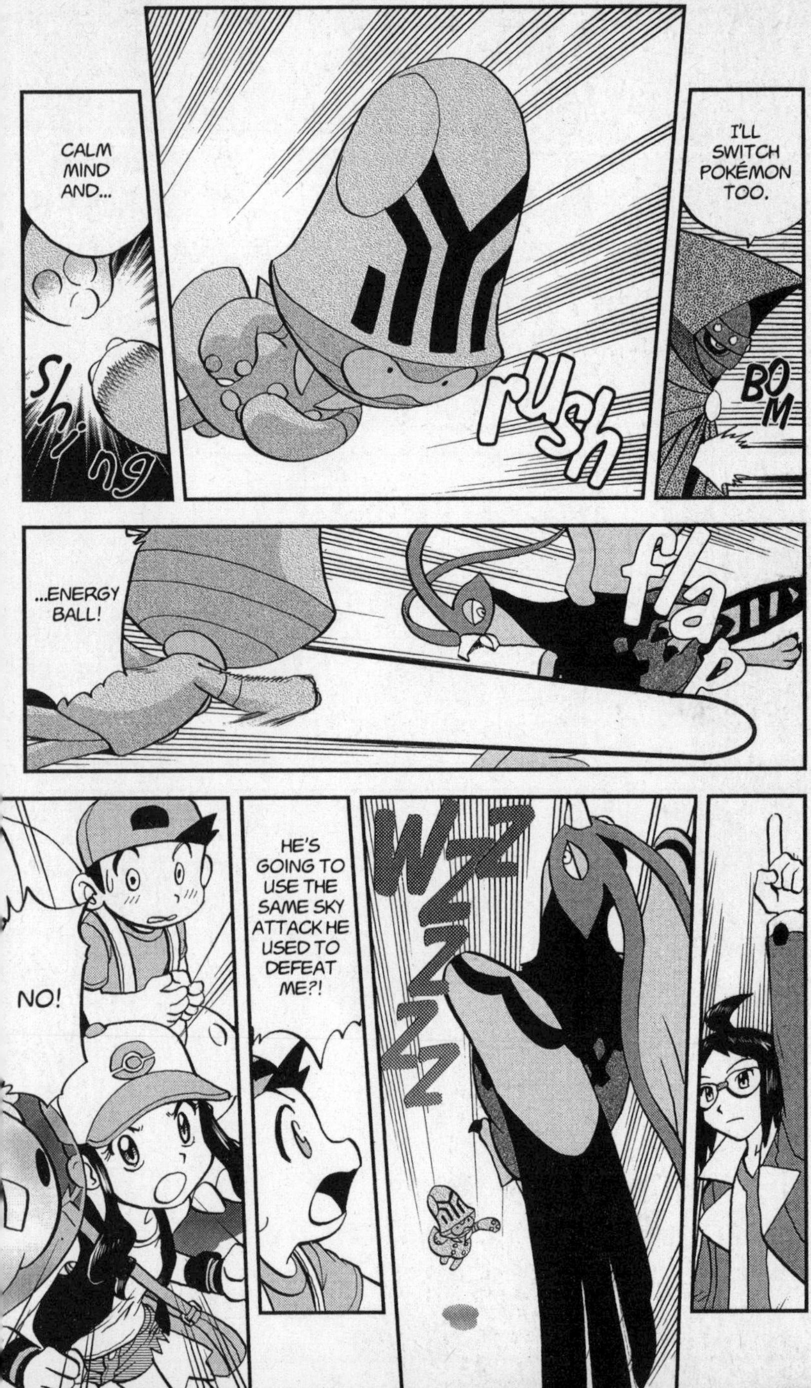
I'LL SWITCH POKÉMON TOO.
BOM
rush
CALM MIND AND...
shing
flap
...ENERGY BALL!
WZZZZZ
HE'S GOING TO USE THE SAME SKY ATTACK HE USED TO DEFEAT ME?!
NO!

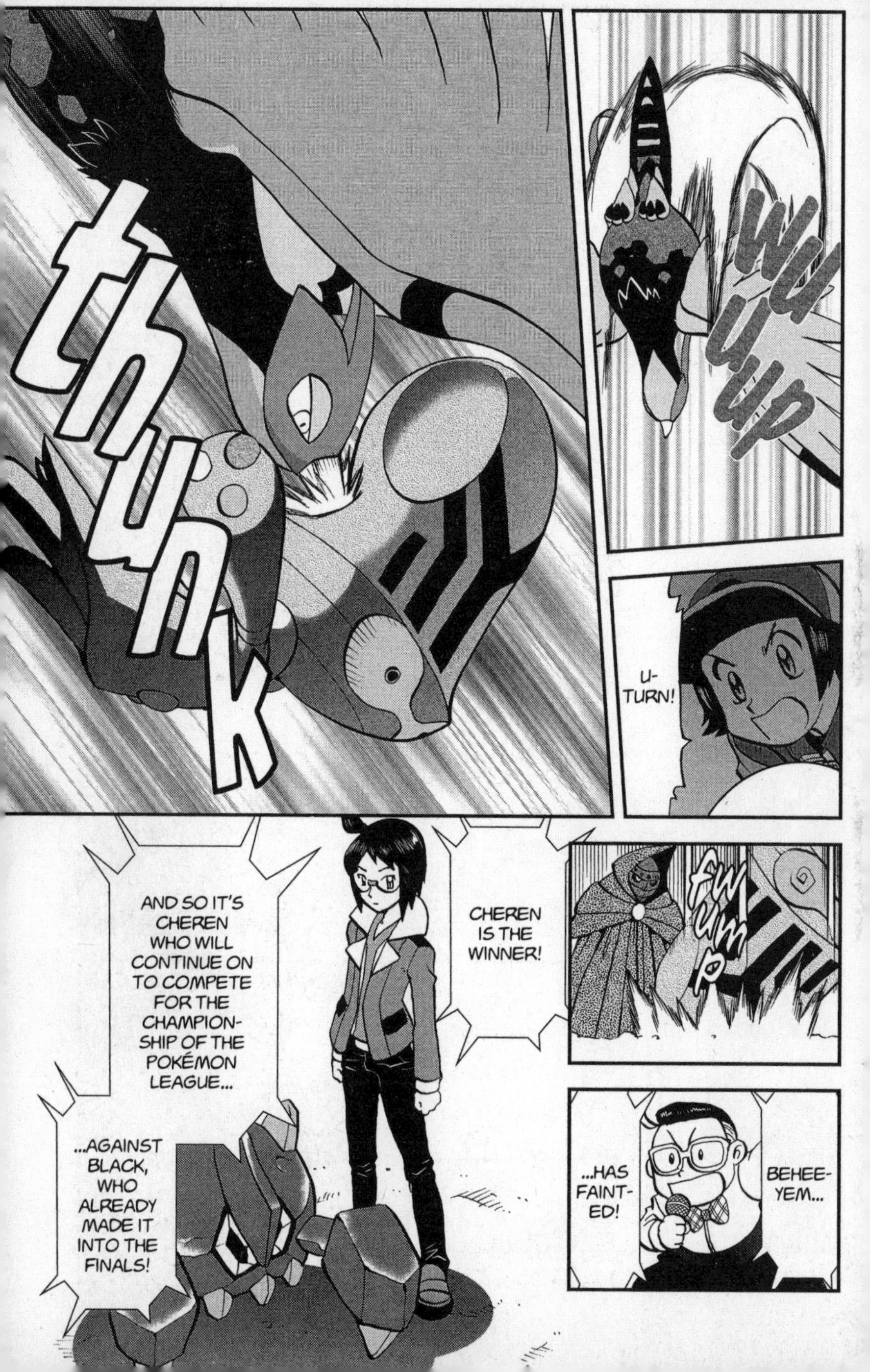
WUUUP
U-TURN!
thunk
FWUMP
BEHEE-YEM...
...HAS FAINT-ED!
CHEREN IS THE WINNER!
AND SO IT'S CHEREN WHO WILL CONTINUE ON TO COMPETE FOR THE CHAMPION-SHIP OF THE POKÉMON LEAGUE...
...AGAINST BLACK, WHO ALREADY MADE IT INTO THE FINALS!

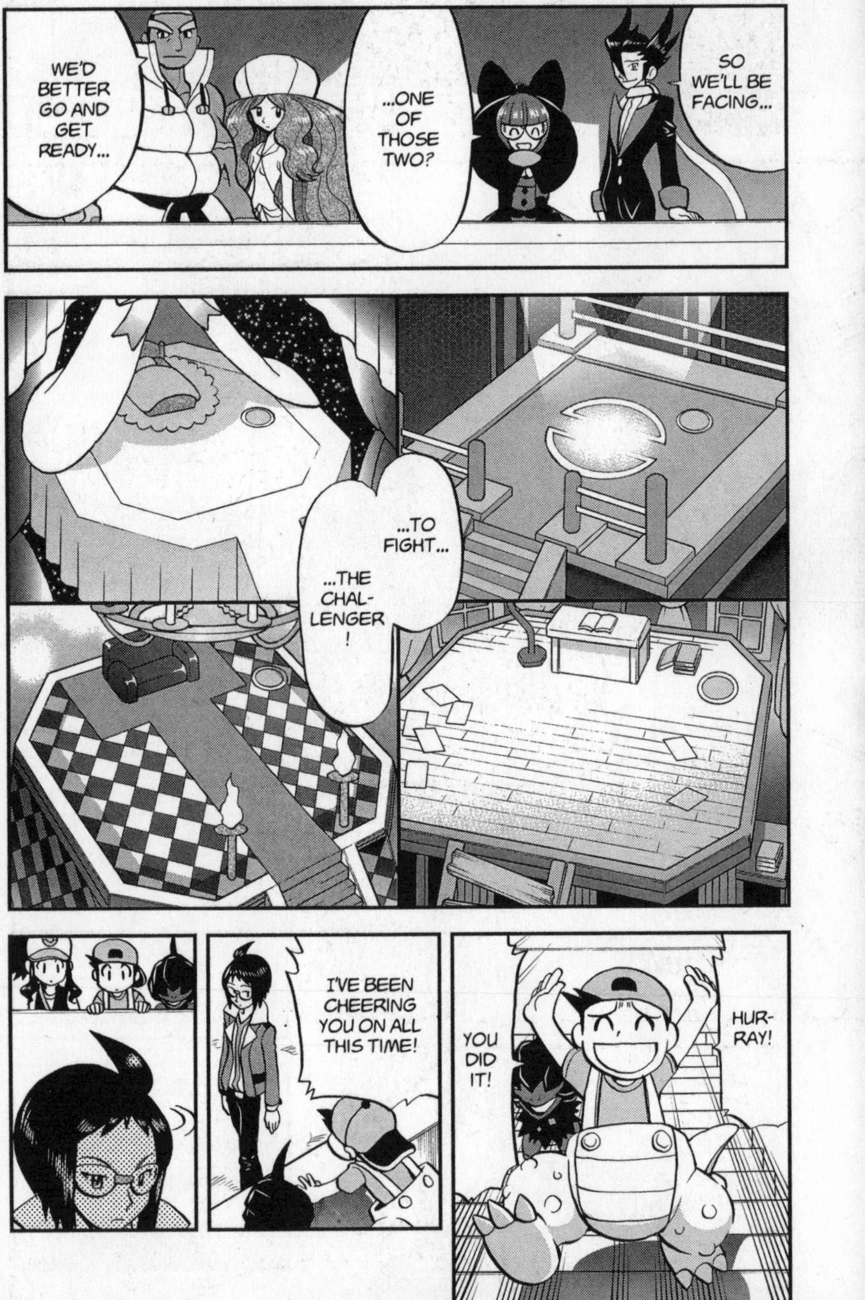
SO WE'LL BE FACING...
...ONE OF THOSE TWO?
WE'D BETTER GO AND GET READY...
...TO FIGHT...
...THE CHALLENGER!
HURRAY!
YOU DID IT!
I'VE BEEN CHEERING YOU ON ALL THIS TIME!

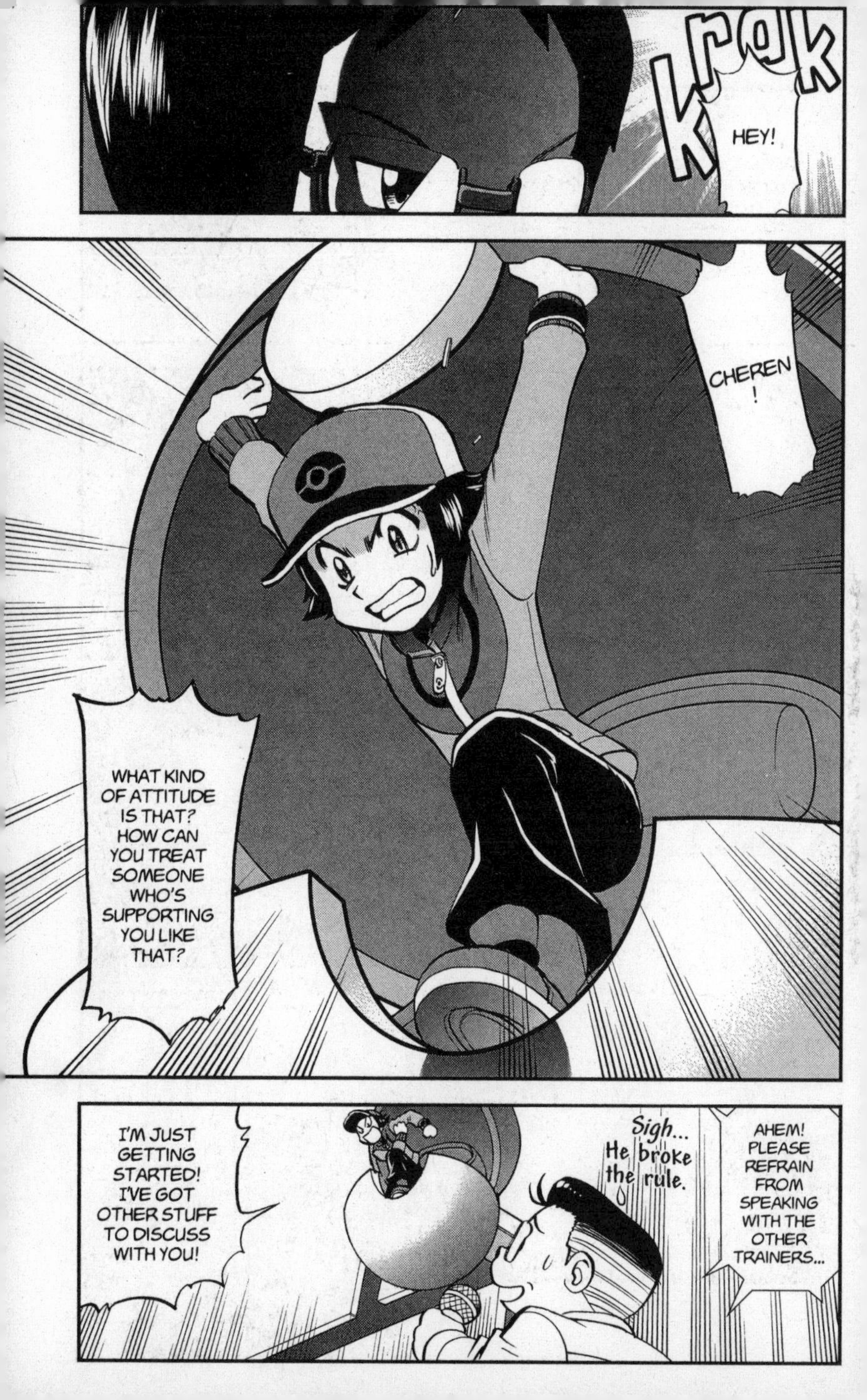
krak
HEY!
CHEREN!
WHAT KIND OF ATTITUDE IS THAT? HOW CAN YOU TREAT SOMEONE WHO'S SUPPORTING YOU LIKE THAT?
AHEM! PLEASE REFRAIN FROM SPEAKING WITH THE OTHER TRAINERS...
Sigh... He broke the rule.
I'M JUST GETTING STARTED! I'VE GOT OTHER STUFF TO DISCUSS WITH YOU!

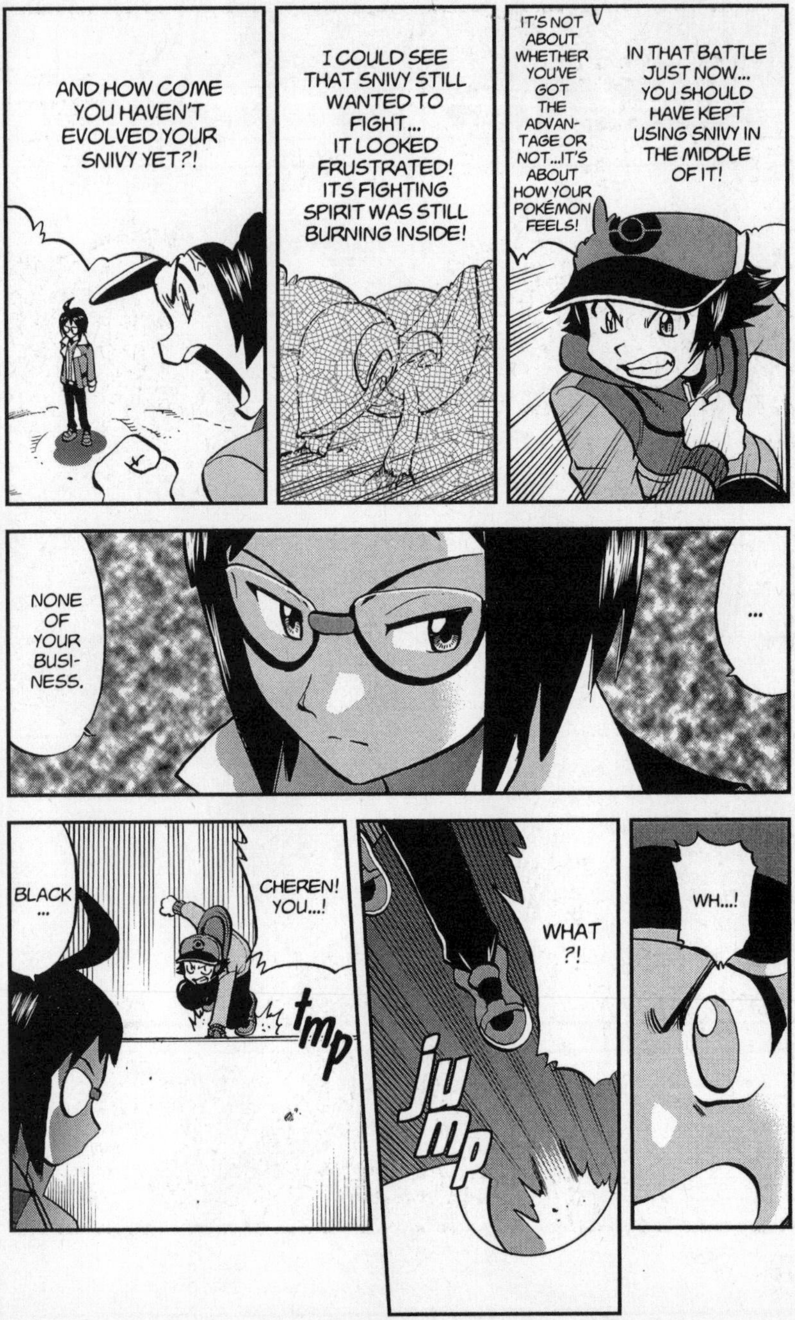
IN THAT BATTLE JUST NOW... YOU SHOULD HAVE KEPT USING SNIVY IN THE MIDDLE OF IT!
IT'S NOT ABOUT WHETHER YOU'VE GOT THE ADVANTAGE OR NOT...IT'S ABOUT HOW YOUR POKÉMON FEELS!
I COULD SEE THAT SNIVY STILL WANTED TO FIGHT... IT LOOKED FRUSTRATED! ITS FIGHTING SPIRIT WAS STILL BURNING INSIDE!
AND HOW COME YOU HAVEN'T EVOLVED YOUR SNIVY YET?!
...
NONE OF YOUR BUSINESS.
WH...!
WHAT ?!
jump
CHEREN! YOU...!
tmp
BLACK ...

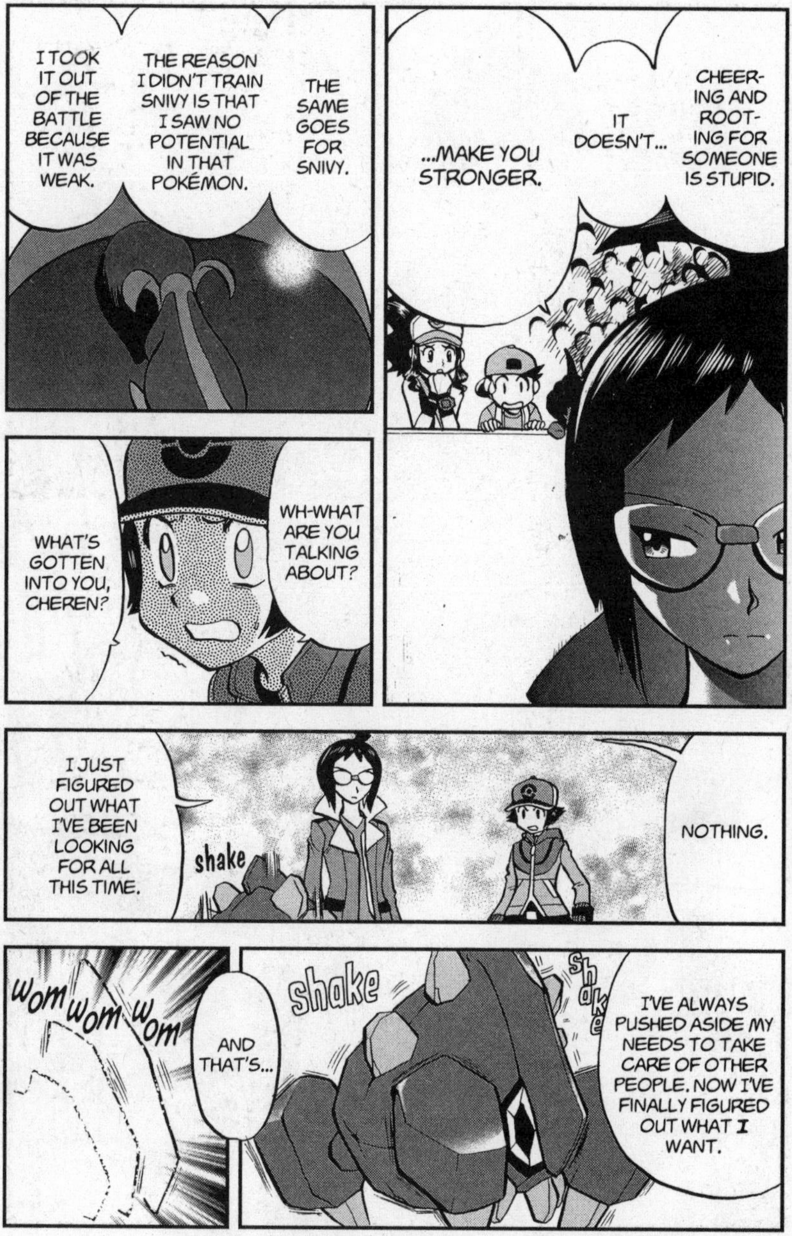
CHEERING AND ROOTING FOR SOMEONE IS STUPID.
IT DOESN'T...
...MAKE YOU STRONGER.
THE SAME GOES FOR SNIVY.
THE REASON I DIDN'T TRAIN SNIVY IS THAT I SAW NO POTENTIAL IN THAT POKÉMON.
I TOOK IT OUT OF THE BATTLE BECAUSE IT WAS WEAK.
WH-WHAT ARE YOU TALKING ABOUT?
WHAT'S GOTTEN INTO YOU, CHEREN?
NOTHING.
I JUST FIGURED OUT WHAT I'VE BEEN LOOKING FOR ALL THIS TIME.
shake
I'VE ALWAYS PUSHED ASIDE MY NEEDS TO TAKE CARE OF OTHER PEOPLE. NOW I'VE FINALLY FIGURED OUT WHAT I WANT.
shake
shake
AND THAT'S...
wom wom wom

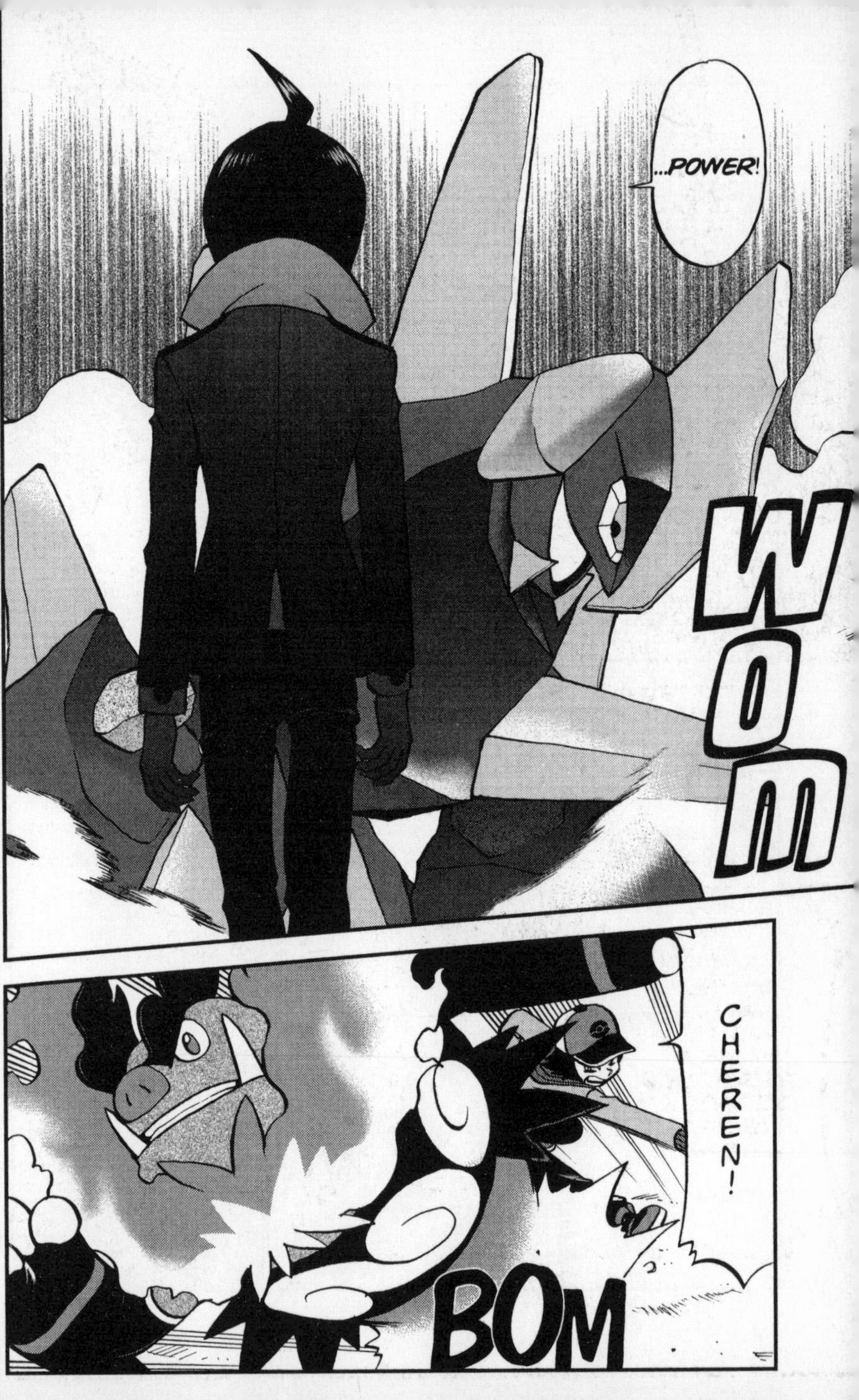
...POWER!
WOM
CHEREN!
BOM

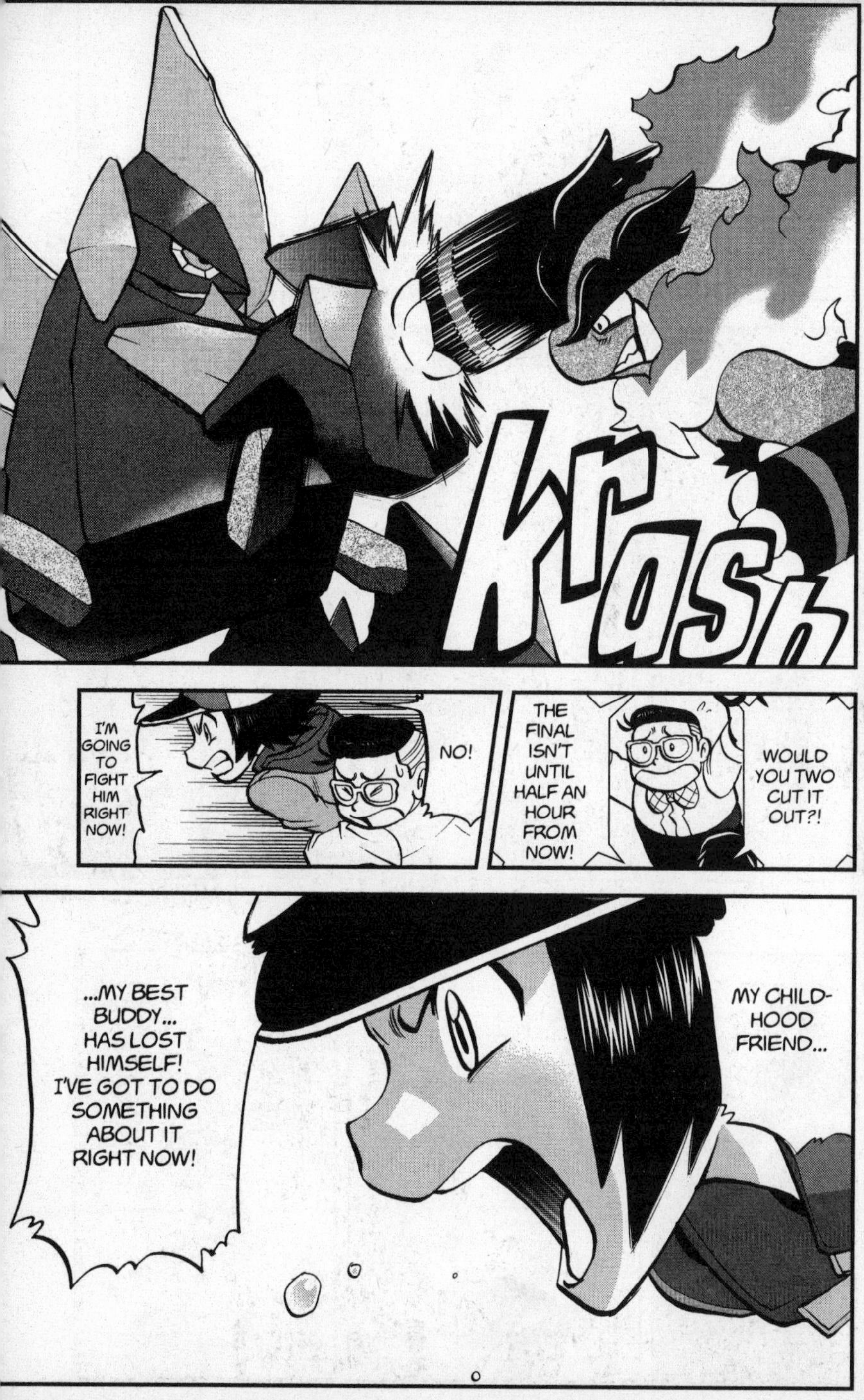
KRASH
WOULD YOU TWO CUT IT OUT?!
THE FINAL ISN'T UNTIL HALF AN HOUR FROM NOW!
I'M GOING TO FIGHT HIM RIGHT NOW!
NO!
MY CHILD-HOOD FRIEND...
...MY BEST BUDDY... HAS LOST HIMSELF! I'VE GOT TO DO SOMETHING ABOUT IT RIGHT NOW!

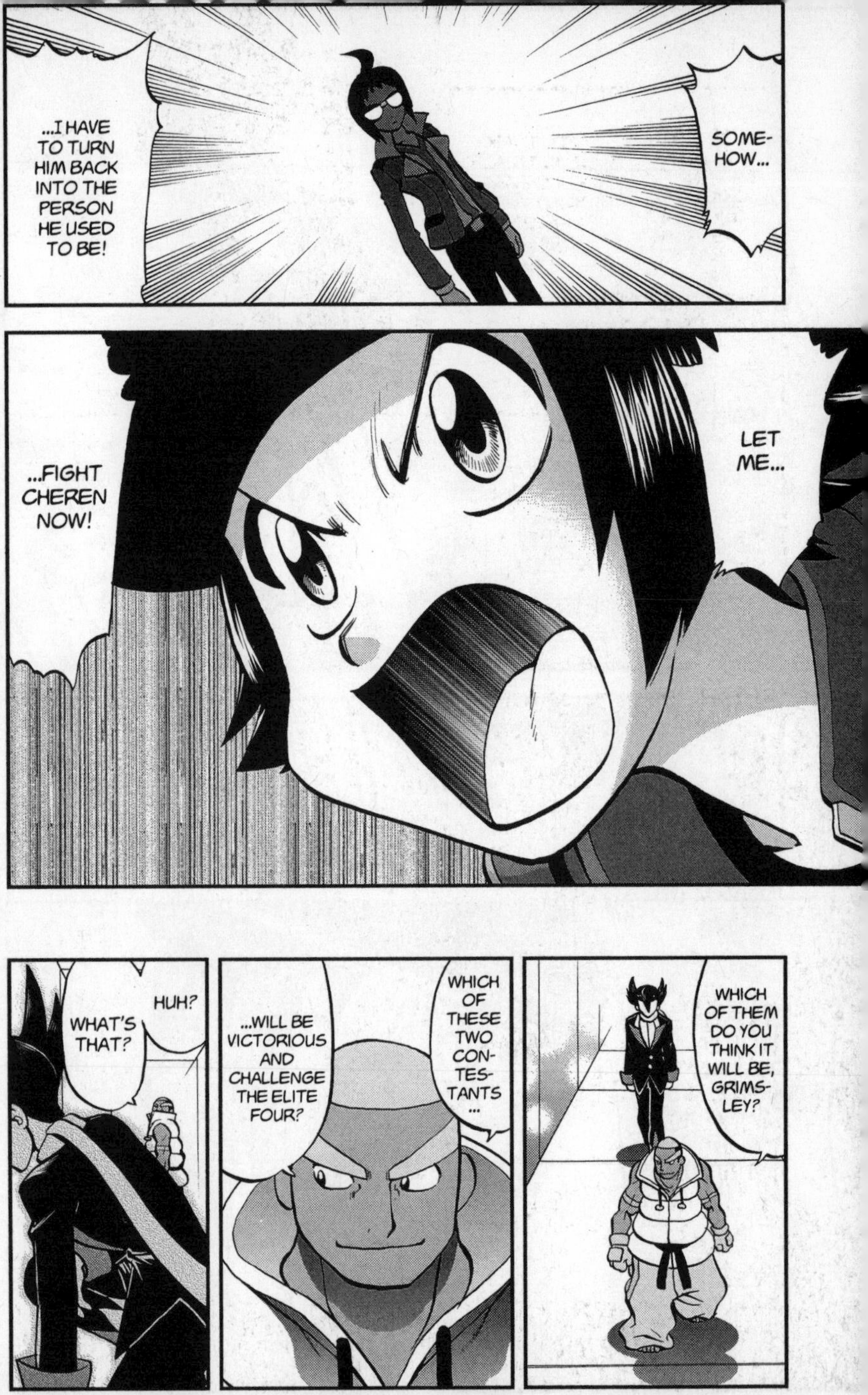
SOME-HOW...
...I HAVE TO TURN HIM BACK INTO THE PERSON HE USED TO BE!
LET ME...
...FIGHT CHEREN NOW!
WHICH OF THEM DO YOU THINK IT WILL BE, GRIMS-LEY?
WHICH OF THESE TWO CON-TES-TANTS...
...WILL BE VICTORIOUS AND CHALLENGE THE ELITE FOUR?
HUH?
WHAT'S THAT?

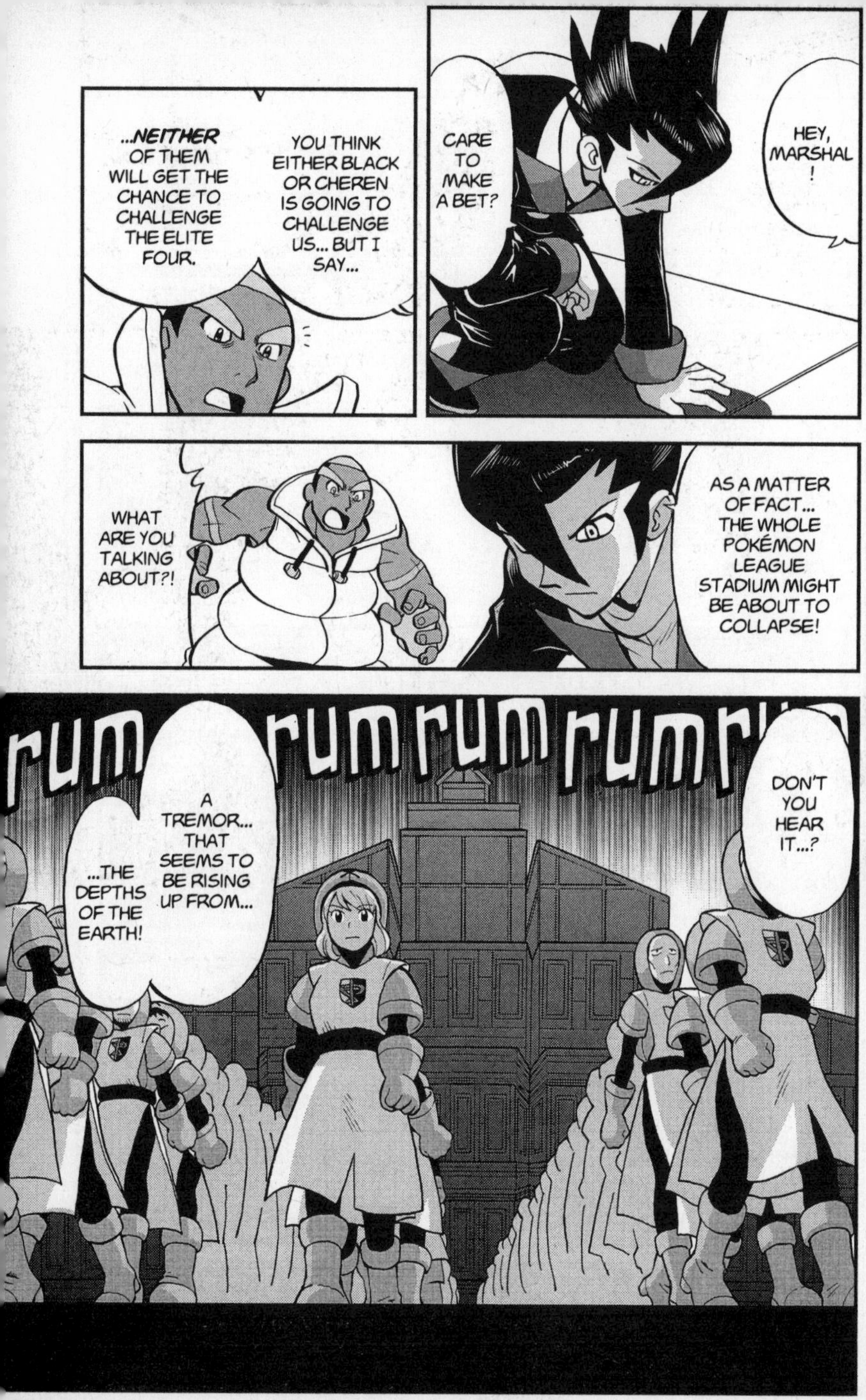
HEY, MARSHAL!
CARE TO MAKE A BET?
YOU THINK EITHER BLACK OR CHEREN IS GOING TO CHALLENGE US... BUT I SAY...
...***NEITHER*** OF THEM WILL GET THE CHANCE TO CHALLENGE THE ELITE FOUR.
AS A MATTER OF FACT... THE WHOLE POKÉMON LEAGUE STADIUM MIGHT BE ABOUT TO COLLAPSE!
WHAT ARE YOU TALKING ABOUT?!
rum rum rum rum
DON'T YOU HEAR IT...?
A TREMOR... THAT SEEMS TO BE RISING UP FROM...
...THE DEPTHS OF THE EARTH!

# ADVENTURE MAP

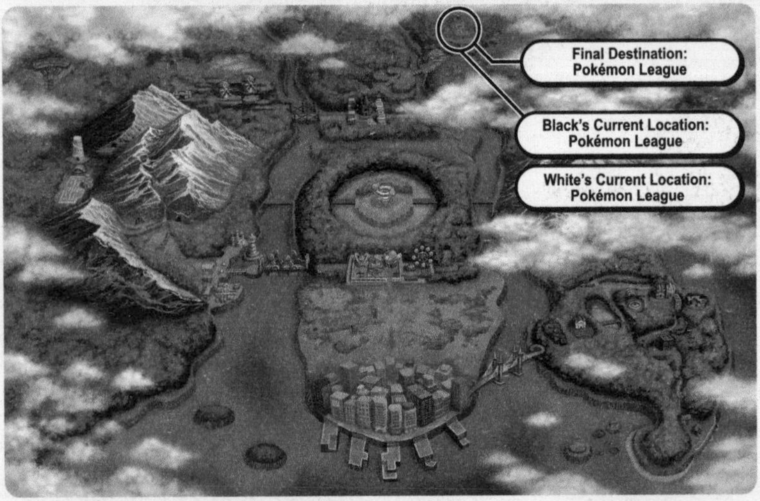

Final Destination:
Pokémon League
Black's Current Location:
Pokémon League
White's Current Location:
Pokémon League


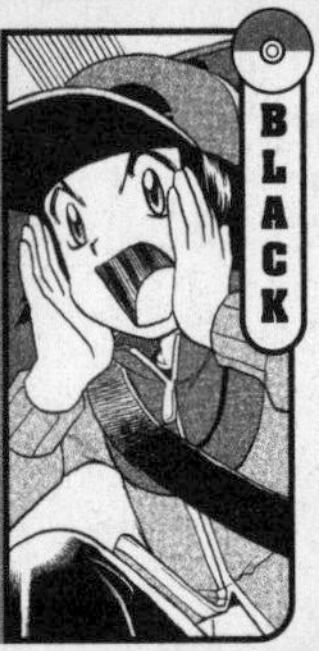

BLACK


**Bo** — Mega Fire Pig Pokémon
Emboar ♂ | Fire | Fighting
Lv.49 Ability: Blaze

**Brav** — Valiant Pokémon
Braviary ♂ | Normal | Flying
Lv.59 Ability: Sheer Force

**Tula** — EleSpider Pokémon
Galvantula ♂ | Bug | Electric
Lv.59 Ability: Unnerve

**Costa** — Prototurtle Pokémon
Tirtouga ♂ | Water | Rock
Lv.43 Ability: Solid Rock

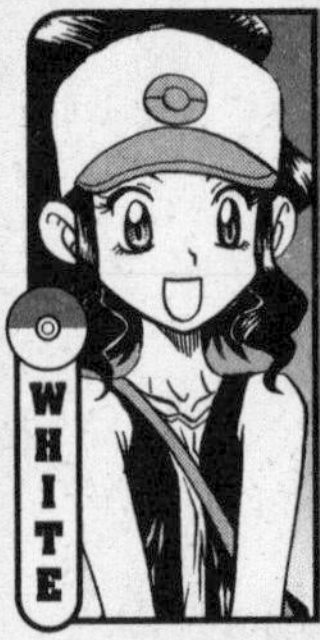

WHITE


**Amanda** — Grass Snake Pokémon
Servine ♀ | Grass
Lv.40 Ability: Overgrow

**Darlene** — Season Pokémon
Deerling ♀ | Normal | Grass
Lv.31 Ability: Chlorophyll

**Dorothy** — Trap Pokémon
Stunfisk ♀ | Ground | Electric
Lv.34 Ability: Limber

**Nancy** — Caring Pokémon
Alomomola ♀ | Water
Lv.35 Ability: Healer

**Barbara** — Diapered Pokémon
Vullaby ♀ | Dark | Flying
Lv.39 Ability: Big Pecks

**Solly** — Cell Pokémon
Solosis ♂ | Psychic
Lv.29 Ability: Magic Guard

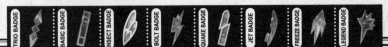

TRIO BADGE | BASIC BADGE | INSECT BADGE | BOLT BADGE | QUAKE BADGE | JET BADGE | FREEZE BADGE | LEGEND BADGE

POKÉMON™ ADVENTURES BLACK & WHITE

UNFEZANT

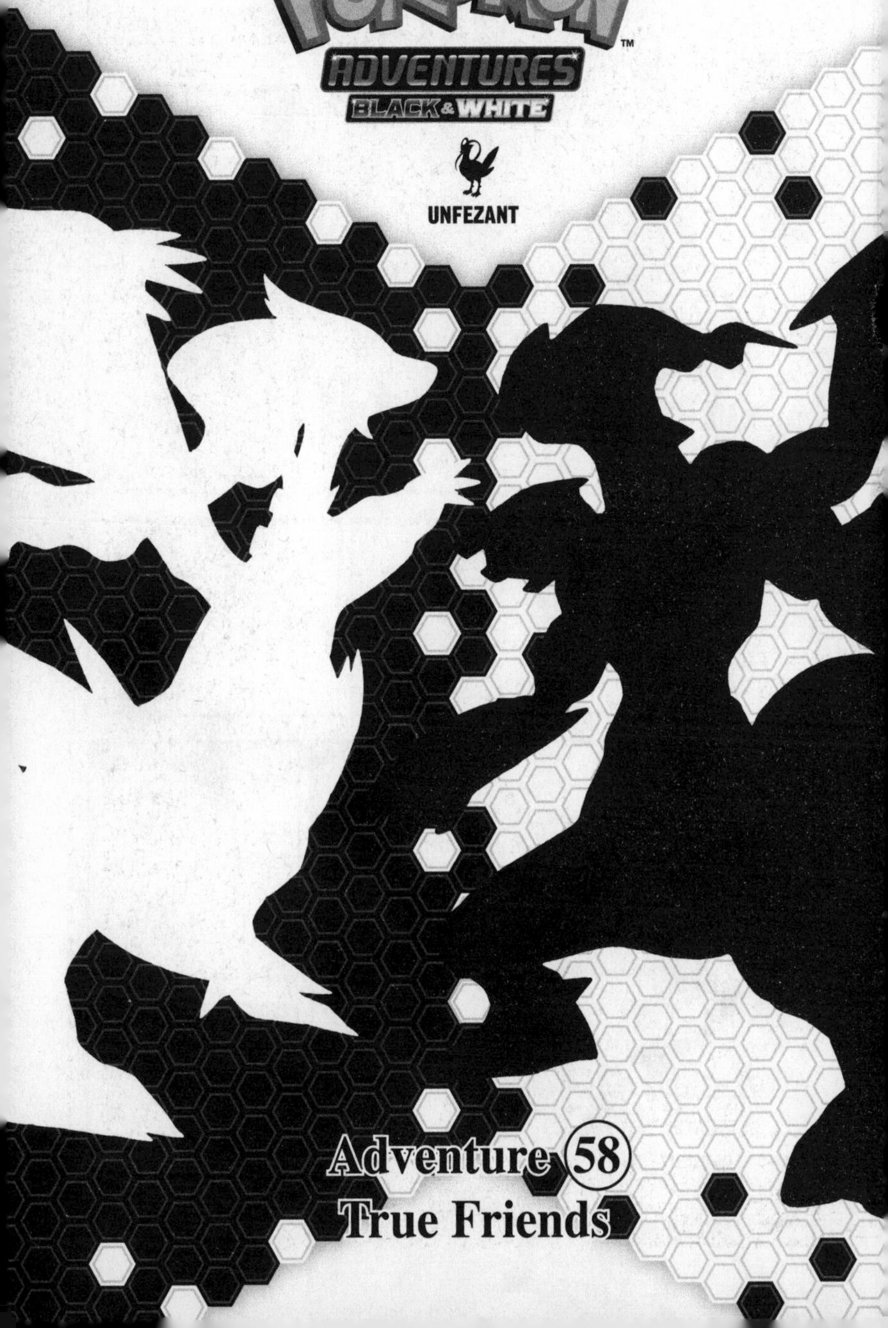

# Adventure 58
## True Friends

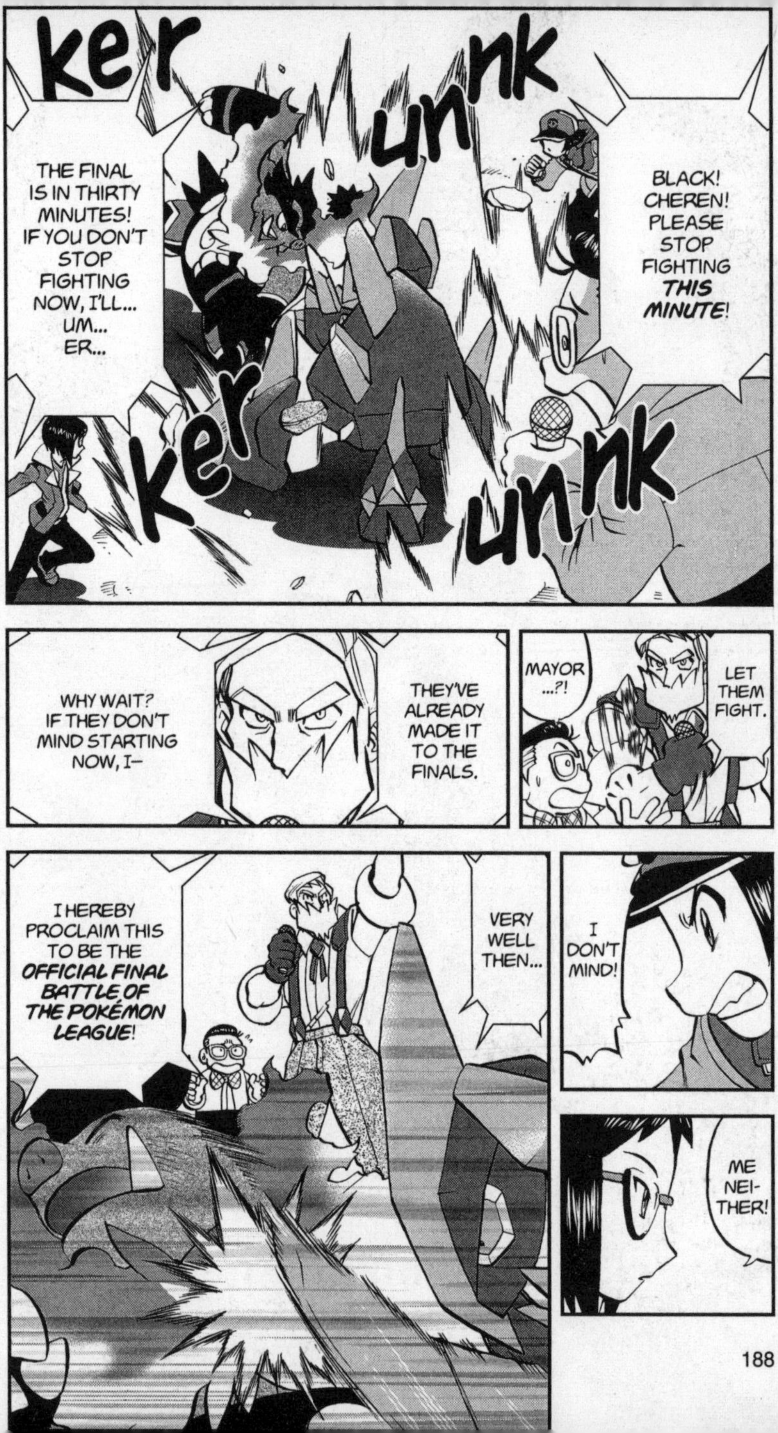

ker
unnk
BLACK! CHEREN! PLEASE STOP FIGHTING **THIS MINUTE**!
THE FINAL IS IN THIRTY MINUTES! IF YOU DON'T STOP FIGHTING NOW, I'LL... UM... ER...
ker
unnk
LET THEM FIGHT.
MAYOR ...?!
THEY'VE ALREADY MADE IT TO THE FINALS.
WHY WAIT? IF THEY DON'T MIND STARTING NOW, I—
I DON'T MIND!
ME NEI-THER!
VERY WELL THEN...
I HEREBY PROCLAIM THIS TO BE THE ***OFFICIAL FINAL BATTLE OF THE POKÉMON LEAGUE***!

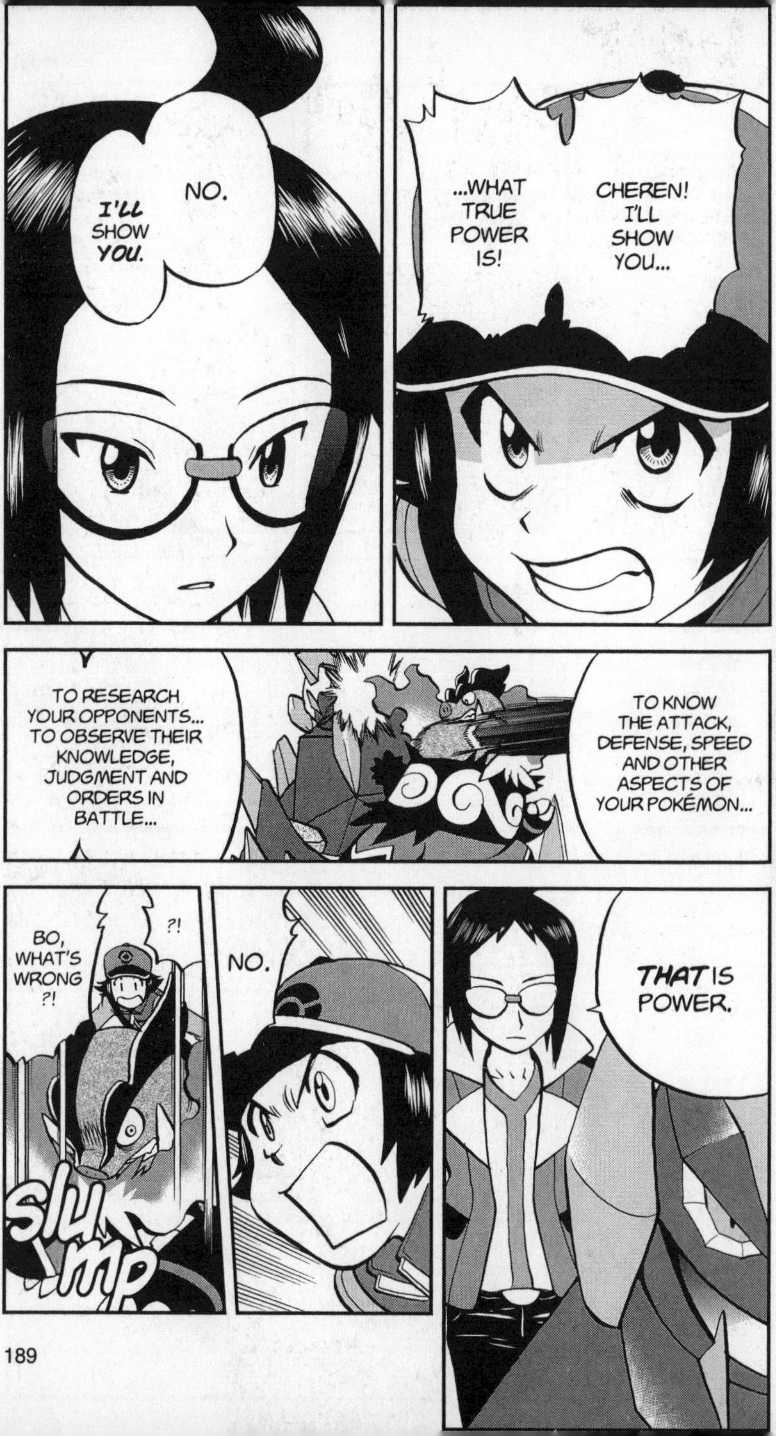
CHEREN! I'LL SHOW YOU...
...WHAT TRUE POWER IS!
NO.
I'LL SHOW YOU.
TO KNOW THE ATTACK, DEFENSE, SPEED AND OTHER ASPECTS OF YOUR POKÉMON...
TO RESEARCH YOUR OPPONENTS... TO OBSERVE THEIR KNOWLEDGE, JUDGMENT AND ORDERS IN BATTLE...
THAT IS POWER.
NO.
?!
BO, WHAT'S WRONG ?!
slump

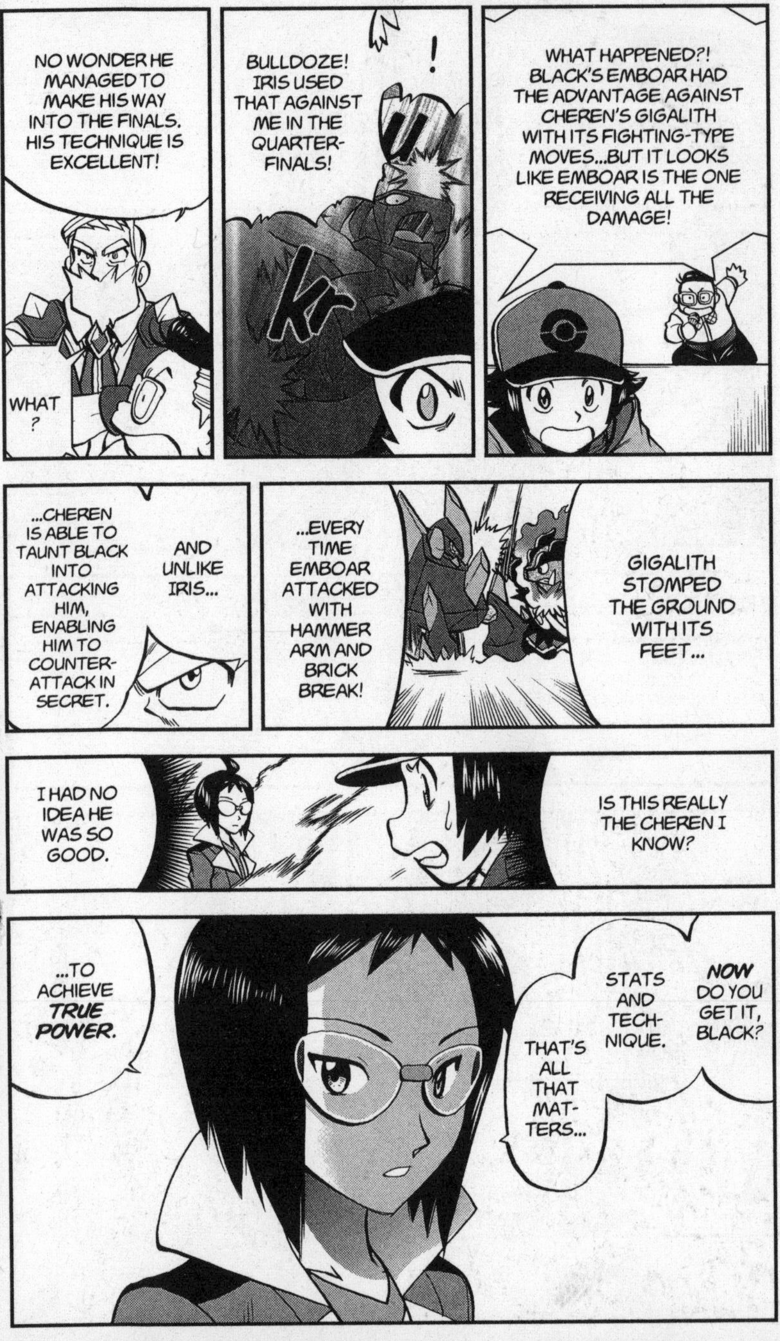
WHAT HAPPENED?! BLACK'S EMBOAR HAD THE ADVANTAGE AGAINST CHEREN'S GIGALITH WITH ITS FIGHTING-TYPE MOVES...BUT IT LOOKS LIKE EMBOAR IS THE ONE RECEIVING ALL THE DAMAGE!
!
BULLDOZE! IRIS USED THAT AGAINST ME IN THE QUARTER-FINALS!
kr
NO WONDER HE MANAGED TO MAKE HIS WAY INTO THE FINALS. HIS TECHNIQUE IS EXCELLENT!
WHAT ?
GIGALITH STOMPED THE GROUND WITH ITS FEET...
...EVERY TIME EMBOAR ATTACKED WITH HAMMER ARM AND BRICK BREAK!
AND UNLIKE IRIS...
...CHEREN IS ABLE TO TAUNT BLACK INTO ATTACKING HIM, ENABLING HIM TO COUNTER-ATTACK IN SECRET.
IS THIS REALLY THE CHEREN I KNOW?
I HAD NO IDEA HE WAS SO GOOD.
*NOW* DO YOU GET IT, BLACK?
STATS AND TECH-NIQUE.
THAT'S ALL THAT MAT-TERS...
...TO ACHIEVE ***TRUE POWER***.

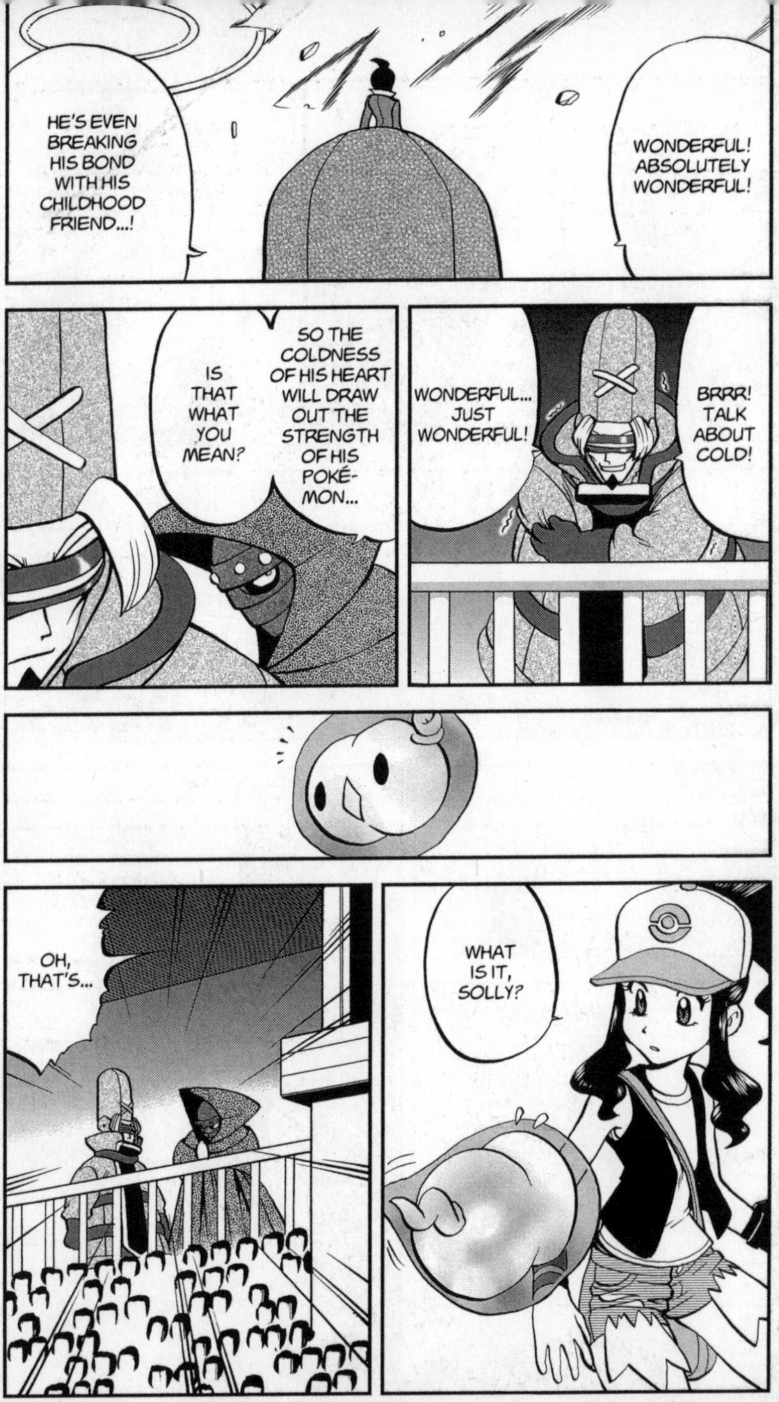
WONDERFUL! ABSOLUTELY WONDERFUL!
HE'S EVEN BREAKING HIS BOND WITH HIS CHILDHOOD FRIEND...!
BRRR! TALK ABOUT COLD!
WONDERFUL... JUST WONDERFUL!
SO THE COLDNESS OF HIS HEART WILL DRAW OUT THE STRENGTH OF HIS POKÉ-MON...
IS THAT WHAT YOU MEAN?
WHAT IS IT, SOLLY?
OH, THAT'S...

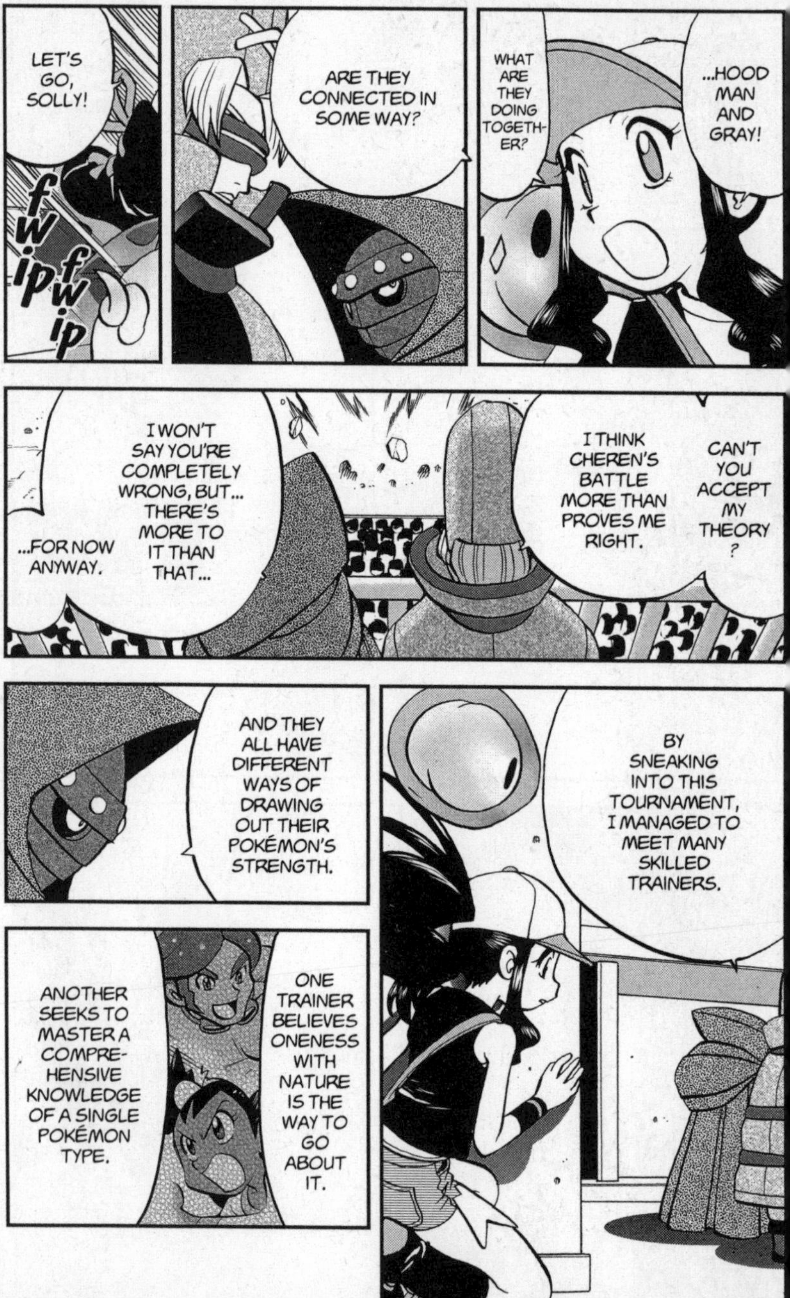
...HOOD MAN AND GRAY!
WHAT ARE THEY DOING TOGETHER?
ARE THEY CONNECTED IN SOME WAY?
LET'S GO, SOLLY!
fwip fwip
CAN'T YOU ACCEPT MY THEORY?
I THINK CHEREN'S BATTLE MORE THAN PROVES ME RIGHT.
I WON'T SAY YOU'RE COMPLETELY WRONG, BUT... THERE'S MORE TO IT THAN THAT...
...FOR NOW ANYWAY.
BY SNEAKING INTO THIS TOURNAMENT, I MANAGED TO MEET MANY SKILLED TRAINERS.
AND THEY ALL HAVE DIFFERENT WAYS OF DRAWING OUT THEIR POKÉMON'S STRENGTH.
ONE TRAINER BELIEVES ONENESS WITH NATURE IS THE WAY TO GO ABOUT IT.
ANOTHER SEEKS TO MASTER A COMPREHENSIVE KNOWLEDGE OF A SINGLE POKÉMON TYPE.

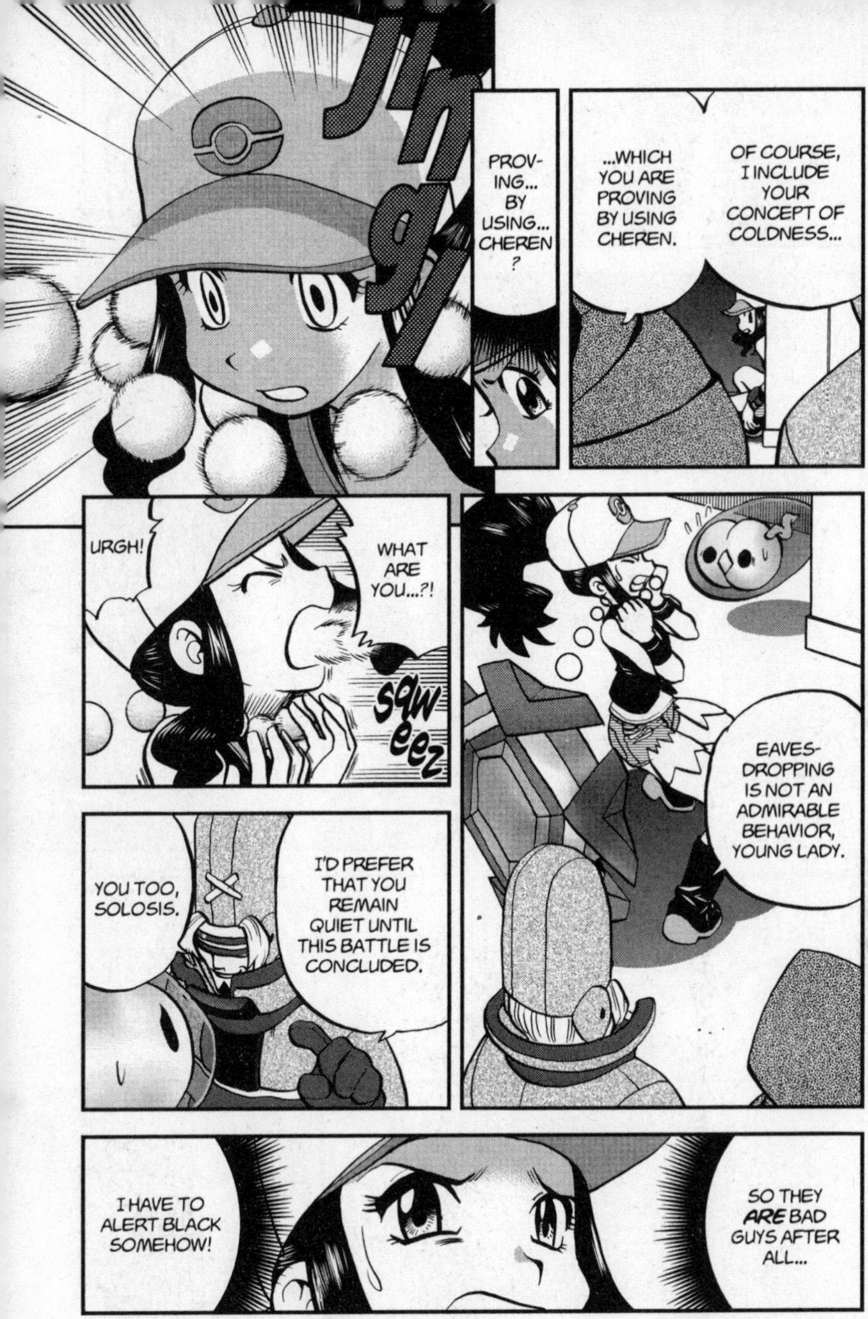
OF COURSE, I INCLUDE YOUR CONCEPT OF COLDNESS...
...WHICH YOU ARE PROVING BY USING CHEREN.
PROV-ING... BY USING... CHEREN?
EAVES-DROPPING IS NOT AN ADMIRABLE BEHAVIOR, YOUNG LADY.
WHAT ARE YOU...?!
URGH!
sqweez
I'D PREFER THAT YOU REMAIN QUIET UNTIL THIS BATTLE IS CONCLUDED.
YOU TOO, SOLOSIS.
SO THEY *ARE* BAD GUYS AFTER ALL...
I HAVE TO ALERT BLACK SOMEHOW!

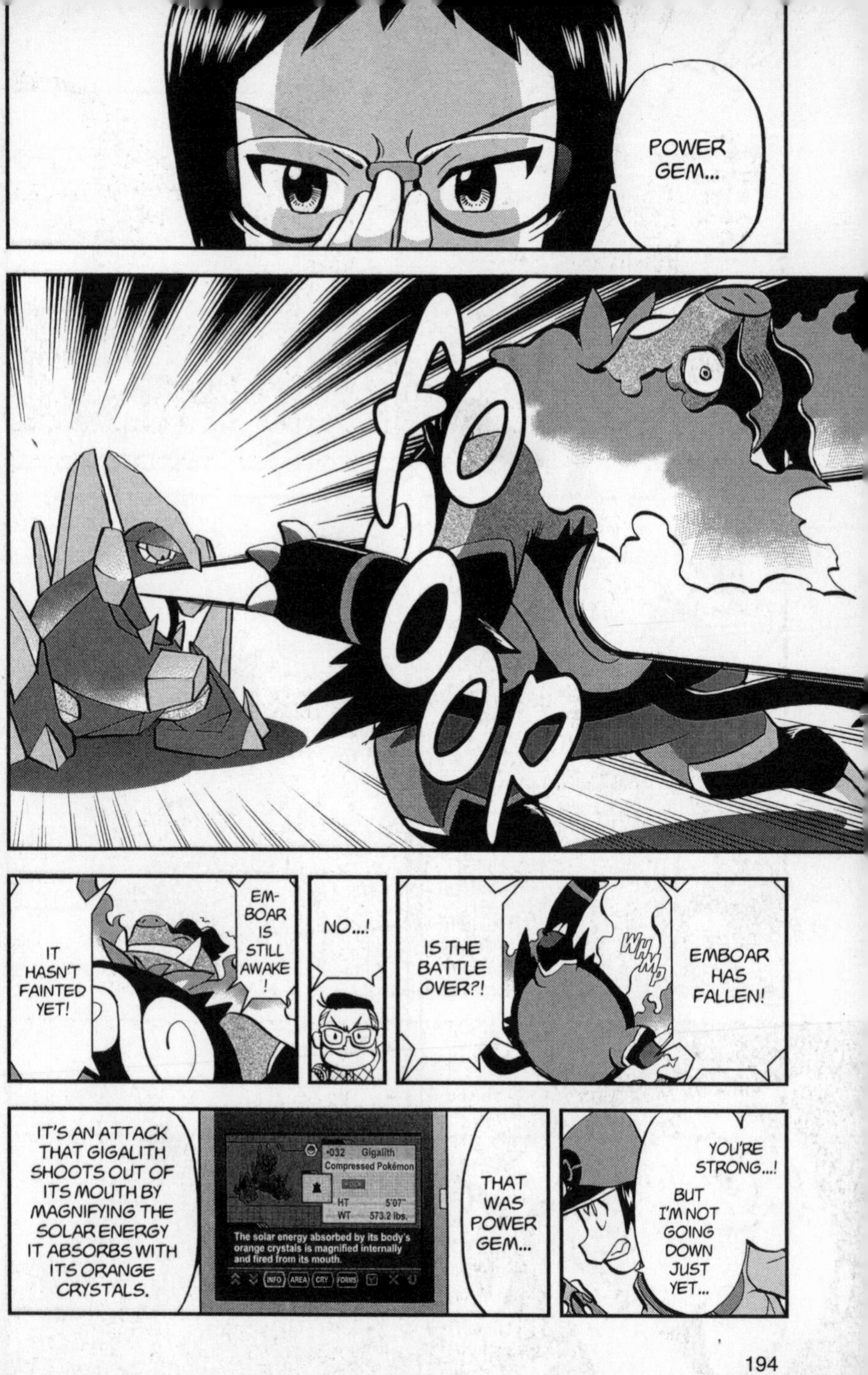
POWER GEM...
FOOOOP
EMBOAR HAS FALLEN!
WHMP
IS THE BATTLE OVER?!
NO...!
EM-BOAR IS STILL AWAKE!
IT HASN'T FAINTED YET!
YOU'RE STRONG...!
BUT I'M NOT GOING DOWN JUST YET...
THAT WAS POWER GEM...
•032 Gigalith
Compressed Pokémon
HT 5'07"
WT 573.2 lbs.
The solar energy absorbed by its body's orange crystals is magnified internally and fired from its mouth.
INFO AREA CRY FORMS
IT'S AN ATTACK THAT GIGALITH SHOOTS OUT OF ITS MOUTH BY MAGNIFYING THE SOLAR ENERGY IT ABSORBS WITH ITS ORANGE CRYSTALS.

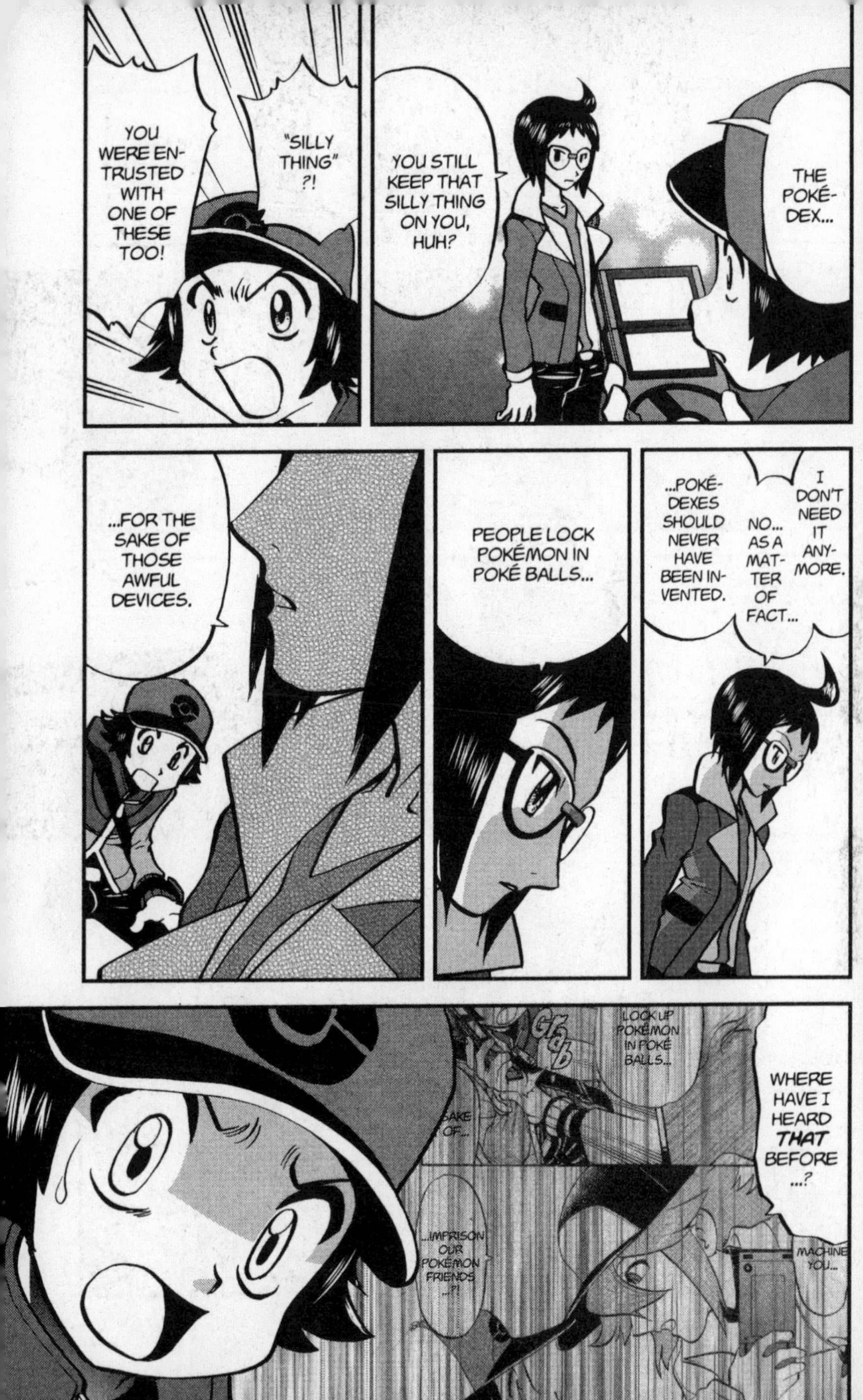
THE POKÉ-DEX...
YOU STILL KEEP THAT SILLY THING ON YOU, HUH?
"SILLY THING"?!
YOU WERE EN-TRUSTED WITH ONE OF THESE TOO!
I DON'T NEED IT ANY-MORE.
NO... AS A MAT-TER OF FACT...
...POKÉ-DEXES SHOULD NEVER HAVE BEEN IN-VENTED.
PEOPLE LOCK POKÉMON IN POKÉ BALLS...
...FOR THE SAKE OF THOSE AWFUL DEVICES.
WHERE HAVE I HEARD ***THAT*** BEFORE ...?
LOCK UP POKÉMON IN POKÉ BALLS...
Grab
SAKE OF...
MACHINE YOU...
...IMPRISON OUR POKÉMON FRIENDS ...?!

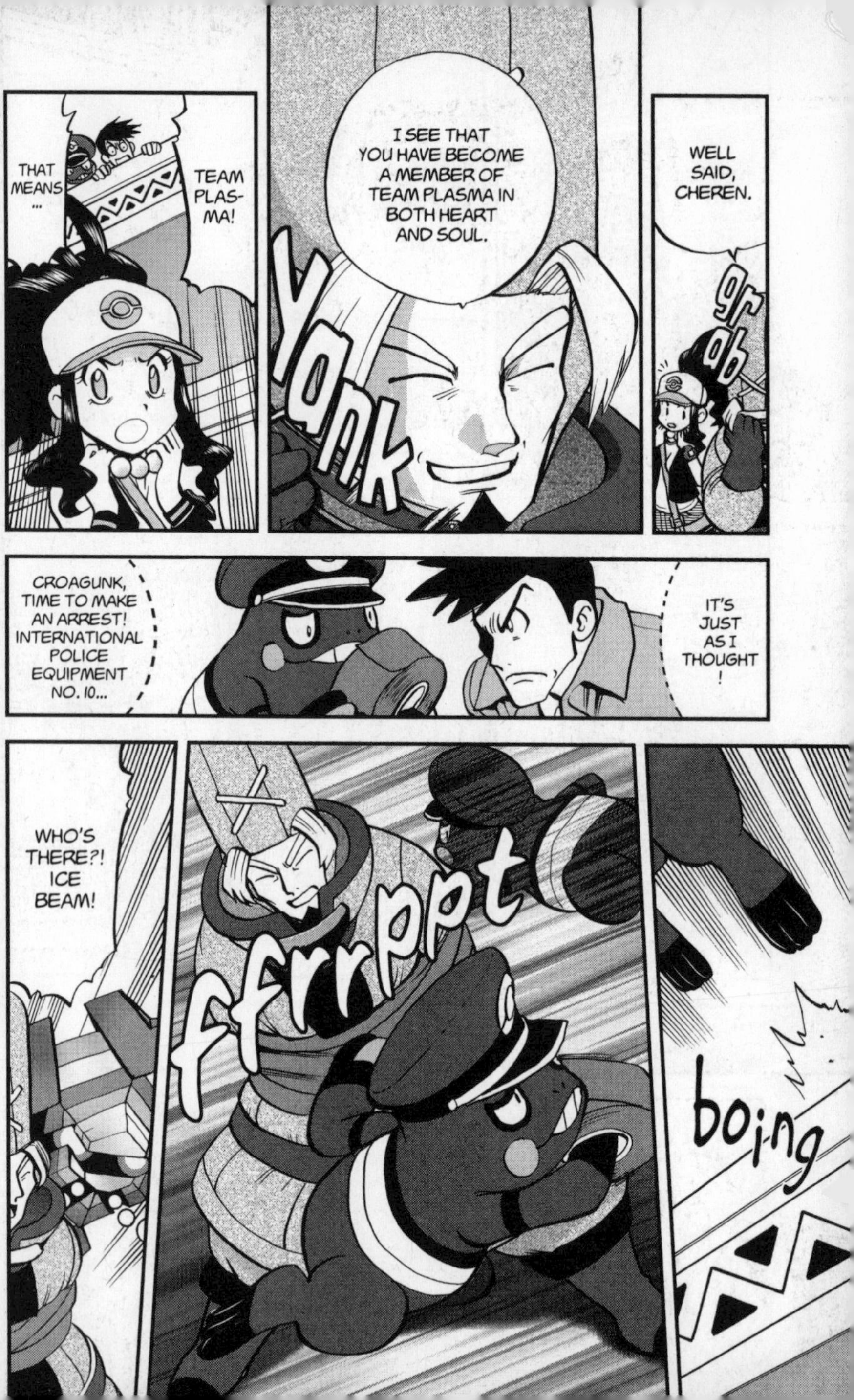
WELL SAID, CHEREN.
grab
I SEE THAT YOU HAVE BECOME A MEMBER OF TEAM PLASMA IN BOTH HEART AND SOUL.
Yank
TEAM PLASMA!
THAT MEANS...
IT'S JUST AS I THOUGHT!
CROAGUNK, TIME TO MAKE AN ARREST! INTERNATIONAL POLICE EQUIPMENT NO. 10...
boing
ffrrppt
WHO'S THERE?! ICE BEAM!

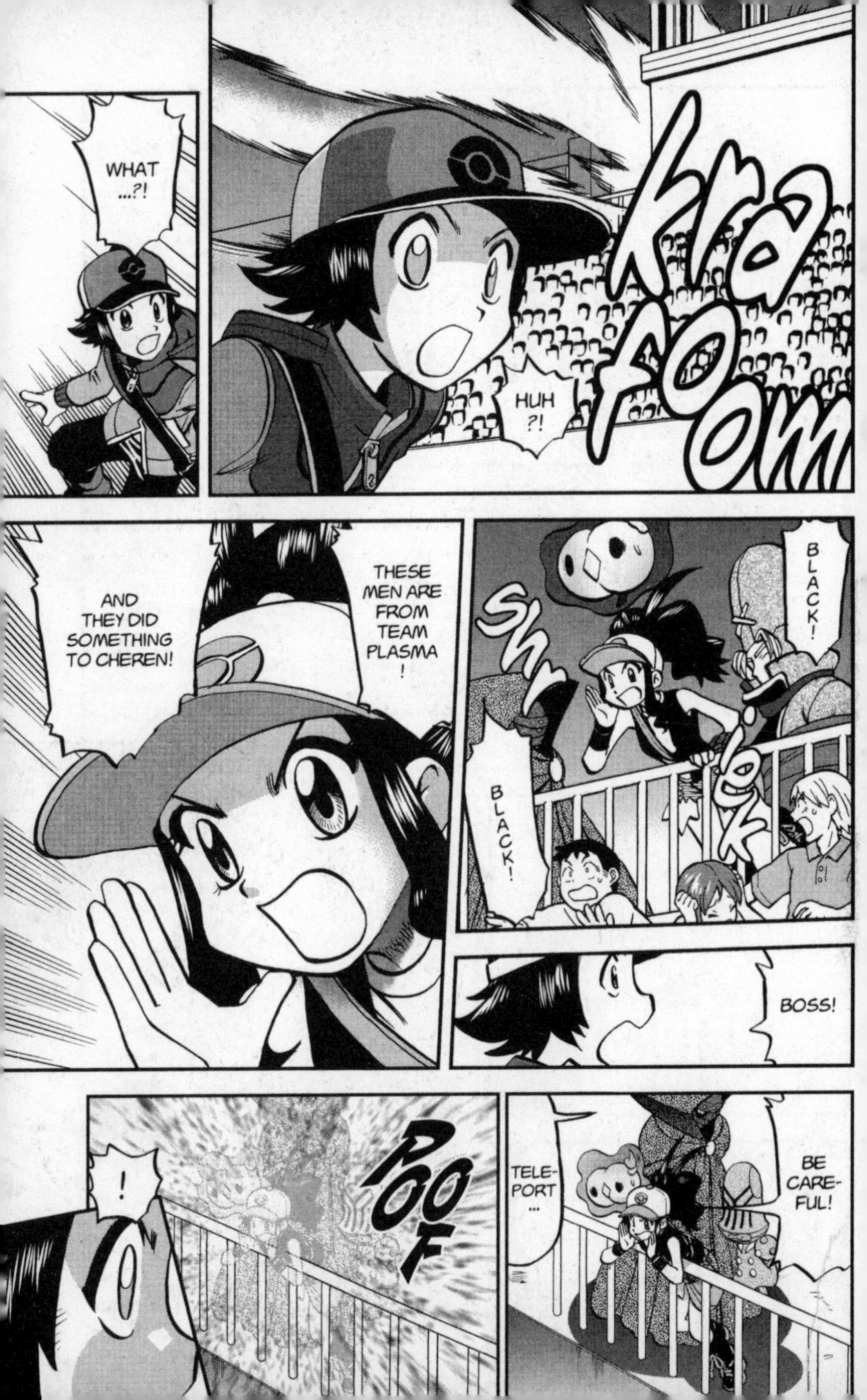

kra
foom
HUH ?!
WHAT ...?!
BLACK!
BLACK!
BOSS!
THESE MEN ARE FROM TEAM PLASMA!
AND THEY DID SOMETHING TO CHEREN!
BE CAREFUL!
TELEPORT ...
POOF
!

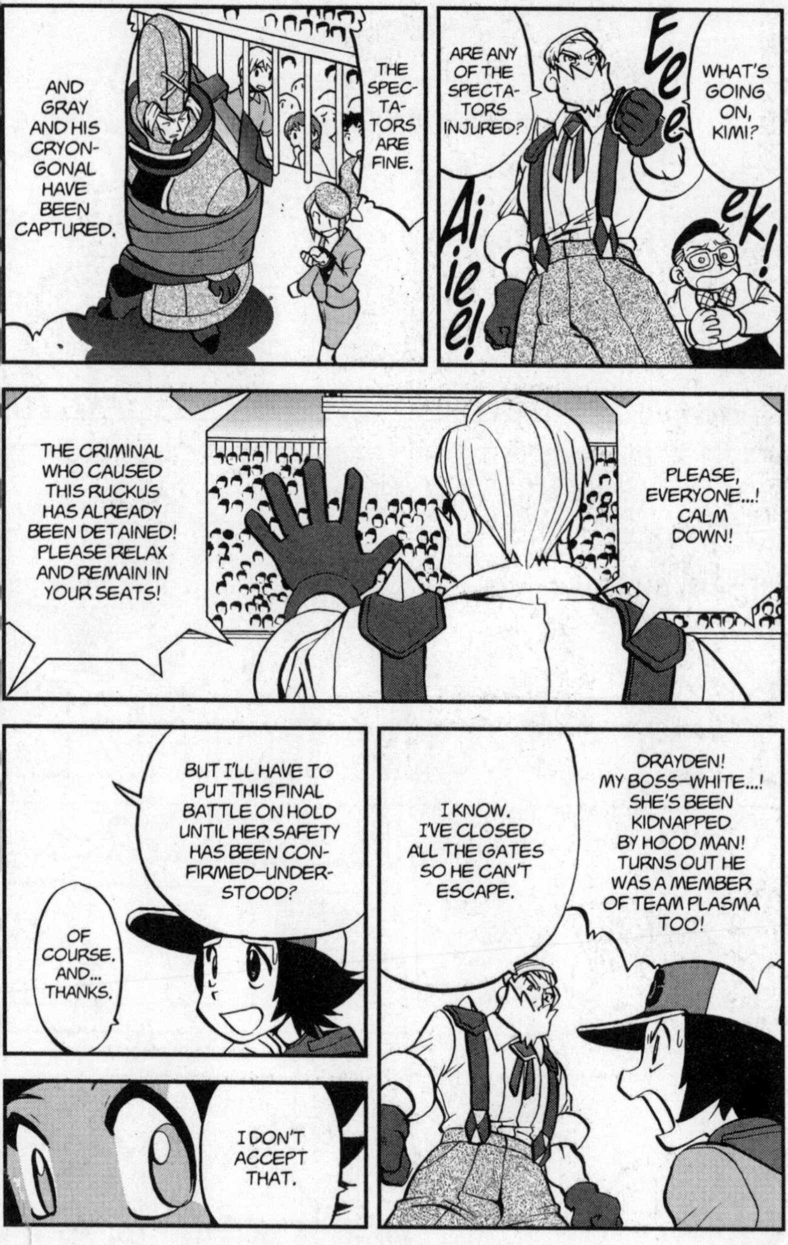
WHAT'S GOING ON, KIMI?
Eeee
ARE ANY OF THE SPECTATORS INJURED?
ek!
Aieee!
THE SPECTATORS ARE FINE.
AND GRAY AND HIS CRYONGONAL HAVE BEEN CAPTURED.
PLEASE, EVERYONE...! CALM DOWN!
THE CRIMINAL WHO CAUSED THIS RUCKUS HAS ALREADY BEEN DETAINED! PLEASE RELAX AND REMAIN IN YOUR SEATS!
DRAYDEN! MY BOSS—WHITE...! SHE'S BEEN KIDNAPPED BY HOOD MAN! TURNS OUT HE WAS A MEMBER OF TEAM PLASMA TOO!
I KNOW. I'VE CLOSED ALL THE GATES SO HE CAN'T ESCAPE.
BUT I'LL HAVE TO PUT THIS FINAL BATTLE ON HOLD UNTIL HER SAFETY HAS BEEN CONFIRMED—UNDERSTOOD?
OF COURSE. AND... THANKS.
I DON'T ACCEPT THAT.

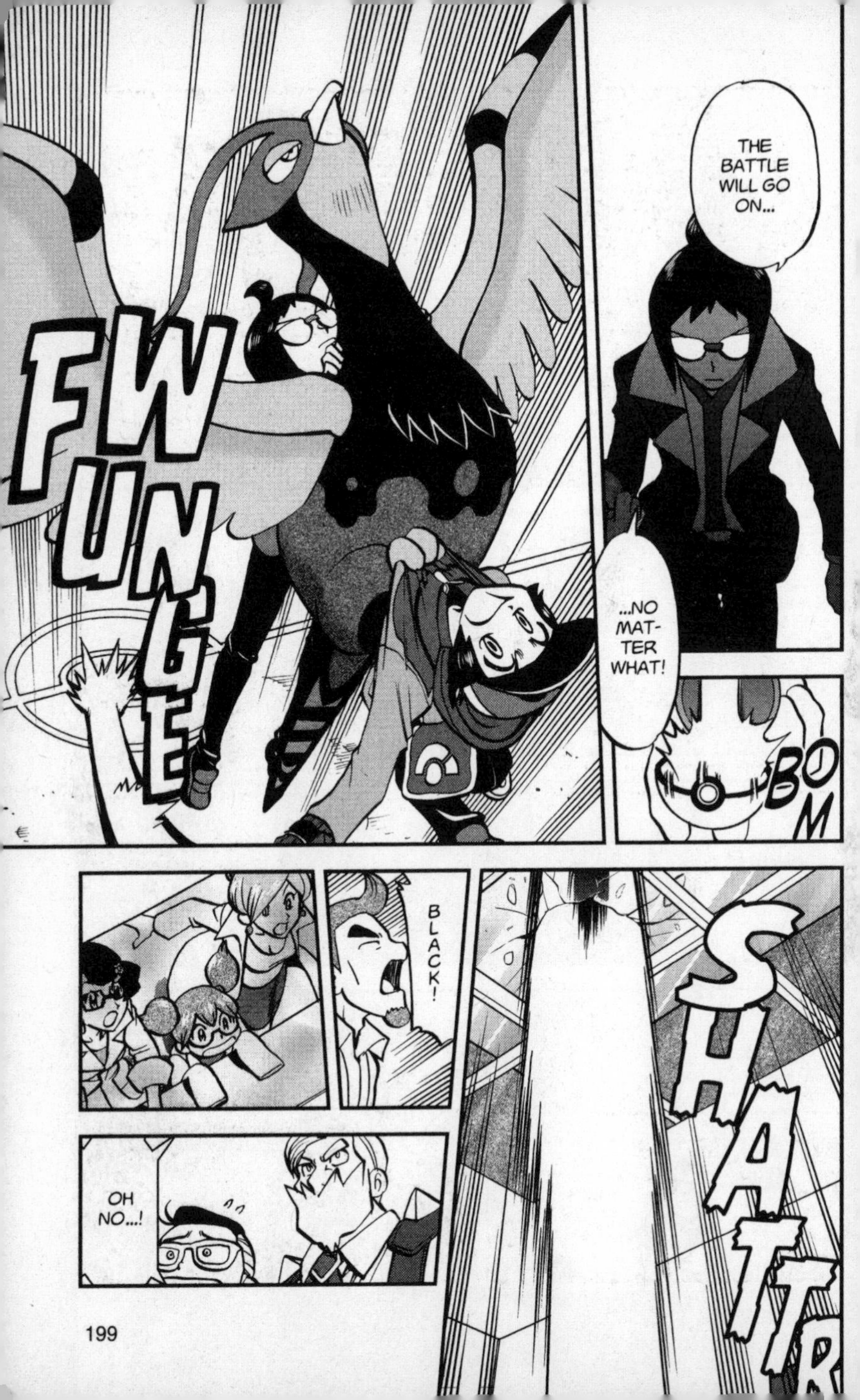
THE BATTLE WILL GO ON...
...NO MATTER WHAT!
BOOM
FWUNGE
SHATTR
BLACK!
OH NO...!

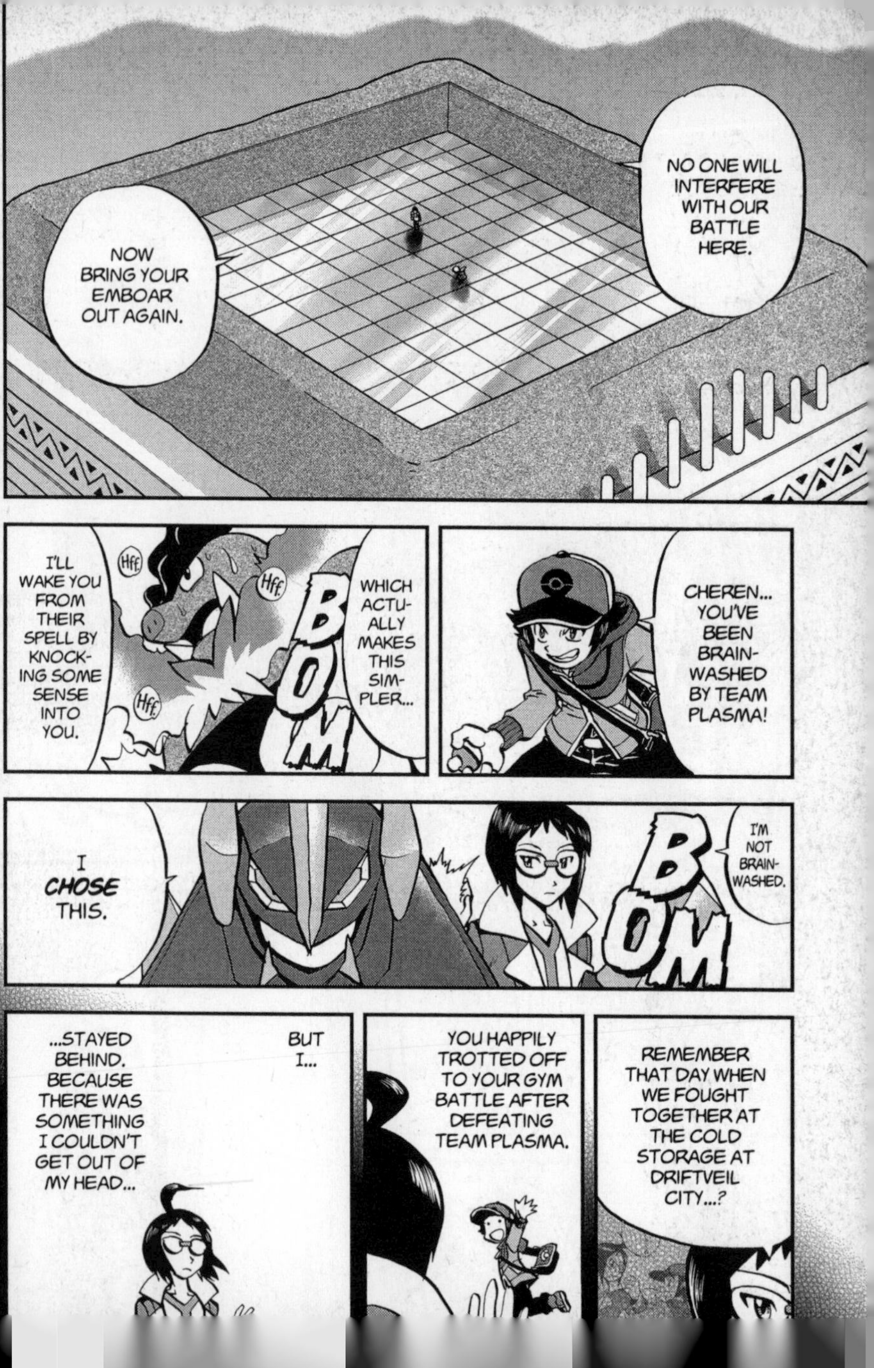
NO ONE WILL INTERFERE WITH OUR BATTLE HERE.
NOW BRING YOUR EMBOAR OUT AGAIN.
CHEREN... YOU'VE BEEN BRAIN-WASHED BY TEAM PLASMA!
WHICH ACTU-ALLY MAKES THIS SIM-PLER...
BOOM
Hff
Hff
I'LL WAKE YOU FROM THEIR SPELL BY KNOCK-ING SOME SENSE INTO YOU.
Hff
I'M NOT BRAIN-WASHED.
BOOM
I CHOSE THIS.
REMEMBER THAT DAY WHEN WE FOUGHT TOGETHER AT THE COLD STORAGE AT DRIFTVEIL CITY...?
YOU HAPPILY TROTTED OFF TO YOUR GYM BATTLE AFTER DEFEATING TEAM PLASMA.
BUT I...
...STAYED BEHIND. BECAUSE THERE WAS SOMETHING I COULDN'T GET OUT OF MY HEAD...

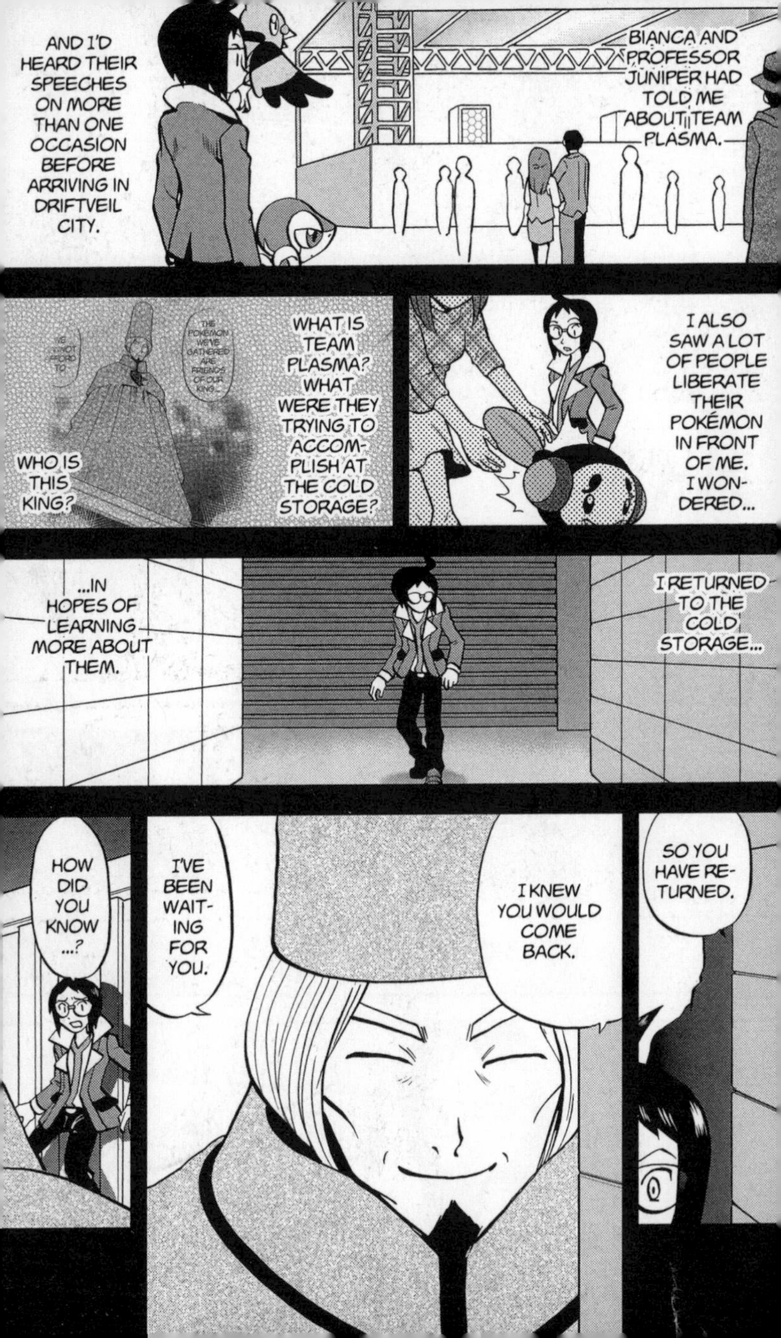
BIANCA AND PROFESSOR JUNIPER HAD TOLD ME ABOUT TEAM PLASMA.
AND I'D HEARD THEIR SPEECHES ON MORE THAN ONE OCCASION BEFORE ARRIVING IN DRIFTVEIL CITY.
I ALSO SAW A LOT OF PEOPLE LIBERATE THEIR POKÉMON IN FRONT OF ME. I WONDERED...
WHAT IS TEAM PLASMA? WHAT WERE THEY TRYING TO ACCOM-PLISH AT THE COLD STORAGE?
THE POKÉMON WE'VE GATHERED ARE FRIENDS OF OUR KING...
WHO IS THIS KING?
I RETURNED TO THE COLD STORAGE...
...IN HOPES OF LEARNING MORE ABOUT THEM.
SO YOU HAVE RE-TURNED.
I KNEW YOU WOULD COME BACK.
I'VE BEEN WAIT-ING FOR YOU.
HOW DID YOU KNOW ...?

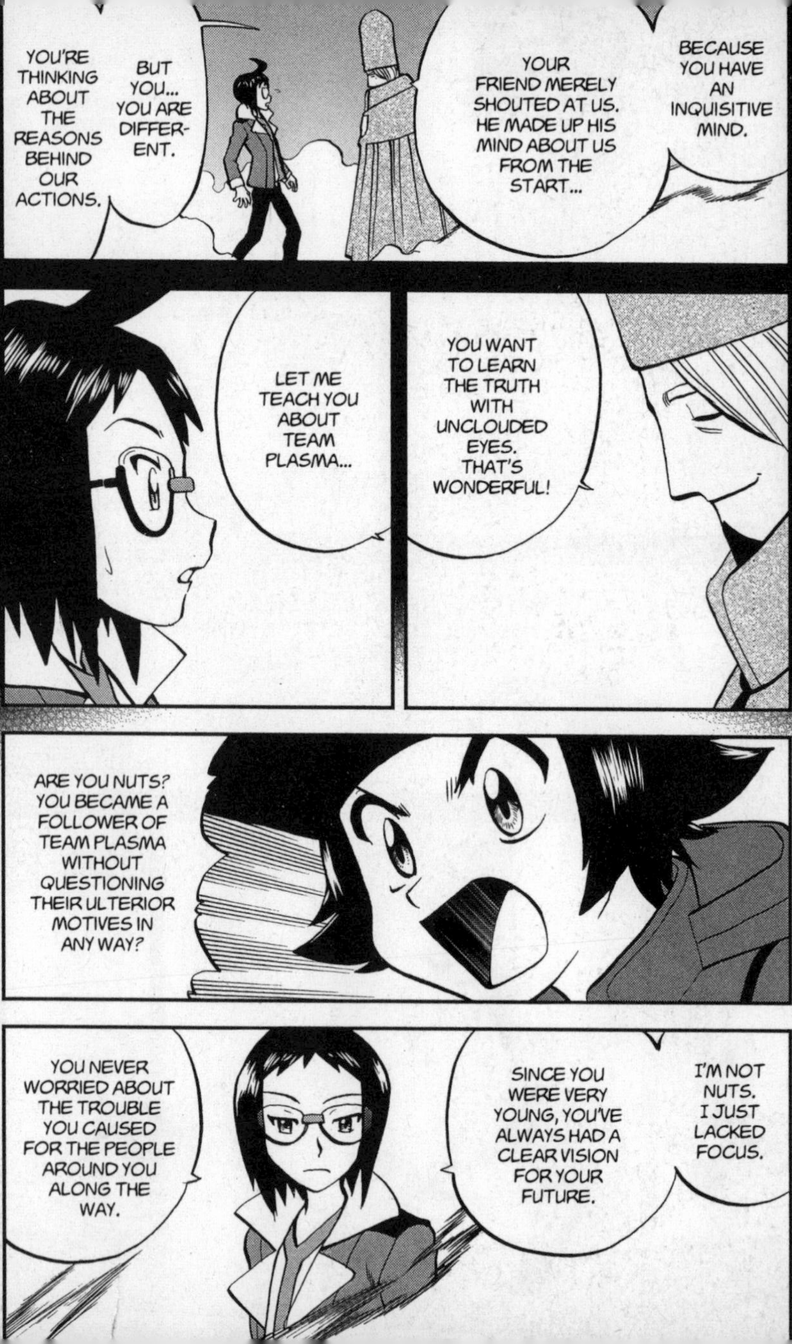
BECAUSE YOU HAVE AN INQUISITIVE MIND.
YOUR FRIEND MERELY SHOUTED AT US. HE MADE UP HIS MIND ABOUT US FROM THE START...
BUT YOU... YOU ARE DIFFER-ENT.
YOU'RE THINKING ABOUT THE REASONS BEHIND OUR ACTIONS.
YOU WANT TO LEARN THE TRUTH WITH UNCLOUDED EYES. THAT'S WONDERFUL!
LET ME TEACH YOU ABOUT TEAM PLASMA...
ARE YOU NUTS? YOU BECAME A FOLLOWER OF TEAM PLASMA WITHOUT QUESTIONING THEIR ULTERIOR MOTIVES IN ANY WAY?
I'M NOT NUTS. I JUST LACKED FOCUS.
SINCE YOU WERE VERY YOUNG, YOU'VE ALWAYS HAD A CLEAR VISION FOR YOUR FUTURE.
YOU NEVER WORRIED ABOUT THE TROUBLE YOU CAUSED FOR THE PEOPLE AROUND YOU ALONG THE WAY.

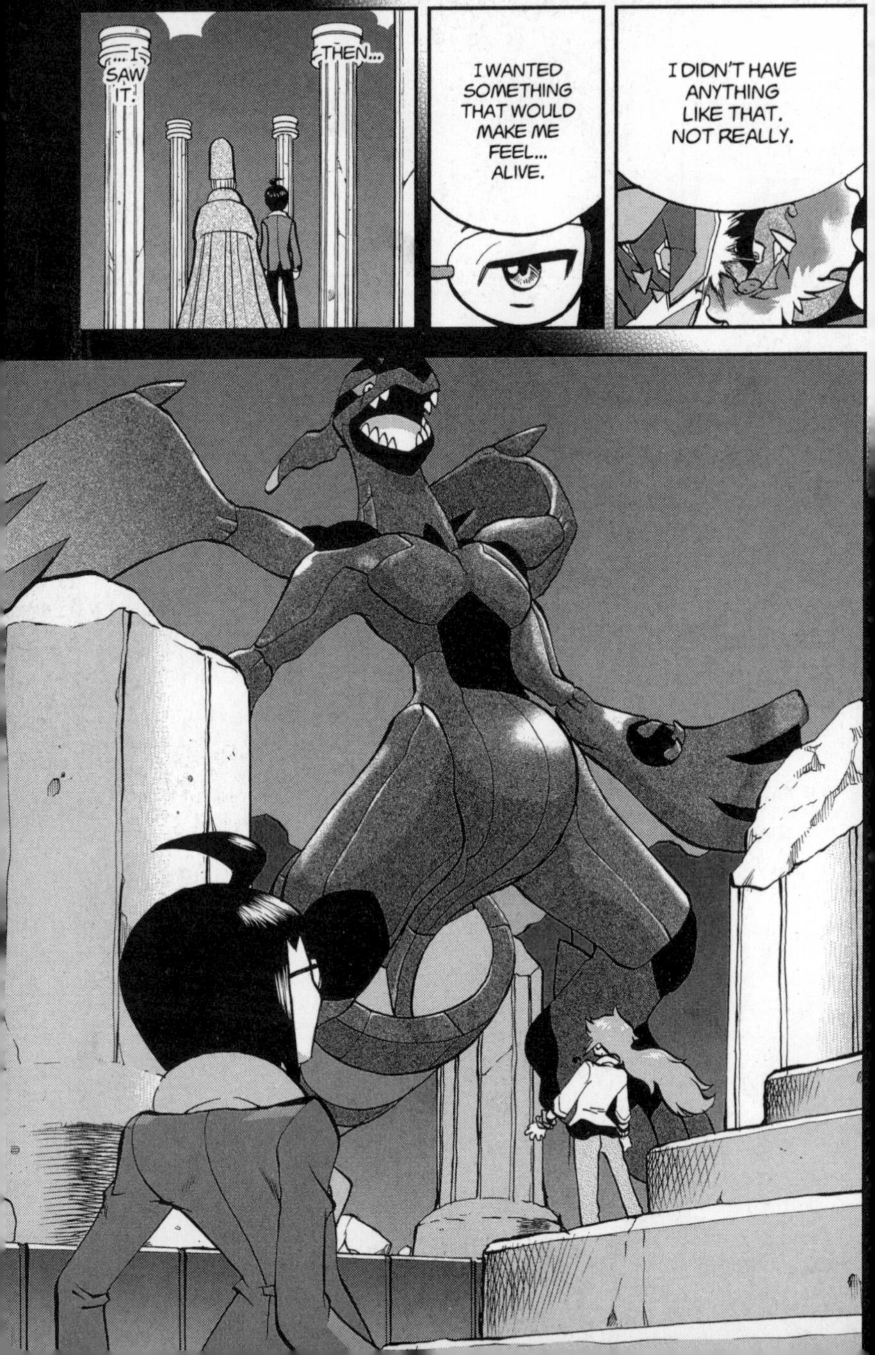
I DIDN'T HAVE ANYTHING LIKE THAT. NOT REALLY.
I WANTED SOMETHING THAT WOULD MAKE ME FEEL... ALIVE.
THEN...
...I SAW IT.

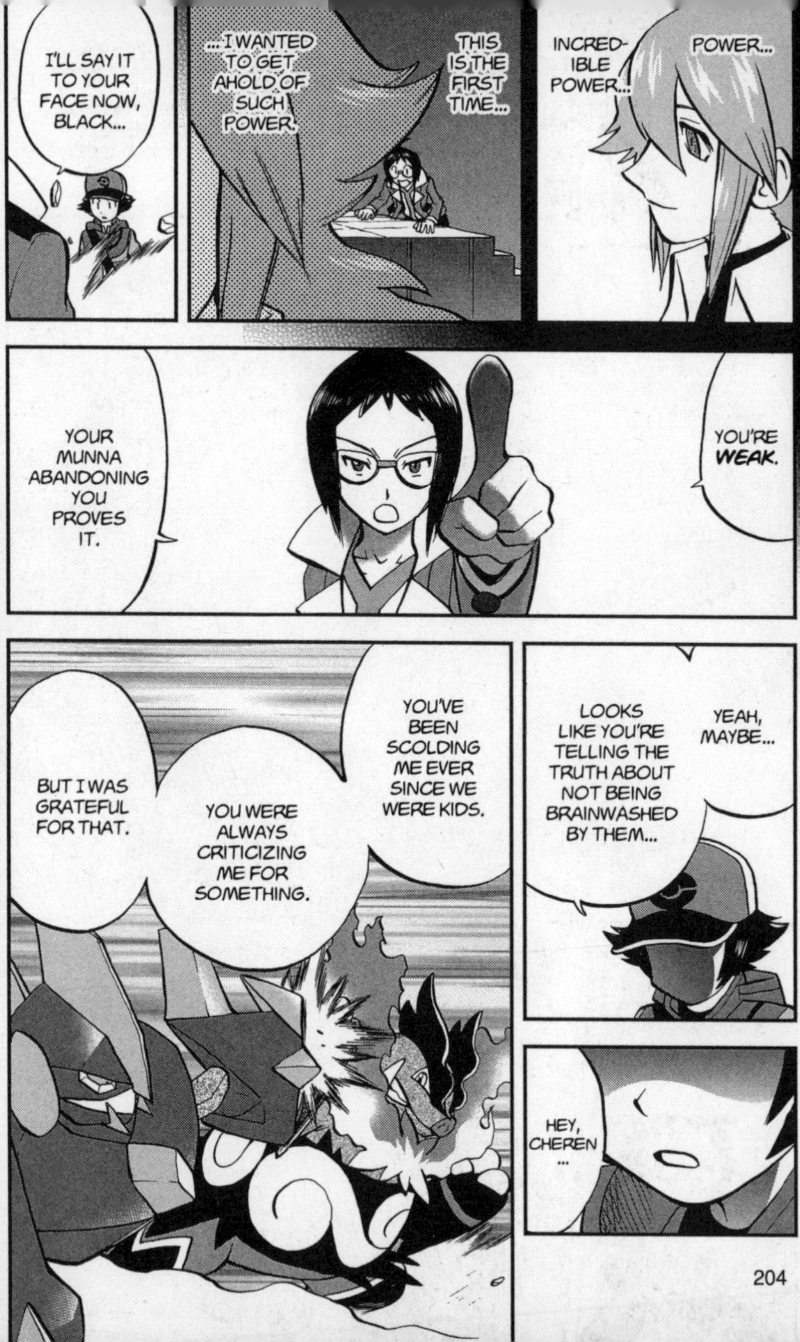
POWER...
INCRED-IBLE POWER...
THIS IS THE FIRST TIME...
...I WANTED TO GET AHOLD OF SUCH POWER.
I'LL SAY IT TO YOUR FACE NOW, BLACK...
YOU'RE **WEAK.**
YOUR MUNNA ABANDONING YOU PROVES IT.
YEAH, MAYBE...
LOOKS LIKE YOU'RE TELLING THE TRUTH ABOUT NOT BEING BRAINWASHED BY THEM...
HEY, CHEREN...
YOU'VE BEEN SCOLDING ME EVER SINCE WE WERE KIDS.
YOU WERE ALWAYS CRITICIZING ME FOR SOMETHING.
BUT I WAS GRATEFUL FOR THAT.

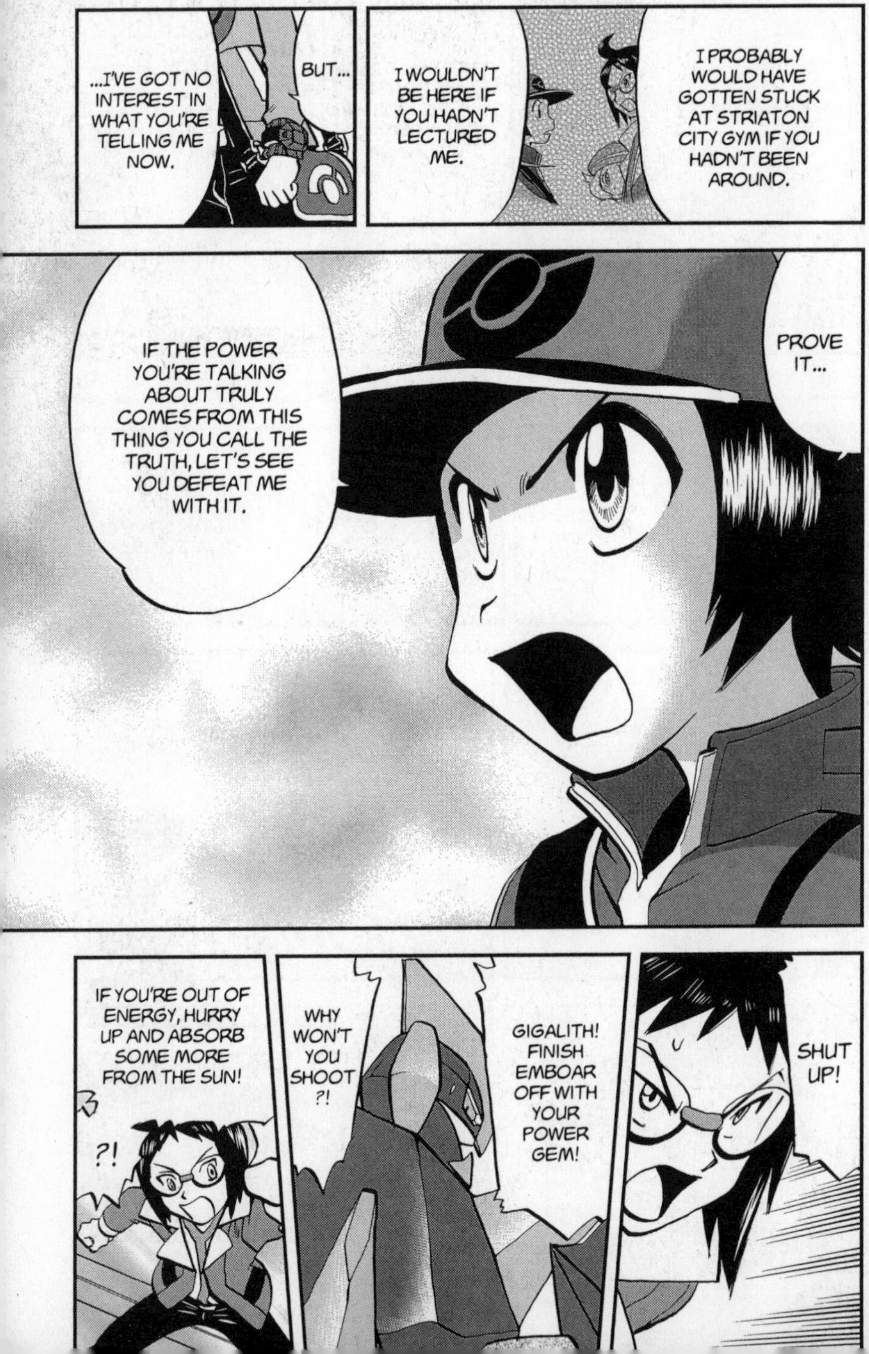
I PROBABLY WOULD HAVE GOTTEN STUCK AT STRIATON CITY GYM IF YOU HADN'T BEEN AROUND.
I WOULDN'T BE HERE IF YOU HADN'T LECTURED ME.
BUT...
...I'VE GOT NO INTEREST IN WHAT YOU'RE TELLING ME NOW.
PROVE IT...
IF THE POWER YOU'RE TALKING ABOUT TRULY COMES FROM THIS THING YOU CALL THE TRUTH, LET'S SEE YOU DEFEAT ME WITH IT.
SHUT UP!
GIGALITH! FINISH EMBOAR OFF WITH YOUR POWER GEM!
WHY WON'T YOU SHOOT ?!
IF YOU'RE OUT OF ENERGY, HURRY UP AND ABSORB SOME MORE FROM THE SUN!
?!

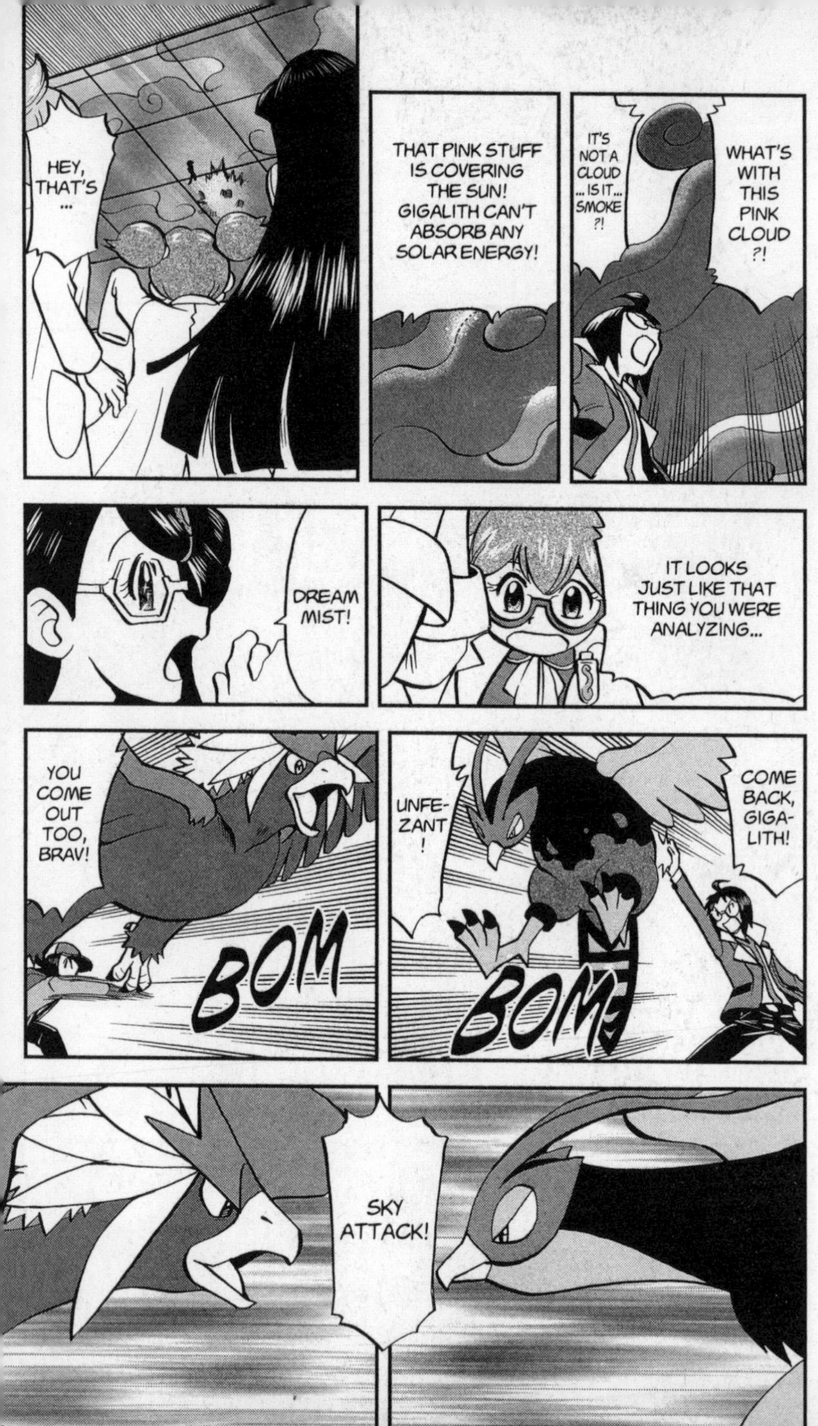

WHAT'S WITH THIS PINK CLOUD ?!
IT'S NOT A CLOUD ...IS IT... SMOKE ?!
THAT PINK STUFF IS COVERING THE SUN! GIGALITH CAN'T ABSORB ANY SOLAR ENERGY!
HEY, THAT'S ...
IT LOOKS JUST LIKE THAT THING YOU WERE ANALYZING...
DREAM MIST!
COME BACK, GIGA-LITH!
UNFE-ZANT !
BOM
YOU COME OUT TOO, BRAV!
BOM
SKY ATTACK!

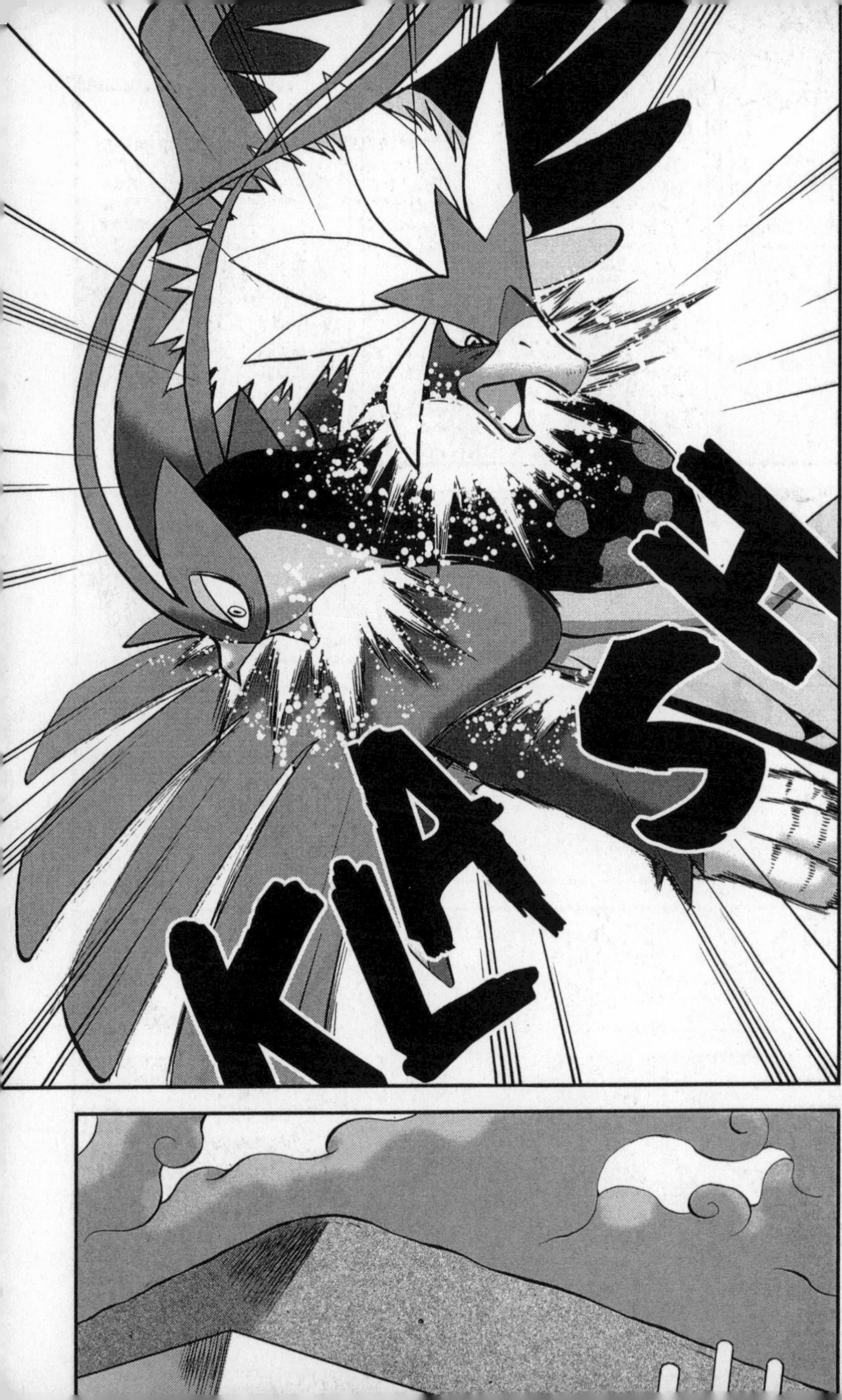
KLASH

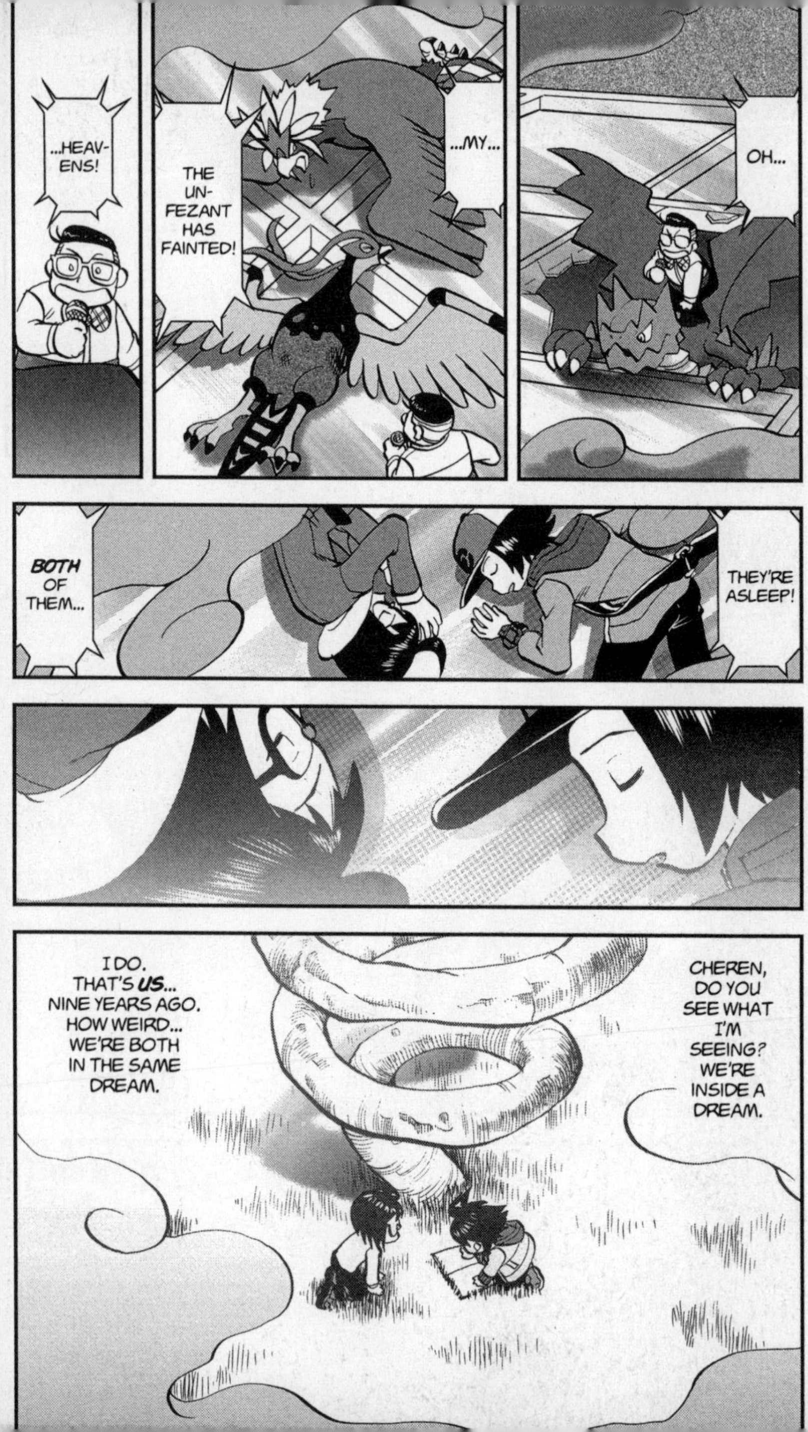
OH...
...MY...
THE UN-FEZANT HAS FAINTED!
...HEAV-ENS!
THEY'RE ASLEEP!
BOTH OF THEM...
CHEREN, DO YOU SEE WHAT I'M SEEING? WE'RE INSIDE A DREAM.
I DO. THAT'S US... NINE YEARS AGO. HOW WEIRD... WE'RE BOTH IN THE SAME DREAM.

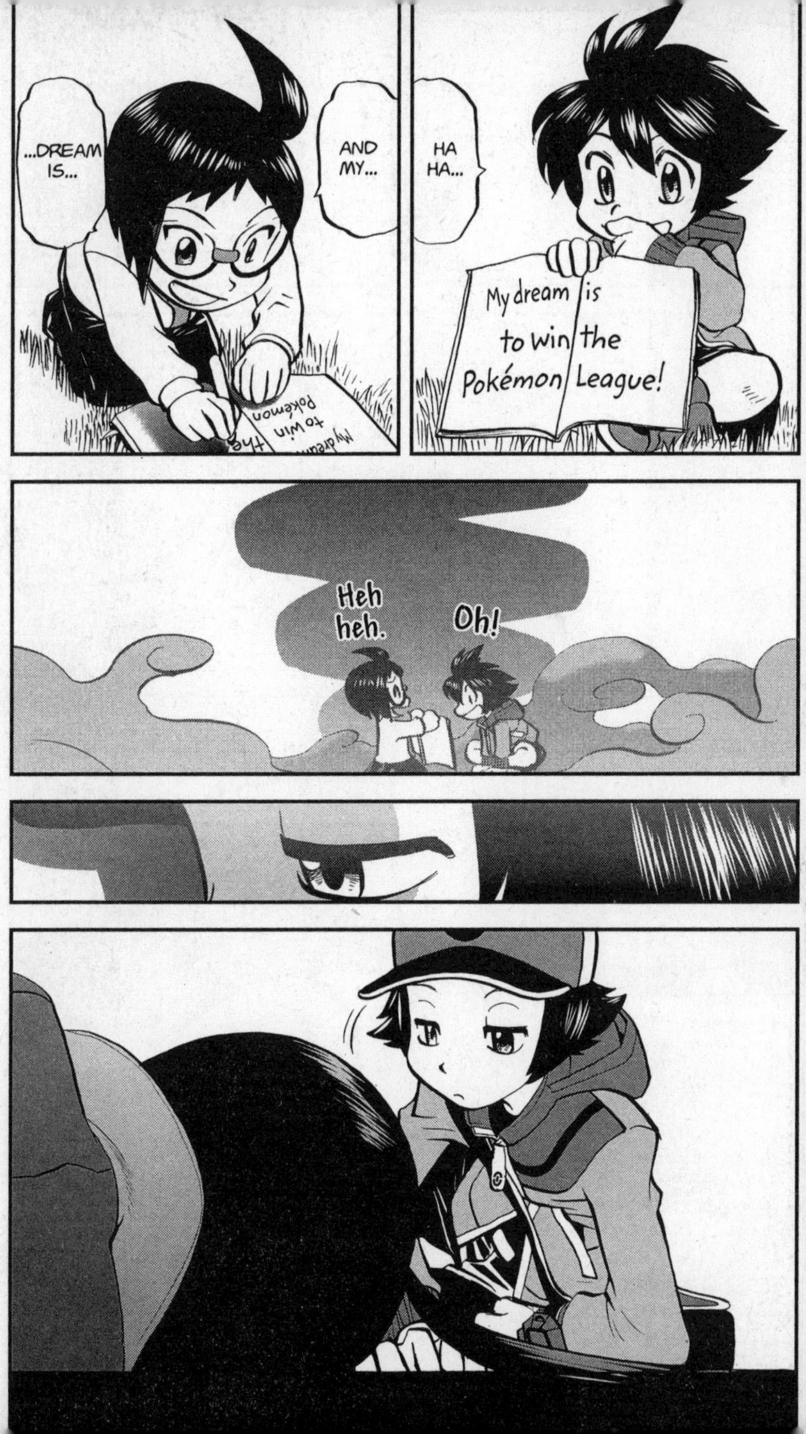
HA HA...
My dream is to win the Pokémon League!
AND MY...
...DREAM IS...
Oh!
Heh heh.

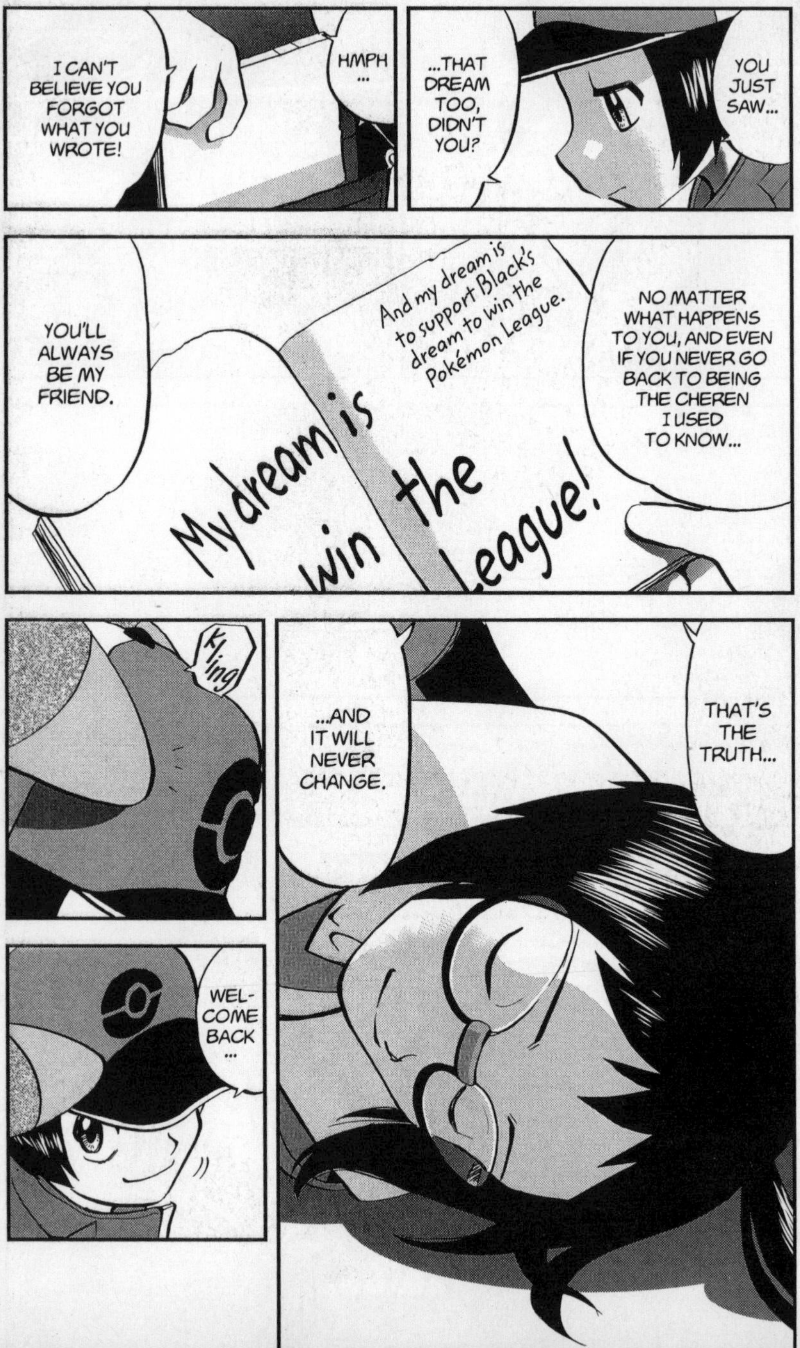
YOU JUST SAW...
...THAT DREAM TOO, DIDN'T YOU?
HMPH ...
I CAN'T BELIEVE YOU FORGOT WHAT YOU WROTE!
NO MATTER WHAT HAPPENS TO YOU, AND EVEN IF YOU NEVER GO BACK TO BEING THE CHEREN I USED TO KNOW...
And my dream is to support Black's dream to win the Pokémon League.
My dream is win the League!
YOU'LL ALWAYS BE MY FRIEND.
THAT'S THE TRUTH...
...AND IT WILL NEVER CHANGE.
Kling
WEL-COME BACK ...

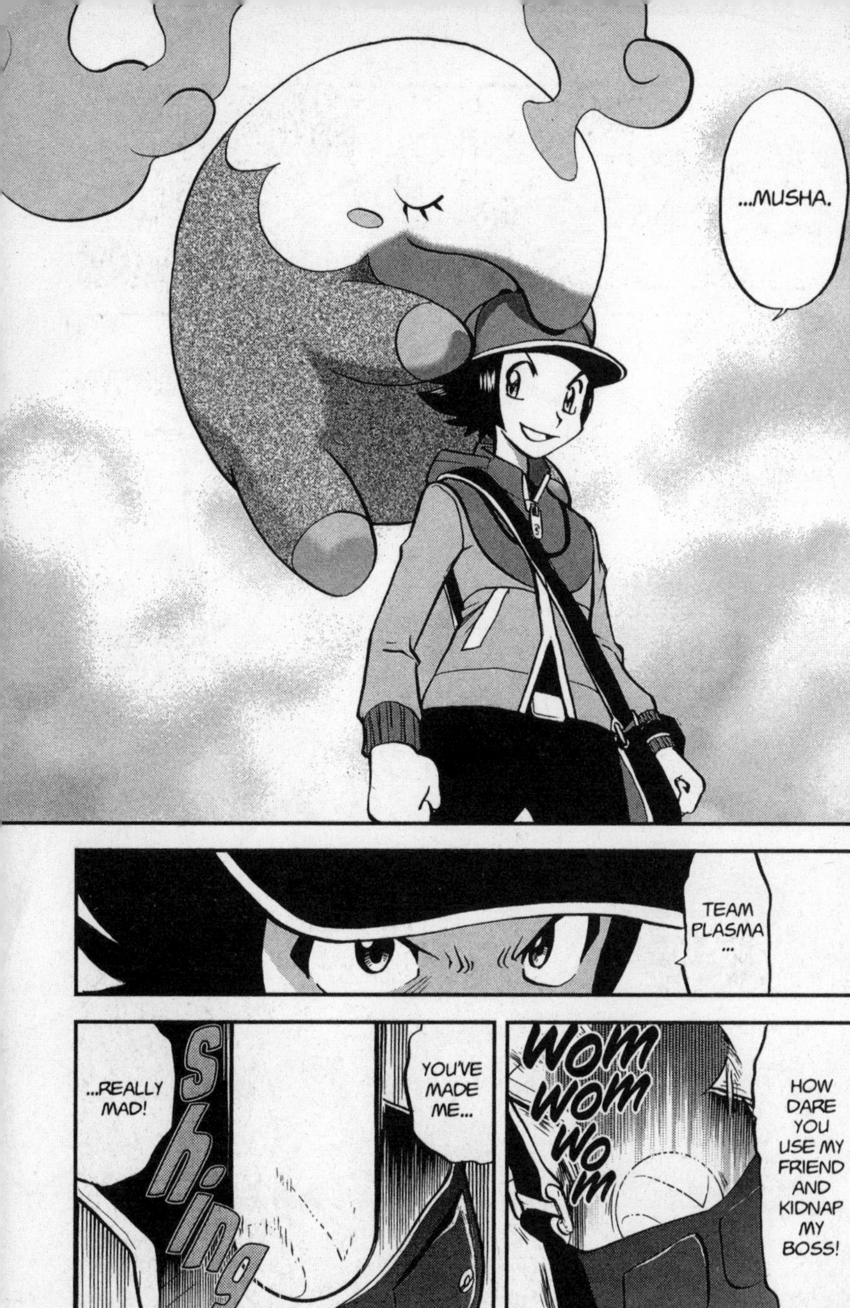
...MUSHA.
TEAM PLASMA ...
WOM WOM WOM
HOW DARE YOU USE MY FRIEND AND KIDNAP MY BOSS!
YOU'VE MADE ME...
...REALLY MAD!
Shing

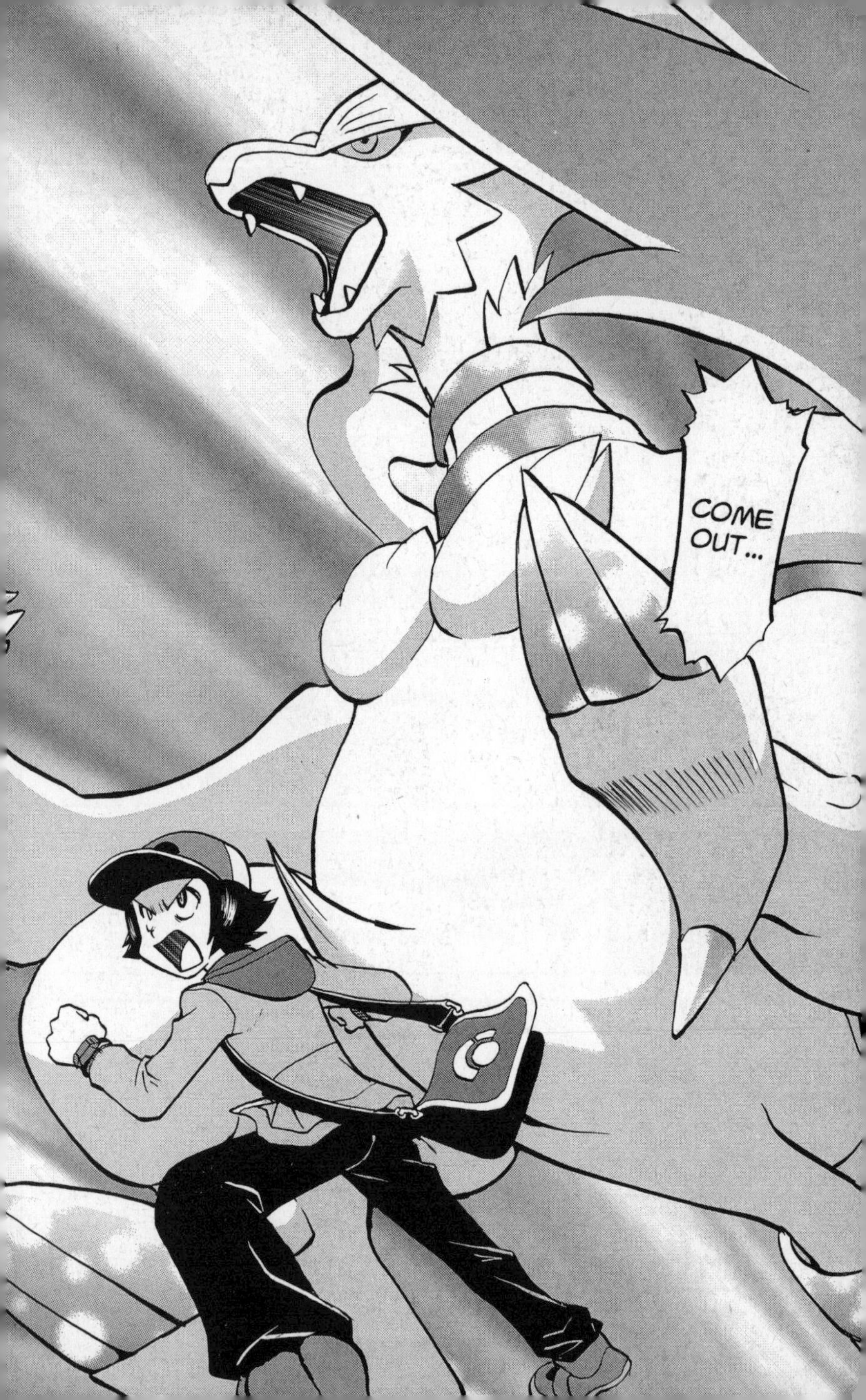
COME OUT...

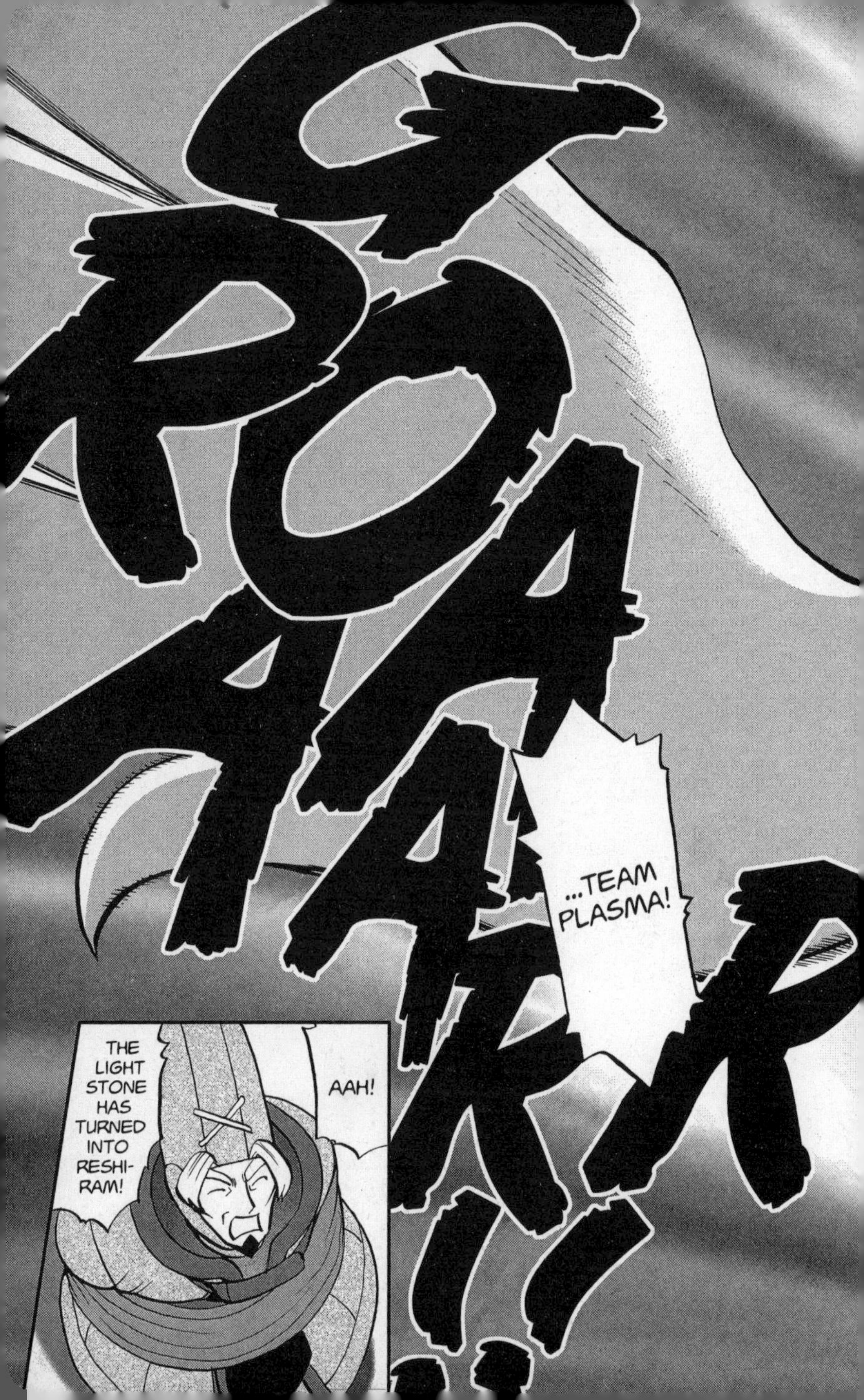
ROAAARR!!
...TEAM PLASMA!
AAH!
THE LIGHT STONE HAS TURNED INTO RESHI-RAM!

TO BE CONTINUED

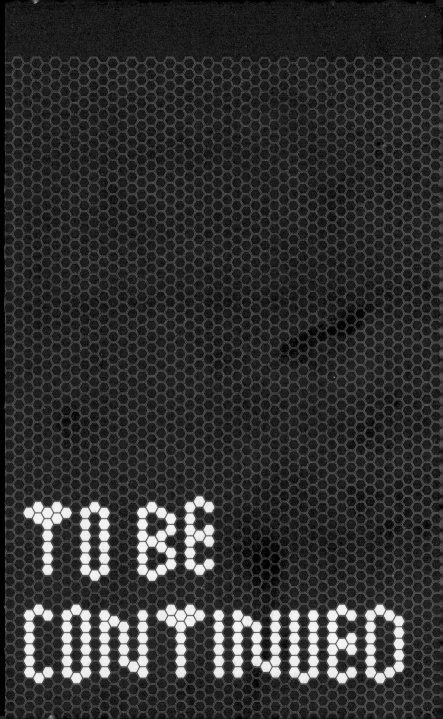

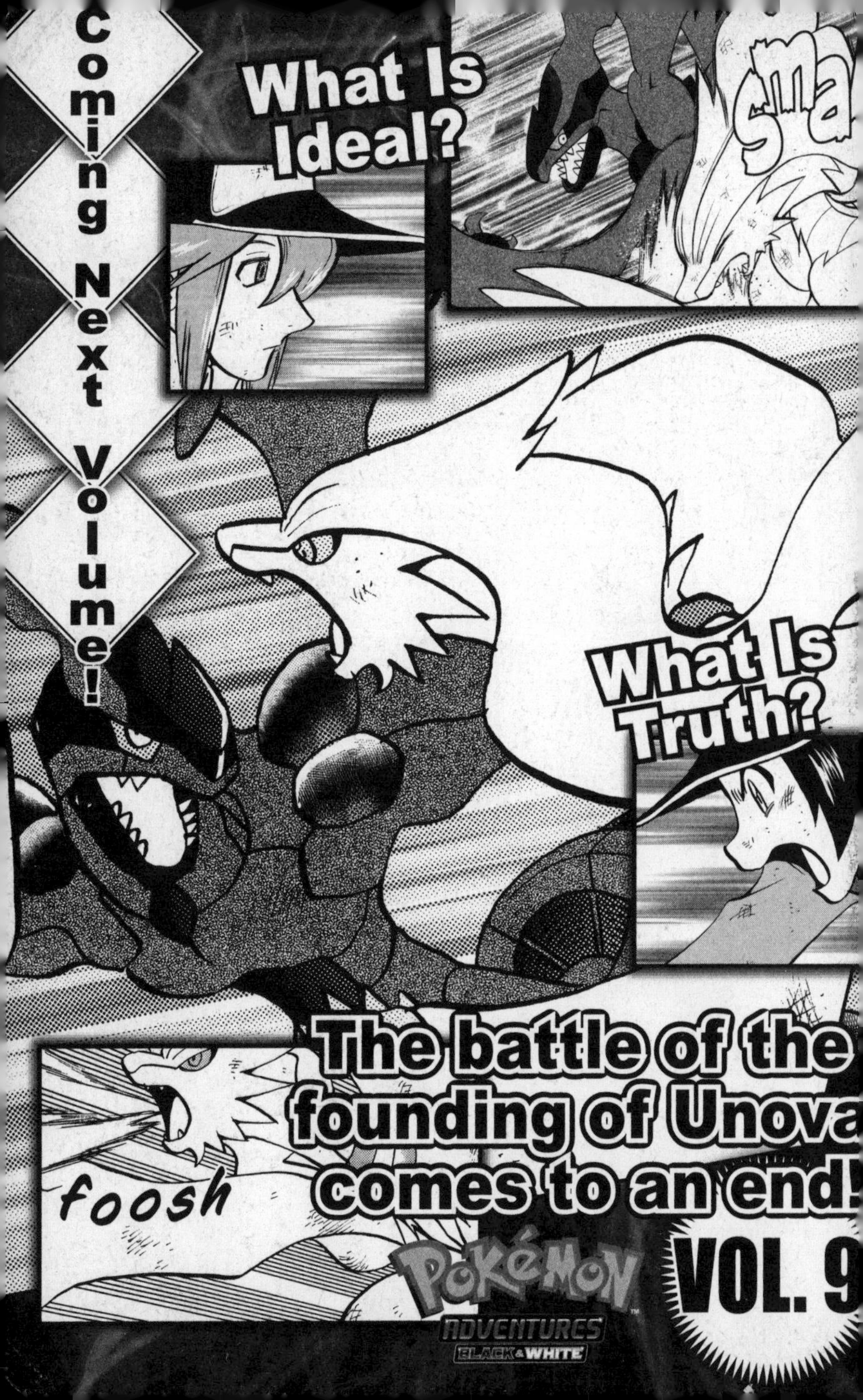
Coming Next Volume!
What Is Ideal?
What Is Truth?
The battle of the founding of Unova comes to an end!
foosh
POKÉMON ADVENTURES BLACK & WHITE
VOL. 9

## Team Plasma's Seven Sages

# The final battle begins!

## Where are they and what are they up to...?

TEAM PLASMA HAS EAGERLY BEEN WAITING FOR THE POKÉMON LEAGUE TO COMMENCE. AND NOW THAT RESHIRAM HAS BEEN AWOKEN BY BLACK, THEY ARE ALL BOUND TO CLASH. BUT ONLY ONE OF THE SEVEN SAGES HAS APPEARED SO FAR. WHAT OF THE OTHER SIX? LET'S GET TO THE BOTTOM OF THIS MYSTERY BY ANALYZING WHAT'S HAPPENED SO FAR...

### GHETSIS

GHETSIS IS THE LEADER OF THE SEVEN SAGES, AND THE SPOKESPERSON FOR TEAM PLASMA. HIS POWERS OF PERSUASION ARE IMPRESSIVE. HE'S ABLE TO WORM HIS WAY INTO PEOPLE'S MINDS...

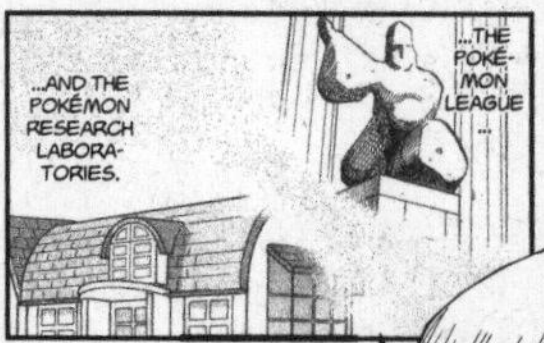
...THE POKÉMON LEAGUE...
...AND THE POKÉMON RESEARCH LABORATORIES.

↑ COULD GHETSIS BE THE ONE WHO TAUGHT N THAT THE POKÉMON LEAGUE AND RESEARCH LABORATORIES WERE TO BLAME FOR HIS TROUBLES?

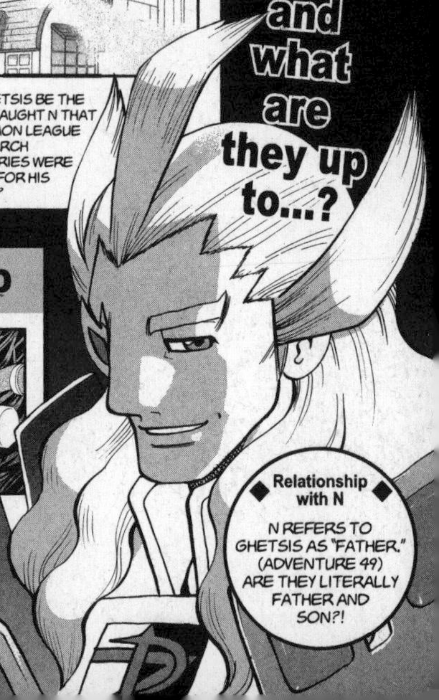

◆ Relationship with N

N REFERS TO GHETSIS AS "FATHER." (ADVENTURE 49) ARE THEY LITERALLY FATHER AND SON?!

### GORM

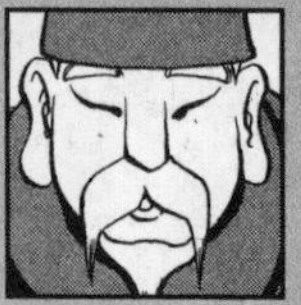

○ NACRENE/THEFT OF THE DRAGON POKÉMON FOSSIL

GORM WAS THE SAGE BEHIND THE STEALTHY THEFT OF A COMPLETE FOSSIL SKELETON ON DISPLAY AT THE NACRENE MUSEUM.

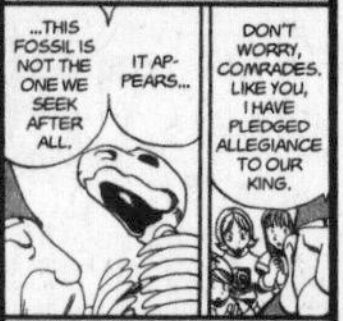
DON'T WORRY, COMRADES. LIKE YOU, I HAVE PLEDGED ALLEGIANCE TO OUR KING.
IT APPEARS...
...THIS FOSSIL IS NOT THE ONE WE SEEK AFTER ALL.

↑ IT COMES AS QUITE A SHOCK TO HEAR THAT HE HAS "PLEDGED ALLEGIANCE" TO A "KING"!

◆ GORM'S GRUNTS ◆

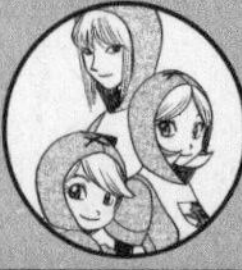

### BRONIUS

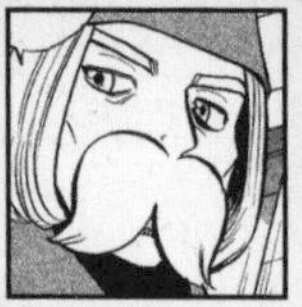

○ CASTELIA/THE CASE OF THE DISAPPEARING POKÉMON

BIANCA'S POKÉMON WAS ONE OF THE ONES THAT DISAPPEARED. IT WAS BRONIUS WHO CAME UP WITH THE AUDACIOUS IDEA OF LOCATING TEAM PLASMA'S HIDEOUT RIGHT IN FRONT OF A POKÉMON GYM. (ADVENTURE 19)

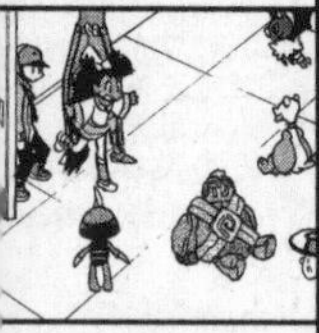

↑ THANKS TO BLACK, ALL THE MISSING POKÉMON WERE RESCUED.

◆ BRONIUS'S GRUNTS ◆

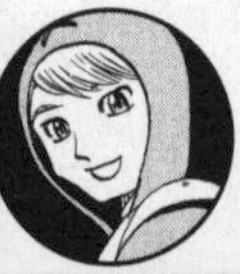

### ◆ GHETSIS'S GRUNTS ◆ SHADOW TRIAD

GHETSIS'S RIGHT-HAND OPERATIVES, THE SHADOW TRIAD, ARE CURRENTLY FIGHTING THE STRIATON TRIPLETS AT THE P2 LABORATORY. COBALION AND THE OTHERS HAVE APPEARED THERE TOO. THIS IS ONE MORE BATTLE YOU WON'T WANT TO MISS!

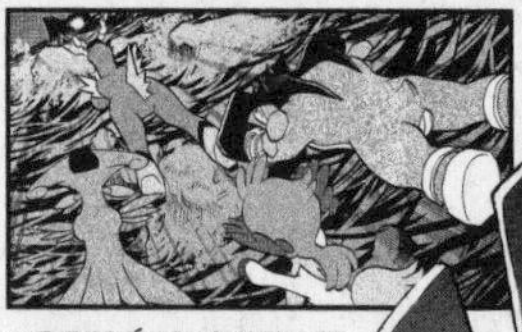

↑ THE POKÉMON SWORDS OF JUSTICE ARE CONVINCED THAT PEOPLE WILL NEVER STOP FIGHTING EACH OTHER. WILL THEY WATCH OVER THE FINAL BATTLE WITH TEAM PLASMA?

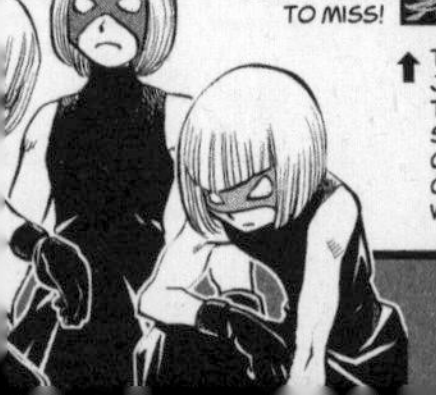

## RYOKU

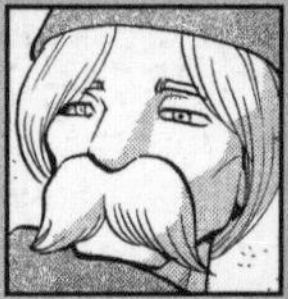

### DESERT RESORT & RELIC CASTLE/SEARCH FOR VOLCARONA

THE GRUNT WHO SNEAKED INTO THE CONSTRUCTION SITE WAS ONE OF RYOKU'S OPERATIVES. TEAM PLASMA HAS INFILTRATED EVERY LOCATION IMAGINABLE. (ADVENTURE 22)

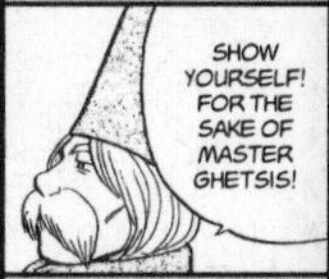
SHOW YOURSELF! FOR THE SAKE OF MASTER GHETSIS!

⬆ RYOKU IS A FANATICAL FOLLOWER OF GHETSIS. HE STRIVES TO STRENGTHEN TEAM PLASMA'S FORCES.

◆ RYOKU'S GRUNTS ◆

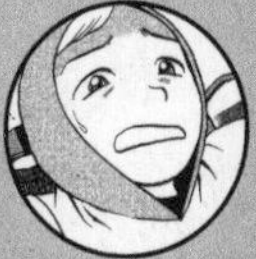

## GIALLO

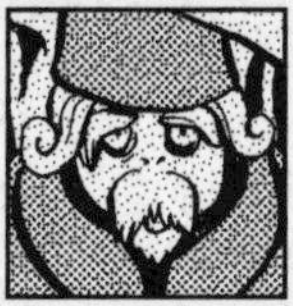

### NEAR ANVILLE TOWN/CAPTURING TORNADUS, THUNDURUS AND LANDORUS

A LEGENDARY BATTLE BETWEEN WIND AND THUNDER TAKES PLACE. A THIRD ENTITY, LAND, JOINS THE BATTLE, BUT IN THE END GIALLO SUCCEEDS IN CAPTURING ALL THREE POKÉMON. (ADVENTURE 30)

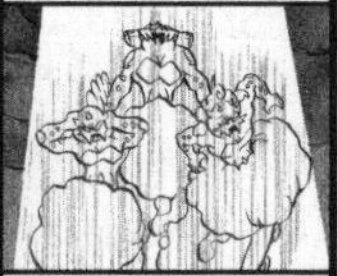

⬆ TEAM PLASMA GETS AHOLD OF UNPARALLELED POWER.

◆ GIALLO'S GRUNTS ◆

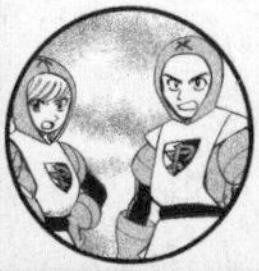

## ROOD

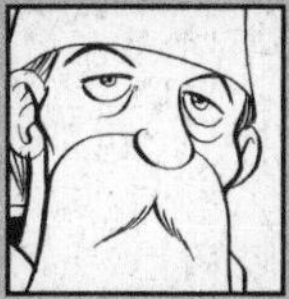

### LIBERTY GARDEN/INVESTIGATION OF VICTINI

UNLIKE THE OTHER SAGES, ROOD DOESN'T PERSONALLY LEAD HIS TROOPS. HIS TROOPS WERE SENT TO A SOLITARY ISLAND WHERE THEY ALMOST—BUT NOT QUITE—CAPTURED THE VICTORY POKÉMON. (ADVENTURE 20)

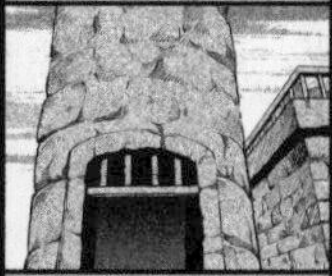

⬆ ROOD IS A MILD-MANNERED SAGE WHO APPARENTLY ONLY ORDERED HIS MEN TO PROTECT VICTINI.

◆ ROOD'S GRUNTS ◆

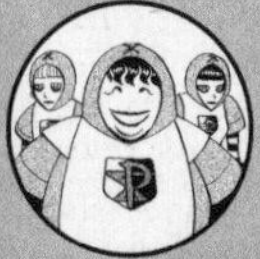

## ◆ GODDESSES ◆

THESE TWO WOMEN ARE WITH N WHEN HE TRIES TO APPROACH ZEKROM, AS WELL AS AT HIS CORONATION. THEY ARE DIFFERENT FROM THE SAGES, GRUNTS AND SHADOW TRIAD.

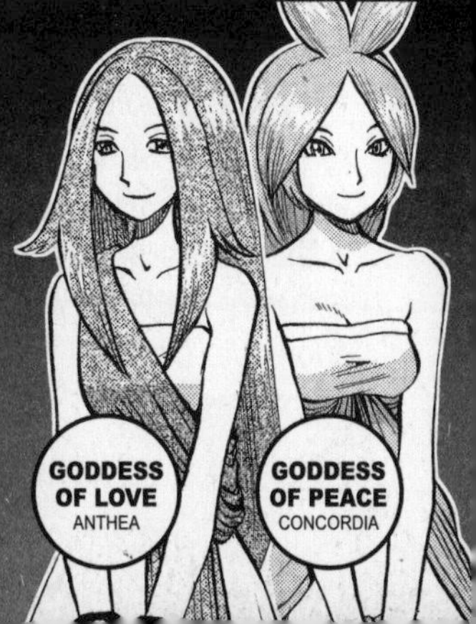
GODDESS OF PEACE
CONCORDIA
GODDESS OF LOVE
ANTHEA

## ZINZOLIN

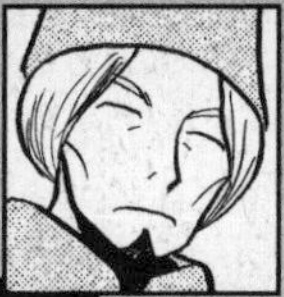

⬇ HE GETS COLD EASILY AND IS VERY WARMLY DRESSED. HE SEEMS TO ENJOY BEING COLD THOUGH... WHICH IS ODD.

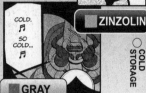

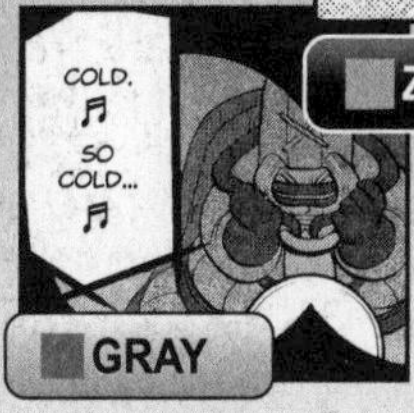
COLD. ♬ SO COLD... ♬
GRAY

### COLD STORAGE

### POKÉMON LEAGUE/INFILTRATION OF THE FINALS

AN EERIE RUMBLE IS HEARD FROM BENEATH THE POKÉMON LEAGUE STADIUM. THE FACE HIDDEN BENEATH THE MASK IS FINALLY REVEALED. IT TURNS OUT THAT THE MAN WHO MADE IT INTO THE TOP EIGHT FINALISTS UNDER THE NAME OF GRAY IS ACTUALLY ZINZOLIN. HE IS THE ONLY SAGE WE'VE SEEN FIGHTING IN THE FRONTLINES SO FAR. WHY DID HE APPEAR AT THE POKÉMON LEAGUE IN DISGUISE?

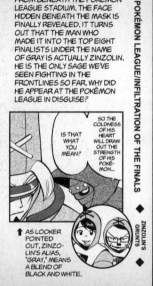

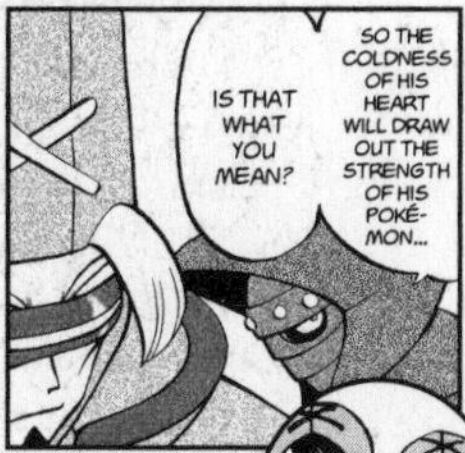
SO THE COLDNESS OF HIS HEART WILL DRAW OUT THE STRENGTH OF HIS POKÉMON...
IS THAT WHAT YOU MEAN?

⬆ AS LOOKER POINTED OUT, ZINZOLIN'S ALIAS, "GRAY," MEANS A BLEND OF BLACK AND WHITE.

◆ ZINZOLIN'S GRUNTS ◆

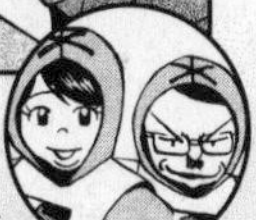

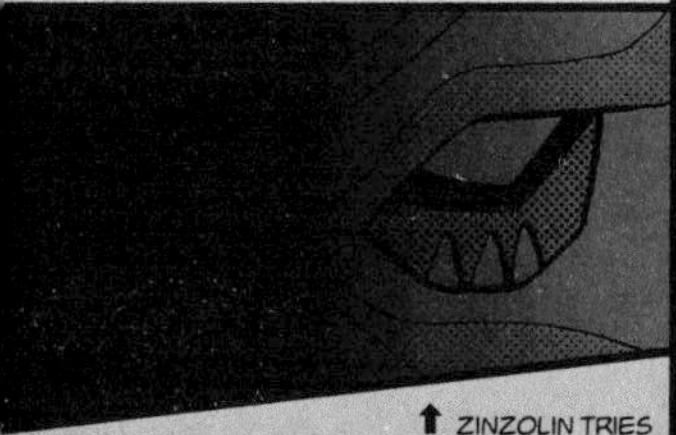

⬆ ZINZOLIN TRIES TO PROVOKE BLACK BY MANIPULATING AND USING HIS FRIEND CHEREN. ZINZOLIN WAS GATHERING POKÉMON BACK AT THE COLD STORAGE. WHAT'S BEHIND HIS OBSESSION WITH COLD TEMPERATURES?

# Message from
## Hidenori Kusaka

I moved to the Shinjuku Ward of Tokyo when I was in elementary school. I've lived in that area ever since. Every now and then, I think about the people I knew before I moved. I remember the friends I met in kindergarten and wonder what they're up to now. Pearl's image of Dia... Cheren and Bianca's image of Black... I'm sure they have a very special relationship. I'm envious because I don't have anyone like that in my life: a childhood friend. What a sweet relationship that must be.

# Message from
## Satoshi Yamamoto

The last time I drew the Pokémon League was in the *Pokémon HeartGold*, *SoulSilver* and *Crystal* story arc. That was 37 volumes ago! But that was an exhibition match, so the last real Pokémon League appeared in volume 3, which was 47 volumes ago. To top it off, this is the *Pokémon Adventures* series, so this will be no ordinary battle between skilled trainers... No way will I allow it to be an ordinary battle! So prepare for battles full of passion and sinister strategies!

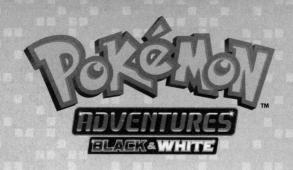

Pokémon™ ADVENTURES BLACK & WHITE

Pokémon ADVENTURES
BLACK AND WHITE
Volume
Perfect Square Edition

Story by HIDENORI KUSAKA
Art by SATOSHI YAMAMOTO



Translation/Tetsuichiro Miyaki
English Adaptation/Annette Roman
Touch-up & Lettering/Susan Daigle-Leach
Design/Shawn Carrico
Editor/Annette Roman



Printed in the U.S.A.

Published by VIZ Media, LLC
P.O. Box 77010
San Francisco, CA 94107

10 9 8 7 6 5 4 3 2 1
First printing, July 2015

www.perfectsquare.com

www.viz.com

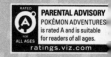

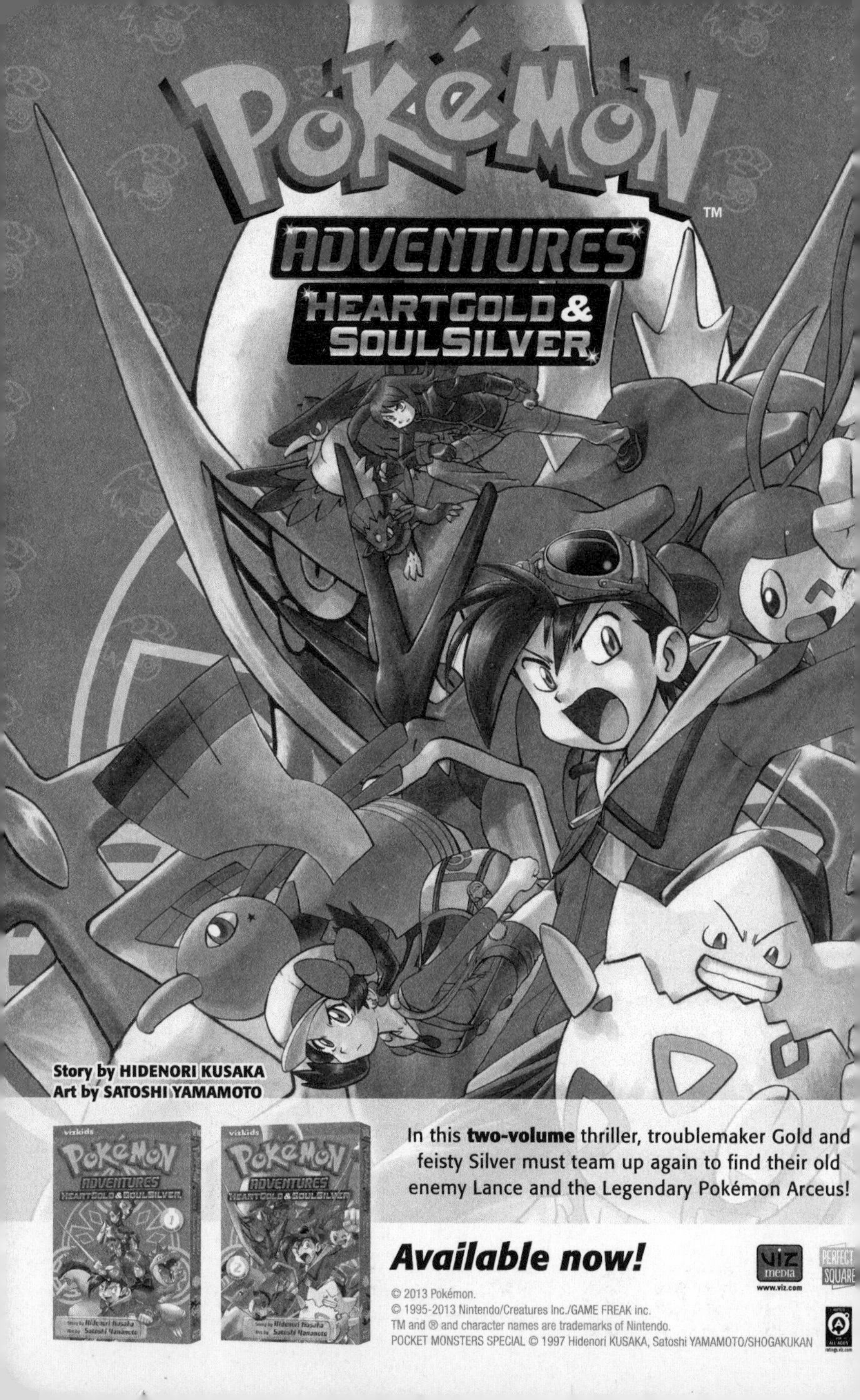
POKéMON™
ADVENTURES
HEARTGOLD & SOULSILVER
Story by HIDENORI KUSAKA
Art by SATOSHI YAMAMOTO
In this two-volume thriller, troublemaker Gold and feisty Silver must team up again to find their old enemy Lance and the Legendary Pokémon Arceus!
Available now!
© 2013 Pokémon.
© 1995-2013 Nintendo/Creatures Inc./GAME FREAK inc.
TM and ® and character names are trademarks of Nintendo.
POCKET MONSTERS SPECIAL © 1997 Hidenori KUSAKA, Satoshi YAMAMOTO/SHOGAKUKAN
VIZ media
www.viz.com
PERFECT SQUARE